Praise for
THE OTHER WOMAN

"Whiplash-inducing."

—*The New York Times Book Review*

"Monster-in-law! The love triangle in this twisted psychological thriller is between Emily, her new boyfriend Adam, and Adam's mother, Pammie, who refuses to let her son go and wants Emily out of his life!" —*InTouch* (Book Report, A–)

"Excellent . . . Jones delivers a tightly coiled story in *The Other Woman* and fills it with believable characters." —Associated Press

"Pammie is every young woman's worst nightmare: a mean mother-in-law (on steroids) in this addictive debut thriller. Readers' pulses will race as they anticipate how she might strike next and be completely knocked off balance by the shocking ending."

—*Library Journal* (starred and boxed review)

"*The Other Woman* is an absolute corker—wickedly relatable story, wonderful characters, and a great twist. Should definitely be on your reading list for this summer." —T.M. Logan

tone to her relationship's incremental slide toward discontent is uncomfortably familiar. Emotionally tense, with layers of deception offering strong appeal for fans of Clare Mackintosh, Christobel Kent, and Karen Perry."   —*Booklist*

"Many women worry about another woman coming into their relationship, but what if the other woman is your partner's mother? That's the concept in the thriller *The Other Woman* by Sandie Jones."
                                          —*National Examiner*

"For anyone who's dealt with an unsavory in-law, this thriller will hit close to home."
                    —Refinery29 ("Summer Thrillers That
                                 Will Have You at the
                                 End of Your Chaise Lounge")

"What happens when a mother won't let her grown son pursue a life of his own? Sandie Jones's debut thriller examines the relationship between mother and son, and what can happen when another woman is brought into the picture."   —POPSUGAR ("10 Bingeworthy
                                 Books to Read After
                                 The Woman in the Window")

"It's a page-turner like no other, and the ending will knock your socks off."   —HelloGiggles

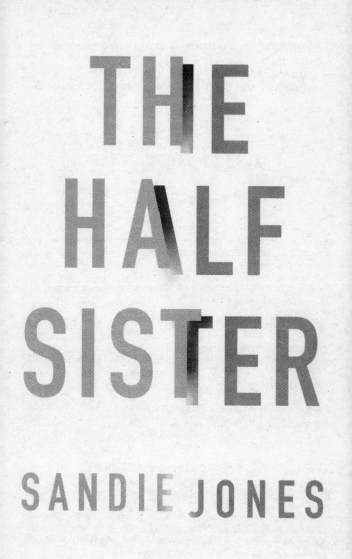

THE HALF SISTER

SANDIE JONES

St. Martin's Paperbacks

This is a work of fiction. All of the characters, organizations, and events portrayed in this novel are either products of the author's imagination or are used fictitiously.

Published in the United States by St. Martin's Paperbacks, an imprint of St. Martin's Publishing Group

THE HALF SISTER

Copyright © 2020 by Sandra Sargent.
Excerpt from *The Blame Game* copyright © 2022 by Sandra Sargent.

For information, address St. Martin's Publishing Group, 120 Broadway, New York, NY 10271.

www.stmartins.com

Library of Congress Catalog Card Number: 20200141299

ISBN: 978-1-250-84871-0

Our books may be purchased in bulk for promotional, educational, or business use. Please contact your local bookseller or the Macmillan Corporate and Premium Sales Department at 1-800-221-7945, ext. 5442, or by email at MacmillanSpecialMarkets@macmillan.com.

Printed in the United States of America

Minotaur hardcover edition / June 2020
Minotaur trade paperback edition / June 2021
St. Martin's Paperbacks edition / July 2022

10 9 8 7 6 5 4 3 2 1

For Oliver
You make me proud every day
Keep being you

1

KATE

Kate sees the familiar nameplate on Dr. Williams' office door and feels a knot in her stomach. She doesn't know why, after all this time, it still affects her like this—she should be used to it by now. But every time she walks through his door she's filled with hope, and every time she walks back out, she feels utter despair and sadness, unable to believe that fate could be so cruel.

As if he knows what she's thinking, Matt grabs hold of her hand as they sit in the clinic's waiting room. Squeezing it, as if he is somehow able to transfer his boundless optimism onto her.

He kisses her head as she leans into him. "I think this might be the one," he says, over-enthusiastically, as if believing it hard enough will prove him right.

"It's certainly the *last* one," she says wearily.

"Let's see," says Matt with forced joviality.

"Kate!" exclaims Dr. Williams as he opens his door.

She should call him Ben, as he's requested a hundred times. But using his first name means she knows him well, and if she knows him well, it would be admitting how long this has been going on for.

"Doctor," she says, as she stands up and walks toward him with an outstretched arm.

"Good to see you," says Dr. Williams. "Matt, how are you?"

The two men greet each other as if they're old friends, meeting at a football match. Kate finds herself wondering at what point the bonhomie will be replaced with the business in hand. She suspects it's when her legs are in stirrups and said hand is gloved.

"So, are we all ready?" asks Dr. Williams, now seated in front of them at his desk. He doesn't look up from his computer screen to see Matt's determined nod.

"Okay, so all your numbers are looking good," he says, almost to himself. "We've identified the strongest embryo which, I'm pleased to say, is of the highest grade."

Kate feels Matt looking at her, knowing that he'll be beaming from ear to ear, but she doesn't have the energy to return his eagerness because she's heard it all before. *"Highest grade," "4AAA blastocyst," "It doesn't get much better than this"*—all had been bandied around during their last three attempts, but it hadn't made that line go blue on the pregnancy test, had it?

Matt's enthusiasm had propped Kate up at first, when test after test proved inconclusive. She'd relied on his positivity to bring her back around the right way after they were told that the reason they couldn't get pregnant was due to "unexplained infertility."

"It means there's nothing wrong," he'd said as he practically skipped out of Dr. Williams' office three years ago.

Kate didn't have the heart to tell him that it also meant that there was "nothing right."

Instead, she'd adapted her diet, stopped drinking, and stood on her head after sex. But nothing had resulted in them being able to conceive, hence they now find themselves in the clinic. *Again.*

Once Kate's lying on her back with her legs in the air, she sings Queen's "Bohemian Rhapsody" in her head, to distract herself from the fact that there is a doctor, an embryologist, a nurse and a medical student all staring intently at her lady parts. *Galileo Galileo*, she hums, in an attempt to take herself to another place.

"Once you've had a baby, a smear test will be like just going to the hairdresser's," her sister Lauren had offered when they'd inadvertently run into each other at the doctor's. Kate hadn't wanted to share her infertility struggles, so had been caught on the hop. Of all the things she *could* have said she was there for, a smear was the first thing that popped into her head. She could have kicked herself.

You would have thought that an older sister with three children would be the perfect antidote to the situation that Kate finds herself in. Someone who would sympathize, offer unbiased advice and a shoulder to cry on. But Lauren is not *that* person, or perhaps, more to the point, Kate doesn't *see* that person in her. Instead, she sees a woman who is living the life she had assumed *she'd* be living, and sisters or not, Lauren's perfect little set-up is not the kind of support network Kate feels she needs to be immersed in right now. *And anyway,* she thinks, *how could she possibly understand what I'm going through when she only has to look at her husband to get pregnant?*

She jumps as she feels a sharp pain in her groin.

"Okay, so we're inserting the embryo now," says

Dr. Williams, though Kate doesn't know if he's talking to her or the eager student, who can't seem to get close enough to see what's happening.

As it turns out, it doesn't matter how many times you've been poked and prodded, it will *never* feel like going to the hairdresser's.

She wants to push the invasive hands and instruments away, restore her dignity and tell them she's had enough of being treated like a laboratory rat. But then she looks at Matt, with his gentle smile and hopeful eyes. She could so easily take herself down the *why is life so unfair?* route, but in the rare moments of clarity, when she knows that having a good life isn't dependent on having a child, she is so grateful to have *him*.

She'd always wanted a baby with the husband she loves, more than anything in the world. Had been consumed by it at one point. But the pain and constant disappointment were taking their toll. If she'd had her way, they would have stopped at the third IVF attempt. She was exhausted, both physically and mentally; her nervous energy depleted by the tales she'd had to spin to friends and work colleagues who raised a knowing eyebrow whenever she refused an alcoholic drink.

"This is it," she'd said to Matt, a couple of nights ago, as they were snuggled on the couch watching TV.

She felt him stiffen and sit up straighter. "What, this is our last chance?" he asked, seemingly floored.

Hadn't he noticed how tired she was? Seen her desolation every time they looked at a blank pregnancy test? Couldn't he see how their whole lives had been taken over by the process of getting pregnant?

"I've had enough," she'd said quietly.

"But we . . ." he stuttered. "Darling, we're so close now—I know it. We can do this."

Something inside her had snapped. "You keep saying *we*, as if we're going through this together."

He'd looked at her, hurt. "Aren't we?"

She chastised herself for taking her frustrations out on the person she loves the most. But isn't that always the way?

She thinks back to how carefree they'd once been. How they'd met on the newsroom floor of the *Gazette* and bonded over mutual banter about a loathsome editor. It had made the day go quicker, made the shifts under the editor's watch seem a little easier to bear. Whenever he'd march into the open-plan office, shouting his morning mantra, "Who are we going to throw to the lions today?," Kate and Matt would race to send each other an email with "*YOU?*" in the subject heading. It was a regrettable day when the editor himself received Matt's email.

"I'll miss working with you," said Matt, as he and Kate sat in the pub ruing their stupidity. "But every cloud has a silver lining."

She'd thought he was referring to his new job at rival newspaper the *Echo*. She couldn't stop grinning when he added, "Because now I can ask you out."

They'd spent blissful evenings trawling the pubs of South London and lazy weekend mornings reading the papers in bed. But now she can't remember the last time they'd done either.

Instead, they'd been referring to ovulation charts before they made love and subliminally avoiding social events with their pregnant and blessed-with-children friends, which seemed to be just about everyone they knew.

In their effort to have a baby, they'd lost the ability to be spontaneous. Ironically, they'd given up what should have been the halcyon days of pre-parenthood to the restrictions of being responsible for another human, despite the painful absence of one.

"Done!" says Dr. Williams with a flourish. He puts the catheter back on the tray and pings his gloves off.

"So, we've got two more in the freezer?" asks Matt. "Before we have to go through egg retrieval again, I mean?"

"Yes, we've got two more good quality embryos left to go on this cycle."

"But even if they don't work, we can still go again, can't we?" Matt continues.

Kate doesn't want to have this conversation. She has an urgent need to empty her painfully full bladder and all the time there's a viable chance of a baby being inside her, she refuses to acknowledge that they'll have to go through this again. Because that would mean that the little human being who is having to work so hard right now isn't going to make it.

"Let's concentrate on the here and now," says Dr. Williams, as Kate swings her legs down to the floor. "So, just carry on as normal, and I'll see you in a couple of weeks' time for the blood test to see where we're at."

Kate looks to Matt and smiles. She can't help but notice that he's got his fingers crossed.

2
KATE

"So, no Matt today?" asks Rose, Kate's mum, as she bustles into the dining room carrying a tray of roast potatoes.

Lauren deftly lifts one out as Rose sets the tray down and bites into it, groaning with pleasure as it crunches.

"Afraid not," says Kate. "He got called into the office at the last minute."

"Ah well, no bother," says Rose, going back into the kitchen. "I'll do you a plate to take home."

"So, what's the big scoop of the day?" asks Lauren's husband Simon, as he carves into the beef joint that's resting in the middle of the table. Kate can't help but feel that he's taking her dad's job away from him. "Or are you not allowed to tell?" he goes on.

"I could"—Kate lowers her voice—"but then I'd have to kill you."

He laughs heartily at the joke he thinks she's made, but, truth be known, nothing would give her more pleasure. She and Matt had often lain in bed thinking of ways to commit the perfect murder, and her sister's husband always topped the list of potential victims.

He's tolerated rather than liked, and if it wasn't for her mother wanting to keep the Sunday-lunch ritual going, Kate could quite easily never see him again. But hey, you can't choose your family.

"Come on, seriously, I wanna know," says Simon. "Do you and Matt share stories or are you bitter rivals? Fighting each other to the death for the best ones."

Kate wonders whether he'd prefer to hear about the imminent cabinet reshuffle or the prostitute who's claiming to have kept a Premiership footballer up the night before a cup final, both of which she knows Matt is working on. She decides not to give Simon the satisfaction of either.

"I couldn't possibly divulge our pillow talk," she says. "Lauren, pass me the carrots, will you?"

"I can't remember the last time we were all together," says Lauren.

Kate can. It was three weeks ago, and on the way home, she and Matt had discussed how they might be able to stretch the weekly lunches to maybe every other week.

"I only do it for Mum," Kate had said. "You know how she loves having us all over."

"I know," Matt had replied. "But it's dictating our weekends. I don't get much time off as it is, and when I do, no disrespect, I'd rather us two do something together."

But in the last three weeks, that hadn't happened either, as Matt had worked, then Kate had been at a film festival, and now, this weekend, he's had to go into the office again.

"It's just that everyone's busy," says Kate.

"Everyone but me," laughs Lauren. "I'll be sitting at this table waiting for the roasties until my dying day."

"Well, maybe you need to get a life!" Simon laughs.

It's funny how words are dependent on who says them. If Matt had said that, Kate would have taken it in the spirit it was meant: banter between two people who gave each other as good as they got. But from Simon's lips, the joke is lost, turning a flippant comment into something that sounds far more disrespectful.

The flash of disdain that crosses Lauren's eyes tells Kate she's not the only one who feels it.

"I'd imagine being a mother keeps you very busy," Kate interjects.

Lauren rolls her eyes. "You have *no* idea."

You're right, I don't, thinks Kate.

"In all honesty, now that I'm back on maternity leave, I don't know how I had time to go to work," Lauren says, laughing.

"It's all about time management," says Simon. "Imagine Kate when *she* has children; it'll be like a military operation." He laughs again.

"Not everyone wants children," says Lauren, and Kate can't help but feel dismayed at how misplaced and ill thought out her words are.

She fixes an insincere grin on her face, wondering how much longer she has to keep up with this charade of happy families. If Matt were here, he'd at least take some of the flak for her, stepping in to bat away the barbs.

"Some women want careers instead," Lauren goes on.

Kate struggles to keep her expression neutral, but it feels like her cheek's been slapped. "I don't think you have to make a choice between having a career and having children," she says.

Simon looks at her with an amused expression. "You can't have both."

"Why not?" asks Kate brusquely. "We're perfectly capable. Just because we're the ones who have babies shouldn't mean our careers have to suffer while we have them."

Simon rolls his eyes.

Kate looks to Lauren, shaking her head in the hope that she'll get some sisterly support, but Lauren has turned away. Kate wonders when her sister became so spineless when faced with her husband's old-fashioned views.

Up until their first child, Noah, was born five years ago, Lauren had dedicated her life to bringing *other* people's babies into the world. In fact, Kate couldn't remember a time when her sister *wasn't* surrounded by children. She'd babysat for family friends as a teenager and had studied midwifery as soon as she'd finished secondary school, which was why she was well placed to make comments about forgetting your dignity when you give birth. Logically, Kate knew she should take her sister's words as they were probably intended, yet she couldn't help but feel they were aimed at her personally.

Simon sighs theatrically. "The proof's in the pudding. Someone like Lauren, who has worked for the good old NHS for fifteen years, isn't as high up as her peers who have chosen not to have children. Fact."

"When do you think you'll go back to work?" asks Rose in an attempt to change the subject, although Kate is quite sure that she already knows the precise date. Lauren and their mum are close like that.

Lauren throws a glance at her husband. "I'm not due back until the end of the summer, but if we need the money, I might go back sooner."

"Let's hope that she still has a job by then," says Simon. "If the current government have *their* way, the NHS won't last for much longer."

Now, you just wait a minute. This government have gone all-out to secure the future of our healthcare system.

Those are the words she knows her conservative father would normally have said, but there's a deafening silence. Kate looks at the chair he'd once occupied, now sitting woefully empty in the corner of the room, and feels a very real physical tug on her heart.

It's coming up to a year since he died, yet Kate can still hear him, still see him, sitting at his place around the table. They'd left his chair empty for the first six months, none of them able to remove it from where they gathered every Sunday, but gradually they'd moved a little this way and that, shuffling ever closer, until suddenly it had been banished to where only cobwebs grew. Kate had been a reluctant visitor ever since, finding the slow removal of the man she adored too painful to accept. Where she'd once looked forward to the family getting together, excited to hear about her father's week at work and revelling in the heated debates between him and Matt, it had now become an effort. Without her ally, the dynamics seem to have shifted, and the once light-hearted, evenly matched pairings of her and her father versus Lauren and their mother now feel heavily weighted in her sister's favor.

Whenever Kate calls her mother, Lauren seems to be adding her two pennies' worth in the background.

And on the odd occasion Kate's dropped in to see the children, Rose is there, preparing dinner in Lauren's kitchen. Maybe it's always been this way, but now that her father isn't round at *her* flat, helping her out with odd jobs, Kate notices it more.

She'd lost count of how many cups of tea she'd made him on a Saturday morning when Matt was invariably on a weekend shift, and Harry had taken it upon himself to fix a leak in the shower in his DIY-shy son-in-law's absence. Kate had always managed to find a creaky door for him to oil, or a shelf to put up, despite being more than capable of doing it herself, the pair of them as good as each other for finding excuses to spend time together.

"I thought I'd get out from under your mother's feet for a bit longer," he used to say when he'd appear on her doorstep on his way back from watching Chelsea play at Stamford Bridge. By then Matt would be home, and they'd all sit and watch the late kick-off on the telly together.

"Do you think you two will have kids one day?" her dad had asked once, ever so casually. She and Matt had looked at each other as they weighed up whether to share their desperate struggle. If any member of the family were to know about it, it would only have been him, but then Kate thought of the sadness that would cloud his features as he contemplated his daughter's childless future. She'd discreetly shaken her head at Matt and said instead, "We'd love them when the time's right."

"I'm going to make sure that whenever it happens and whatever it is, it's going to be a Blues fan," he'd said, smiling. "It'll be chanting 'blue is the color, football is the game' before it can say 'dada.'"

"I don't think so," Matt, a lifelong Arsenal fan, had said, laughing. "I'm all right with its first words not being daddy, but if you think for one second that its favorite color is going to be blue instead of red, then I think we might have to put a restraining order in place."

They'd all laughed together as Kate dared to imagine her father holding the hand of his grandchild, the pair of them wrapped in blue and white scarves as they made their way to the stands. The thought of it had made her want to cry even more than the prospect of it never happening. Now, though, the impossibility of both scenarios threatens to engulf her.

Kate takes her plate into the kitchen, unable to stomach her food or the conversation any longer. She stands facing the units with her hands spread wide on the worktop. *Just count to ten*, she can hear Matt's voice saying.

It would be a hell of a lot easier if you were here, she replies silently.

She pictures him in the high-rise tower of the *Echo*'s offices, pacing up and down, raking a manic hand through his hair as he is forced to go to the wire on tomorrow's front-page exclusive. Will the government insider get the names to him on time? Will the prostitute want more money, now that Real Madrid are rumored to be interested in signing her one-night stand?

Despite both of them being in the business for over ten years, the pressure never lessens, and the reliable sources were proving to be ever more *un*reliable. That's why Kate had opted to stay where she was, on the *Gazette*'s showbusiness desk, instead of rising up through the ranks where the stakes and stress increased tenfold. She chose not to acknowledge that the bigger reason for not putting herself forward for promotion was that she'd not expected to be there for that much longer. But that was four years ago, when she'd thought that she'd have to hand over coverage of the next Oscars because she'd be too heavily pregnant to fly to Los Angeles. She honestly hadn't expected to be reporting on the fashion faux pas of Hollywood actresses ever again, but she'd been there for the last three years in a row, without even the merest hint of a bump.

"Are you okay, darling?" asks Rose, coming into the kitchen to fetch more gravy. "You look a little pale."

For the briefest of moments, Kate considers telling her why she might look peaky, why her temper seems to be on a short fuse and why *everything* everybody's saying seems to be rubbing her up the wrong way. But no, she and Matt had decided they'd do it together, when there was something to say, and anyway, Rose has already disappeared through the side door and into the garage.

"I don't like vegetables," says Noah, spitting out a mouthful of chewed-up swede as Kate walks back into the dining room.

"Come on, darling, just a few more for mummy," says Lauren patiently.

"No! Vegetables are yucky."

Lauren looks at Kate, as if to say, *Aren't you glad you're not me?*

You're exactly who I want to be, Kate says to herself.

Over the years, she's fallen into the trap of gauging everyone's good fortune and sense of self-worth on whether they have children or not, using their ability to have a baby as some kind of currency that makes them rich beyond their wildest dreams. So in *her* eyes, Lauren is a multimillionaire. Though when she looks a little closer, she notices the finer details of what her sister's life might *really* be like. For example, the fact that her husband has almost cleared his plate while she is yet to start her dinner, as she's too busy cutting up carrots for eighteen-month-old Emmy, chasing the peas that Noah is flicking onto the table, and maneuvering baby Jude's hungry mouth onto her breast.

The juxtaposition of the scene and her selfish thoughts jolt Kate into action.

"Here," she says, moving around the table to stand behind Emmy's highchair. "Let me do that."

Lauren gratefully gives her sister a child's plastic knife and fork while throwing a sideways glance at her oblivious husband.

"Thanks," says Lauren, as Kate cuts up Emmy's vegetables before kneeling to retrieve the errant peas.

It somehow feels easier to be under the table than sitting around it. A place to hide from all the words that are said and unsaid. Kate can hear them forcing a conversation, changing the subject to one that isn't deemed to be in the least bit controversial, so that nobody gets on their high horse and threatens the equilibrium again.

She's still on the floor when the doorbell rings, and Rose huffs before putting her knife and fork down. "Who can that be on a Sunday afternoon? Simon, be a love and go and get that, will you?"

Kate watches as Simon walks out of the room, and waits to hear his voice at the door. The conversation is muffled and she strains to hear, relishing his discomfort as he no doubt listens to a Witness regaling him about the power of Jehovah, or a landscaper who just happens to have finished a garden down the road and has a few pergolas and statues left over.

Emmy is hitting Kate on the head with her plastic bowl and she waits expectantly for more peas to rain down on her.

"Oi, you little rascal," she laughs, grabbing hold of Emmy's bare foot. Just feeling her soft skin in the palm of her hand makes Kate's chest tighten and she swallows the tears that are prickling the back of her throat.

"It's someone looking for Harry," says Simon, as he walks back into the dining room with a young blonde woman behind him.

"*What?*" asks Rose abruptly, looking from the woman to Simon and back again.

Kate is still on her knees, surveying the scene across the top of the table.

"Yeah, it's actually Harry I'm after," says the woman. "Harry Alexander. Is he around?"

Kate feels her blood run cold as her brain struggles to comprehend what this woman might want. But whichever way she looks at it, asking for a man almost a year after his death can't be a good thing.

"Sorry, what is it we can help you with?" asks Kate, rising to her full height.

The woman looks at her feet as they shuffle from side to side. "It's probably best if I speak to Harry first," she says.

"Well, he's not here," says Kate tightly, her chest feeling like a coiled spring. "What is it you want with him?"

"Are you Lauren?"

Kate feels her mum shift beside her, but Lauren, she notices, is stock still. Even her swaying to comfort the baby has stopped.

"Sorry, who *are* you?" asks Kate, ignoring the question.

"I'm Jess," says the woman, before clearing her throat.

"And what do you want with Harry?" asks Rose shakily.

Jess eyes her warily. "I need to talk to him. It's really important."

Kate looks to Rose. "I'll let him know you came by," she says, as her mother's and sister's heads turn in her direction. "What should I say it's about?" she goes on, ignoring their perplexed stares.

The woman looks down at the floor again, as if summoning the courage she needs to say what she's about to say.

"I'm his daughter," she says eventually. "Tell him his daughter came to see him."

3

KATE

"What?" gasps Kate, as the room spins around her. She looks to her mother, who is standing open-mouthed, as if frozen in time. "But . . . but that's not possible," she stutters, her voice sounding as if somebody has a hand around her throat.

"I think you'd better leave," are the first words that Rose says. "I don't know who you are or what you want, but you've no business coming here."

"My name's Jess and I just want to see my father—that's all."

"Well, he's not here," says Kate, feeling ever more present. "You've come to the wrong place. You've got the wrong man."

"I'm sorry—I just wanted to—" begins Jess.

"You need to go—now!" barks Rose, in a tone that Kate hasn't heard before.

"Can we not at least talk about it?"

"There's nothing to say," hisses Rose. "As my daughter says, you've come to the wrong place."

Jess reaches into the handbag on her shoulder, pulls out a crumpled piece of paper and reads it. "It's Rose, isn't it?" she says, extending her hand, but Rose doesn't even flinch.

"And you must be Kate, or are you Lauren?" She attempts a smile.

Kate stands firm, her jaw set, staring at the woman who has just thrown a grenade into her world.

"Look, I can see this is a huge shock to you all," says Jess. "And I'm sorry—I had no idea you didn't know. Otherwise I would never have . . ."

Rose is beginning to shake, and Lauren sidles up beside her and puts a firm arm around her back.

"You need to leave," says Kate, her voice belying the panic that is raging within her.

"But if I could just—"

"For God's sake, he's—" starts Rose, before Kate grabs her mother's wrist, cutting her words off.

". . . not the man you're looking for," says Kate, feeling as if her airways are being crushed.

"I just want him to know—" starts Jess.

"Get out!" screams Rose, making Emmy jump and dissolve into frightened tears.

"Look, I'm sorry, but you need to leave," says Simon, stepping forward and holding an arm out toward the hall.

"I'm sorry," says Jess tearfully, as Simon ushers her into the hall. "I thought you knew . . ."

"Just get out!" Rose yells again.

A moment later the front door shuts and everyone takes a sharp breath, none of them wanting to be the first to speak.

Simon coming back into the room breaks the almost hypnotic spell that seems to have been cast.

"Well, what the hell . . . ?" he smirks, stifling a laugh. Only *he* could make this worse.

Kate falls back onto a chair, feeling the air in her body rush out. She thinks of the embryo inside her and forces herself to take deep, steady breaths. In for three, out for four. But her chest constricts, making it feel as if it's trapping what little air there is inside of it. She imagines blowing into a brown paper bag and closes her eyes as she pictures it inflating and deflating.

"M-mum?" stutters Lauren. "Are you okay?"

If Kate feels floored by the unwanted guest's announcement, she can't even begin to think how her mother must be feeling. Rose's eyes are glazed. "Yes, yes, I'm fine," she says eventually. Her voice is barely more than a whisper and she coughs to clear her throat.

"So you don't know who she is?" asks Lauren.

Rose numbly shakes her head.

"Well if you ask me," says Simon, "there must be *something* in it. You don't just interrupt some random family's Sunday lunch and deliver a bombshell like that."

"I have no idea what she's talking about," says Rose. "It doesn't even make sense. None of what she said makes any sense."

Kate's head is in her hands as she contemplates what just happened, knowing that if she says the wrong thing or asks the wrong question, she won't ever be able to retract it.

"Mum, could it be . . . ?" starts Lauren, looking to Rose, who turns to her with a face like thunder.

Kate looks to her mother and sister, their expressions mirroring each other's: their eyes wide with fear and confusion, their lips pinched tight as if they're biting down on the words that are threatening to spill from their mouths.

"Could it be *what*?" asks Kate.

"Nothing," snaps Rose. "The girl's got her wires crossed. It's as simple as that. There's no other explanation."

Kate doesn't know whether her mother is speaking about Lauren or the young woman who's just turned up claiming to be her father's daughter. *Her father's daughter*. Just hearing those words in her head makes Kate's throat clench as it battles the tears that are teetering behind her eyes.

For once in her life, she agrees with her mother—it's just not possible. Harry was devoted to his family and devoted to *her*. She was Daddy's little girl and they were like two peas in a pod, in every way, except for their looks. Where Kate had inherited her mother's auburn hair and fair skin, that freckled whenever she so much as looked at the sun, Harry could be seen in Lauren's wide-set eyes, straight narrow nose and one-sided dimple. The blonde hair that they'd once shared had grown more ashen on Harry in his later years, but he'd always looked distinguished—like the man she knew him to be. But what if he wasn't? What if he was distinguished in an entirely different way? Conspicuously marked with the stigma of *another* family; a family he had kept secret from the rest of the world.

Her mind races back to the time when Jess would have been born. She looked young—early twenties maybe? Which would have made Kate barely a teenager. Those were the years when, during the school holidays, she used to accompany her father to his office, where he worked as a lawyer. She was adamant she'd follow in his footsteps, convinced she wanted to right people's wrongs.

"You're a real-life superhero," she'd once said, watching in awe as he spent the morning fighting for a mother's custody and the afternoon negotiating a fair divorce deal for a husband who had been cheated on.

He'd smiled modestly at her through crinkled eyes, but she knew her words mattered to him. As did everybody else's whose lives he touched. He wasn't how lawyers are so often cast: the epitome of a vulture preying on the vulnerable. He was an upstanding citizen who treated each and every one of his clients like a good friend. He had *always* been a superhero in Kate's eyes.

Yet now, she dares to contemplate the possibility that he might have been the very opposite.

"Why didn't you tell her he was dead?" asks Lauren, almost accusingly.

It takes a while for Kate to realize that she's talking to her.

"Because it's none of her goddamn business," Kate snaps. "Though I suppose if it were up to you, you'd sit her down, make her a cup of tea and tell her the whole story."

"And what's *that* supposed to mean?" says Lauren.

"It means that this would suit you, wouldn't it?" Kate glares at Lauren. "You'd love nothing more than to have Dad's memory tarnished."

"Why would I want that?" asks Lauren, fixing her sister with a cold hard stare.

"Because then you'd feel justified for treating him with such contempt for all these years."

"Girls, girls, please," says Rose, who's still visibly shaking and wringing her hands in her lap. "None of this is helping."

"So, what are we going to do?" asks Lauren.

"Nothing," says Kate.

"Don't you think she deserves to be heard?" asks Lauren incredulously. "You can't just dismiss what she said and ignore her."

"That's *exactly* what we're going to do," says Rose icily as she stares at her daughters.

4

LAUREN

"Well, what d'ya know?" Simon smirks, as soon as Lauren has strapped all the children into the backseat of the car and gets into the front. She exhales, letting out the breath she feels she's been holding in for an eternity. She doesn't want to talk about it, but she doubts her husband will give her the choice. "Do you think there's something to it?" he asks.

Lauren turns to look out the window, watching the pavement fall away as Simon pulls off. Jess's sudden appearance is hard enough for *her* to get her head around. She hasn't got the energy to face an interrogation from her husband.

"Who knows?" she says quietly.

"Who would have thought it?" Simon says, chuckling to himself. "The man who spent his life dealing with everyone else's infidelities was up to no good himself."

"It might not be all that it seems," she says. "We shouldn't jump to conclusions until we know the facts."

Simon snorts, and she knows he's about to do exactly

that. He'll enjoy flying in the face of controversy, especially if it will give him a ringside seat.

"All those times he spoke to me like I was a piece of dirt on the bottom of his shoe. All those times he tried to make me feel as if you were too good for me . . ."

Lauren bites down on her lip, to stop herself from saying, *I am*.

"And all the while he was up there, in his ivory tower, he had a secret lovechild."

Lauren takes a deep breath. It's all very well having her own thoughts and feelings about her nearest and dearest, but she can't bear to hear Simon saying them out loud. She'd never dream of airing her opinions on his own dysfunctional family, so she doesn't expect, or want, to hear his views on hers. But she can sense he's looking for a row, and she just doesn't have the strength for another evening of arguments and sleeping on the sofa.

Although, if the truth be known, sleeping alone, even if it *is* on a secondhand couch, where no matter how she lies a spring sticks into her ribcage, is preferable to lying beside her husband right now. The admission saddens her, but these past few months it's felt like every night has been a war zone which she's had to navigate her way through, judiciously avoiding the grenades that Simon throws at her.

"What is it you do all day exactly?" he had tactlessly said when he came in from work the other night to find Lego on the living room floor and a pile of dirty laundry on the landing.

She used to wonder that herself, especially when she'd only had one baby to get up, change, feed and put back to sleep again. Some days, she'd not had time to shower, or even get dinner ready for when Simon got home.

But ironically, the more children they'd had, the more efficient Lauren had become with *her* time and *Simon's* money, as she learned to stretch both to their full capacity. She'd mastered multi-tasking, and had become a wise shopper, searching out the best deals on meat and vegetables and eking the most out of every meal.

When Simon was working, the pressure eased off a little, as Lauren didn't need to worry so much about where the next penny was coming from. But on the occasions he was laid off, which as a laborer on a building site were often, both their purse strings *and* Simon's moods, Lauren noticed, were more difficult to manage.

"I cannot *wait* to see how this all plays out," says Simon, still grinning, although his eyes are fixed firmly on the road. "It's almost a shame that he's not here to repent his sins. I'd love to see how he'd wriggle his way out of *this* one."

Lauren's chest tightens. She's not going to respond, but she doesn't suppose that's going to stop him saying what he wants to say.

"Can you imagine your mum?" he goes on. "She's going to go fucking ballistic if this all turns out to be true."

"Don't use that language in front of the children," says Lauren, although what she really wants to say is, *Don't you dare talk about my family as if we're just some sideshow put on for your own amusement.*

"They're asleep," snaps Simon, without checking.

A car pulls out in front of them. "Careful," calls

out Lauren, dramatically slamming her hand onto the dashboard, hoping that the diversion will dispel the increasingly uneasy atmosphere. Simon honks his horn unnecessarily, but it doesn't distract him from his train of thought.

"Either way, I think we should all take some time out," he says.

"Meaning?"

"Meaning," says Simon, turning to look at her for far longer than feels comfortable, "that we should take this opportunity to back off a bit."

"Back off what?" says Lauren, her patience wearing thin.

"From your family!" he exclaims. "With all this going on, there's really no need for us to be getting together every Sunday. We should wait for all this to calm down."

Lauren can't believe what she's hearing. "Are you serious?"

"Of course I'm serious. We only go through this farce every week to appease your mother, so that she can fawn over the kids and play the doting grandmother. But it seems that there's one or two bad apples in your family and until we find out exactly how rotten they are, it's probably best if we keep the kids out of it."

"This has got *nothing* to do with the kids," Lauren snaps, knowing that he's probably only saying it to rile her and get a reaction. She wishes she were strong enough not to give him one.

"I don't want them in a toxic environment," he says.

Lauren lets out an involuntary snort of disbelief. Can he hear himself? Does he honestly believe that being with her family for Sunday lunch is more damaging to their children than the ominous black cloud that is hanging over their parents' marriage?

"You're being ridiculous," she says, as forthrightly as she dares. "The children enjoy seeing everyone and it's important to give them a sense of family." She refrains from adding that between his own alcoholic father and his mother's penchant for corresponding with prisoners, her family is, by far, the least dysfunctional, even in light of Jess's appearance.

He grunts derisorily. "Who are you trying to kid? You can cut the atmosphere between you and Kate with a knife. You honestly think that gives the kids a true semblance of family?"

"But—" she starts defensively.

"I don't know why you bother," Simon says over her. "There's not exactly much love lost between you two, is there?"

As much as it hurts to hear the words out loud, maybe he's right. Why *do* she and Kate keep up the pretense that they get on? That they have things in common?

"She's my sister," says Lauren.

"Well, now you have another one," says Simon snidely. "Maybe you'll get along a bit better with her."

Lauren's stomach turns over as she thinks back to the events of the past hour. When Jess had walked into the dining room of her parents' house, she'd known instantly who she was. She'd been rooted to the spot as she looked into eyes that were so like her own. She'd felt the air being sucked out of her as she watched the way Jess, startled like a rabbit in headlights, had overused her hands to combat her nervousness—a mannerism so like her own.

She'd wanted to go to her, to tell her the truth instead of sending her on a wild goose chase, looking for a man who doesn't exist, but Kate had stepped in. As Kate *always* does, looking to take control.

For the first time, it occurs to Lauren how Jess's appearance will have affected her mother. She'd seemed shocked, as if it was so far removed from reality that it couldn't possibly be true, but surely she can't be that naive? You can't live with someone for all those years and not know them. She chooses to ignore the voice in her head that says, *Isn't that exactly what you're guilty of?*

When they pull up outside their terraced house, Lauren lifts Emmy out and deftly unclips baby Jude's car seat, while Simon goes ahead carrying a sleeping Noah. She watches as he disappears up the narrow staircase, his shoulder knocking off a chip of peeling paint. She instinctively climbs the four steps to retrieve it from the threadbare carpet. Maybe, when he's in a better mood, she'll ask him again when he might be able to redecorate. The last four times she's asked, his stock answer has been "when I get round to it," but the paint chips are sharp and she worries about one of the children hurting themselves, especially Noah, who's taken to sliding down the stairs on his stomach.

"Right, I'm going to the pub," says Simon, as he comes back down the stairs a little while later.

"What, now?" asks Lauren from the sofa, where she's giving Jude his bedtime feed.

He looks at her. "I assume you haven't got a problem with that."

It's a statement rather than a question. There used to be a time, before the children, when they'd run something like that by each other first, not to ask permission exactly, but as a common courtesy. Now, on the rare occasion that *she* wants to go out, she has to clear it with him weeks in advance. When it gets to the event itself, the children's food, bath and bedtime are planned with precision so that Simon doesn't have to do anything. He then proceeds to call her at least three times, to ask questions that fully grown men should really know the answer to, resulting in Lauren coming back home sober, and earlier than intended. She'd end up thinking that it really wasn't worth her while going out in the first place, and then she'd wonder if that was actually Simon's intention.

She watches as he walks into the kitchen, opens the fridge and drinks the milk from the carton. God, how she hates him doing that. Why can't he get a glass, like everyone else? He wipes his mouth with the back of his hand.

"Right, I'm off," he says, coming back into the living room with his car keys in his hand.

"Why don't you leave the car?" braves Lauren. "Get a taxi. You've already had a couple of drinks."

"I didn't know you were counting."

"I'm just saying . . ."

He leans over her, with one hand on the arm of the sofa and the other behind her head. She instinctively holds Jude tighter to her as she feels his hot breath on her face.

"Why don't *you* worry about women's stuff and leave me to deal with the men's?" he whispers.

She *could* take the comment as an attempt by her

husband to divvy up their responsibilities, albeit chau-
vinistically. Certainly a few years ago, that was all it
would have meant. But things have changed, and Lauren knows that Simon's words are loaded, specifically
chosen to intimidate her.

"*I'm* the man!" she remembers him shouting eighteen months ago as he pinned her up against a wall,
smashing his fist into the door beside her head. Her
legs had threatened to give way as wood splintered
around her. "*I'm* the provider," he'd gone on. "That's
my job—not your fucking father's."

She'd naively thought Simon would be happy that
her dad had discreetly deposited five thousand pounds
into their joint account. He'd obviously known they
were struggling to make ends meet after Simon had
been laid off work two months before. She, for one,
had been grateful. It meant that she could do a food
shop without worrying and not have to constantly justify the need to use the car instead of walking. But
Simon hadn't quite seen it like that, choosing instead
to see it as Harry undermining his alpha-male status,
wounding his fragile ego.

"If I'd wanted your parents' money, I would have
asked for it," he'd yelled, his face turning a putrid
shade of red. "But yet again, your father has seen fit to
wield his almighty sense of self-worth."

"He's only trying to help," Lauren had offered, desperate to defuse the hostile situation she found herself in.

"So you asked him?" he'd said accusingly. "You
went to your parents with your begging bowl?" Bubbles of anger had formed on his lip and Lauren could
see the vivid red marks on his knuckles as his arms
flailed in fury.

"No!" she'd said, though it sounded more like a yelp. "I would never ask them for money."

"So, he just used his initiative, did he?" Simon had sneered, his face still too close to hers. "He decided out of the goodness of his heart to help us, without you saying a word?"

Lauren had nodded feverishly. "Yes, yes. I swear I had no idea he would do that."

Simon had hit the door with his open palm one more time before turning away. If the wall wasn't there to support her, Lauren might well have fallen to the floor in a heap, drained of nervous energy.

"It doesn't have to be a bad thing," she'd chanced, after a minute or two of silence. "It will take the pressure off you—off us."

Simon had laughed and shaken his head in apparent derision. "You think that's why he did it?"

"Well, yes," she'd said, confused. "Why else would he . . . ?"

"It's not done to help us," he said. "It's done with the sole intention of making me look stupid—making me look less of a man."

"But . . ." started Lauren.

"Don't you see?" he'd said, grabbing hold of her arms. She'd instinctively flinched, but something in his eyes had changed. They had a look of what she'd fallen in love with all those years ago.

"This is what your dad does," he'd said softly. "He makes you think he's doing you a favor, but it's all about making himself feel superior."

Was it? Lauren had thought about the man she'd grown up with and couldn't help but wonder if Simon might be right. Was her father's incessant need to help everyone that crossed his path, always keen to champion the underdog, a pretense? She certainly remembered a time when he'd pretended to help *her*.

"You're right," she'd said. "We'll give it back—tell him we don't need it."

She'd hated herself for sounding so conciliatory, but she learned that night that if that's what she needed to do to keep the peace and create a happy home for her children, then so be it. It was a relatively small price to pay.

"I won't be too late," Simon says now, leaning in for a kiss. She can't help but recoil at his ability to switch between Jekyll and Hyde in an instant.

"Okay," she says quietly, suddenly desperate to get him out of the house.

As soon as she hears the front door close, her shoulders slump forward, the pent-up nerves and tension flooding out. How had this happened? When had their marriage become so fraught with anxiety?

Lauren thinks back to when they first met eight years ago, at a bar close to King's College Hospital, where Lauren worked on the labor ward. Simon was on a job in nearby Lordship Lane and was obviously the joker in his crowd. He was charming and made her laugh which, after years of dating self-obsessed numbnuts, was a breath of fresh air. He also happened to be in the right place at the right time, as with her thirtieth birthday behind her, the old biological clock was ticking loudly in her ears.

She'd thought she loved him, or had at least convinced herself that she *could*. Yet gradually, as each year had passed, his ambivalence toward her had driven her insane. One day she was his be-all and end-all, the next he would casually cast her aside, as if she meant nothing to him. It was the not knowing *which* Simon would walk through the door each night that gave her the most anxiety. And despite being together for all this time, she is no nearer knowing what triggers him one way or another. The realization that she doesn't know what makes her husband tick, and even more importantly, what makes him stop, shames her.

5

LAUREN

Lauren's hand hovers over her phone. She should call her mother, just to make sure she's okay, but as she's about to press a thumb on *Mum* in her contact list, the front doorbell rings. Lauren instinctively looks at the time on the screen and relaxes when she realizes it's not as late as she thought it was.

She imagines the momentary awkwardness that will hang between her and Kate, who she's sure will be standing on the other side of the door. They'll eye one another warily, sussing out each other's moods, trying to pre-empt their reaction to the bombshell that's just befallen their family. Lauren will invite her in, and Kate will make a show of checking her watch and saying, "Okay, but just for a minute." As if she's the only one of them who is constantly chasing time.

"Jess!" Lauren blurts out as she swings the door open.

"Lauren," says Jess softly. "Or is it Kate?"

"What . . . ? I mean . . . how did you know where I lived?"

"I followed you from Rose's house," says Jess matter-of-factly, as if it's completely normal. "Can I come in?"

"Well, I don't know if that's a good idea . . ." starts Lauren. "What . . . what if someone sees you?"

"Your mother or your sister, you mean?"

Lauren nods, as her mouth dries out. She swallows in an attempt to summon the ability to talk.

"So, can I come in?"

Lauren nods numbly again and steps aside, peering up and down the road before she closes the door.

"S-so what do you want?" asks Lauren.

"Answers," says Jess, looking around the small living room.

A heat rises up from Lauren's toes, making every blood cell that is circulating around her body feel like it's on fire. She falls down onto the sofa, more out of necessity than choice, and silently signals to Jess to take a seat on the armchair opposite. *I wish Kate was here*, she thinks, before pulling herself up, surprised by her own admission.

"So, what do you want to know?" she asks, as she runs through the million and one questions of her own that are flying around her head.

"Everything," says Jess, taking a seat.

Lauren feels winded as she sits there, opposite Jess, without any other distractions. The similarity between them is uncanny and the juxtaposition of how close they are, but yet so far apart, makes Lauren shudder involuntarily.

"You didn't seem that surprised to see me," says Jess. "At least, not as surprised as your sister or your mother."

Lauren can't pull her eyes away from Jess, transfixed by her every move and idiosyncrasy. "I don't know what you want me to say," she says, when she eventually finds her voice.

"I want to know where my father is," says Jess. "Because it felt like you were all hiding something."

Lauren coughs, clearing her throat. "I . . . I'm afraid that my father . . ."

Jess looks at her expectantly, her blue eyes, so like Lauren's, wide and hopeful.

"My father . . ." she starts, ". . . passed away."

Jess's mouth falls open. "But . . . but . . ." she stutters as tears pool in her eyes. She bows her head as they fall silently onto her cheeks.

Lauren's chest caves in as she fights the instinct to get up and go to her. "I'm so sorry."

"Wh-when?" croaks Jess.

Lauren looks down at her hands, visibly shaking in her lap. "Ten months ago," she says quietly. "He had a heart attack. It was very sudden."

"Was he at home? Who was with him? Did he say anything? Anything at all to the people who were with him?"

Lauren looks at her, taken aback. "No . . . no . . . I don't think so. He was at a client's house when it happened."

"Who was it? Do you know who it was?"

"It was a woman who he'd been helping with a divorce," says Lauren, confused by the line of questioning. "I don't remember her name—she was just a client."

"I need to speak with her," says Jess abruptly. "I need to know who she is."

"What for?" asks Lauren, suddenly going on the defensive.

"Did he say anything to her?" asks Jess frantically. "Anything at all?"

"About what?"

"Me!" exclaims Jess. "Did he say anything about me?"

Lauren lets out a derisory laugh. "Do you honestly believe that *your* name would be the first to leave his lips when he was dying? Before his wife and the two daughters he brought up?"

Jess bites down on her lip and Lauren immediately feels remorseful. "I'm sorry, I didn't mean—"

"I *know* what you meant," says Jess tearfully. "I just thought it might have been the moment that he told the truth. That he might have redeemed himself and confessed the secret he's been hiding for twenty-two years."

"I'm sorry," says Lauren. "It was very quick, and he never regained consciousness. If it's any consolation, none of us got to say goodbye."

Jess sniffs and puts her head in her hands.

"You look like me," blurts out Lauren. She'd not meant to say it out loud.

"I know," says Jess, looking up, with the tiniest hint of a smile.

"Did you ever meet him? Do you remember anything about him?" asks Lauren.

Jess stands up and walks to the front window. The light is fading and the street lamp outside the house is burning with a low orange light.

"No."

Selfish relief rushes out of Lauren's body as her overactive imagination is silenced. She was worried that Jess would have memories that she didn't want to hear. She couldn't bear to think about her father bouncing her up and down on his knee, or taking her to the zoo with another woman.

"I can't believe he's gone," says Jess, as another tear falls onto her cheek. "I had so many questions to ask him. So many things I wanted to say."

Lauren forces herself to stay where she is, even though every natural fiber in her body makes her want to reach out to the broken young girl in front of her.

"Could your mother not help you?" asks Lauren. "Might she be able to fill in some of the gaps?"

Jess pulls herself up, taking a deep breath. "She might, if I knew who she was. I was given up for adoption when I was a baby."

A heaviness weighs down on Lauren's chest at the thought of what this young woman has been through. "I'm so sorry," she says.

"Don't be," says Jess, with a hollow laugh. "It was for the best. For whatever reason, my birth parents obviously didn't feel they could care for me in the same way that someone else could. And I'm truly grateful to them for that. I've had a good life, probably better than they could ever possibly have given me. My adoptive parents were amazing. I couldn't have asked for a better start in life. They've given me the best of everything."

Lauren smiles, consoled by the image of a baby being rocked in the arms of parents who really loved and wanted her. A couple who had fought long and hard, with a courage and determination that most birth parents didn't need to possess, because everything they'd wanted had come naturally to them. People like her father, who'd had a baby with reckless abandon, but who was too cowardly to take responsibility for it.

Shame threatens to overwhelm her as she contemplates how he could have let his own flesh and blood go through the trauma of an adoption, just because he wasn't man enough to tell his wife what was going on. Who knows what might have happened if he had? Perhaps the three girls could have grown up as sisters, rather than endure the shock of finding each other twenty-two years later.

"I'm so pleased to hear that," says Lauren eventually.

"If only I'd found him earlier," says Jess, blowing her nose into a tissue. "I had so many things to ask him. Now I'll never get the chance."

"You can ask *me*," says Lauren, softening to Jess's plight. "I might not have all the answers, but I can certainly try and build you a better picture of who he was." Though even as she's saying it, she wonders how well she really knew her father after all. Her childhood memories of him jar noisily against those from her adult years.

Lauren remembers the night a woman came to the door, crying hysterically and demanding to see him. Her mother had done all that she could to placate her, even offering to make her a cup of tea, but she wouldn't believe that Harry wasn't home. "I *must* speak to him," she'd shouted. "I keep calling, but he's refusing to talk to me." In Rose's infinite wisdom, or perhaps naivety, she'd tried to assure the woman that he was very busy at work and had hundreds of distressed spouses desperately in need of his time and expertise, but it seemed to fall on deaf ears.

"She's still there," Lauren had called out to her mum, while looking onto the street below from behind the net curtains in her bedroom.

"Come away from the window," Rose had remonstrated. "Your dad will deal with it when he comes in."

Had Harry told Rose about this neurotic client of his? Warned her even, that she might show up at their home, because that's the kind of woman she was? Had they laughed about it together, as he'd regaled Rose with the juicy stories of his day? Or was his wife sitting downstairs, alone with her thoughts, and wondering if this was more than a manic plaintiff in a divorce case?

The memory throws Lauren back out with a jolt and she's almost surprised to find Jess still sitting in front of her. An overwhelming sense of guilt consumes her as she imagines how differently this could have all played out.

"Do you think he even knew I existed?" asks Jess, looking at Lauren square-on.

Lauren's stomach turns as her brain rapidly takes her back, offering her distorted flickering images and barely audible soundbites of a time that she'd tried so hard to forget. There are raised voices and a palpable sense of disappointment and betrayal, though whether they're coming from Harry, Rose or her imagination isn't clear.

"Yes, I think he knew you existed," Lauren says carefully.

"And you?" Jess presses. "Have you always known I was out there?"

Tears prick Lauren's eyes. "Yes," she says, swallowing the lump in her throat. "I've just been waiting for you to show up."

6

KATE

"Wow!" Matt exhales the next morning, as he sips his coffee while leaning against the kitchen worktop. "So, do you think there's anything in it?"

Kate looks at him as if he's crazy and forces a laugh. "I don't think so, do you?"

"So, you don't think your dad . . ."

She switches the food blender on full power, drowning out his absurd words. There's no part of her that wants to drink the celery, kale and spinach smoothie that's being spun around the glass jug. But if it stops Matt from going there, then she'll gladly down three pints of it.

As much as Kate had tried to stop thinking about the woman who called herself Jess, her face seems to be indelibly printed on the inside of her eyelids. As soon as she'd closed her eyes last night, there she was, goading her.

She's hit by the sudden recollection of her dream, which until that very moment had buried itself within her subconscious. How do dreams do that? How does an inane thought or action the next day recall such a vivid collection of images, so real and lifelike that it feels as if you've been thrown straight back into them?

Kate can see Jess's pinched face in all its clarity, mocking her from afar, as she taps on her watch—a ticking timebomb. They're at a party, it's her father's sixtieth, though he'd died at fifty-nine, and she can see him dancing, surrounded by his family and work colleagues, having the time of his life. Kate had wanted to freeze-frame that moment, because she knew that she was about to stand on the stage and deliver the truth about the much-loved man, stunning the party into silence.

She kept looking at Jess as she made her way to the microphone, silently begging her not to make her do this. But Jess just tapped at her watch again and smiled, leaving Kate in no doubt that if *she* didn't do it, Jess would.

"Ahem," she said over the loudspeaker, into a room that suddenly resembled London's O2 arena. "Excuse me."

The music ground to a halt and the lights went up, illuminating every inch of the vast space. Kate looked down at her mum and dad, who smiled up at her, their arms wrapped around one another. She cleared her throat and tried to speak, but couldn't, and stumbled toward the edge of the stage, desperate to reach her parents before they realized what was happening. She felt herself fall and the next thing she remembers is being held by Matt.

"You were having one hell of a nightmare last night," he says now, as the blender grinds to a halt.

"Was I?" says Kate, her grief suddenly magnified by the memory of the dream. She can recall her father so clearly—see him standing there, smiling up at her, willing her on—how could he not be here in real life? It makes her want to clamber back into her night-time vision so she can see him, touch him, smell him. The realization that that will never happen again snakes around her heart.

Matt puts his mug in the sink and takes her in his arms, folding himself around her, and she wishes she could stay here all day. Protected from the outside world, keeping their baby safe. *How ironic*, she thinks. *That I want nothing more than for this baby to have a life, yet I'm already scared I won't be able to shield it from what life may have in store.*

"Will you be okay?" Matt asks, as if he can hear the exhausting thoughts that are filling her brain. He knows her so well that he probably can.

She gives a little nod into his chest.

"Do you want to talk to me when you're ready?"

She looks up at him, smiling gratefully. "Thank you."

"Look after yourself," he says. "I'll see you tonight."

She doesn't want him to go, because when he does, she's going to be forced to face the day and the very real problems that Jess's appearance has caused.

She waits until she's had a shower and done her make-up before making the call, her confidence strangely bolstered by a flick of mascara and swipe of lipstick. As Lauren's phone rings, Kate's still inspecting herself in the mirror, leaning in closer to retrieve the gloopy residue that sits in the corner of her eye.

"Hey, it's me," she says, over-cheerfully.

"Hi." Lauren sounds wary and Kate can't blame her.

"Look," says Kate. "I'm sorry about how I acted

yesterday. I said some unfair things that I really didn't mean."

"About how Jess turning up suited me?" Lauren says pointedly.

"Mmm, yes, I don't know why I said that."

"So how are you feeling today?" asks Lauren.

"Honestly? Like shit. I dreamed about it all night and when I woke up this morning, I honestly thought Dad was still alive and that woman was a character from my worst nightmare."

"I had a pretty rough night as well," admits Lauren.

"Have you spoken to Mum?"

"Not yet, you?"

"No, I think it might be better if you have a chat with her first, just to see how she's feeling."

As much as Kate tries to ignore it, it pains her that that is the natural default setting of their family dynamic. It had become even more so since Lauren had had children. Kate supposes that's what happens when a woman's daughter has her own babies; the two of them instinctively come together, as if it's an exclusive club that only those who have borne a child can be members of. Kate caresses her stomach, as if hoping to find a bump there. She can't help but feel disappointed when she doesn't.

"Yeah, I think you're right," says Lauren. "I was going to pop round there once I've dropped Noah off at school."

"Okay, let me know how it goes, will you?"

"Are you not going to talk to her yourself?" her sister asks.

"I will do later," says Kate. "But I'm at work all day, and anyway, I'm sure that now we've all had a chance to think about it, we know that what that woman said yesterday was just completely farcical."

"So, you don't believe her?" asks Lauren.

Kate feels her hackles rise, unable to believe that Lauren would even feel the need to ask.

"Of course not!" she exclaims. "Why, do you?" There's a delay at the other end, just a few seconds, but it's enough to give Kate a clue as to what's coming.

"I . . . I just think we should listen to what she has to say," says Lauren hesitantly.

Now it's Kate's turn to go quiet, as she tries to make sense of what Lauren's suggesting.

"I just think we should hear her out," Lauren goes on. "You never know, she might have unequivocal proof."

"And this is how you're going to approach it with Mum, are you?" asks Kate eventually.

"Well, I'll play it by ear," says Lauren.

"May I make a suggestion?" says Kate, unable to keep the frustration from her voice.

"Sure."

"This woman—"

"Jess," cuts in Lauren.

"This *woman*," repeats Kate, ignoring her, "turns up, out of nowhere, at our family home, claiming to be our father's daughter."

"Yes," says Lauren.

"And your immediate thought is that it might be true?"

"Well, yes," says Lauren. "Isn't it yours?"

"No!" exclaims Kate. "See, this right here is what I'm talking about. It wouldn't occur to me to believe it, not for even a second, yet you, having had time to sleep on it, have decided that it's a possibility. That's the difference between you and me, Lauren. I trusted Dad with all my heart, and I will continue to do so until my dying day. No matter what that woman may *say*, or what you may *think*."

"Well, then I think you're deluded," says Lauren, under her breath.

"Just do yourself a favor," says Kate, forcing herself not to rise to the bait, "don't ever let Mum know your true feelings. The man she loved and lived with for the past forty years has been suddenly taken away from her. We might think we know what that must feel like—he was our father after all—but I don't think we can possibly imagine how it must feel to lose your life partner, the person you woke up to every morning, the person you shared your innermost thoughts with—"

"But—"

"She won't thank you for it," says Kate. "And she might never forgive you for it either."

"So, you think we should lie to her," says Lauren. "Just to keep her memory of Dad preserved."

"*I* won't need to lie," says Kate abruptly. "Because the father *I* remember is the father I had. Nothing you or anyone else says will ever change that."

"We can't just ignore what Jess is saying. If what she's saying is true, it might just make the pain of losing Dad that little easier to bear."

"You're willing to believe her because you think it'll somehow ease our grief?" Kate exclaims incredulously.

"I just think that it might give us all some perspective, especially Mum, who's not been herself since he's been gone. If she realized that maybe he wasn't the man she thought he was, she might not feel his loss so profoundly."

"Now who's deluded?" hisses Kate.

"You never know," says Lauren. "Jess might even bring us closer."

"Over my dead body."

"Let's hope it doesn't come to that," says Lauren, before hanging up.

7

LAUREN

Lauren was going to tell Kate that she'd seen Jess, but their conversation hadn't gone the way she'd hoped. She doesn't know why Kate is so adamant in shutting herself off to the possibility that their father might not have been all that they thought he was. She naively hopes that their mother isn't going to be quite so opposed to the idea.

"Hi, it's only me," she calls out, at pains to sound normal as she lets herself into her parents' semi-detached home. A familiar warmth immediately wraps itself around her, the smell of baking merging with the dulcet tones of BBC Radio 2's Ken Bruce, as he quizzes a contestant on PopMaster. This is Lauren's safe place, though she has to admit it doesn't feel quite so dependable since her father's been gone. It shouldn't make a difference, not in the scheme of things, not when she hadn't confided in him about what was going on with Simon. But still, if she was honest, she'd known that if it ever hit the fan, like *really* kicked off, her dad would have been the first in line to protect her.

"I'm in here," says Rose, sticking her head around

the kitchen door. Lauren gently puts the car seat down, with a sleeping Jude inside, and carries Emmy, who's kicking her little legs with excitement, down the hallway toward her Nana.

"Hello, my precious girl," says Rose as she discards her oven glove and takes Emmy in her arms. Lauren looks at her quizzically, noting that nothing about her mother is any different. She looks just the same as she looked yesterday, *before* a girl arrived claiming to be her dead husband's lovechild.

"You okay?" she asks hesitantly.

"Absolutely," says Rose, and Lauren hears that lilt in her voice that gives the game away. She's far from okay.

"Listen, I just wanted to talk about Jess and what happened," says Lauren. "I can't imagine how you must be feeling about it all."

"I'm fine, absolutely fine," Rose insists. "Now, what does this baby girl want for breakfast?" She tickles Emmy and the little girl squirms delightedly in her arms.

Lauren *could* leave it. She almost feels compelled to, so that they can go back to pretending that they're just like every other family. But this isn't about them. This is about Jess, and Lauren knows that she has set something in motion that she can't stop.

"We need to talk," says Lauren, more assertively.

"Honestly, darling, there's really no need. I'm absolutely fine."

Lauren swallows and picks an imaginary piece of fluff off her trouser leg. "But it's not just about you or us," she says, without looking up. "This is about a woman who thinks . . ."

Rose goes to her daughter and cups her face. Emmy giggles and reaches out with her own hand to touch her mother's other cheek. The two women can't help but smile. "Your father was a good man," says Rose earnestly. "Don't let a stranger destroy your faith in him."

"But she's not a stranger," says Lauren, pulling away. "And while I can understand you not wanting to have anything to do with her, I want the chance to get to know her. I want the *children* to get to know her."

Rose retracts her hand as if she's been burned. "You can't possibly be serious," she says, looking at her daughter as if she's mad. "You don't know the first thing about this woman. She turns up here, out of nowhere, professing to be my late husband's child, and you're honestly going to believe what she's saying? You're going to allow her to denounce the memory of your father? She could be absolutely anybody. But I tell you one person she's not . . ."

Lauren waits with raised eyebrows.

"Your sister."

"But Mum, I—" starts Lauren, before Rose holds her hand up.

"Enough."

It's what her mother has always done when she doesn't want to hear something she doesn't like. *Maybe that's why we're in this predicament*, thinks Lauren.

"You can't just shut me down like that," she says, sounding more confident than she feels. She may be thirty-eight years old, but she'll *always* be her mother's daughter—she only needs to get a certain look from Rose to make her feel five again.

Rose purses her lips tightly together and takes Emmy to the oven to see the rising sponge cake. "Yum," she says, as Emmy giggles and blows raspberries.

Lauren's chest tightens and she stands up straighter,

in the hope that it will give the impression that she's feeling far more forthright than she actually is. "A woman came to our house one time . . ."

Rose shoots her that look and Lauren's stomach rolls over, but she refuses to back down.

"Do you remember?" she pushes on, a gentler tone to her voice.

Rose shrugs her shoulders.

"She was demanding to see Dad," says Lauren, trying to jog her mother's memory, but feeling wretched for trawling up something she may have spent years burying. "She said that she'd been calling him, but he'd been avoiding her."

"He avoided a lot of women," says Rose. "Because they all felt that they held the monopoly on his time. That's just the way he made his clients feel. That's why he was so good at what he did, but it was also his downfall."

"She didn't *look* like a client."

Rose laughs. "None of them ever did! I remember this one time, when we were at a charity function at one of the big London hotels, and this woman sashayed up to him as we were eating our meal. She looked straight at me as she whispered something that made your father choke on his chicken. He was going all red and I didn't know whether to give him the Heimlich maneuver or throw a bucket of cold water over him."

Lauren can't help but smile. "Did you ever find out what she'd said?"

"Your father couldn't bring himself to repeat it, but suffice to say, the woman was a recently divorced client who had perhaps misread the signals. You have to understand that a lot of the women he worked for were lonely and would do anything to feel loved and wanted again."

"Including going to bed with their married divorce lawyer?"

"If your father had been that way inclined, yes," says Rose. "But he wasn't, so . . ."

"But—"

"You need to stop with this now, Lauren," says Rose, putting Emmy down on the floor. "Before it gets out of hand."

"But there must be something to all this," says Lauren, knowing this is her one and only chance. She'll not be brave enough to bring it up again.

"You need to drop this nonsense."

"I know this must be painful for you," says Lauren. "And I'm sorry for that—truly I am—but I can't deny a young girl the chance of knowing who she is, just because Dad made one mistake twenty-two years ago."

"She is *not* your father's daughter," hisses Rose.

"Mum, please . . ." says Lauren.

"She is *not* your father's daughter," Rose repeats.

"But Mum, I *know* that she is."

Rose looks at her, momentarily stupefied. "How could you possibly *know* something like that?"

Lauren shifts, unable to look her mother in the eye. "Because it's in her DNA."

8

KATE

It's taking all of Kate's willpower not to fall asleep during the conference meeting. She can hear her editor's monotone voice drifting in and out of her psyche, something about an American pop star dating an electrician from Croydon, but she doesn't feel present in her surroundings. At one point, her head drops unconsciously onto her chest. A sharp elbow in her ribs rouses her enough to sit up straight and she looks at Amy beside her, confused, but thankful.

"Rough night?" asks her colleague as they file out of the boardroom.

"Something like that," says Kate, smiling.

"You look awfully pale," says Amy. "You sure you're feeling all right?"

Now Kate comes to think of it, she doesn't feel well, and she instinctively puts a hand to her stomach. Her mind has been so preoccupied by yesterday's events that she had hardly given the baby a second thought.

Her brain goes into overdrive, recalling the significant dates of the last three IVF attempts. How could she not have remembered that day seven, *today*, was usually the day she found out she *wasn't* pregnant.

She immediately feels a tug in her groin, as if a weight is pulling her down to the floor. If it was her first cycle, she'd optimistically think that it was a psychosomatic symptom that came with anxiously willing herself to be pregnant. But on her fourth, she knows it's the prelude to a heart-wrenching visit to the toilet.

As Kate rushes to the bathroom, she's riddled with guilt that she's allowed Jess's appearance to monopolize her thoughts. But in the split second that follows, she acknowledges that it's almost a relief to have something else to worry about. For three years, every waking moment has been filled with the anticipation, excitement and the ultimate disappointment that descends on her when she finds out she's not pregnant. It's been a never-ending cycle of hope and despair, and these two weeks, after the embryo transfer and before the pregnancy test, are always the worst. She suspects that it's because she has nothing to do except wait, which after months of injections, appointments and scans, feels interminable.

She lets out an audible "Oh," when she realizes that nothing appears to be wrong, and calls Matt from the cubicle, suddenly desperate to hear his voice.

"Hey, you okay?" he asks nervously when he picks up the phone. Maybe *he* knows what day it is too.

"Yeah, just tired," says Kate.

Matt lets out a deep breath. "That's a good thing, no?"

"I guess," she says. "Unless you're me. How's *your* day going?"

"Well, so far I've interviewed five applicants for a

job I know they're not going to get within a minute of shaking their hands."

"That bad, eh?" sighs Kate.

"Honestly, I can't tell you," says Matt, laughing. "They may well have all the right qualifications on paper, but put them in front of a human being and they can barely make eye contact."

"That's because they're much more at ease engaging with a computer screen or mobile phone," she says. "They can't communicate in normal social situations. This is the way it's going to be from now on."

"And yet this is the world we're preparing to bring a baby into."

Kate can't tell him that the same thought kept her awake sometimes, wondering whether they were doing the right thing.

"How many more interviews have you got this afternoon?" she asks.

"Thankfully only three more. I'd like to at least feel today hasn't been a complete waste by the time I leave the office, but I'm not holding out much hope."

"Well, good luck."

"Thanks—I'm going to need it. How are you feeling about what happened yesterday? You spoken to Lauren or your mum yet?"

"I spoke to Lauren earlier—she's gone to see Mum this morning. The more I think about it, the more ridiculous it is. I mean, my dad would have never . . . He just wouldn't."

"And what's Lauren's take on it?" asks Matt. "Does she share your confidence?"

"You know Lauren," says Kate wearily. "She and

Dad never really saw eye to eye, so I'm sure she's more than happy to pick this up and run with it for as long as she can. But it's honestly the most ridiculous thing I've ever heard. I cannot even tell you."

"You don't have to," says Matt. "I knew your father . . ."

"Exactly," says Kate, grateful that she doesn't have to justify herself any further.

"I'll make dinner," says Matt, changing the subject. "Something light."

"That'll be great," she says. "Love you."

"Love you too."

If she leaned her head on the tiled wall for just a few minutes, she's sure she could fall asleep.

"Kate! Are you in here?" calls out Daisy, the new intern on the entertainment desk.

She must have dropped off, as she jumps up with a jolt, the blood rush to her head making her feel dizzy.

"Er, yep, I'll be out in a sec."

"No rush—there's just somebody downstairs for you."

"On my way."

A few minutes later, Kate takes a deep breath as the lift doors open onto the lobby.

The only problem with having her byline on show-biz stories in the paper is that would-be hacks turn up to hawk their tales about the first wife of a lead singer of a seventies rock group who's now residing in their village. It also wasn't unusual for a man to arrive in reception claiming to be the ghost of Elvis Presley. Kate tended to pass those ones on to the science team, under the guise of being a supernatural feature.

Chloe on the front desk nods her head toward a woman who is standing with her back to them, watching the bank of TV screens that showcase the channels the media conglomerate also owns. Kate's relieved to see that she's dressed sensibly—the first sign that she can't be *too* eccentric—and hopes that whatever she has to say won't take up too much time.

"Hi," she says as cheerily as she can manage. "I'm Kate Walker, how can I help you?"

As the woman turns around, Kate feels winded and sways in an effort to keep herself upright.

"Hi," says Jess, holding out her hand.

Panicked, Kate looks to Chloe, and is relieved to see that she's too busy answering a call to notice the heat that is sure to be radiating from her glowing cheeks.

"You?" she hisses. "What the hell are you doing here?"

Jess, who Kate can now see is a little older than she first thought, cocks her head to one side and smiles sweetly. There's an air of professionalism to her that she didn't have yesterday. In her ripped jeans and T-shirt, she'd looked like a student from a reputable university. Today, dressed in a smart black trouser suit, with a crisp white blouse underneath, she looks a good few years older, and as if she means business.

"I wonder if I might have a word."

"I thought we made ourselves quite clear yesterday. Whatever information you think you have is wrong. You have nothing to do with us—you are *not* our family."

"I'm not here to cause any trouble," says Jess.

"So, what do you want?" asks Kate, before holding her breath for the answer.

"I just wanted to say sorry. I should never have turned up like that yesterday, not without knowing what I now know."

"Which is?" asks Kate hesitantly.

Jess looks down at the floor. "That . . . that my father is dead."

"H-how do you know that?" Kate stutters, all too aware that she'd not divulged that information the day before.

"Your sister told me."

"Lauren?" says Kate, far louder than she'd intended. She looks around the vast lobby as a few heads turn in her direction. She suddenly wishes she *was* dealing with the ghost of Elvis.

"If I'd known that he wasn't . . . here, I'd have never burst in on your family like that." Jess looks close to tears. "I was hoping to find *him*."

Kate feels a band pull tight around her abdomen and she's reminded to try and stay calm, if not for herself, then for the baby she's trying to grow. Taking Jess forcibly by the arm, she steers her toward the doors and out onto the street. "What do you mean Lauren told you he'd died? When? How?"

Jess looks at her, as if surprised she needs to ask. "Last night," she says. "I saw her last night."

"Wh-what?" Kate can't even begin to comprehend what she's being told. "When?"

"At her house."

"You . . . you went to her house?" Kate feels all the air inside her rush out. "After you came to my parents'?"

Jess nods and looks away, as if it's finally beginning to dawn on her that she might be speaking out of turn.

Kate puts her hand out to steady herself against the mirror-like glass of the building's exterior. As she looks around, everything feels out of place, like she's just landed from another universe. It's as if she's in a bottle and Jess's distorted features are peering in, laughing and goading her.

"I'm sorry, did she not tell you?" asks Jess. "I assumed you would have spoken this morning."

"I need to go," says Kate, breathlessly, turning on her heel and heading back into the building. She's grateful for the blast of cool air that hits her like a slap across the face, but she feels like Bambi on ice as she walks across the polished marble floor, her legs seemingly struggling to hold the rest of her body up.

She rushes from the lift onto the open-plan news and features floor. Her desk is, thankfully, a little removed from the main melee, nestled in a corner, overlooking Cabot Square twelve floors below. She grabs her phone and slings her leather bucket bag onto her shoulder.

"I've got a lead I need to follow up," she calls out, to no one in particular. "I'm going to meet a source."

There are murmurs of acknowledgment and a look of awe from Daisy.

Kate makes her way to the station, but as she's about to go into the bowels of the London Underground, she stops to call Lauren, who picks it up on the first ring.

"Hello?" her sister says, tentatively.

Hearing her voice makes Kate want to climb down the telephone line and put her hands around her throat.

"What the hell is going on?" she almost shrieks.

"Please tell me you know nothing more about this Jess girl than the rest of us do."

There's a deafening silence at the other end. "Lauren!" barks Kate.

"I'm with Mum," says Lauren quietly. "You'd better come over."

9

LAUREN

As soon as Lauren hears Kate's key turning in the lock, she jumps up, wide-eyed, and starts chewing on the skin around her thumbnail.

Rose sits on the other side of the kitchen table, her face ashen, staring into space.

Lauren waits for the front door to shut, knowing that how it closes will offer a clue as to how mad Kate is. It bangs with such ferocity that it makes her shudder. This is going to be far worse than she could have ever imagined.

"You'd better start talking," says Kate, coming in and throwing her handbag onto the table, "and it had better be good, because I swear to God . . ."

Lauren looks from her sister to her mother and back again. "I was just explaining to Mum . . ." she starts, wishing her voice sounded far more authoritative than it does. She doesn't know why she's so nervous—she's not done anything wrong.

"So, I'll start from the beginning again," she goes on, sitting down and spreading her hands out on the table. She hopes and prays that Jude will wake up and need to be fed, or Emmy grows bored of the brightly colored toys that are littered all over the floor. Anything to create a distraction, to give her more space, as the intensity of the moment is making her feel claustrophobic. She loosens the neck of the top she's wearing as heat burns her ears and makes her brain feel as if it's boiling in its own fluid. *You've done nothing wrong*, she says to herself again, though even *she's* not convinced.

"Ever since Dad died, it's felt like the three of us have grown apart." She looks to Kate, whose jaw is set, lips pulled tight as she glares back. Rose is staring blankly down at the table, but Lauren hopes she's at least listening. "It's as if there's just been this huge hole, a vortex that felt like it was sucking us in."

"It's called grief," says Kate tartly, seemingly unable to keep the vitriol from her voice. "That's what happens when someone you love dies. Though I'm surprised you'd feel it to that degree."

Lauren swallows the barbed comment, refusing to let it get to her, but in some respects Kate's right. She can't possibly claim to have felt their father's death in the same way as Kate did. Lauren's relationship with Harry was complicated, multi-layered, the result of a firstborn being taught hard lessons by a father who didn't know any different. They say ignorance is bliss, but she'd paid a high price for his.

"He was *my* father too."

Kate curls her lip disdainfully.

"So, I was wondering how to close this divide that seems to have opened up between us. If we're all honest, our Sunday lunches have become strained and it doesn't feel as if some of us even want to be here. But just because Dad is no longer with us, it doesn't mean that we should give up something we once looked forward to."

Kate shrugs her shoulders.

"I thought that if we had something in common, a shared interest, that it might bring us closer together."

"So what has any of this got to do with the girl?" asks Kate impatiently.

"I thought it would be a good idea to look back over our heritage and find out more about who we really are," Lauren continues. "It's ironic really, to feel compelled to do something like that after losing the very person who could answer all our questions for us."

"*Isn't it?*" snipes Kate.

"Anyway," Lauren goes on, "I registered with a website that finds your ancestors and distant relatives and . . ."

Kate sits more upright in her chair, while Rose seems to crumple in hers.

"So, you've made a clumsy attempt at tracing our family tree and ended up with a woman who claims to be related to us." Kate exhales, showing visible signs of relief. "There are a lot of lonely people out there looking for a family, *any* family, to attach themselves to. This woman must have thought she'd struck gold when she found you."

Lauren offers a tight smile. "I'm afraid it's not quite that simple."

"Why not?" asks Kate. "We all know that there's absolutely no way that Dad would ever have had an affair, least of all one that resulted in a child." She looks to Rose and laughs, but Lauren can hear that it's hollow. "Right, Mum?"

Rose starts at the sound of her name and looks around, as if seeing the scene for the first time.

"Dad would never have had an affair, would he?" Kate pushes. "It's the most ridiculous thing I've ever heard."

Rose's hands are shaking so violently that Lauren puts her own hand on top of them.

"Well, how else do you explain it?" asks Lauren.

"There's nothing to explain," says Kate. "This is just a classic example of how badly managed these websites are. It's just names in a hat that anyone can pick up and run with. I can't believe you've allowed yourself to be taken in by it." She looks at Lauren scathingly.

Lauren swallows hard, wondering what part of this Kate is missing. "It's not just names," she says bluntly. "It's moved on from family trees. This is about science—this is about DNA."

Kate looks at her blankly, her mouth slowly dropping open.

"This isn't a case of mistaken identity," Lauren goes on. "Or some fly-by-night who fancies their chances at infiltrating a random family. I uploaded my DNA profile."

Kate stands up, looming over Lauren and Rose, gripping hold of the table that sits between them. "Mean-ing?" she says in two slow syllables, her eyes flickering rapidly.

"Meaning, Jess also uploaded her DNA profile, and we're a match."

Rose lets out an involuntary sob and puts a tissue to her mouth to absorb the sound. But little Emmy has already heard it and looks at her grandmother, perplexed, before standing herself up and waddling over to her, as if she knows that something's wrong. The innocence of the moment makes Rose cry even more.

"So, you *knew* she was coming," hisses Kate.

"No, I didn't know she was coming," says Lauren, the words catching in her throat. "I just knew that we'd been matched when she sent me an email."

"Saying what?" demands Kate, her features twisted with anger.

"It was just a couple of lines about who she was and that she'd been looking for her dad for a long time."

"And what did *you* say?"

"I . . . I went back to her to say that I was shocked, but happy to hear from her and gave her our names. That's all. The next thing I know she's at the house."

"So, you didn't give her our address?"

Lauren looks at her, shocked. "Of course not! I was intending to tell you both in the fullness of time. I just hadn't found the right moment."

"So that's it, is it?" snaps Kate. "We're all supposed to believe that she's Dad's secret daughter?"

Lauren has to stifle her surprise at Kate's reticence to accept the scientific proof. Her sister is an intelligent woman, who never misses an opportunity to belittle her with her career achievements, so why is she finding this so hard to grasp?

While Lauren worked twelve-hour shifts on nigh-on minimum wage, Kate had gleefully regaled her with her regular jet-setting jaunts to meet the stars. If she wasn't in LA interviewing A-listers, she was on tour with pop stars. Lauren has lost count of how many times Kate had attended the red carpet at the Oscars, but she knows that she was loaned a couture dress on every occasion. Lauren doesn't even *own* a dress, aside from her midwife's uniform, as Simon only likes her to wear trousers these days.

"But Kate's life just *looks* more exciting," Rose had said, in an attempt to pull Lauren out of a downward spiral of low self-esteem when she was eight months pregnant with her third child. "What *you* do is far more worthwhile." But it didn't feel like it, at two o'clock in the morning, when sick and hungry children had not yet let her sleep and she'd received a picture of Kate in a stunning red dress, holding a bottle of champagne in one hand and some kind of award in the other.

Woo-hoo! Guess who's showbiz reporter of the year?!? she'd written on the group text.

Naturally, it was their father who had replied the fastest. *That's my girl!*

Lauren looks at Kate now and battles the inferiority complex that always hits her whenever her sister's in the room. "It is what it is," she says, and immediately regrets how laissez-faire she sounds.

"It *is* what it *is*?" repeats Kate irritably.

"I didn't mean to sound so glib," says Lauren. "But it's up to each of us, as individuals, what we choose to do next."

"And you choose to do what?" asks Kate.

Lauren clears her throat. "*I'd* like to get to know her, and I'd really like you to get to know her as well."

Kate *tsks* and Rose looks from one daughter to the other. "You can't honestly expect me to take on your father's child with another woman."

"If that's even who she is," says Kate.

"For God's sake," snaps Lauren. "Listen to the pair of you. We're talking about a young woman who is trying to find her way in life. Trying to find where she belongs. Imagine looking for your father for years, only to find him ten months too late."

"Well, she doesn't belong *here*," says Rose defiantly. "This is *my* family and I will not let some interloper come in and destroy it."

"I can't imagine how hard this must be for you, Mum," says Lauren, going to Rose and crouching next to her. "But this doesn't have to mean that everything will change. We've still got each other and you're right, no one should ever be able to take that away. But getting to know Jess and letting her into the fold might do us some good."

"Well, you can count me out," says Kate acerbically.

Rose gets up, throwing Lauren's hands off her lap. "I can't believe you would do this," she says. "Why couldn't you just leave things be? You had no right."

"She has a right to know her family," says Lauren, incensed. "To know where she's from. Are you honestly going to deny her that?"

"She's not from here," screeches Kate. "And she's not my family—she never will be."

Lauren refuses to let the tears fall. Why is everybody conspiring against her, when all she ever wanted to do was bring her family closer together?

10

KATE

Kate is still seething as she sits on the train back to Canary Wharf, unable to believe her mother's reluctance to stand up for their father, and Lauren's naivety. The man opposite looks at her oddly and she glares back with a look of defiance, but then she realizes that her lips are moving, so if she's not been mouthing her dissension, she's been saying it. She wonders which would have made her look madder.

"Oh, for Christ's sake," she says out loud as the train sidles into North Greenwich station. She knows that despite the call of the office—she's got a thousand and one things she should be getting on with—she's not going to be able to ignore the pull of her flat and what's hidden there.

She'd not wanted to root around in the eaves cupboards to find it—she didn't think she would ever need to, but now that Jess has turned up, she doesn't feel she has a choice.

She knows where it will be—in the furthest, darkest

corner—and she crawls behind the wall of their spare bedroom, using the torch on her phone to guide the way.

This box belongs to Kate Alexander.
Top Secret—Do Not Enter.

The words are written in faded black marker across the taped-down lid. Kate can't remember the last time she would have looked in here—probably just before she sealed it up, which must have been when they upped and left Harrogate to move to London twenty-odd years ago. The brown masking tape comes away easily, its underside having long lost its stickiness. That unmistakeable mustiness of nostalgia permeates her nostrils as she lifts the lid—the sight of a Polly Pocket diary almost making her cry, as its very existence transports her to a place and time she's long forgotten. She can hear TLC's "Waterfalls" playing on the CD player in her bedroom, smell her mum cooking a roast dinner and see herself sniveling into her pillow because Freddie Harris had chucked her. They'd seemed like such desperate times back then, but now, with the benefit of hindsight, it was nothing compared to being a grown-up and all that it entails.

She reaches under the teddy she'd named "Bert," who she'd refused to go to sleep without until Lauren had called her a crybaby. Her eyes pass fondly over the cards that the aforementioned Freddie had written her, as an eleven-year-old, when he'd still been in love with her. She'd like to pore over them, and feel the intensity of that first love, but they're not what she's here to look at. She'll do that another time.

She can see the smaller white box under the oversized quill pen that her father had claimed he'd found in the bowels of his chambers in London.

"That'll be from one of the barristers that used to walk the floors in the fifteenth century," he'd enthused.

"I doubt quill pens were even invented then," Lauren had haughtily remarked as she passed by.

"Of course they were," said their father, laughing.

"Well then I bet barristers hadn't been invented then," she'd quipped, ever ready with a cynical comment, especially where their father was concerned. Why *had* there been so much animosity between them?

Kate carefully lifts the smaller box out and lays it on the carpet, as if psyching herself up to open it. She *knows* what's inside it; she just can't remember the details. She takes a deep breath, not knowing whether she wants to be proved right or wrong as she lifts the lid.

The romper looks just as pink as she remembers it, though she'd forgotten about the white embroidered rabbits that hopped across its chest. She picks up the velvet-soft teddy bear that sits nestled in the corner and instinctively holds it against her cheek. Did he hold the key that would unlock their family's secret?

She is suddenly struck by a recollection, so vivid that it's overwhelming. She's standing on the landing, at the bottom of the loft ladder, listening to her dad huffing and puffing.

"Have you found them yet?" she'd called up to him.

"Nope," he'd shouted back, the insulation making him sound as if he was speaking from inside a box. "I'm telling you, they're not up here. Call down to your mother."

"Mum!" Kate had yelled over the bannister. "Dad says the Christmas decorations aren't up there."

"Of course they are," Rose had said in a sing-song voice, breaking away from the duet she was performing with Bing Crosby in the kitchen. "They're in the back corner; there's a couple of bags and a few boxes of red and green baubles."

"Mum says they're red and green and in the corner," Kate called up the ladder.

"I'm telling you, they're *not* up here," he'd said, exasperated.

"Can I come up?" asked Kate. "To help you look."

"Come on then," he'd said, appearing at the hatch with an outstretched arm.

She'd balanced on the beams as if her life depended on it, remembering her father's warning years previously not to go up to the loft without him. "If you fall through the lagging you'll end up in your mother's lap in the front room," he'd said sternly.

Kate was sure that he was spinning her a yarn, but she wasn't taking any chances as she slowly worked her way over to the corner.

While Harry busied himself with trying to find the decorations, Kate had begun to open a few boxes and peer inquisitively inside. The quill pen had been sat on top of a pile of dusty law books. "Can I take this downstairs?" she'd asked, holding it up.

"Yes," Harry had said absently, without even looking at what she was referring to.

She'd pulled out a carrier bag that she'd spied stuffed down between two boxes and put the feathered nib in with the small box that was in there.

"Have you found them yet?" called out Rose. She'd sounded closer than the kitchen.

"The only ones I can find are silver and purple," Harry replied.

There was a lengthy silence and Kate and Harry had looked at each other, as if they knew what was coming—trying not to giggle.

"They're the ones!" Rose exclaimed.

Harry had clenched his fists in exasperation and mouthed a frustrated scream as he looked imploringly at Kate. "You said I was looking for red and green."

"I must have chucked them out," said Rose, blithely oblivious. "I bought silver and purple for last year—I remember now."

Kate had gleefully covered her face with her hand, while her father had blown out his cheeks.

It wasn't until later that day, when her dad had gone out to play golf, that she remembered the box in the bag that she'd brought down. She'd taken it to her mother, holding it open at arm's length.

"What's this?" she'd asked innocently.

Rose gave it a cursory glance. "I have no idea."

Kate had opened the box and lifted a romper suit out, so tiny that it would have easily fitted one of the dolls that she'd only recently thrown out.

Rose had flown across the room, as if she'd sprouted wings, snatching the all-in-one out of her hand. "Where did you get this?" she'd breathed, barely audible.

"It was in the loft," said Kate. "Was it mine?"

"No, no," said Rose, roughly pulling the box out of Kate's hand and inadvertently dropping it to the floor. She'd scrambled to pick up the teddy that had fallen out of it, but hadn't noticed the minute plastic tag that had slid under the oven. "It was Lauren's," she'd said breathlessly, shoving the bear and romper back into the box.

"And what's this?" asked Kate, picking up the piece of plastic that she could now see was a hospital ID tag.

"Nothing!" Rose barked, whipping it out of Kate's hand and shoving it all into the cupboard where they normally kept the saucepans. "Now go," Rose had said, turning back around. "Run along and I'll call you when dinner's ready."

Kate had watched, through the crack in the kitchen door, as her sobbing mother had gone into the sideway and thrown the box into the dustbin.

When she was sure the coast was clear, Kate had crept out there to retrieve the box and all its contents, and hid it under her bed. If it wasn't for Jess, it would most likely have stayed hidden until a time when she might have wanted to show her own children some-thing of the person she used to be. But now, that tag is ringing alarm bells in her head that refuse to be si-lenced.

She can see it, wrapped around the teddy bear's foot, its numbers facing away from her. The significance of what those digits are, and what they might mean, weighs heavily on Kate's chest. She has to be sure that she's ready to face the consequences of what they're going to reveal.

As she twists the tiny tag, the numbers blur as Kate squints, knowing that once she sees them, she will never be able to unsee them. Can she live with that? She tells herself to read the date from the left, but her eyes have already fast forwarded to the last two num-bers: the year. She so wants it to be Lauren's date of birth. It won't help the predicament they find themselves in with Jess, but it would mean, for the most part, that her family is the one she thought it was, the one she now desperately wants it to be.

But the numbers burn indelibly onto her brain, like scores on a punch card.

15/09/96

It's not Lauren. It's not her. It has to be Jess.

11

LAUREN

Lauren is driving around the South Circular, cursing every red light that stops her in her efforts to get Jude to fall asleep. He'd woken up among all the commotion at her parents' house and despite being fed, winded, changed and rocked, he's still screaming an hour later. She used to feel compelled to find a reason for her children's distress, but since her mother had reassured her that "sometimes babies just cry because that's all they can do," Lauren had tried to be a little more relaxed. Though it isn't easy when his cries are beginning to hurt her ears and little Emmy keeps repeating "poo poo" over and over again.

Unable to bear it for a moment longer, she pulls into a petrol station, even though her tank is almost full, and climbs out of the car, slamming the door behind her. The silence that follows almost makes her cry, but the respite is only temporary, for as soon as she drowns out the demands of her children, her thoughts are dragged back to Jess, Kate and her mother.

Lauren knew it was never going to be easy to bring Jess into the fold, but she'd hoped that the way she'd done it would have been better received. Though she had to admit that she had had three months since Jess's email to get used to the idea before she'd turned up at her parents' house. Kate and her mother hadn't even had time to take a breath.

Lauren had known she was potentially opening a can of worms by essentially inviting anyone with a tenuous family link to stake their claim. She'd thought she'd find nothing more than a great-grandfather's cousin, so to find Jess was a shock she was still absorbing when Jess had turned up at the house. Lauren wonders if Jess had known that, and decided to force her hand. But she wishes she hadn't, as all it's served to do so far is to make people say things and hear things they weren't ready for.

"Can I get some paracetamol please?" she says absently to the man behind the counter. He reaches behind him for a box of tablets and hands them to Lauren.

"Anything else?" he asks dourly.

Lauren eyes the miniature bottles of gin that line the shelves and wonders whether it would make her pounding head better or worse.

"Erm, no thanks, just these," she says, instantly regretting it.

He hands her change from a five-pound note, and she turns, practically bumping into the man standing behind her.

"Lauren?" he says, startled.

She looks at him, before pulling back, as if she's trying to shrink herself. She wishes she could turn back around and become anonymous again, because nothing about this encounter is how she'd imagined it being for all these years.

"Justin!" she says, once she's made the split-second decision that there's no way out of this. She instinctively runs a hand through her hair, as if hoping that by some small miracle, her straggly ends have transformed themselves into lustrous curls. Are her cheeks still mascara-stained from when she'd sobbed at the traffic lights earlier? Does she look like a crying clown? Or had she even put make-up *on* this morning? She doesn't know which she'd rather right now.

"Oh my God," says Justin. "Lauren! I can't believe it. How . . . I mean . . . how *are* you?"

She allows her hair to fall forward, in the naive belief that it will cover the color in her furiously burning cheeks.

"I'm good," she says. "Gosh, it's been a while—a long while. I heard you moved to Chicago."

He nods animatedly. "Yes, about twenty years ago. Not long after we—you know."

Lauren looks at the floor, wishing it would open up and swallow her whole.

"But I've been back for a few months now."

She wants to ask him all the questions she's spent the last two decades asking herself. Who did he marry? Does he have children? Has he changed? Why did he leave when she needed him most? The only one she can safely answer is he looks even better than he did when he was eighteen. A few gray hairs pepper his temples and his jawline isn't quite so defined, but his eyes are still the kindest she's ever seen.

Sweat is prickling under her arms, and although her heart wants to stay in this moment forever, her practical head is yelling at her to say what needs to be said and get out of there.

"So, what are you doing now?" she says, finally finding her voice.

"Well, I got divorced a year or so ago," he starts, and Lauren can't help herself from doing a virtual leap. "So when my company asked if I'd be interested in running the UK operation, it seemed like the right time to come home."

The weight of the next question lies heavy on her lips, knowing that the answer will impact her far more than she'd like. Yet still she can't stop herself.

"And . . . children," she says. "Do you have children?"

He looks away, out onto the petrol station forecourt, where time seems to have stood still, and swallows hard. Lauren knows what's coming.

"Erm, yep, two," he says, clearing his throat.

She bites down on her lip to stop herself from crying.

"And what about you?" he asks hoarsely. "Married? Kids?"

How could such a simple question be so difficult to answer? She looks out to her car, where, no doubt, Armageddon is in full swing, and before she knows it, she's shaking her head.

"N-no," she mutters, feeling as if she's lost control of her senses. She's sure her brain is telling her head to nod, but no matter how hard she tries, she can't seem to comply.

"Wow," says Justin, shaking his head from side to side. "I've just always assumed that . . ."

"No," she says, more assertively. "It just wasn't to be."

"Wow," he says again, before laughing nervously. "It's so good to see you."

Lauren can't help but feel disappointed. In herself, for how she looks and what she's said, but most of all because she knows this chance meeting is coming to its natural end.

Ever since Justin had told her it was over, not a day has gone by when she hasn't thought about him, wondering how their perfect life together had gone so wrong.

"But how can you say that?" she'd cried down the phone, the day before her seventeenth birthday.

"It's just how I feel," he'd said, matter-of-factly.

"You told me you loved me two days ago. You promised we'd be together forever. What's changed?"

"*You!*" he'd said. "You're not the person I thought you were."

None of what he was saying made any sense. "Of course I am. I'm still me."

"I'm sorry, but I just don't love you anymore," he'd said before putting the phone down.

No matter how many times she'd tried calling him back and no matter how many times she'd pleaded with his mum to let her see him, he'd never spoken to her again. Just like that, he'd destroyed two and a half years of a love so intense that she didn't think she'd ever breathe again.

Why why why? she wants to scream now, as he pulls her into an awkward embrace. She closes her eyes as her chin rests on his shoulder, his familiar smell transporting her back to those painful teenage years. Despite the harrowing memories, she wishes she could stay here, because no matter what, Justin had always made her feel safe. He'd never treat her like Simon does.

"Good to see you too," she says, removing herself from his arms.

She's already working out whether she's got enough

time to get to her car and drive off before he pays for his fuel. She doesn't know why she lied to him, but now that she has, she can't run the risk of him seeing two red-faced babies screaming in the backseat.

"Take care," she says, backing out the shop door.

He offers a sad smile and raises his hand.

She turns and hurriedly makes her way to her car, just managing to get a grip on the handle when she hears her name being called.

"Lauren, wait up."

"Shit, shit, shit," she says under her breath before turning and almost running back to him.

Justin laughs nervously. "Listen, I know this may sound completely crazy, but do you want to get together?" He looks everywhere but at her. "For a catch-up."

Lauren's mouth dries up and she feels as if she has a tennis ball lodged in her throat.

"No, you're right," he says, without her saying a word. "It's probably not a good—"

"I'd love to," she says, without even realizing it. What the hell was she thinking?

Justin grins. "Really? Wow, great, can I give you my number?"

Her head's racing at a million miles an hour, wondering how she's got herself into this situation and how to get herself out of it. All the time, knowing that she doesn't want to.

"Or perhaps I can take yours?"

She shakes her head, thinking of Simon and what he would do if he found out that she'd given her number to another man. It'd be bad enough if he thought it was a stranger. She can't bear to think what he'd do if he knew it was the boy she once loved more than anything.

"No, I'll call you," says Lauren quickly, before realizing in a hot-headed panic that her phone is in the car. She hops from one foot to another as she contemplates what to do. If she goes to get it, he's likely to follow, and then what will he think? She hedges her bets, hoping that the one she puts money on won't let her down.

"Listen," she says. "I really need to be somewhere, but if you call my number now, I'll have your details, and I'll give you a call in the next couple of days."

Justin punches the digits into his phone with a quiet determination as she recites them. "If I don't hear from you, I'll ring you."

"No!" says Lauren, far too abruptly. "*I'll* call you."

"You promise?"

She can't help but go back to him and reach up to give him a kiss on the cheek. "I promise," she says, walking away, wondering how she's leaving the petrol station with even more problems than she came in with.

12

KATE

"Hey," says Matt, smiling as he emerges from the re-volving door of his office building. He slips an arm around Kate's waist and kisses her cheek. "You okay?"

She could be honest and say, *No, my mother and sister are being the worst versions of themselves, and Jess might well be my sister*, but she smiles and says, "yes," instead.

"To what do I owe this pleasure?" he asks, as they hold hands and fall in step with each other. "You don't normally come up to meet me." His offices are only four blocks away from Kate's, but they're farther from the station, so on the rare occasions they leave work at the same time, Matt would always walk down to Kate.

"I just needed to get out," she says. It's not a lie. Since her suspicions had been confirmed, she'd found it difficult to concentrate, but she wasn't sure she wanted to share her muddled thoughts just yet. At least not until she'd managed to unravel them in her *own* head.

"It was pretty quiet this afternoon," she goes on. "So once I'd put tomorrow's stories to bed, I wanted some fresh air."

"You're okay though, right?" he asks, stopping and turning to look at her.

Commuters tut as they're forced to sidestep around them on the pavement.

Kate instinctively touches her stomach and nods.

"Nothing's happened?" Matt presses.

She shakes her head. "I'm just tired."

"That's all it is?" asks Matt, in a way that suggests he thinks she might be hiding something.

"Yes," she says, smiling at his concern. "That's all." She links her arm through his, encouraging him to start walking again.

"Mmm," he mutters, looking at her through narrowed eyes, as if he's still not quite convinced.

"Anyway, how's *your* day been?" she asks, eager to change the subject. "How did the interviews go? Find anyone suitable?"

Matt groans. "Everyone pre-lunch was a write-off, but there were one or two candidates this afternoon that are promising."

"Is that because you had a couple of drinks in you by then?" she asks, laughing. "Did your beer goggles make them a more attractive proposition?"

Matt nudges her playfully with an elbow. "I'll have you know I've remained sober all day, thank you very much."

"That's unusual for *you*," Kate teases. "For a Monday."

He smiles as he swings open the door into the station, holding it for an attractive woman and her canine companion. "Ah cute," he comments after her.

Kate raises her eyebrows. "Is that the dog or the human?"

Matt rolls his eyes. "So, there were two stand-out applicants this afternoon, but with very different backgrounds. One's straight out of university, having graduated in journalism. The other left school at eighteen, took a work experience position at the local paper and never left. She's having to supplement her minimum wage by working in a bar in the evenings and at weekends."

"Okay," says Kate.

"So, who would you plump for?"

"The one who's working on a paper," says Kate, without hesitation.

"Really?"

"Absolutely. She *really* wants it, so much so that she's prepared to work for next to nothing. I assume she's writing for the paper?"

"Yeah, but only at a very local level."

"But that doesn't matter, because you'll be training her up anyway. You'll want her to do things your way and it'll be a hell of a lot easier teaching someone who's willing to learn versus someone who's spent the last three years in a classroom and thinks they know everything already."

"Speaking from experience, are we?" he says, smiling.

"Actually, I *did* know everything by the time you took me on."

Matt rolls his eyes in mock exasperation. "Or so you thought."

"I think you'll find *I* taught *you* things," says Kate with a cheeky glint in her eye. "Not the other way around."

Matt laughs. "So, you'd do yourself out of a job? You'd take the worker over the slacker?"

"Oi, just because I went to university doesn't make me a slacker," says Kate, breaking away from Matt to tap in at the ticket barrier. "I worked my arse off when I was there."

"So, you'd definitely go for experience over education?" asks Matt, as they jump on the escalator.

"If that's all that's separating them, yes."

"Okay, on your head be it," says Matt. "Have you heard anything from your mum or Lauren?"

Kate tells him about this morning, and the DNA match that Lauren is claiming to have found. Just the thought of her putting their personal details online makes Kate's chest tighten. How could she have been so stupid?

"It might not be your sister's finest hour," he admits. "But it doesn't necessarily mean that the girl is who she says she is."

"How do you mean?" asks Kate, desperate to find any other scenario than the one that's whirring around her head, making her feel as if she's going mad.

"Well, there's got to be some semblance of a match there, especially if they've used an ancestry website, but it doesn't necessarily mean that the players are playing by the rules."

Kate looks at him confused. "So you're saying there's room for error?"

"Put it like this; these big genealogy sites are not in the habit of making mistakes, otherwise we'd all be running around thinking our mother was our sister and our children weren't our own."

Kate can't help but laugh. When he puts it like that . . .

"So, it's safe to say," he goes on, "that if you've uploaded your DNA, you'll only be shown your proven matches."

"O-kay," says Kate hesitantly, unsure where he's going with this, but open to all suggestions.

"So essentially, the DNA *has* to have been a match to have brought Lauren and this girl together. But— bear with me here—what if, crazy as it sounds, the girl has somehow cooked the results."

"By doing what?" asks Kate, stopping stock still on the platform.

"I dunno," says Matt, shrugging his shoulders. "She might have uploaded *your* DNA, for example."

"What?" shrieks Kate, the idea too far-fetched for her to take it even remotely seriously.

"I'm just saying," says Matt. "There are other ways that a match could have occurred, without her actually being related to you."

"But why would anyone go to those kind of lengths?" asks Kate, her investigative mind beginning to whir at the possibility.

"They wouldn't," says Matt decisively, as if sensing the runaway train Kate's just jumped on. "And certainly not where you're concerned, because, let's face it, you're not exactly an intriguing dynasty that someone would commit forgery to be a part of."

Kate playfully slaps his arm.

"I'm just saying that it's a possibility," says Matt. "That's all. You might not want to take this girl at face value."

She had no intention of doing so. "So how come you're a genealogy expert all of a sudden?" teases Kate, keen to inject some light-heartedness to lift her mood.

"Aha," says Matt, tapping a finger to his nose conspiratorially. "Funnily enough, I had an interesting pitch come through from a freelancer today."

"If you're prepared to tell *me* about it, it can't be *that* interesting," says Kate sarcastically.

Matt smiles. "Well, it was a feature about police forces uploading DNA from unsolved crimes to genealogy websites in the hope of finding a match to their suspect."

"Oh," says Kate. "Go on."

"Well, it got me thinking, what with you finding yourself in this rather unsettling position, and I decided to do a bit of digging."

Kate looks at him expectantly.

"It's already bringing in results in the States, on cold cases from decades ago," Matt goes on.

Kate shakes her head. "How?"

"Because despite DNA being left at almost every crime scene, unless the suspect was already on the police database, there was no way of tracking him down. Now, with the help of these websites, the police are able to trace relatives of the suspect and track him down by working backward through the family tree."

"Wow," says Kate. "So from millions of suspects, they're now able to narrow it down to one family."

"Yep, and some offenders have already been charged and are awaiting trial," says Matt as triumphantly as if he'd made the arrests himself.

"So that means that anyone dead, alive or otherwise has the potential to be identified," says Kate.

Matt nods. "It's a game-changer."

Indeed it is, thinks Kate.

"So now that Lauren has put herself in this position, what does she make of it?" Matt asks.

"She seems pretty set on this girl being the real deal, but that's because it would suit her to have Dad's name dragged through the mud."

Matt pulls a disbelieving face. "I know she and your father were never close, but still . . . it's a bit of a leap. I mean, why would she want that?"

"Because she knows that it would hurt me, and he's no longer here to defend himself."

"But that just doesn't make sense," says Matt through a frown. "I know you don't always see eye to eye, but no more than me and my brother. That's how siblings are; you love each other, but don't necessarily like each other all of the time."

"I don't think she has the first clue as to what she might have unleashed," says Kate bitterly.

"Woah, let's not get ahead of ourselves," says Matt, holding his hands up. "This girl might be exactly who she says she is. And if that's the case, it's not exactly going to be rocket science to work out whose child she is."

Kate bites down on her lip. If only it were that simple.

"But then again, maybe Lauren knows something you and I don't?"

Kate's hackles rise. "Like what?"

"I just think she might know more than she's letting on . . . about your dad, I mean."

Kate had had a lifetime of defending her father to Lauren, but she didn't ever envisage having to do it to Matt, who had so often teamed up with Harry whenever a family debate had ramped up unexpectedly.

They had a middle-class background in common, both erred slightly to the right on the political spectrum and shared a love of football that was only eclipsed by their love for her.

As was always the case in the Alexander household, as soon as talk turned to politics, the gloves were off and it became a free-for-all. To an outsider looking in, it might have seemed stacked against Simon, but for everyone there, it was deemed good banter. Everyone that is, except Lauren, who would often end up in the kitchen crying over the Yorkshire puddings.

"Why does Dad *always* have to do this?" she'd sobbed one Sunday. "He winds Simon up just to get to me."

"Oh, don't be ridiculous," Kate had said, coming to their father's defense. "Why do you always think it's about you?"

"Because it always has been," said Lauren. "I can do no right in his eyes and now he's just using Simon to get to me."

"Listen to yourself," said Kate. "You're almost forty years old. Whatever you have against Dad, don't you think it's time to let bygones be bygones?"

"Just leave it, Kate," their mother had warned. "Now, can we all please be civil to each other? It's surely not too much to ask."

The sisters had sulkily picked up a bowl of vegetables each and gone into the dining room, where the talk had turned to who was going to win the *X Factor* final, with all three men agreeing with each other.

Kate hadn't been able to resist looking at Lauren and raising her eyebrows, as if to say, *See, it's not al-*

ways about you. Now, it seems, Matt's suggesting it might be.

"Are you saying that Lauren might know something about Dad that I don't?" A heat is beginning to creep up Kate's neck and muffle the sound in her ears.

Matt holds his hands up. "I just think you should stay open-minded, that's all."

Kate looks at him, her thoughts too rushed to be able to make sense of anything.

"It might be that Lauren isn't as surprised by Jess's appearance as she's making out," he offers, non-committally. "Maybe she already knew she existed, because it seems odd that she'd just accept a stranger as her sister as easily as she seems to have."

"She's not my father's daughter," says Kate bluntly.

"Well, then you're going to need to find out exactly what grounds that theory is based on," says Matt. "Because DNA doesn't lie."

"Oh, don't you worry," says Kate. "I'll get to the bottom of it."

"Okay," says Matt. "But if you're going to dig around, be careful."

"Of what?"

"You might discover something you don't want to find."

13

LAUREN

"You smell of smoke," says Simon, leaning in to kiss Lauren's cheek as she walks through the door.

She'd not had a cigarette for years, not since she was nineteen, but then she'd not seen Justin in all that time either and, ashamed as she is to admit it, a smoke was what was needed to calm her down.

Both children were mercifully asleep by the time she'd got back to the car and she'd driven around the block before heading back to the same petrol station to buy a pack of ten Marlboro. When the man behind the counter informed her that tens had been banned since 2017, she'd coughed awkwardly, asked for a pack of twenty and some chewing gum, and almost run out of the door, half expecting him to run after her. She'd felt like a teenager again as she inhaled her first drag, pulling it in deep to calm her nerves. Her heart had pumped blood around her body far quicker than was normal and every breath felt lodged in her chest, as if in anticipation of what might happen if she let it out. She didn't want to admit it, but as uncomfortable as the sensation was, it had made her feel alive. Seeing Simon's car parked up outside the house had sapped that feeling away again.

"Do I?" she says, recoiling from him.

"Where have you been?" he asks, as if the answer means nothing to him, yet she can tell by his demeanor that what she says next will dictate the atmosphere for the rest of the day.

"Only over to Mum's," she says as ambivalently as she can. She lifts her shirt to her nose and sniffs for effect. "Oh, but I did just stop off for petrol and there was a guy there smoking." As soon as the words are out of her mouth, she realizes how stupid they are.

If she was brave enough to look at him, she'd notice that his eyes have narrowed. "In a petrol station?"

"No," she says, far too quickly. "I meant in the hand car wash next door."

"So, you got the car cleaned?"

It feels like she's on the witness stand, facing a judge and jury. "Er, no, we waited in the queue for a while but gave up—it was taking too long."

"You shouldn't take the kids in there."

The lie is getting worse by the second and Lauren's brain is banging against the side of her head as she attempts to stop it unravelling altogether. "We normally stay in the car," she says. "But I was hoping to get the inside cleaned as well, so we went to the waiting room."

"Well, I don't want the kids there—it's dirty and reeks of all kinds of shit. Now you smell like an old ashtray."

If she's going to fail at the first interrogation, when

she's done nothing wrong, how is she going to fare when she *has*? The thought of seeing Justin again makes her insides somersault. She looks away in case Simon can see it in her eyes.

"Anyway, why are you home so early?" she says, while thinking, *today of all days*.

"Why do you think?" he says, and Lauren's heart sinks. Her eyes follow him into their tiny galley kitchen, where he opens the fridge and takes out a beer.

"Have you been laid off?" She just stops herself from saying, *again*.

"Yep."

"What are you going to do?" she asks.

"I've asked around. Bill says he might have something for me toward the end of the week. I'm going to go down the pub in a bit—see if there's anything knocking around down there."

"And if there isn't?" she asks, treading carefully.

"Then I'm going to be around more than I usually am," he says tightly.

Not so long ago, back when she was working, the thought of them spending a day together excited her. They'd drive to Brighton and eat fish and chips on the promenade, the smell of vinegar and sea air taking her back to day trips with her parents. She'd contemplate their life together and lean into the husband she loved as they watched the waves crashing onto the pebble beach. But that was when they got on, when they were both working and bringing in money. Now, Lauren wonders if she lost his respect when she lost her salary.

"Great!" she says through gritted teeth. "Why don't you go and start the kids' baths? You know Noah loves it when you do it."

"Yeah, I could do," he says, his expression beginning to soften, giving Lauren a rare glimpse of why she fell for him in the first place.

A ringing phone pierces the silence and Lauren looks to Simon, hoping that if she pretends not to hear it, he somehow won't either.

"Aren't you going to get that?" he asks.

Her blood feels like it's stopped flowing and frozen inside her veins. Simon stands there watching her as she slowly reaches toward her bag. She hopes it's her mother. She even hopes it might be Kate, because the alternative doesn't bear thinking about. The unknown number flashes urgently on the screen and a whirling pool of nausea rises up from her stomach. She tries to keep her face expressionless, but she fears the pulsation in her bottom lip is making it quiver.

Simon's looking at her expectantly, leaving her with no choice but to slide to answer. She almost cowers, waiting for the person on the other end to speak first, knowing that if it's a male voice, she's going to have to think fast.

"Hel-lo," she offers, when she can bear the protracted silence no longer.

"Lauren?" says a voice. A female voice.

Lauren has to bite down on her lip to stop an involuntary sob of relief from escaping.

"Lauren, it's Jess. Are you okay to talk?"

"Yes, of course," she says, before mouthing *It's Jess* to Simon.

"I was just wondering if you'd managed to speak to Kate at all," Jess is saying on the other end of the line. "I tried to see her today, to talk to her, but she really doesn't want to hear anything I've got to say, and I'm not sure she ever will. She just seems so angry with me, with you . . ."

Lauren walks into the door-less kitchen, where she's afforded marginally more privacy. "I know," she says. "She's going to need a bit of time to get her head around all this. You have to remember that you and I have had that luxury—she hasn't, so we just need to be patient."

"She hates me," says Jess, her voice cracking.

"Hey, hey, she doesn't hate you," says Lauren, her mothering instinct coming to the fore. "She has no reason to. We just need to give her some space." Lauren looks at her watch. "Listen, I'm about to bathe the kids and get them ready for bed. Do you want to come over?"

"Yes," squeaks Jess. "Yes please."

Lauren does a quick calculation in her head, knowing that Simon will be out of the door as soon as Noah's head hits the pillow.

"Give me an hour," she says, cradling the phone under her chin to pick up a pile of clean laundry that's been sitting on the end of the sofa for the past two days. If not for Jess's imminent arrival, it would have stayed there a lot longer.

"Thank you," says Jess. "I really appreciate it."

"No worries," says Lauren, making her way upstairs. "See you shortly."

Lauren busies herself with putting the children's clothes into their chests of drawers, wishing they had more space. At the moment, Noah and Emmy have a bedroom each, but once Jude is out of her and Simon's room, someone is going to have to share. She dared to dream that one day they would be able to afford their own four-bedroom house, instead of a three-bedroom rental.

"Remember what I said," says Simon as she walks into the bathroom, where he's flicking soap suds at Noah and Emmy, who are giggling incessantly. The coldness in his words are in contrast to the cozy scene. "Don't go getting us into anything with your family, and if she's *got* to come over, I want her gone before I get home."

"Yep, sure," says Lauren, just to keep the peace.

She checks her phone a hundred times between Simon going out and Jess arriving, though what she's looking for she doesn't know. She's already logged Justin's number into her contacts as "Sheila," and mentally given "her" the profile of a fellow midwife from the hospital that she's still on maternity leave from. It feels like she was there in another life.

Her thumb hovers over the disingenuous contact, imagining what her first words will be if and when she's brave enough, or stupid enough, to call him. The ringing doorbell infiltrates her thoughts.

"Hi," says Jess, holding a small bouquet of flowers and a bottle of white wine.

Lauren looks at her, a younger, slimmer version of herself, and feels a very real tug in her chest. Without even knowing she was going to do it, she pulls Jess into her, hugging her tightly and breathing her in.

"It's good to see you," she says, before holding her at arm's length to look at her.

Jess smiles. "You too. I bought you these." She holds up her offerings. "I don't know if you drink wine, or like flowers . . ."

"Thank you," says Lauren, taking them from her. "Come in, come in."

They talk their way through their first glass of wine, chatting about anything and everything that has nothing to do with why Jess is here.

"So, I guess your mother hasn't taken it too well either," Jess eventually says.

Lauren shakes her head. "No, I'm afraid not."

"I'm not surprised," says Jess. "It must be very hard." She looks at Lauren, as if gauging whether she should say what she's about to. "Especially now that your dad has passed."

Lauren nods. "It's a shock for everyone."

"But not so much for you, it seems."

Lauren looks at her, meeting her gaze. "As I said, I've had time to get used to the idea."

"Am I who you came looking for?" asks Jess.

Lauren swallows, taking time to formulate her answer. "I don't know who I was looking for. I just wanted to find a way to bring my family together and I thought that widening our circle, finding other family members, might be a way to do it."

"Yet it's had the opposite effect," says Jess.

Lauren clears her throat and tears immediately spring to her eyes. "I . . . erm . . ."

Jess gets up from the armchair she's sitting in and goes to Lauren on the sofa, putting an arm around her shoulders.

"This is silly," Lauren chokes. "I should be the one comforting *you*."

"What's upsetting you?" asks Jess.

"It was just a horrible time," says Lauren.

"What was?"

"When . . . when you were born . . ." Lauren clamps a hand to her mouth, knowing she's already said too much.

"What do you mean, how do you . . . ?" falters Jess. "Do you *know* when I was born?"

Lauren's head scrambles to backtrack, trying to get herself out of the precarious position she finds herself in.

"I was young, and it was . . . it was . . ."

"What do you know?" pushes Jess.

Lauren rubs at her head, frustrated with herself. This wasn't the plan. "As I say, I was young and . . ." She feels Jess's arm fall away from her back. "It was a really difficult time and . . ."

"And?" urges Jess.

"I was seventeen and on my way home from school when I saw Dad." She dares to look at Jess. "It was nothing. I shouldn't have . . ."

"Please," begs Jess. "I need to know."

Lauren clears her throat. "He was with another woman, a beautiful woman, and he was pushing a pram."

Jess's mouth falls open. "You *saw* him?" she croaks. "With *me*?"

Lauren nods and a tear falls onto her cheek. "I think so."

"You *saw* my mother?" Jess cries in a high-pitched voice. "Who was she? What did she look like?"

"She was beautiful," says Lauren.

Jess lets out a sob. "Where were they? Do you remember where you saw them?"

"It wasn't far from where we lived in Harrogate," says Lauren. "Just on the other side of town."

"I was born in Harrogate?" says Jess, almost to herself, as if in a trance. "I'm from Yorkshire?"

Lauren can't begin to comprehend the enormity of how it must feel to know where you were born, after a lifetime of wondering.

"Would you know the road?" asks Jess, suddenly more animated. "Might you recognize it? I could go there and ask around. Someone might remember her. Oh my God, she might even still be there."

Lauren feels under siege as Jess's questioning gathers pace. "I couldn't tell you exactly where it was," she says. "I just know the area of town. Where did you *think* you were from? What did your adoptive parents tell you?"

Jess's palpable excitement immediately dissipates. "Just that I'm from the north of England and was put into foster care as a baby. They didn't know anything about my birth parents, or at least claimed not to."

"But they've cared for you and loved you."

"As if I were their own," says Jess, smiling. "I've had the best education, went to a really good university . . . I couldn't have asked for more."

"And do you have any brothers or sisters?"

"No, I'm a spoiled only child."

"And where did you grow up?" asks Lauren, eager for as much information as she can garner.

"On the south coast," says Jess dreamily, her eyes glazing over as if caught up in a fond memory. "Near Bournemouth. We had a beautiful house overlooking the sea and every day after school, I'd take the dog down onto the beach and walk for miles."

Lauren smiles. "It sounds idyllic. Are your parents still down there?"

Jess's jaw tightens and her brow furrows. "No, not anymore. They've both passed away, sadly."

"Oh, I'm so sorry," says Lauren.

"That's why I decided to upload my DNA," says Jess. "After they'd gone, I realized I didn't have anyone who I could call family. Sure, I had a couple of aunts and a few cousins, but I felt detached, as if I didn't really fit in anywhere. I couldn't have done it when they were here. I didn't want to hurt them and make them think that everything they'd done for me had been a waste of their time. They were so proud of everything I've achieved."

"You should be proud of *yourself*," says Lauren. "Despite everything you've been through, you've turned into a wonderful young woman."

"Thank you," says Jess. "If only everyone thought so."

"Kate, you mean?"

Jess nods, pulling at the tissue that's in her lap.

"Just give her time, she'll come around," says Lauren, all the while thinking, *not in a million years.*

14
KATE

The motion of the train is making Kate feel sick, its rhythmic movement matched by her swaying reflection in the window opposite. It'd probably be best to focus on something else, something still, but every time she looks down to read her book, the words swim on the page.

She closes her eyes and the nausea immediately subsides, until she remembers the jabbing of a needle into the inside of her arm, as the nurse had struggled to find a juicy enough vein to draw blood from. Kate's hand instinctively goes to the site, her fingers able to feel the ball of cotton wool that is taped over the puncture through the fabric of her jacket.

"It's not normally this difficult," the nurse had commented as she'd tried, and tried again, to tap a vein into action. "It's probably because you're slim."

Kate refrained from saying that only a bad workman blamed his tools. She'd had enough blood tests to know that *she* wasn't the problem.

It had only been two weeks since the embryo transfer, but it had felt like a month—a year even, as she'd spent every second wondering whether she might be pregnant. Yet in just a few short hours, Kate will find out one way or another, and whatever the outcome, she knows that she's in this moment, the right here and now, for the last time. Because whether she *is* or *isn't*, she's not going through this again.

"Nice of you to join us," Lee, her editor, calls out, as she walks into the open-plan office twenty minutes later. "We're going into conference in five."

She waves a nonchalant hand in the air. "Okay guys," she says, in a hushed tone to the three reporters on the desks facing hers. "What have we got?"

Her team run through some potential stories, but it's all pretty thin gruel: a sacked manager; a couple of film premieres that evening; a soap star walking their dog. Daisy, the intern, has picked up on an interview in an American magazine, where an A-list actress admits to having had cosmetic surgery.

"Mmm," says Kate, thinking on her feet. "So let's pull the article, rewrite it and get some photos through the years? I'll offer it up as a picture-led spread."

"Sure," says Daisy, all too eagerly, and Kate can't help but love her for it.

"Two minutes!" barks Lee.

Kate hastily collects today's celebrity magazine spreads that are strewn across her desk and flicks through them as she makes her way to the boardroom. In the absence of a strong lead story, she's got one more option up her sleeve.

"So, what have you got, Kate?" asks Lee, once they've decided that a surprise announcement from the Home Secretary isn't enough for a front page of its own.

"Well, it's a bit left field and it might be something

the features team want to take up, but police in the States are using a new tactic to catch criminals."

"Is this where they're uploading a suspect's DNA to genealogy websites?" questions Lee.

"Yeah, that's the one," says Kate.

"I like the story, but it doesn't work for the front page, unless your desk has found a celebrity element to it? Any of the crimes in or around LA?"

Kate nods. "I can look into it."

"Great, if we can find a celebrity connection, it might make a splash. Do we know of anyone famous who was *almost* a victim in one of these crimes? Maybe a celebrity's parent knows one of the guys they've caught using this method? Were friends with him? Maybe their kid played with his kid—that kind of thing."

Kate's heart drops, not just at the enormity of the task, but because she just doesn't have the appetite for this kind of journalism anymore. She wants to report on stories that matter, not the tenuous links between a suspected murderer and the parents of someone who was once on *The Voice*.

She feels a bubbling sensation in the pit of her tummy and smiles knowingly to herself, hoping that maybe it won't be too long before she can take a break from both.

"Okay, so follow the celebrity lead, Kate, and Lara, maybe you can run alongside to develop the true crime element or see if you can find a strong real-life example of how Joe Bloggs is using an ancestry website to find his long-lost mother or something."

Kate can't help but flinch as Lara, the features editor, nods enthusiastically and jots a note down on her pad.

"That's all," says Lee, standing up. "Back to work."

Despite having tons to do, Kate finds herself day-dreaming for the rest of the day, unable to concentrate on the simplest of things. Even Karen, her deputy, telling her about a Tinder date she had last night, which Kate is usually keen to hear about, leaves her bored and uninterested. The minutes feel like hours as the clock ticks slowly toward four o'clock, the time she can ring the clinic for the results. Yet as soon as her phone displays 16.00, she suddenly feels reluctant to call, knowing that once she does, she will no longer be in limbo. If she doesn't get the answer she wants, she'd now almost prefer to be in this state of uncertainty, where there's still a chance that her life is about to change. Where she can dare to believe that this time next year, she'll be out of this job, holding her longed-for baby with another twelve months separating her from her father's passing.

She knows that the pain of losing him will never leave her, but as each week comes and goes, a tiny part of her starts to heal. Sometimes she can almost feel herself being sewn back together again—as if a needle is darning the holes that have been left by his death. Yet now, with Jess turning up, it feels as if they're all about to be unpicked again.

Kate takes her phone and grabs a tissue from her handbag, knowing that whichever way this phone call goes, she will probably need one. She walks through the office painstakingly slowly, almost willing someone to stop and talk to her—anything to hold off the inevitable for a few more minutes. Even Stan, the normally chatty post guy, who she bumps into on the way out of the building, lets her pass without comment.

"Bloody typical," she says out loud, as she walks

through a throng of smokers adding to the already pol-
luted streets of E14. She holds her breath as the clouds
of smoke billow around her, forcing her to step off the
curb. A black cab toots its horn and she holds up an
apologetic hand. She has to apologize again when the
cabbie pulls over next to her, thinking she's hailed him.

"Sorry," she says. "I don't need . . . I was just . . ."
He tuts and joins the line of traffic again.

She hopes that once she's made this call, her brain
will return to its usual levels of awareness.

Her fingers fumble for the numbers on the keypad
and she waits for the familiar options to present themselves:

"Welcome to Women's Health at Woolwich Hospital.

Press one for appointments.

Press two for test results.

Press three to speak to a doctor.

Press four for anything else."

Kate's hand hovers over the phone and she takes a
deep breath before pressing two.

"Women's Health, can I help you?" asks a monotone voice.

Kate wonders how you can sound so miserable when
your job is to relay good news. But then she catches
herself as she realizes that more often than not, it's *bad*
news this woman has to dispense. Kate wonders where
she's going to feature in the stats.

"Oh hi," she says, cheerily, as if it will make a difference to the outcome of the conversation. "I'm calling for pregnancy test results."

"What's the name?" asks the woman.

"Kate Walker."

"Date of birth?"

"Fourth of August 1984."

"Hold on," says the woman, sounding as if it's like every other call she's received today.

What you're about to say next will dictate my future, Kate wants to scream down the line. She thinks of Matt and feels a flutter in her chest. *Our future.*

She chews on her lip as she listens to a piped version of Beethoven, watching the people in Costa Coffee on the other side of the street as they go about their everyday lives. None of them knowing what's happening to her, none of them aware that her life may be about to change forever.

Her eyes are drawn to a young woman working on a laptop, and she allows her imagination to build a world around the girl she names Bryony. She's working on her dissertation in the coffee shop because she can't bear the mess in the kitchen she shares with her lazy flatmate Ned. It drains her inspiration, yet she refuses to clean up someone else's debris.

When she gets her 2:1 degree in politics and international relations, she wants to work for local government because she's still naive enough to believe she can make a difference.

What a waste, Kate says to herself, cynically writing the girl's aspirations off, even before she's started.

The girl looks up out of the window and across the street to where she's standing. Kate pulls her jacket around her to keep out the chill of the cold wind that whistles through the shadows of Docklands' skyscrapers. Their eyes momentarily lock, and Kate is struck by the fact that this woman has seen her and is, no doubt, wondering what *her* story is. She can't possibly begin to imagine the momentous occasion she might be about to witness. Kate smiles at her and the woman, seemingly embarrassed, returns to the screen in front of her. *When did it become more awkward to smile at someone than pretend to ignore them?* Kate wonders. She will never see this woman again, never give her another moment's thought, yet while Kate goes about her life, so will this young woman, neither of them aware of each other's existence and how important each of their lives are—to them at least.

"Mrs. Walker?" says the woman down the phone, cutting off Beethoven just as he was about to reach his crescendo.

"Erm, yes," says Kate, her mouth suddenly dry.

"Your test came back positive."

That was it. No gentle build-up. No advance warning. Just that.

"What?" cries Kate, steadying herself against a wall for fear that her knees will give way. "I'm pregnant? Are you sure?"

"Well, that's what the results say," says the woman, with not an iota of understanding of how big this moment is. "Kate Walker. Fourth of August 1984."

"Yes, that's me," says Kate in barely more than a whisper.

"Well, if that's *definitely* you, then you're *definitely* pregnant." The woman gives a little laugh, making her suddenly sound like a human being rather than a robotic voice on the end of an automated line.

Kate clamps a hand to her mouth and tears spring to her eyes. "I *am*?" she says, still waiting to be told it's a mistake.

"Congratulations!" the woman says warmly, and

Kate wishes she could leap down the telephone to give her a kiss.

"Oh my God, I'm pregnant!" she says under her breath as she paces up and down the same five-meter stretch of pavement. Back and forth she goes, wiping her tears, only stopping when she momentarily forgets how to put one foot in front of another. Her chest feels as if it's about to burst open as she thinks of Matt and how she's going to tell him, but then she immediately pictures her dad, who she'd always imagined giving a "Congratulations Grandad" card with an ultrasound scan of his new grandchild inside. He would have cried, she knows he would, and he'd have hugged her tight, not wanting to ever let her go. *I knew you'd do it, kid*, he'd say to her, letting on that he'd instinctively known what she and Matt had been going through all this time. She wouldn't have been surprised if he had; he was so intuitive of her feelings that he often knew she was unhappy even before she did. And he was *always* there when she was. An invisible support system that held her up, whenever she needed him.

"I need you now, Dad," she cries, floored by the unexpected grief that washes over her. She'd always known how proud of her he was; he'd shout it from the rooftops whenever he was given half a chance. But this . . . this would have made him so happy. His little girl finally getting the one thing that will make her feel complete. Her heart breaks that he's not here to see it. "He'll *never* be here to see it," she whispers, wiping a tear away.

"Excuse me," says a voice, interrupting her thoughts. She instinctively moves aside, imagining that she's holding someone up from where they want to go. What other reason would there be for unsolicited interaction between strangers in London?

"Er, hi, excuse me," says the voice again.

Kate sniffs and drags a tissue under her eyes.

"I'm really sorry to intrude, but you look upset and I just wanted to make sure you were all right."

Kate looks from the girl to the empty place in the coffee shop window and back again.

"Are you okay?" asks the girl, with a sympathetic smile.

"I'm pregnant!" says Kate, feeling a warmth wrap itself around her, though she's not sure if it's the knowledge that she has a baby inside her or that her faith in human nature has been restored.

"Congratulations?" says the girl hesitantly, as if waiting for confirmation that it is, indeed, good news.

Kate instinctively pulls the girl into her, hugging her tight. "Thank you," she says.

"For what?"

"For not being afraid to show you care."

15

LAUREN

Lauren had cited an unnecessary food shop to her mother to get a child-free half an hour to make the call. Now, she sits in the car outside her own house, staring blankly at her phone, as if willing it to ring. But she doesn't suppose Justin's telepathic, and anyway, that wasn't the agreement. *She's* supposed to call *him*. If she's brave enough.

Her hands are shaking as she looks at "Sheila," unable to believe that just eleven digits separate her from a past she never imagined she'd have to face again. When Justin dumped her, it was the start of a downward spiral that she feels she never truly escaped from. She'd got in with the wrong crowd when they moved to London and started experimenting with drugs. She lost all sense of self-respect, sleeping with anyone who showed an interest, in the misguided belief that sex was love. And when she'd run out of ways to punish herself, she decided to get control back over her life, in the only way she knew how: by limiting the food she allowed herself. She thought she was being clever, that nobody would notice, so when her dad put her into hospital for two weeks, it only made her hate him even more.

But he's gone now, she says to herself, with her thumb hovering shakily over "Sheila." *And I'm an adult.* But even as she's saying it, she knows that no matter how old you are, you're *still* your parents' child.

She's almost surprised when she presses the number, as if somebody else has done it on her behalf.

"I didn't think you'd call," says Justin, before Lauren even hears it ring.

"Hi," she says, not knowing what else to say, before adding unnecessarily, "it's me."

"How are you?"

"I'm good," she says. "You?"

"Better now," he says. "I haven't been able to stop thinking about you since the other day."

I haven't stopped thinking about you for the last twenty years, thinks Lauren.

"I want to see you again," he says.

Lauren feels like she can't breathe. How can this be happening? After all this time. And why now? It's as if it's a sign.

"I'd like that," she says, hesitantly.

"When?" he asks. "What about tonight?"

"No, I can't, not tonight."

"Tomorrow?"

She suddenly feels claustrophobic, as if he's crowding her, demanding something she can't give. But then she reminds herself that he doesn't know any different. Why *wouldn't* he think she might be available tonight or tomorrow? That's the short notice that single, unencumbered people can work to.

"I might be able to do something tomorrow," she

says, though her brain's already registering how unfeasible that is. If Simon's working, he'll go to the pub straight from the job. If he's not got any work, he might stay at home. She panics when she realizes that it doesn't matter, as either way she can't go anywhere.

"When will you know?" he asks.

"I, er . . . I don't know. I'll need some time to sort things out." She imagines him asking what there is to sort out and her telling him that it's just the small problem of getting rid of her controlling husband and drafting in her mother to look after the three children she's denied having.

"I'll see what I can do," she says. "I'll call you later."

"Okay," he says. "But Lauren . . ."

"Yes?" she says, feeling as if every word she utters is catching in her throat.

"Do your best."

She puts the phone down, his urgency resounding in her ears, not knowing whether it's that which is causing her stomach to flip or the nostalgia that hearing his voice evokes. They were so young, *too* young to be able to cope with the responsibilities that came with a teenage relationship turning into an adult one. If only they'd met later, when they both knew who they were and what they wanted.

"Mum, can you do me a favor tomorrow night?" she says as she walks into the house. She puts the solitary bag of shopping on the counter and absently clicks the kettle on.

"Is that it?" Rose asks, nodding toward the half-full bag.

Lauren can barely remember being in the supermarket, let alone what she'd bought.

She nods. "I might nip out and if Simon's not about, I wondered if you would mind the kids for a bit."

"Of course," says Rose. "What are you up to?"

The words are accusing, but the tone in which she says them tells Lauren they're not meant to be. Nevertheless, Lauren can feel her cheeks going red and she turns to put a jar of coffee in a cupboard already overstocked with caffeine.

"Erm . . . I'm going to try and get Kate out." It's the first thing she can think of.

"Oh, that would be lovely," enthuses Rose. "It would do you two the power of good to get together and sort out your differences."

"I'm sorry for the trouble this has all caused," says Lauren.

"It can't be helped," says Rose, in the sing-song voice she puts on when she means the exact opposite. "But you would have been wise to have thought about the consequences beforehand."

"I hate him," says Lauren, with such vitriol that she surprises even herself.

"Don't say that, darling," says Rose, sidling up beside her. "It would break his heart. He was your father and he loved you so very much."

"If he loved me, he'd never have done what he did," she cries. "How could he have had a baby with someone else, when all the time . . . he . . . he . . . ?" Her shoulders convulse and a sob escapes from her chest.

"Lauren," implores Rose, taking her daughter's hands in her own. "You have to leave this alone. You need to leave this in the past where it belongs. You can't continue punishing yourself like this."

"I shouldn't be the one being punished," cries Lauren. "*He* should."

"And don't you think that *not* seeing his sixtieth birthday is punishment enough?"

Lauren looks down at her feet as tears fall onto her cheeks.

"And don't you think he knew what he'd done?" soothes Rose. "That he knew how wrong he was."

"So why didn't you stop him?" sobs Lauren, feeling an overwhelming desire to lash out at her mother, *at anything*, just so she can release the years of pent-up frustration that swirl relentlessly around her body.

Rose takes her daughter in her arms and holds her tight, making Lauren cry even louder.

"There was nothing I could do," says Rose into her ear. "I tried everything—but no matter what I said or did, he wouldn't listen."

"There must have been something . . ." says Lauren.

"You know what your dad was like," says Rose softly. "Once his mind was made up, that was it. But it didn't mean he loved you any less."

Lauren's tears fall onto Rose's shoulders as her mother strokes her hair, just like she used to when she was younger. Lauren feels as if she's on the outside of herself, looking onto the same scene of some twenty-two years ago.

"It's not good for you to be around Jess," Rose says, holding Lauren at arm's length. "I don't think you should see or talk to her again."

"She deserves to know the truth," says Lauren.

Rose shakes her head. "No!" she says abruptly. "Look at the state of you. Look at what it's doing to you."

Lauren contemplates telling her mother that Justin showing up after all this time is the straw that's broken the camel's back, but she thinks better of it.

"I can handle it," she says.

"If you honestly believe that, then you're in denial. If you carry on with this, it will rip this family apart— look at what it's done to you and Kate already. Why don't you concentrate on sorting out *that* relationship, rather than go on a wild goose chase after someone you don't even know?"

"I'm going to deal with Kate," says Lauren. "Tomorrow night."

The reminder of who Rose thinks Lauren is seeing seems to calm her, and Lauren immediately feels guilty.

"I'll only need to call on you if Simon's not in," she goes on, knowing that that's the only scenario that'll allow her to go.

"Fine," says Rose tightly. "But only on the understanding that you sort things out with Kate. Keeping this family together means everything to me, and I will not allow anyone to destroy it."

16

KATE

"I don't think I can order until we know," says Matt, sitting opposite Kate in their favorite Italian restaurant in Soho. "What time did they say you can call?"

"Six o'clock." Kate battles with her expression, trying hard not to convey that she already has the answer to the question that's threatening his appetite. But she can't stop the corners of her mouth from turning upward and she's sure that the glint in her eye is undisguisable.

"What are you going to have?" he asks, without looking up from his menu.

"I was going to have the burrata to start," she says.

"Do you think you should?" he asks, clearly concerned that her favorite cheese might be unpasteurized.

"Mmm, maybe not, just to be on the safe side." She's quite enjoying playing this game, but she needs to put Matt out of his misery soon. She needs to put *herself* out of misery, as she can barely keep her bottom on the seat due to her pent-up excitement.

"So, how's work been today?" she asks, forcing herself to sound normal.

"Well, I've offered the Junior Reporter job."

"Oh great, which one did you choose?"

Matt screws his face up. "Mmm, you're not going to be happy."

Kate falls back in her chair in mock outrage. "Don't tell me you went for the uni graduate."

Matt nods and holds up his hands. "But in my defense, when we got them both back in for a second interview, she nailed it."

Kate shakes her head. "Well, don't come running to me when it all goes wrong."

"O ye of little faith," Matt laughs.

Unable to contain herself any longer, Kate reaches into her bag and pulls out a wrapped gift box, putting it in front of Matt on the table.

"What's this for?" he asks.

"Do I need a reason?"

"Normally, yes," he says, eyeing her suspiciously.

"Just open it," she says impatiently.

Her eyes don't leave him as he unwraps it, far too slowly.

"Hurry up," she urges.

He smiles and rips the paper off impatiently, looking quizzically at the pen-shaped box he's left with. As he lifts the lid, his face crumples.

"Are you . . . are you really?" he cries, holding up the pregnancy test with its two blue lines prominently displayed.

Kate can do no more than nod her head for fear that the *pair* of them will end up sobbing. They look at each other, alternating between crying and laughing, unable to say anything.

"When did you find out?" he asks incredulously.

"About an hour ago," she says, smiling. "I couldn't wait, and I didn't want to tell you on the phone. I wanted to see your face."

"Well, you're definitely not having the burrata!"

"I know!" She laughs. "I'm already missing it."

"I . . . I don't even have the words," says Matt. "I truly don't know what to say. How do you feel? Do you feel different?"

Kate had spent the past hour wondering that herself. She'd taken herself off to the toilets as soon as she got back into the office, leaning against the locked door, inhaling and exhaling deeply. She'd felt her breasts, checking for signs of tenderness, and questioning whether she could make it to the shop to get some ginger biscuits, because she was sure she felt sick. She'd read enough *Mother & Baby* magazines to last her a lifetime, so she knew what she was *supposed* to feel. It was all very well *saying* she was pregnant, but she doubted that she'd truly believe it until she actually *felt* it. Though standing there, waiting for all the symptoms to present themselves, was probably a pointless exercise.

"I think my boobs are bigger," she says.

"Already?" says Matt, with his eyebrows raised in surprise.

Kate laughs and drops her head onto the table. "Oh my God, listen to me. I'm going to be one of those women, aren't I?"

Matt looks at her expectantly.

"I'm going to think I'm the only woman in the world to have a baby."

He laughs. "I can't even begin to imagine how high-maintenance you're going to be."

"You *will* go and mine for coal if I develop a craving for it, won't you?" She can't keep the mirth from her voice.

"The best you're going to get is ice cream at midnight."

"Häagen-Dazs?" she questions playfully. "*Any* flavor?"

"Within reason," he says, smiling. "I can't believe we've done it. It just doesn't feel real. Can we go around to your parents' house tonight?"

It catches Kate off guard, her mind playing tricks on her for that split second, making her believe that her dad is still there. She's ashamed to acknowledge how differently she feels about going once she realizes he's not. Perhaps it's time to start calling it her mum's house.

"It's very early days," she says.

"I honestly don't think I can keep this a secret," says Matt, his expression struggling to hide his unadulterated joy.

For so long, Kate hadn't even allowed herself to dream that the IVF was going to be successful, so to find herself in this position, having to decide when to share the news, is not something she'd given much thought to.

"Can't we just tell our mums?" asks Matt, looking like a kid on Christmas morning.

"It's not really a great time at the moment," says Kate.

"Because of that girl?"

Tears unexpectedly spring to Kate's eyes and she quickly wipes them away.

"Hey," says Matt, stretching across the table and taking her hand in his. "What's up?"

"I think it's all just beginning to get a bit on top of me," she admits.

"The family stuff or the pregnancy?"

"All of it," cries Kate, half laughing. "I think the hormones are playing havoc with my emotions."

"You're pregnant! We're pregnant!" A tear falls onto Matt's cheek. "Let's concentrate on that. I know the stuff going on with Lauren and this girl is difficult, but no matter what, it will never change your feelings for your dad."

"No," Kate sniffs. "It won't."

"So, step away from it—don't get involved."

If only it were as easy as he makes it sound.

"She came to see me," says Kate, looking at him.

"Who, Lauren?"

"No, the girl," says Kate. "She came to the office."

"Jesus!" exclaims Matt. "How did she know where you worked?"

Kate shrugs her shoulders nonchalantly, though she feels anything but. "I guess Lauren told her. They clearly know each other better than I thought."

"What the hell are they playing at?" says Matt, agitated.

"I honestly don't know," says Kate. "I've always thought we were a close family, but since losing Dad, it just seems that we're all hiding secrets from each other. That's not what normal families do."

"You'd be surprised," says Matt. "I think there are very few families who are what they claim to be. We all say one thing and think another."

Do we? wonders Kate.

"If you need to *say* how close you are," Matt goes on, "you'll normally find it's the exact opposite."

"Mmm, maybe," muses Kate.

"And what's your mum's stance on all this?"

"She's just in denial about the whole thing."

"So what are you going to do?"

"I was hoping it wouldn't come to this," says Kate. "But I'm going to have to prove Lauren wrong."

"And how are you going to do that?"

She looks at him, her jawline twitching involuntarily.

"By getting the DNA that's going to prove the girl isn't who everyone thinks she is."

17

LAUREN

The nerves circling Lauren's stomach have already seen her rush to the toilet three times and her hand shakes as she puts her mascara on, knowing that she'll have to go at least once more before she leaves.

Her hair's gone well, falling in silky curls on her shoulders, and she's refraining from overdoing the make-up. *Less is more*, she remembers Kate saying when they were discussing the virtues of Lady Gaga's transformation in *A Star Is Born*.

She eyes the blue jumpsuit she's laid on the bed and applies the same theory. Leggings would be better; give off the impression that she hasn't tried too hard. She refuses to acknowledge that their stretch waistband might also be easier to fit her post-pregnancy belly into.

"Mum!" calls out Noah from downstairs. "Jude's been sick."

"I'm coming," she says, quickly pulling her leggings from their hanger and stepping into them. She grabs a white top that she's always felt comfortable in, before throwing it to the bottom of the wardrobe and selecting a royal-blue shirt instead. Justin always used to comment on her eyes and this color will make them stand out even more. She doesn't put it on yet though, as she's already over-heating and cleaning up Jude will only exacerbate the problem.

He's gurgling happily through his milky vomit as he watches Noah and Emmy dancing to *Sesame Street*, and as Lauren picks him up, she wonders what the hell she's doing. What is a married mother of three children under five doing going to meet a man she was in love with over twenty years ago? She looks at the children she adores, knowing that what she's about to do can only end badly. But she feels powerless to stop it.

"Hello, my gorgeous boy," exclaims Rose, as she opens her front door to see Noah bounding up the garden path toward her.

"Hi, Nana," he says, as he wraps his chubby arms around her neck.

"Goodness," says Rose, as Lauren follows him with the car seat in one hand and Emmy clinging onto the other. "You look gorgeous too. Are you sure it's not some fancy man you're going to see instead of your sister?"

Lauren instantly feels her cheeks redden, knowing she's going to have to get better at this if she's going to get away with it.

"I'll get going, if you don't mind," says Lauren on the front doorstep. "I won't be too long."

"Listen, if it means you having a good chat with Kate and sorting everything out, you can take as long as you like."

Lauren smiles tightly, gives each of the children a kiss and waves as she pulls away.

By the time she gets to the Fox and Hounds pub, her stomach is in knots and she can't even remember the route she took to get there. She flips down the sun visor and inspects herself in the mirror one last time, smoothing her eyebrows with a finger adorned with gold jewelry.

"Oh my God," she says, unable to believe that she was about to walk in with the proof that she's married to someone else sparkling on her ring finger. She eases off her wedding band and wonders if Justin had seen it when they'd met at the petrol station. Surely it would have been the first thing he'd looked for, just as she had. It clangs unceremoniously as she drops it in the ashtray on the center console—the irony not lost on her.

Lauren steps furtively into the unfamiliar pub, unable to remember the last time she walked into somewhere like this on her own. She crosses her fingers that Justin is going to present himself immediately, as the little confidence she's enforced upon herself is fading fast.

Her eyes scan the low-ceilinged room, frantically peering into the darkest nooks in the corners, hoping to see him. Fear clasps itself around her diaphragm, as the possibility of recognizing someone else infiltrates her brain, or worse, someone recognizing *her*. What if a former colleague of Simon's, one of the hundreds that she's been introduced to over the years, is here and sees her? Would she pretend that she's waiting for a girlfriend and ignore Justin when he arrives? Or should she introduce him as her brother? What would he think of her if she did? How would she explain it away?

Stop! she silently screams as the never-ending questions circle in her head.

"Hi, what can I get you?" asks the smiling girl behind the bar.

Lauren hadn't even realized she was standing at it. "Oh, erm, can I get a gin and tonic please?" she says, still looking nervously around.

"Is that a large?"

She wants to say yes because she feels she needs it, but she's driving, and she'd never go over the limit.

"No thanks," she says. "Just a small one."

"You're early," says a voice beside her. "I was hoping to get here before you."

She spins around and locks eyes with the man she loved and lost over two decades ago.

"Am I?" is all she can say. She was quite sure she timed it so that she would arrive ten minutes after the agreed time. The nerves must have got to her more than she thought.

Justin leans in to kiss her cheek, his skin soft and stubble-free. "You look amazing," he says, drinking her in with his eyes.

"What, in this old thing?" she says, out of habit whenever anyone pays her a compliment. She pulls at the bottom of her blouse and remembers Kate's words. "Why do you always do yourself down whenever anyone says something nice?" She remembers being at one of Kate's swanky do's and a handsome man telling her that she had beautiful hair. She'd immediately put a hand to it and said, "I imagine it looks like I've been dragged through a hedge backward."

"Just say thank you," Kate had said, as they watched the man make a hasty retreat. It saddens Lauren that she was so insecure about how she looked, even before having children, when she felt like a different woman entirely. She wishes she knew then what she knows now.

"It brings out the color in your eyes," says Justin.

"Thank you," says Lauren, looking at the floor.

He orders a lager top, and a surge of melancholy engulfs her as she's transported back to when she'd managed to blag her way into Zen's nightclub wearing a crop top and pleated miniskirt, thinking her attempt at looking like Britney Spears as a schoolgirl was a good idea to try and pass as someone older. It had worked though, and with Justin being over eighteen, they'd happily drunk lager tops and vodka until the early hours before crashing at someone's house whose parents were away.

As they move away from the bar with their drinks, Lauren feels Justin's hand in the small of her back, guiding her, reassuring her. If she were with Simon, he'd either be stomping off in front of her or holding her arm territorially, as he pushed her to where *he* wanted to go.

"Where would you like to sit?" asks Justin.

"Just over there," says Lauren, seeking out the quietest, darkest corner.

They sit down and look at each other for what feels like an interminable amount of time, as if disbelieving that they're really here.

"You haven't changed one bit," says Justin eventually.

Lauren pictures the stretch marks streaking her stomach, the sagging breasts that he will remember being pert, both a testament to the three wonderful children she has denied exist. But it's not just the physical changes Justin will be shocked by; it'll be the parts of her he can't see.

"A lot has happened since," is all she says, before taking a long slug of her drink, desperate for the alcohol to numb her nerve endings.

"Not a day has gone by when I haven't thought about you," says Justin. "I'd tell myself, *convince* myself, that we were too young for it to ever work, but deep down I knew we were meant to be."

"*You* made the decision to end it," says Lauren quietly.

"Only because that was clearly what you wanted," says Justin.

"What *I* wanted?" she says, a little too loudly.

"Let's not," says Justin, putting his hand on top of hers. "It all happened a long time ago, in another lifetime. Let's concentrate on the future."

"But we're different people now," says Lauren.

"True, but who knows? Maybe we should be thankful for what we went through."

"Thankful?" says Lauren.

"Yes, because look where we ended up," says Justin enthusiastically. "Maybe we needed to go through all that we've been through, to go off and experience another life, to bring us back together again. It's like starting over . . . we've been given a second chance."

Lauren pictures Simon, Noah, Emmy and Jude, and thinks, *If only you knew.*

18

KATE

"Kate!" exclaims Rose, as she opens her front door. Kate has a key, but given what happened the last time she was here, it doesn't feel appropriate to let herself in.

"Mum," says Kate, nervously. "Look, I'm so sorry . . ."

"What's happened?" says Rose, panic etched on her features. "Is it Lauren? Is she all right?"

"Lauren?" says Kate, confused. "What's Lauren got to do with anything?"

Rose ushers her into the hall. "You were seeing her tonight—to sort things out. What happened?"

Kate shakes her head. "I was seeing Lauren? Since when?"

"Well, that's where she's gone," says Rose, her voice high-pitched with rising panic. "She's gone to meet you to talk about the whole mess with that girl and . . ."

It's only then that Kate notices the brightly colored paraphernalia that litters the hall carpet, leaving a trail into the front room. A sure sign that Lauren's children are here.

"Where's Lauren now?" she asks.

"Out with you," shrills Rose.

"But I was never meant to be meeting Lauren tonight," says Kate. "We haven't spoken since I left here on Monday." She'd thought of calling her several times in the three days since, especially given the news that she was pregnant, but she and Matt had decided that they'd keep it to themselves, at least for a few weeks, or until they couldn't hold it in anymore.

"So where's she gone then?" asks Rose, her lips pursed in thought.

Kate shrugs her shoulders nonchalantly. "I don't know, and anyway, I didn't come here to talk about Lauren."

Rose fixes her with a steely glare. "So, what *did* you come here for?"

Kate's stomach turns as she wonders where she should start, the bravery she'd felt driving over here dissipating with every passing second.

"I want to talk about Jess."

Rose grimaces as if there's a bad taste in her mouth. "I have nothing more to say."

"But we need to talk about it," says Kate. "Because if Lauren has her way, this isn't going to go away."

Rose's face changes, as if she's been hit by a sudden recollection. "That's where she'll be," she says abruptly. "She'll have gone to see Jess."

They may not be the closest of siblings, but the thought of Lauren playing sisters with someone else cuts Kate deep.

"I knew she was up to something," continues Rose bitterly. "She was all dressed up, looking like she used to. She's not made as much effort since before the kids." She tuts blithely. "She must take me for a fool."

The realization that Lauren's forging a strong bond with the same girl that *she's* trying to cut loose makes Kate feel adrift without a paddle.

"You *know* Jess isn't Dad's child, don't you?" asks Kate, without looking up. She counts as she waits for her mother to answer. She gets to twelve and wonders what the hell is taking her so long. "*Don't* you?" she presses.

"I hope she isn't," is all that Rose offers. "But the DNA seems hard to ignore."

"You can put an end to all this," says Kate. "You can tell Lauren that she's got it all wrong. That Dad would never have done what she's accusing him of . . ."

Rose shrugs her shoulders. "But how do we know? How will we *ever* know?"

"Why wouldn't you want to nip this in the bud, before it goes too far?"

"I don't know what you want me to do," says Rose.

Kate looks at her mother's sorrowful face, her peachy complexion smooth, aside from a few expression lines that show the life she has lived has been full of love and laughter.

If she's not going to do the right thing, Kate supposes that she's going to have to force her hand. It feels wrong, but she's given her mother enough chances to stop this.

"Have you got any paracetamol?" she says. "I've got a terrible headache."

Kate knows where they'd usually be kept and prays that her mother doesn't magic the tablets out of her handbag on the kitchen worktop.

"I've got some in the medicine cabinet in the bathroom," says Rose, going to get up.

"Don't worry," says Kate, beating her to it. "I'll go."

The stairs that she's run up and down a million

times now feel like a crime scene. For some reason, she doesn't even want to touch the bannister for fear of leaving any incriminating evidence.

She wants to close and lock the bathroom door but is sure Rose would think that weird. There's a toilet downstairs, so why would Kate go upstairs? Any other time it would have felt totally natural, but when she knows she's being devious, it feels anything but. She opens the mirrored cabinet above the sink and scans the shelves, not knowing what she's looking for. There's an ointment for nigh on every ailment, though when Kate picks up the menthol vapor rub, she sees that it's five years out of date.

She puts two paracetamol into her pocket and eyes the two toothbrushes that stand proudly in a glass. Knowing that the bristles hold all the evidence she needs, she looks at them, disappointed that she's unable to distinguish whose is whose. Though even if she could, she'd never be able to take either away, as Rose would instantly notice that they were gone. A folded flannel sits neatly in the chrome bath tray and a loofah sponge hangs from the taps, but again, both would be noticed if they weren't there.

Careful to avoid the creaky floorboard, Kate steps over the landing into her parents' bedroom. The curtains are half drawn, and the room is shrouded in the fading light of the setting summer sun. Kate hasn't been in her parents' bedroom since she doesn't know when, but the memories it evokes instantly bring tears to her eyes and a tightness in her chest.

She watches through the eyes of her six-year-old self as she tiptoes into this room at their old house in Harrogate, dragging her misshapen pillowcase stuffed with presents behind her. Her dad's face is ruckled into his pillow, his mouth wide open as he loudly snores.

"Daddy," she'd whispered. "Daddy, are you awake?"

He murmured momentarily and her heart had soared, but then he'd snuggled back down into the duvet and snored even louder. She'd stood there, waiting for what seemed like an eternity, desperately wanting him to wake up, but not wanting to be the one who woke him.

"Father Christmas has been," she'd whispered loudly into his ear.

He'd suddenly opened one eye, staring straight at her, and she'd momentarily been too scared to move, but his face had dissolved into the biggest smile. "Has he left any presents for the best little girl in the world?"

She'd grinned and hauled her makeshift stocking into the air. "Look how many."

Her father had swung Kate up onto the mattress, onto this very same Laura Ashley bedspread, where they'd quietly shared a Terry's chocolate orange, waiting for Rose and Lauren to wake up.

Kate wipes a tear away, wishing that she and Lauren were as close now as they were then. But it seems that any chance of returning to those times has been blown out of the water by Jess. The realization makes Kate hate her even more.

She inches across the beige carpet, toward the hairbrush that is lying upturned on the dressing table. Her father's ash blond hair is entangled with her mother's auburn strands, and she wonders if it's been left like this for a reason. Had Rose found it too painful to clean and throw away? Believing it to be the last semblance of her living, breathing husband who she misses so much? Kate is racked with guilt as she tries to lift just a couple of strands, knowing that if she's going to prove Jess isn't her father's daughter, she *has* to get the evidence. She wraps what she manages to disentangle in a tissue and puts it in her pocket.

She ought to get out of here before Rose wonders what she's up to, but she feels compelled to look inside the built-in wardrobes that run the length of one wall. She slides across the last door and runs her fingers along the sleeves of the suits that hang there. A sob catches in her throat as she brings a cuff to her nose and breathes in her father's scent—its muskiness still so distinctive.

Kate's eye catches sight of a candy-striped hat box, hidden under a shelf beneath her father's clothes, and she looks out onto the landing before carefully sliding it out. Her chest flutters when she opens it to find dozens of handwritten envelopes, some in her mother's handwriting, but most in her father's, each addressed to the other. She wants to take them all, hurry home and settle into the corner nook of her L-shaped sofa to read each and every line carefully, but she's sure she heard a creak and quickly takes the top one and stuffs it in her pocket.

"What are you doing?" asks Rose, with a furrowed brow.

Kate's just pulling the door closed.

"I . . . I was just looking for the tablets," she stutters.

"I told you, they're in the bathroom."

"Did you?" says Kate, feigning ignorance. "Sorry, I thought you said your bedroom."

"Since when have I kept medicines in the wardrobe?" Rose's voice is tight and clipped.

"I . . . just thought . . ."

"I'll go and get them," says Rose, turning and walking into the bathroom. Kate has a hot panic that she'd not put the tablets back as they were; that it was going to be obvious that she'd already found them. It would only take a tiny spec of foil from the blister pack to give the game away.

A few seconds later, Rose comes back into the bedroom with the intact box in her hand and Kate breathes a sigh of relief.

"Do you want to tell me what's really going on?" asks Rose, through narrowed eyes.

"What do you mean?" says Kate, far too defensively.

"This whole headache thing," says Rose. "Is that *all* it is?"

"I don't understand," says Kate, feeling uncomfortable with where this is going. She wishes she'd done this another time, when her mother was out. But as usual, she'd been too impatient, desperate for the truth, believing that it was somehow going to run away, and she'd be too far behind to catch it up.

"I think this has all had a far more adverse effect on you than you're prepared to admit," says Rose.

"Meaning?"

"All this carry-on with the girl," says Rose.

Kate bats away the anxiety that's making her breathless. "It doesn't help knowing that Lauren is with her right now and lying to you and me about it."

Rose nods. "Try and talk to her, will you? I can't bear to see the two of you going against each other like this." Her voice cracks. "I've tried so hard to keep this family together and since your dad . . . well, it's been even harder. It's as if he was the only person holding us all in place. We used to be so close, but now it feels as if you don't want to be here."

"I've found it hard," says Kate honestly. "Being here without Dad is . . ."

A tear falls onto her cheek and Rose goes to her, pulling her in. "I know, I know," she soothes. "But he wouldn't want to see us all like this, would he?"

Kate imagines Jess turning up when Harry was still alive and shudders. What would he have made of it? How would he have reacted to being told that she and Lauren had another sister? Kate shocks herself by thinking that she's glad that he's not here to witness it.

"Talk to Lauren," pleads Rose. "For the sake of the family."

"If you really want to protect our family, then you're going to *have* to tell us the truth," says Kate, letting her mother's hands fall from her own. "Because you're the only one who can."

19

LAUREN

Lauren is on cloud nine when she wakes up and realizes that the plethora of dreams she'd had were just a realistic extension of the evening she'd had. She smiles, desperate to stay in her happy cocoon for just a little bit longer, but there's hot breath on her face and she sleepily opens one eye, expecting to see Noah lying beside her. She gasps out loud when she's faced with Simon, his head just inches from her, his eyes wide and staring.

"Who were you expecting to see?" he asks.

"Wh-what?" she stutters, clawing to get up.

"Who were you expecting to see?"

"Noah," she says. "Who else?"

"You were talking in your sleep."

"Was I?" she says, her body immediately taut with tension. She daren't ask what she was saying, but *not* knowing is almost as nerve-wracking.

"You sounded like you were having a good time," says Simon. There's a cold edge to his voice that she doesn't like.

Lauren reaches for her dressing gown at the end of the bed.

"Who were you with?" he asks.

Pinpricks of sweat rush to her pores as she struggles to remember what she told him, or even where she told her mother she was going. Words, names and places fly about in her head as her brain goes into overdrive, hoping that something is going to start making sense. She pictures Kate and feels instantly calmer.

"I told you," she says, as if affronted. "I went out with Kate."

Simon pulls himself up onto the headboard. "Why would you think I was talking about last night?"

"What?" She's tired of playing these stupid mind games.

"I was asking who you were with in your dream," he says. "Because you seemed to be having such a good time."

"For God's sake," she says, getting up and tying her gown in a double knot around her waist.

He looks at her through narrowed eyes. "But now you've made me wonder about last night."

She's sure her heart skips a beat as she looks at him, forcing herself to hold his gaze. "I'm going to start breakfast."

As she walks down the stairs, a notification on her phone lights up her dressing gown pocket, and as she scrambles to pull it out, she's hit by the sudden realization that she's not cut out to be an unfaithful wife.

It was so good to see you—I can't wait until we do it again, reads the text from "Sheila."

Heat rushes to her ears as she remembers Justin's

hand on the back of her neck, pulling her toward him as they stood outside the pub.

"I can't," she'd said, turning her head just as his lips were about to touch hers.

"I'm sorry, I don't . . . I . . . I shouldn't have."

Lauren had caught hold of his wrist as he'd taken his hand away from her neck. "It's okay," she'd whispered, desperate to hold on to that tingling sensation, as his skin touched hers, for just that little bit longer. He'd cupped her cheek and it had taken all her willpower not to kiss his palm as he traced the outline of her jaw, his fingers outlining her lips.

"What are we going to do?" she'd said, looking into his pale blue eyes, knowing that if she weren't a married mother of three, going home with him would be a foregone conclusion.

"Whatever you want to do," he'd said, and she felt herself falling in love with him all over again.

"It's complicated," she said.

"I know, but if we just take things slow . . ."

"I need to go," she said, before she did anything she might regret.

"Wait, when can I see you again?"

"I'll call you," she said, rushing off to her car, even though she couldn't remember where she'd parked it. She'd clicked the key fob in her hand and headed in the direction of the flashing hazard lights. She kept her head down, refusing to look back at him, fearing that if she did, she'd run straight into his arms and never leave.

"How did it go?" Rose had asked enthusiastically, when Lauren went back to collect the children.

"Good," Lauren had replied, far too quickly. "Really good."

"So, you made some inroads?" asked Rose. "You can see a way through."

Lauren had nodded.

"Because I can't bear the thought of you two being at loggerheads. It breaks my heart."

As if Lauren hadn't felt bad enough, her mother was sending her on one hell of a guilt trip.

"I'm sure it will be fine," she'd said, all the while thinking that she'd better call Kate first thing in the morning, to forewarn her.

Last night, with a gin and tonic inside her and buoyed by an adrenaline rush she hadn't experienced since she was a teenager, she'd felt she could justify her actions to her sister. But now, in the cold light of day, Kate's sanctimonious views on marriage burn deep into Lauren's psyche and she knows she's not going to get off lightly if she tells her she was with Justin.

She's watching a saucepan of water boiling furiously, lost in the bubbles, when Simon comes into the kitchen.

"Are you going to put anything in that?" he asks, making her jump.

"God, you scared me," she says, and he offers a self-satisfied smile.

"Emmy's up," he says, tilting his eyes to the ceiling.

She wants to say, *Well, why didn't you bring her down then?* but thinks better of it. The last thing she needs is to rile him, which it seems she can now do even when she's asleep.

She stiffens as he comes up behind her, reaching around to kiss her cheek. "I'll see you tonight," he says. "Maybe we can recreate that dream you had."

She drops two eggs into the saucepan, unable to

think of anything worse. There used to be a time when she wouldn't have let him leave the house in the morning without making love to her first. But that was before having children, when she had the energy and no inhibitions. If she can convince herself that's the real reason, she can convince herself of anything.

As soon as she hears the front door close, she breathes a sigh of relief, but the problems of the day don't offer much respite. She overboils the eggs and hopes that Noah and Emmy don't notice that their soldiers can barely penetrate the yolks.

"My egg's not runny," is the last thing she hears Noah cry as she gently closes her bedroom door.

She calls Kate's mobile, hoping that it goes to voicemail, but knowing that she'll only have to summon the courage to call her again later if it does. She looks at the digital clock on her bedside; it's not yet eight and she imagines Kate and Matt still nestled under the duvet together, probably making love, uninterrupted, in their swanky apartment. Kate will probably travel into town to meet a celebrity in a fashionable hotel for breakfast this morning before heading into the office to work on an exclusive for tomorrow's front page. Lauren wonders what it must be like to lead such a glamorous life, with a husband you adore and nothing to tie you down. She tries to push the bubbling envy aside as the phone rings.

"Hello," Kate finally answers groggily. Perhaps they're not making love after all.

"It's me."

"Are you okay?" asks Kate, her voice laced with concern. "Has something happened?"

"No, why would you think that?"

There's a momentary pause before Kate says, "Because you were out last night."

Lauren's shoulders slump forward. Rose had obviously beat her to it.

"About that," says Lauren. "Did Mum say anything?"

"Unfortunately, I went round there," says Kate.

"Shit!" says Lauren, under her breath.

"So, do you want to tell me what's going on?"

Lauren feels like a blunt instrument is being ground into her chest. "I'm sorry, I told her I was with you."

"I know," says Kate. "But we all know that you weren't."

"Shit!" says Lauren again.

"If you'd given me the heads up, I might have been able to cover for you, but . . ."

"Well, she did a good job of pretending," says Lauren. "Look, I'm really sorry, I didn't mean to put anyone in an awkward position."

"No, but now that you have, do you want to tell me where you were?"

Lauren's jaw tightens as her teeth grind against each other. "I don't want you to get mad . . ." she says, surprising herself that it still matters to her what Kate thinks. "But, it's just that . . ."

"You know this is never going to end well, don't you?" says Kate, cutting her off.

Lauren pulls herself up. How could Kate possibly know that she met Justin? Had someone seen them after all? Would that same person tell Simon? An icy terror courses through her veins, as she imagines what he might be capable of. The thought of him using the children against her makes it feel as if her heart's stopped working.

"Can I just explain . . . ?" says Lauren.

"I can't tell you what to do," says Kate. "You're just going to have to find out the hard way."

"But you have no idea what it's been like for me," says Lauren.

"Listen, spare me the 'woe is me' line. We're all in the same boat, but if you want to see Jess for whatever reason, that's up to you."

"Jess?" Lauren exclaims. "But . . ."

"Just know that it's your problem when it all goes wrong, because it *will* all go wrong."

Lauren's brain feels as if it's about to explode as she weighs up using Jess as her excuse for lying, wondering which is the lesser of two evils.

"I'm sorry I lied," she says, opting to go with what Kate believes. "But I know you'd rather I didn't see her."

"You can do what you like," says Kate. "But you need to be absolutely sure you know what you're getting yourself into."

She makes it sound as if Lauren's doing something dangerous, but then she reminds herself that she wasn't with Jess. The realization of who she *was* with chills her to the bone.

"I know what I'm doing," she says hesitantly.

"I hope, for *all* our sakes, that you do," says Kate.

20

KATE

Being pregnant doesn't feel how Kate thought it would. After the interminable wait to get here, she expected fireworks to be going off and an instantaneous rounding of her tummy. But at six weeks, all she feels is really nauseous and a bit weirded out that there is a human being growing inside of her.

She's glad to be almost done for the day, but the rush hour has already started as she heads back to the office from her last appointment in Soho. The summer heat from above ground has turned the Underground into a furnace and the labyrinth of tunnels becomes hotter and hotter the further down she goes, with the only relief being the whoosh of air that precedes the train. Though even that feels like she's stuck in the diffuser of a high-powered hairdryer.

She gets caught up in the throng of people clamoring to get on the already packed carriage. There's pushing, tutting and the occasional shout of, "Move the fuck down," which, if it had been winter, would have been, "Can you move down please?" The heat does funny things to you.

Kate clings on to the rail, eyeing the healthy-looking young guy who is slouched in the preferential seat for the elderly and pregnant. She fantasizes that in the weeks and months to come she'll bare her bump and demand that he give up his seat, but right now, she looks like she's just had a heavy lunch. She'd be happy if that was the truth, but she can't remember the last time she had a decent meal, her insides unable to cope with the mere thought of carbohydrates and protein. So, to save herself from starving to death, and on Matt's insistence, she'd taken to carrying a box of cereal around in her bag—the cardboard-tasting flakes being the only thing she can stomach right now.

She gets off at Canary Wharf and watches in awe as fellow commuters rush past her on the escalator. Men, with sweat staining their shirts, race up the steep risers toward civilization. The women take their time, preferring to be taken down in the apocalypse than display a wet patch on their blouse.

The coolness of the air-conditioned office building is a welcome relief, but as she's waiting for one of the lifts, her phone rings.

"Hello, darling, it's only me," says Rose. "I'm glad I caught you."

Kate can't help but sigh. "What's up?"

"Well, I just wondered if you'd spoken to Lauren at all."

"Not for a couple of weeks, no," says Kate.

"It's only that I wondered if there was a problem between you . . ."

"I don't know, is there?"

"She won't admit it to me," Rose goes on. "But I'm

pretty sure she's still talking to that girl, or maybe even seeing her."

For a split second, Kate doesn't know who her mother's referring to, but then the cold hard realization hits her. She'd spent the last couple of weeks desperately trying to silence the noises in her head, refusing to let Jess infiltrate her thoughts, which had been easier to do without Lauren to constantly remind her. Though she had to admit that, even for them, two weeks was a long time to go without speaking and she missed her. Could she dare to hope that the next time they spoke, any thought of Jess being their half sister would be forgotten? It didn't sound like it.

"I'm really not interested," she says.

"It's breaking my heart, all of this," says Rose, her voice cracking. "I can't bear it when you two aren't talking."

"We're just busy," says Kate, by way of an excuse, but even *she's* not falling for it.

"Goodness knows the girl's caused enough grief as it is, let's not let her ruin *everything*."

Kate stops herself from saying, *She already has.*

"Lauren is a grown woman," she says instead. "She can do what she wants."

"Not if it's at the expense of the family."

"You keep talking about this wonderful family of ours, as if it's the Holy Grail," says Kate, seeing red. "That we're somehow untouchable by anything immoral or unethical. But guess what, Mum—right now, we're in the middle of a shitstorm, all lined up like sitting ducks, waiting for the bullet that is going to blow us all to smithereens."

"If you're referring to your dad—" starts Rose.

"I'm referring to *you*," snaps Kate. "When are *you* going to stand up and take responsibility for what *you're* putting your precious family through?"

There's a deathly silence at the other end of the line and Kate instantly wishes she could suck her words back in. She'd not intended to say them. She hadn't expected to be brave enough.

"We obviously need to talk," says Rose eventually.

Kate breathes out. *Finally we're getting somewhere.*

"Can you come over at some point this week?" asks Rose.

"Yes, of course," says Kate, suddenly eager to sound conciliatory. "I can probably pop in the day after to-morrow."

"Fine, I'll see if Lauren can get cover for the kids for an hour," says Rose. "But Kate . . . ?"

"Yes, Mum."

"Be ready for some home truths."

The poor signal in the lift ends the call and Kate spends the twenty seconds of peace it affords her to try and control the apprehension that is tightening her chest. It's not long, but it gives her the time she needs to arrive at the news floor with a smile on her face.

"Those pictures have come in," says Daisy eagerly, as soon as Kate reaches her desk.

"Great, what are they like?"

"I'll ping them over to you now."

Kate throws her bag onto the desk and stands over her computer terminal. If these mobile-phone shots of a pop star they've been promised are good enough, it'll be a front-page lead and all she'll have to do is write a quick caption before she heads home.

Her phone rings again as she taps impatiently on her keyboard, waiting.

"Yes," she says, without knowing who's calling.

"Hey, it's only me," says Matt. "You okay?"

She wants to tell him that no, she's not okay. Her family are driving her insane, the heat is killing her, she could fall asleep standing up and she's sure that her ankles have swollen, but she's already bored of herself.

"I've been rushing around all day, so I'm a little bit tired," she says instead. "I'm just going to wrap things up here, head home and have an early night."

"Ah, okay," says Matt. "A few of us are going for a quick drink after work. I was going to ask if you fancied coming with us."

"Mmm, I think I'll give it a miss if you don't mind."

Matt's colleagues on the news desk are far more testosterone-fueled than she's in the mood for right now. Standing in a packed pub with all her ailments is bad enough. Having to do it while being lectured on the merits of a 4-4-2 formation over a 5-3-2 would be a bridge too far.

"Okay, do you mind if I go for a quick one?"

"Go for as many as you like," she says, laughing.

"Are you sure you don't want to come?"

"Tempting as it is, I have a rather pressing engagement with a book and a scented candle."

Matt laughs. "Okay, as long as you're sure. I'll give you a call as I'm heading home."

"Have fun."

Her head drops onto her chest and she lets out a sigh of disappointment as a flurry of grainy images fill her screen. She doesn't know whether it's because you can barely make out it's a woman, let alone an international pop star, or that a member of the public has deemed it acceptable to invade someone's privacy from fifty meters away. Either way, she knows she can't print them.

"We need something else," she says, pulling out her chair and falling heavily onto it.

"There's that premiere tonight," offers Daisy quickly, as if she'd already anticipated Kate's response.

Kate nods thoughtfully. "Have we got a photographer there?"

"Yes, Ben's on it."

"Okay, great," says Kate. "Let's see if we can get a handle on what and who the leads are wearing and as soon as the pics are in, can you write a caption?"

"Me?" says Daisy in surprise.

Kate normally wouldn't trust anyone but herself or her deputy Karen to write copy, but for some reason, she doesn't feel quite as conscientious as she once did. She suspects it's because she's pregnant, and knows that in a few months from now, her life will be so far removed from the one she's currently living that she won't give two hoots about what film stars are wearing or who pop stars are dating. She's also coming to the conclusion that she's simply lost the taste for exposing the private lives of people who try so hard to keep them private.

"Yes," says Kate. "Do you want to give it a go?"

"Absolutely," says Daisy, smiling enthusiastically. "If you think I'm capable."

"I tell you what," says Kate, looking at her watch. "I'm going to go to the pub for a bit. Give me a call and let me know what you come up with once the pics are in. That way, if there any problems, I can come back to the office."

"Okay," squeaks Daisy.

It isn't quite the evening Kate had envisaged, but if it means she can get off work early, she'll take it. She certainly knows *someone* who will be pleased with the change of plan.

She calls Matt as she's walking up the street toward his office, sidestepping the suits that move toward her like ants as they spill out from the high-rise towers and disperse in different directions, most with the sole purpose of finding the nearest watering hole. She wills him to pick up—although there are only a handful of pubs Matt would head for, in this heat she'd rather not have to do a solitary pub crawl to find him. It goes to voicemail and when she reaches his building she tries again, but still there's no answer.

She sits on a stone bench, reaching surreptitiously into the cereal box in her bag and lifting out a handful of dry cornflakes, unable to determine if the odd sensation in her tummy is hunger or nausea. If she can't reach Matt soon, she might pop to the Tesco on the opposite corner of the square for some ginger biscuits. She'd once run a feature on how Kate Middleton had allegedly relied on them to get her through the severe sickness she'd endured with each of her pregnancies, and if it was good enough for royalty . . .

Her thought process is interrupted by Matt emerging from the revolving door of his building, shielding his eyes from the glaring sun. Relieved to see his lopsided grin, Kate moves toward him, holding her stomach with a protective hand as the tide of bodies moves against her. It doesn't occur to her to wonder what he's smiling about, though if it had, she'd probably hazard a guess that it's the thought of her and the little life that they're incubating.

But as she gets closer to him, something stops her dead, rooting her feet to the concrete. She wants to call out his name, to stop him in his tracks, but her throat is dry and contracting in an involuntary spasm. It's as if she's trapped in a nightmare. She wants to scream, but when she opens her mouth, no noise comes out.

She watches, open-mouthed, as the man she loves guides the woman who's threatening to destroy her family across the concourse. He and Jess are close as they sidestep the horde and move in the direction of the footbridge and the bars of West India Quay. Kate stands there numbly, her brain blocking out the noise of everything but her own thoughts. It's as if they're scratching incessantly at a scab—pick, pick, pick—until they expose the wound. Only then do they throw her back out into the cacophony that surrounds her, raw and bleeding.

A text pings through on her phone and she looks at it as if through a blurry haze.

Had a couple of missed calls—all okay? Matt asks.

She looks up in disbelief as he walks away from her, his head lolling back as he laughs at something Jess says.

What the fuck? Kate asks herself, again and again as she follows them across the bridge. She quickens her step, not knowing whether she wants to catch them up or not, but her warped need to know what's happening pushes her on.

They go into Brown's restaurant on the quayside and Kate lingers outside, debating what she should do.

If she applied her usual forthright mentality, she'd storm straight in there and call them out. After all, she has every right. But there's a tiny part of her that is urging caution. That is trying to offer an explanation as to why her husband is sitting in a bar in Canary Wharf, entertaining the woman who claims to be her half sister.

Before she has a chance to think, they're both coming back out again—Matt with his usual, a pint of beer, and Jess with a glass of rosé. Kate steps backward, stumbling over her own feet, to hide behind a tree. Her heart is thumping and the bitter taste in her mouth is becoming increasingly difficult to swallow as she fights to come up with a logical reason why these two people are together.

Jess leans into Matt as he shows her something on his phone, and she throws her head back laughing. Kate watches with a growing sense of unease as Jess runs a hand through her blonde hair, looking at Matt, almost as if she's in awe of him. He, in turn, smiles at Jess over the top of his pint glass. It's the same playfulness that he used to look at *her* with; is it flirting, or a social nervousness? It would depend on how you want to take it, though Kate has never known Matt to suffer with the latter. If she didn't know better, she'd think they were a couple in the early stages of courtship, when they hadn't quite found that comfortable place where they could truly be themselves. It looks as though they are still testing each other out, seeing how far they should go.

She feels sick, unable to watch any longer as this girl, who she didn't know existed until a few weeks ago, wrecks her world, piece by piece.

21

LAUREN

It's funny how you treat your phone differently when you're doing something you shouldn't be. Lauren used to leave it on the kitchen worktop while she bathed the kids, or in her bag in the hall when she went to bed. But now she keeps it on her wherever she goes and every time it makes a noise, her heart goes to her mouth.

Every one of Justin's six texts today has grown in urgency, begging to see her, and she's fast running out of excuses.

It's been weeks. When can I see you again? he'd texted.

Maybe next week, she'd replied, as frustrated as he was that she'd not found a way for them to spend more time together.

I can't wait that long, he'd written back.

She didn't think *she* could either, because when she wasn't texting him, she was thinking about him, remembering his hand on her neck, the closeness of his lips and imagining how different her life could have been if they'd stayed together.

"I've got a job on Thursday night," says Simon as he

comes down the stairs after putting Noah and Emmy to bed. Jude is lying on his blanket on the floor, kicking his legs as angrily as a five-month-old baby can, while screaming his head off. Lauren refers to this stretch between six and nine o'clock at night as his cranky period.

"Great," she says, finding it difficult to concentrate.

"It's a shop fit in town, so I'll be out late."

Suddenly her ears prick up, as if sensing an opportunity. "Oh, okay," she says, as casually as she can, though her brain is speeding ahead of itself. "What sort of time will you be home?"

"The job doesn't start until eight, so I'll probably work through most of the night."

There's a flutter in her chest as she allows her mind to wander, fantasizing about the hours at her disposal, and the possibilities that abound. But then she's hit by an overwhelming wave of guilt. She's tried so hard to ignore the very real physical tug of needing to see Justin again, concentrating all her energy into being the mother her children need and the wife Simon deserves. Or used to deserve.

Just the other night, she'd cooked a nice meal and put the children to bed early, so they had a chance to talk. But he'd taken one look at the kitchen table, adorned with last year's Christmas tablecloth, and laughed.

"What the hell's that?" he'd smirked.

A cinnamon tea light, that she'd found at the bottom of the decorations bag, confused the senses into thinking that the summer's evening was in the wrong season. But she'd thought it was a nice touch—a romantic gesture.

"I thought we could have dinner," she'd said.

"You'd have been wise to call; I've just had a battered sausage at the chippie."

She should have been disappointed, but she couldn't help but feel relieved that they wouldn't have to make small talk over a dinner that neither of them really wanted, literally or metaphorically.

That doesn't give me the right to embark on a relationship that's only going to hurt the people I love, she says to herself now in an attempt to quell the excited queasiness circling her stomach. Because, for all Simon's faults, she *does* still love him. She chooses to ignore the voice in her head that says, *If you did, then you wouldn't feel the need to go and see another man.*

"I might go and stay with Mum then," says Lauren, knowing that she's already lining her nest, ready to take flight, and hating herself for it. But she already knows that she can't call on her mother again—not after last time, when she lied about where she was. Little did Rose and Kate know that the lie was upon another lie.

"Might be best," says Simon absently. "I don't like the thought of you being here on your own. I hate working nights."

"The money will be good though," says Lauren, encouragingly. "More than a day job, right?"

"What?" says Simon, cupping a hand to his ear as if it will drown out Jude's high-pitched cries.

"It doesn't matter," says Lauren, going to Jude and scooping him up into her arms. He stops for a moment before screwing his face up and letting out another blood-curdling scream.

"What's wrong with him?" asks Simon, as he gets himself a beer from the fridge.

"He's fed, changed and watered," says Lauren, propping Jude up on her shoulder and rubbing his back. "He's probably just got wind."

"Well, can you take him somewhere else for a bit? The football's just about to start."

Lauren looks across the tiny ground floor of the house, unable to see where she can possibly go that will make a difference.

"I might just take him out in the car," she says. "See if that settles him."

Simon barely looks up from the TV as she picks up her bag and heads for the door. Tears of frustration threaten to fall as she pulls away, not knowing where she's going to go, just knowing that she needs to get out just as much as Jude does, away from the overwhelming sense of claustrophobia that's bearing down on her.

Just as she gets to the end of the street, her mobile rings on the passenger seat and she snatches a quick glance at it.

It's Jess, another problem that coils its way around Lauren's insides. She answers it and puts it on loudspeaker.

"Hi, it's me," says Jess. "Can you talk?"

Lauren laughs sarcastically. "I *can* talk, but I doubt you'll be able to hear me over the din of my darling child."

"Is he okay?" asks Jess.

"He's fine—just grouchy. How are things with you?"

"I'm good, I just wanted to ask you a couple of questions actually."

"Okay, fire away!"

"I'd rather do it in person," asks Jess. "Are you at

home? Would it be okay if I popped over? I only need ten minutes."

"Alas, I'm driving around the streets of South London," says Lauren.

"Oh," says Jess. "I was hoping to have a chat."

"Where are you?" asks Lauren.

"At home."

"Didn't you say you live in Hackney?" says Lauren, suddenly feeling as though she has a renewed sense of purpose.

"Well, yes, but . . ."

"I can come to you," says Lauren, grateful for some direction. "I can be there in twenty minutes."

"But—" starts Jess.

"What's your address?"

Jess gives it to her, albeit begrudgingly, and when Lauren pulls up outside a derelict row of shops a little while later, she has half a clue as to why. The windows are either broken or so dirty that you can't see into what were probably once prosperous businesses. The only clue to what used to be there are the half fascias that hang precariously above the shopfronts: *Hair by—*; *Shi—Kebab*; *Tatto—*.

Double decker buses roar past Lauren as she gets out of the car, pinning herself to the bodywork in an effort to be avoided. She moves around to the pavement side to get Jude out, who she suspects finally fell asleep looking at the lights as they rushed overhead hypnotically in the Blackwall Tunnel.

The doorway for number 193 is beside the only open shop in the parade—a Chinese takeaway with yellowing net curtains and cooing pigeons nesting above its entrance. Lauren sidesteps the defecation peppering the paving slabs and presses the buzzer.

She can hear footsteps making their way downstairs and prepares her best, *Well, isn't this lovely?* face, but Jess beats her to it.

"Sorry," she says, as she forces the door over the newspapers and flyers that litter the hall floor. "It's only temporary, until I get myself sorted out."

Lauren forces a smile as she steps inside, suddenly grateful for her tiny but clean house.

"So, how's things?" asks Lauren, as they bypass doors marked A and B and head up the stairs.

"Well, I've got myself a job, which will get me out of this place in the next few months."

"Ah, that's great," says Lauren, already panicking about putting Jude's car seat down when they get into the flat.

"This is me," says Jess as she pushes on a door marked C and holds it open for Lauren.

Once inside, Lauren's relieved to see that despite its outward appearance, Jess's flat is actually very orderly and spotlessly clean.

"What can I get you?" says Jess. "Tea? Coffee?"

"Erm, coffee would be good please."

Jess clicks the kettle on and takes two mugs out of the cupboard.

"So, how's the job going?" asks Lauren. "Are you enjoying it?"

"I love it," says Jess, smiling.

"Is it in town?"

"Canary Wharf," says Jess. "So not too far."

"Kate and her husband work there," says Lauren,

though she doesn't know why. It's not as if Kate's exactly flavor of the month for either of them right now.

"Actually, it's her I wanted to talk to you about," says Jess.

"Oh?"

"Yeah, I just wondered if there was any way you might be able to get us together."

Lauren grimaces before she's even finished the end of the sentence. She's already been summoned to a meeting with Kate and their mother, which will be bad enough. There's absolutely *no* chance of getting Kate and Jess together.

"I just really want us to all get along," says Jess. "You've been so kind, and I just know that if Kate would just give me time, get to know and trust me, then I'm sure we could be the sisters we were meant to be, if circumstances hadn't dictated otherwise."

Lauren looks down at the floor and takes a deep breath. "It's not your fault that Kate's taken this the way she has," she says. "She's a tricky character, who's always been daddy's little princess, so to find out that the man she looked up to wasn't the man she thought he was has been hard for her to accept."

"Does she believe it?" asks Jess.

"No, I don't think she does," says Lauren. "Not yet, but she'll come around."

"How? What can I do to make her see that I'm not here to cause trouble? That I want us all to get along."

Lauren shakes her head. "I don't know, but I'll work on it. It's important to me that you're a part of my family and I'll do whatever I can to make sure you're accepted."

"After everything I've been through, I just want to feel like I belong," says Jess tearfully.

"I know," says Lauren, going to her and pulling her in for a hug. "You don't deserve this."

"Why are you being so kind?" sniffs Jess. "Why aren't you as angry or mistrusting of me as Kate is?"

"Because I know what my father was capable of and I've spent many, many years being angry with him. I would have gone on hating him until my dying day if you hadn't turned up. You saved me from that—you've showed me that some good came from the mistakes he made back then."

"Have you remembered anything more about my mother?" asks Jess quietly. "Anything at all."

Lauren shakes her head.

"I thought I might go up to Harrogate," says Jess. "Just to ask around. See if I can jog anyone's memory."

"It was a long time ago," says Lauren. "I'm not sure that it will help. I can barely remember it myself."

"But you definitely saw your dad with a woman," says Jess. "And a baby."

Lauren nods. "But the memory is getting weaker and weaker."

"Because of what Kate and your mum are saying?"

"I know what I saw," says Lauren. "But it might not have meant what I think it did."

"Why are you backtracking now?" asks Jess.

"I'm not," says Lauren. "I just don't want to give you the wrong information."

"Come with me," says Jess, suddenly animated. "Let's go tomorrow. I've got the day off. We can get the train from King's Cross."

Lauren looks at her as if she's mad. "I can't."

"Why not?"

"Well . . . because . . ." Lauren stutters. "Because I've got three children."

"Okay, so let's take them with us," says Jess through a smile. "We could *all* go. I'll do us some sandwiches and snacks for the train, make a day of it."

Lauren is momentarily stumped for a valid reason to say no. "Look, I don't think there's any point in going up there," she says.

Jess looks at her, crestfallen.

"It was twenty-two years ago. Nobody will remember what happened back then. People who were there then won't be there now. We'd be going on a wild goose chase."

"How do you know?" asks Jess.

Lauren feels a flush of heat creeping up her neck and hopes it's not visible. "Trust me, it will just be a waste of time. You won't find out who your mother is by trekking halfway up the country."

"Okay," says Jess, shrugging her shoulders. "What about if we don't have any expectations? What if we just go up there for the day, just because we can? It would be lovely to spend some time with you and the children."

Lauren is fast running out of excuses. "But it's a long way and I really haven't got the money for the rail fare."

"It'll be my treat," says Jess quickly. "I'm getting my first paycheck on Friday."

"Well, that decides it then," says Lauren, half laughing. "I'm not having you spending your hard-earned money on *me*."

"It'll be a small price to pay if it means spending a day with my sister," says Jess.

Lauren smiles and looks at her through narrowed eyes. "And you won't be disappointed if we don't find anything out about your mum?"

"I promise," says Jess.

The doorbell buzzes around the room, shrill and urgent, making Jude jump and stick his bottom lip out before he's even opened his eyes.

"Oh shit, sorry," says Jess, as Jude launches into a full-on roar. "It'll probably be someone for one of the other flats. I'll go and let them in, otherwise they'll only keep ringing."

Lauren looks at her watch as she goes to lift Jude out of his seat. "He's probably getting hungry again," she says to Jess's retreating back. She bobs Jude up and down on her shoulder, pacing the floor as she walks the hallway of the flat. She walks into the bathroom at the end, before turning around and poking her head into the open door of a bedroom. Like the rest of the place, Lauren notices that it's tidy and immaculately clean. Another door stands closed and she tries the handle, but it won't budge. She twists it the other way and applies a little pressure, but it's locked tight.

Unperturbed, Lauren walks to the front window in the kitchen, to look out onto the street below. There, propped up against a flowering orchid, are three envelopes, all addressed to Harriet Oakley.

"My flatmate," says Jess, taking Lauren by surprise.

"Oh, I didn't mean to . . ." starts Lauren, letting them fall back onto one another. "So the other room . . ."

Jess follows Lauren's eyes into the hall. "Yes, she's away at the moment," she says. "It's *her* flat actually. She's just letting me stay until I get on my feet."

"That's nice of her," says Lauren, still jiggling Jude in her arms.

"Could I hold him?" asks Jess.

Lauren looks at her, still barely more than a child herself as she takes Jude carefully in her arms, bringing his head up to her face to smell him. She wonders what she's thinking; is she questioning how her parents could have ever given her away? Or is she asking why they didn't stop to think about that before creating a human being in the first place?

22

KATE

A cold shower is the only thing that brings Kate out of her numb stupor. As she shampoos her hair, her hands grow more and more urgent as she works up a lather.

"What the hell are they *playing at*?" she says over and over.

Hearing herself out loud makes her realize that she's not trapped in a nightmare, and the harsh reality of the situation has her asking what she's going to do about it. Whenever she's had a problem, she's always been able to turn to Matt, who she knows would have her best interests at heart. But clearly he's not going to help her out on this one. Her dad would always be a close second, ready to hand out wise advice whenever she needed it, but she has to remind herself that he's not here, and once again she feels his absence keenly.

Cooler from the shower, but still desperate for some much-needed air, she opens the balcony doors overlooking the O2 dome—a venue that has been host to a million stars. With its crane-like posts protruding from its roof, it's one of the reasons why she and Matt had bought their apartment on the peninsula. They love that on a warm summer's evening they can sit on the balcony and listen to the thumping bassline of whoever was performing inside. But even that simple joy seems like a lifetime away now.

She's curled up on the bed, her pillow wet with tears, when she hears Matt's key in the lock. Any other time, she'd feel a sliver of excitement that he was home, but tonight there's a weight on her chest and a ball of anxiety lodged in her throat.

It would be easier to stay here in the dark and pretend she was asleep, but she's never been one for the easy option. She wants to watch the husband, who she's loved and trusted for the past ten years, as he explains himself, because seeing his face will tell her if he's telling the truth.

She flicks on the reading light and pulls herself up onto the headboard.

"Hey," he says as he walks into the room. He lowers the book that Kate's just grabbed from the bedside table and leans in to give her a kiss on her forehead. "Jeez, it's hot out there."

She can feel a faint line of perspiration along the top of his lip and offers a tight smile. "How did it go?" she asks, as casually as she can.

He turns his back on her to hang his jacket up in the wardrobe. "How did what go?"

She doesn't even know what she's asking herself. "The pub," she says.

"Oh, you know . . ."

"No, I don't," she says.

He turns to look at her as he unfastens his tie. "I'm detecting a little jealousy," he says.

Kate can't help but flinch at the irony of his statement.

"Or is it regret?" he asks, smiling.

"Regret at what?" she says sharply.

"That you turned down my invitation to go for a drink on a lovely summer's evening." He looks at her with raised eyebrows. "You should have come—you would have enjoyed it."

She wouldn't bet on it. "Who was there?"

He turns away from her again and goes into the en suite bathroom. "Oh, you know, just the usual lot."

If Kate *hadn't* seen her husband flirting with a woman in a pub, if she *hadn't* known it was the woman who was causing the destruction of her family, then perhaps she wouldn't have noticed the flippant, "Oh, you know . . ." A sure sign that he's on the back foot.

"Who? Ben, Jamie . . . ?" she asks.

"Yeah," he calls out from the bathroom. "They came a bit later, along with a few of the others."

"So, what? You were a Norman No-mates until they arrived," she says, piling on the pressure.

These were not the jealous thoughts she was used to having. This was not the kind of marriage they had. Kate prided herself on being a laid-back wife, at one with her husband's career, friends and social life, on the rare occasion it didn't include her. While her girlfriends bickered and bitched about their partners going out without them, berating them when they dared to return later than 10 p.m., she would smugly declare that she trusted Matt with every bone in her body.

Now, she can't shake off the ominous feeling that her complacency might be about to turn around and bite her on the behind.

"No, a couple of us were there," he says. "Including the new junior reporter. You should have come; you'd have liked her. She reminds me of you when you were first starting out."

Kate's head feels as if it's about to explode. She doesn't know whether she feels relieved or even more suspicious. Jess is the girl he *employed*?

"How's she getting on?" Kate asks.

"Really good," he says. "She's got a good nose for a story."

"What was her name again?" Even she can hear the forced nonchalance in her voice. She holds her breath, waiting for him to answer.

"Jess," he says. And in that moment, she flips the resounding question of, *What the hell is he playing at?* to *What the hell is* she *playing at?* There's nothing to suggest that he knows anything more than he's letting on, but it's too much of a coincidence to think that Jess just *happened* to get a job with Matt.

"You okay?" he asks, as he comes back in and lies on top of the bed naked. "You look a bit pale."

She nods, consumed by the unsettling feeling that Jess is up to something. There's no doubt in Kate's mind that she knows what she's doing—the problem is, what is it?

Matt reaches across and pulls her into him, but although nothing's changed between them, she can't help but feel that everything's different. If she doesn't recoil from him physically, she ashamedly shirks from him emotionally, knowing it's not his fault, but blaming him all the same.

"You'd tell me if something was wrong, wouldn't you?" he asks, as if able to sense it.

"Of course," she says, while wondering where she'd even begin.

As soon as she hears Matt's breathing change, she slides herself out from underneath his arm, looking back to check he's asleep. She pads quietly to his side of the bed and carefully unplugs his phone. Their pin codes for everything have always been the date of their wedding anniversary, and although they've often joked that they're a criminal's dream, right now she's thankful that he hasn't changed it.

There's just enough light filtering in from outside for Kate to make her way into the living room, avoiding the brutal corners of the coffee table, to sit on the sofa. She opens up Matt's emails and runs her eyes down the list, waiting for something or someone to jump out. She tells herself she doesn't know what she's looking for, except she does. As her eyes dart over anonymous names and meaningless subject headings, she can no longer tell whether her stomach is churning with nausea because she's pregnant or because she's doing something she never believed she'd do.

Kate is immediately drawn to the numerous emails from "jessica.linley@theecho.com," which prove that she works with Matt. Seeing the evidence that he was telling the truth in black and white is a relief. The content is innocent enough, as they bounce back and forth on news items and feature ideas, but they tell her nothing more of who Jess really is, or where she's from. Kate's eyes trail down the list, looking for something more.

She searches for Jess's name and finds more correspondence under the subject heading of "Junior Reporter." Sent from a personal email address, Kate is taken aback by the image that fills the screen as she clicks on the attached CV, shocked to be face to face with the woman who calls herself her half sister. There's a familiarity about her dirty blonde shoulder-length hair, wide-set eyes and straight nose, but Kate tries to convince herself that it's because they've already met. She will not allow the resemblance to Lauren to infiltrate her brain.

The covering letter, addressed to Mr. Walker, is innocuous enough, with no mention of any supposed connection. As Matt had said, it seems she'd come straight from university in Bournemouth, where she'd studied journalism. *Now*, Jess says in her letter, *I want to work on the country's top-selling newspaper.* Kate groans at the attempted flattery, before forwarding the email onto herself and deleting it from Matt's sent box.

"Kate!"

She jumps up, banging her calf into the "bastard" coffee table and biting down on her tongue to stop herself from screaming out.

"What are you doing?" asks Matt. She can just make out his silhouette in the doorway.

"I was just . . ." she starts, as his phone burns a hole in her hand.

"Couldn't you sleep?"

"I . . . erm . . . no." The panic of getting past him to put his phone back onto his bedside table is messing with her ability to talk. "I had a headache."

"But you're okay now?"

"Yes," she says, thankful that it's dark and he can't see the guilt written all over her face.

"What time is it?" he asks. "I couldn't find my phone."

"Erm, around midnight I think," she mumbles. "Here, let me help you." She scurries past him into the bedroom and rushes round to his side of the bed.

"It might help if we put the light on," he says, flicking the switch.

Kate instantly falls to her hands and knees.

"Are you sure you're okay?" Matt asks.

No, she's not okay. Her heart's thumping through her chest and she feels sick at how he will react if he finds her with his phone. Not because he knows there's anything incriminating on there, but because she's breached the trust that they've always shared.

"Here it is!" she exclaims, far too loudly. "You must have knocked it onto the floor."

"Oh," is all he says, but it's enough to let her know that he doesn't believe her.

23

KATE

Kate's sleep is interspersed with vivid dreams of Matt, Lauren and her mum and dad, each of them vying for screen time in her head. They all float in and out, in various guises—unrecognizable as the humans they are, yet it is still somehow immediately obvious who's who. The only cast member who looks like her real self is Jess, who is ensconced in the corner of a room, beckoning the family members over, one by one, to whisper to them. When it's Matt's turn, she holds his face and kisses him, long and deep, all the while looking at Kate.

When the alarm clock goes off, Kate hits the snooze button, hoping that she'll be thrown back into the dream for just long enough to see what happens in the end. But Matt's already moaning beside her and she feels an intense hatred for him, still so hurt by what he'd done in the dream that she's momentarily unable to separate it from reality.

"I didn't get a wink of sleep," he says, though Kate knows that's not strictly true, as she heard him quietly snoring at least three times. "It's so bloody hot—there's just no air."

Kate sits up slowly, as if trying to fool her body into thinking she doesn't feel well. She groans, for effect, as she lets her head fall heavily onto her bent knees.

"Do you feel rough?" asks Matt, leaning over to her side of the bed to rub her back.

She goes to speak, but clamps her mouth shut and nods instead.

"Okay, you need to lie back down," says Matt. "Slowly." He supports her as she lowers herself back onto the mattress. "I'll go and get a bucket."

As Kate closes her eyes, a replay of her dream flickers on the inside of her eyelids, the image of Matt and Jess branding itself on her memory. She hopes, like most dreams, that it will have all but eradicated itself by lunchtime.

"Here," says Matt, fetching in the spare washing-up bowl from under the kitchen sink and laying it down on the floor beside the bed.

It feels like she's a child again, feigning illness to get off going to school. Her father would take one look at her hot red face, burned by the radiator, and send her straight back to bed. Her mother wasn't quite so easy to deceive and would watch her through narrowed eyes as she took her temperature with a thermometer.

"Why don't you take the day off?" says Matt. "You can't possibly drag yourself in like this."

"Mmm, I think I might," she manages through closed lips.

How ironic that as soon as she makes the decision, a rumbling of nausea circles in the pit of her stomach—like a washing machine on a slow spin.

She watches as Matt gets himself ready for work and can't help wondering what he's thinking as he selects the tie he's going to wear. What would he say if she told him who his junior reporter really was? Would he be surprised? Would he pull her on it? Would he fire her on the spot?

But then Kate is forced to admit to herself that as of yet, Jess hasn't actually done anything wrong. In fact, she's probably the model employee, but if she's expecting Kate to believe that this is all nothing but a huge coincidence, then she's got another think coming.

"Does this go?" asks Matt, holding a pink and gray striped tie up against himself. It works well with his white shirt and charcoal suit. Better than the red one in his other hand.

"I'd go for the red one," says Kate, just to be difficult.

He immediately swaps them over. "Are you going to be okay?" he asks, his face full of concern. "I'm going to struggle to get in early tonight—the Prime Minister's called a press conference up in Birmingham and God knows what crap they're going to announce. Do you want me to see if I can shoot back at lunchtime?"

Kate shakes her head. "No, I'll be fine. I'll wait for this to pass and see how I feel. I've got some work I can do from here anyway."

He leans in and kisses the top of her head. "Okay, look after yourself, and that little one," he says, smiling. "Hopefully this won't go on for too much longer and you can start to enjoy being pregnant."

As soon as Matt leaves, Kate grabs her phone and pulls up Jess's CV from her emails. She quickly scans the salient points before putting a call in to Bournemouth University. She doesn't know what she's looking for or expecting to find, but she refuses to sit by and allow this woman to railroad her life.

"Hello, Student Verification," says the cheery voice at the other end of the line, far quicker than Kate had anticipated.

"Oh hi, I'm looking to employ one of your former students and I'm calling for a reference."

"I'd be very happy to do that for you," says the woman. "But I will need signed consent from the former student in order to release the information."

"Of course," says Kate, her job having taught her to bend the rules when necessary. "I have that already, but I do need this quite urgently."

"We can normally turn it around in five days."

Kate was hoping to get the clarification she needed over the phone, but she doesn't get the impression that this bureaucrat will court such an impetuous request.

"Ah, that's going to be too late I'm afraid," says Kate. "Listen, I'm in the area today, is there any chance I can pop in? I'd hate not to be able to offer your student this opportunity just because I've been a bit slow on the uptake."

And because you're hemmed in by bureaucracy, she says to herself.

"Well, we wouldn't normally accept requests made to the office in person."

"I appreciate that, but I'm really up against it here. It's totally my fault, but if there's any way . . ."

"Okay," says the woman reluctantly. "But I can't promise anything. If the office is particularly busy, we might not be able to do it there and then."

"That's a chance I'm prepared to take," says Kate cheerily.

"If you'd like to give me the student's name now, I

can put it onto the system. It might quicken it up for you and then you only need to show their consent when you come in."

"That's great," says Kate over-enthusiastically. "It's Jessica Linley."

She puts the phone down and types out a two-line letter using Jess's address, prints it out and signs it. How that constitutes consent, Kate doesn't know. But it's clear that Jess isn't playing by the rules, so why should she?

It's predicted to be a record-breaking July temperature today and, in typical British fashion, the DJ on the radio is warning people to stay indoors and check on vulnerable neighbors. Kate wonders how other countries manage to keep functioning when the thermometer goes over thirty degrees, while London's train tracks are buckling and its roads are melting. It's menial thoughts like this that keep her from tearing her hair out, as she tries to figure out what Jess is up to.

She chooses a floral jumpsuit, with cap sleeves and three-quarter-length trousers, in the hope that it will keep her cool on the two-and-a-half-hour train journey. The fabric is light, and the belt can be tied loosely around her waist to allow for its daily expansion.

Even though Kate knows where Bournemouth is on the map, she's still surprised to find the train speeding through the New Forest, a place where she spent many family holidays as a young girl. The pink heathers that adorn the heathlands take her back to the house they rented in Lyndhurst, where they'd have ponies join them in the back garden as they had picnics. The four of them would rent bikes and cycle through the ancient woodland that was peppered with three-hundred-year-old trees and grazing deer.

But the happy memories are suddenly overpowered by the events of their last holiday here, when Kate remembers an almighty row between Lauren and their dad. She could only have been twelve, but never had the four-year age gap between her and her sister felt wider. While Kate was still studying diligently, Lauren had "gone off the rails," in her mother's words. Rose would never have said that to her daughter's face, but it was certainly the opinion she'd aired to Harry after a particularly unpleasant slanging match.

"I don't care what you say," Lauren had shouted. "This is my life and I love him and he loves me."

"But darling," said Harry, in his best placating voice, "you're only sixteen. You've got your whole life ahead of you."

"You met Mum when she was sixteen," said Lauren defiantly. "And that seems to have worked out okay."

"But times are different," said Harry. "You've got so many more opportunities. You can go anywhere. Be anyone."

"I don't want to go anywhere or be anyone. I want to be with him. It's our decision and there's nothing you can do to stop me." Kate had sat at the top of the stairs as the whole house reverberated when Lauren slammed the front door.

"What are we going to do?" Rose had cried.

"It's her decision," said Harry resignedly. "I don't see what else we *can* do."

"You have to do something," said Rose. "We can't let her ruin her life."

"But if that's what she wants to do . . ."

"I will not allow this man . . . this boy," Rose had spat, "to destroy all her dreams. She wanted to go to university. She wanted to go to America. She wanted to be a journalist. She wanted to be so many things, and now she'll be none of them."

Harry had taken Rose into his arms. "You make it sound as if her life is over," he'd half laughed.

"What kind of father lets his sixteen-year-old daughter throw it all away on a whim?" said Rose.

"I don't know what you want me to do."

"She's gone off the rails and it's *your* job to pull her back in."

Kate didn't know what he'd done, but Lauren was never the same again.

"Are you going to the coast for the day or are you on your way home?" asks the lady sitting opposite Kate, interrupting her thoughts. She hadn't noticed her there before—she must have got on at the last station, when Kate was immersed in the memory.

"I'm just going to Bournemouth for the day," she says, smiling politely, a little part of her hoping that it will be enough to signal the end of the conversation. If only to save Kate from having to explain what she's doing there.

"It's a lovely part of the world, isn't it?" says the woman, nodding her head at the window. "I don't know how you townies live among all that smoke and noise."

"It's exhilarating at times," says Kate. "But then I come somewhere like this and I suddenly realize what I'm missing out on."

The woman smiles. "Well, you've certainly got the weather for it. You'll be seeing the south coast at its best. Are you visiting family?"

Despite knowing the question might well be asked, Kate is still caught off guard when it is.

She nods and swallows the bad taste in her mouth. "My sister," she says without even thinking. "It's a surprise."

The woman smiles kindly. "Oh, I'm sure she'll be thrilled."

I wouldn't bet on it, thinks Kate.

24

KATE

There's not a cloud in the sky when Kate gets off the train at Bournemouth. She stands on the platform for a moment, breathing in that unmistakeable sea air and listening to the seagulls squawking overhead.

Despite what she's here for, there's almost a feeling of serenity about the place, a peacefulness that you can't find in London, no matter how hard you try.

"Where to?" asks the driver as she reaches the top of the taxi rank.

"The university please, Talbot campus."

"I assume it's not to study," he says, laughing.

He must see the perplexed look on her face as he quickly follows it up with, "No disrespect, love."

Kate pulls herself up at the slight, knowing that he's only speaking the truth, but it sometimes takes a comment like that, from someone who can only see your exterior, for reality to hit home. The campus is almost deserted, the summer vacation well underway. She spots a few students milling around, their smiles carefree, their optimism for the future almost tangible, and she realizes that she *is* old. She may not *look* a day over thirty-four—though if the truth be told, she'd rather hope that she could pass for closer to thirty— but her mind feels a hundred, scarred by the minutiae of everyday life, cynical of everyone's motive, no longer assured that everything will work out for the best. As she looks at the nondescript building she's about to walk into, she has a sinking feeling that the latter will never be truer.

"Oh hi," she says to the first person who looks at her from across the chest-high counter. "My name's Kate Walker and I'm from the *Gazette*. I called earlier about verifying one of your students for a job offer."

"Oh yes," says the woman, with a frown. "Well, I'm very sorry to have to tell you that we have no record of a Jessica Linley having studied here."

Kate doesn't know what she was expecting, but it isn't this. Still, there is a frisson of anticipation working its way through her as she acknowledges what it means. It will give her no pleasure to inform Lauren that Jess isn't who she says she is, or to tell Matt that his star reporter is a liar and a fraud, but she'll do it if it means putting an end to this ridiculous charade that's been plaguing her family for the past month.

"Are you absolutely sure?" asks Kate earnestly. "There's no way you could have got this wrong?"

The woman shakes her head regretfully. "I've double-checked. The only possibility would be if she attended under a different name. Is that likely?"

Kate considers it for a moment. Anything is possible, especially where Jess is concerned, it seems.

"I don't have another name," she says, rummaging in her bag. "But I do have a photograph. She has only just graduated . . ."

The woman looks at her with a forlorn expression, almost as if she's taking responsibility for Jess's duplicity herself.

"Well, so she says," adds Kate. "You might recognize her."

The woman looks at the photo and back at Kate. "I'm sorry, I don't . . ."

"Don't worry, it was just a thought," says Kate, about to take it back.

"I'm sorry I can't be of more help."

"*I* recognize her," says the woman standing next to her, making Kate's heart feel as if it has frozen in time. The woman takes an inordinate amount of time to lift her glasses, hanging on a beaded chain around her neck, and sit them on the end of her nose, before moving in for a closer look at the photo. "I couldn't tell you her name," she says. "But I've definitely seen her before."

"Are you . . . are you sure?" stammers Kate, feeling as if the small office is closing in on her. She catches the woman shooting a look at her colleague behind the desk, as if in anticipation of a problem.

"You're absolutely sure?" questions Kate.

"Mmm," mumbles the woman noncommittally, as if she's suddenly conscious of breaking some human rights clause in the bureaucracy handbook.

"Maybe it's not who you think it is?" presses Kate.

"I'm usually pretty good," she says. "I know that face, but can't place her for the life of me."

"Might it have been here, at the university?" presses Kate. "Or somewhere in town perhaps?"

"Gosh, I really don't know," says the woman, oblivious to Kate's growing frustration. "I just know I've seen her somewhere before."

"Well, to be honest, if her name's different to the one she used here, it tells me all I need to know anyway," says Kate, slipping the picture back into her bag. "But if you remember anything more, perhaps you'd give me a call?" She hands over her business card.

"Of course," says the woman, a puzzled expression still clouding her features.

Kate thanks the ladies for their help and walks out into the sunshine, wondering where to go next. She'd hoped to at least be able to start tracking Jess's past, but the only lead she has is the university, and with that going cold she has nothing to follow up on.

"Shit!" she says aloud, as soon as she gets around the corner, ignoring the bemused looks of passers-by.

"Hey, excuse me," comes a voice from behind her. "Excuse me . . . Miss!"

Kate turns around, praying that it's the same woman, having had an epiphany. She struggles to contain her buoyed enthusiasm when she sees that it is.

"I don't know if it's going to help you any," pants the woman. "But I've just remembered where I know her from."

It's what Kate had wanted and feared in equal measure.

"Oh," she says, trying to sound nonchalant.

"As odd as this may sound, I think she was working in the cafeteria." The woman looks at her quizzically over the top of her glasses. "What that means, I don't know, but you might want to ask down there."

Kate's brows knit together in confusion. "Working?" she asks.

The woman nods confidently. "She wasn't a student here; she was an employee."

Kate's brain feels as if it's about to explode. "But then why . . . ?" she starts, to which the woman shrugs her shoulders.

"I have no idea, but your best bet is to go down there and ask around. I can safely say I've seen her there in the last six months."

"Erm, okay, thanks," says Kate, hurrying off.

"It's *that* way," says the woman, nodding in the opposite direction to the one in which Kate's heading.

"Thanks," says Kate hurriedly, her feet taking her faster than her brain can think.

It looks more like a cafeteria in an upmarket department store than a university. No wonder it costs nine thousand pounds a year to come here.

Kate heads straight toward the girl on the till, with the photo of Jess in her hand.

"Hello," she says, offering a friendly smile. "I wonder if you can help me. I'm looking for this girl."

She shows Jess's picture and watches the young woman's expression carefully.

"Has something happened to her?" she immediately asks, making Kate's stomach turn over. "Are you the police?"

"No," says Kate softly. "She's my friend and I've lost track of her. The last time we spoke, she was working here."

The girl's face relaxes and she nods. "Yes, Harriet was working here until a couple of months ago."

"Harriet?" Kate repeats, unable to stop herself. She senses the girl tensing up again, so quickly adds, "I've not heard anyone call her that in a long time. I know her as Jess, which is her middle name."

"Oh," says the girl. "Well Harriet, or Jess, left just

before the summer. She said she was going up to London. She wanted to make a name for herself."

Well she's certainly doing that, thinks Kate.

"I've been round to her place in Lancaster Road," says Kate, hoping to give the impression that she knows more than she does. "But they've not seen her for quite a while." She crosses her fingers in the hope that the girl doesn't call her bluff.

"Well, the only place I've known her to live is at Elm House on the Clifford Estate."

"Ah, that must be where she went to after Lancaster Road," says Kate, making a note in her head.

The girl looks taken aback. "How long did you say it had been since you'd seen her?" There's an accusatory tone to her voice and Kate feels hemmed in.

"It's been a while," she says. "But thanks for your help."

The girl nods. "Well, say hello when you find her."

"Oh, I will," Kate replies with a smile.

25

LAUREN

As Lauren walks out of Harrogate Station, she feels like she's stepped back in time. Everything's exactly as she remembers it from when she was last here as a teenager, just before her family suddenly upped and moved to London.

The bench where she spent hours smoking and kissing Justin still sits opposite the station, surrounded by a well-stocked bed of flowers. The council had long since cottoned on that the spa town could be a popular tourist destination and had presented it as such, plowing funds into quaint hanging baskets and attractions such as Valley Gardens and the Royal Pump Room Museum.

It feels odd being back here with her three children in tow, having left this place declaring that she'd remain childless.

"Which way do you think we should head?" asks Jess, interrupting her thoughts.

Lauren shields her eyes from the midday sun as she takes a moment to get her bearings, looking left and right up Station Parade.

"We need to go up the hill," says Lauren, feeling like a reluctant tour guide. "It was one of the roads off on the right, up by the Majestic hotel."

Jess leads the way, pushing the double buggy with Noah and Emmy in, while Lauren follows with Jude in a front-wearing sling. This trip would have been an impossibility on her own, but with an extra pair of hands it just about works.

"Do you think you'll recognize the street if you see it?" asks Jess, reminding Lauren exactly who she's doing this for.

"I don't know," she says honestly.

She can feel Jess throw her a sideways glance as they get to the hotel on the brow of the hill, as if hoping that she'll immediately declare that it was right on this spot that she saw her father push her in a pram almost a quarter of a century ago.

A bus passes by and Lauren is hit by a sudden flashback to when she was coming home from a geography exam. It had gone terribly, like everything else in her life at that time, and she was sitting on the bus, looking out of the window, wondering where it had all gone wrong. Just as she was thinking that it couldn't possibly get any worse, she had seen her dad walking down a side street with one arm draped around the shoulder of a woman and the other pushing a pram. The vision was gone in a flash and she had instinctively jumped up out of her seat and hit the bell, pressing it incessantly until the driver called out, "Okay love, don't get your knickers in a twist." A flippant comment that would cause him all sorts of trouble in today's world.

She'd got off at the earliest opportunity and ran back up the hill as fast as she could, not knowing whether she wanted to be proved right or wrong. The image was already fuzzy in her head and she couldn't be sure if it was the first right turn or the second that she'd seen him. It might even have been the third, but all three were clear by the time she'd got there.

Over the intervening years, her memory had embellished what she'd seen, to give her even more of an excuse to hate the man she'd once loved. She convinced herself she'd seen him kiss the woman and was adamant that he'd scooped the tiny baby up into the air, smiling at it from below. But now, as she stands at the viewpoint from the bus, she wonders whether she ever saw him at all.

"Was it here?" asks Jess.

Lauren looks around pensively, forcing herself to concentrate, while wondering what it's going to achieve even if she does recognize something.

"I don't think so," she says. "Let's go up to the next turning."

The red slate roofs of the houses in the road before are replaced with black tiles, giving the street a more ominous feel.

"This is it," she exclaims, knowing instantly that her memory hadn't lied to her.

Jess stops stock still and looks at her. "Are you sure?" she says.

Lauren nods. "So now what?"

"I'm going to knock on a few doors," says Jess. "See if anyone remembers anything."

Lauren had had a horrible inkling she was going to say that, and tiny pinpricks of sweat spring to the skin of her palms.

"Are you coming?"

Lauren nods half-heartedly, though when they reach the gate of the first house, she holds back. "I'll stay here with the children," she says. "You go."

Jess smiles tightly before walking down the path and as Lauren watches her, she doesn't know what she wants her to find.

"Oh hello," says Jess cheerily to the woman who answers the door. "I'm sorry to trouble you but I'm looking to speak to someone who lived on this street twenty or so years ago."

The woman shakes her head and says, "I'm sorry," before Jess has even finished the sentence.

"I'm not looking to sell you anything," presses Jess, but the door is already closing. This is going to be crueller than Lauren thought, and she berates herself for ever mentioning it to Jess. No good can come of this.

"Come on, let's go," says Lauren with forced joviality. "We can have a walk around town, and I'll treat you to scones and a cuppa at Betty's Tea Rooms."

"We can't give up after just one setback," says Jess. "We need to keep going."

It's not what Lauren wants to hear, but she can't decide whether it's because she doesn't want Jess to get hurt or she is scared for herself. Either way, there's a sense of impending doom as Jess presses on.

The next house is shrouded in shadow, guarded by an imposing oak tree on the pavement. Brightly colored flower boxes line the deep ledges of the ground-floor windows and the front garden is pruned to within an inch of its life. It looks like a home owned by an elderly, but active, house-proud couple. Lauren applauds her observation skills when she sees one of the brilliant-white net curtains twitch. Bingo!

Almost before Jess even navigates the bell pull, an older woman, who reminds Lauren of her late grandma, opens the door and looks at her inquisitively. The sound of the doorbell is still chiming around the house.

"Hello, dear," she says.

"I'm really sorry to bother you . . ." says Jess. "It's just that I'm looking for someone who may have lived here around twenty years ago."

"Well that would be me," says the woman, with a half laugh. "How can I help you?"

Jess turns to look at Lauren hopefully, but a sudden apprehension weighs Lauren down. How could she ever have thought this would be a good idea?

"I haven't got much information to go on, but I'm trying to track down a family that may have lived along this street."

The woman looks at her expectantly.

"A couple and their daughter. He was . . . he was . . ."

"Tall," says Lauren from the curb. "With blond hair and pale blue eyes." As she pictures her father, she unexpectedly feels a pull at the back of her throat.

"You're not referring to the Woods family, are you?" asks the woman, her features darkening.

"I . . . I don't know," says Jess. "Maybe."

"Perhaps you should come in," says the woman, opening the door wider and stepping aside.

Jess looks wide-eyed at Lauren, who shakes her head. "I'll wait with the children out here."

"It's too hot to stand out there," says the woman. "The tree keeps this place lovely and cool—please, come in."

Lauren looks at the pristine hallway, with its pale blue carpet and ornate dado rail, and fast forwards in her head to what it might look like in ten minutes' time, once her little horrors have inflicted their worst, with their sticky fingers and dusty shoes. "This is really very kind of you," she says, as if it will offset the apology she'll have to make on the way out.

"You don't look like reporters," says the woman.

"Reporters?" exclaims Lauren. "Why would we be reporters?"

"They come by here from time to time, every few years, trying to dig it all up again."

The woman was right, the house was lovely and cool, but now there's a ferocious heat coursing through Lauren. *Dig all* what *up again?*

"I'm Jess, and this is Lauren, my . . ." There's a split-second pause that only Lauren would notice. "Sister," she goes on, before smiling to herself.

"I'm Carol," says the woman. "Would you like a cup of tea?"

Lauren wants to say no, but Jess has already said, "That would be lovely, thank you."

They follow Carol down the long hallway, into the kitchen at the very back of the house. Lauren imagines that when the blue and orange cupboards were put in, they were the height of fashion, but although it still looks shiny and new, she can't see this particular trend coming around again anytime soon.

"So, the Woods family?" asks Jess.

"Oh, it was a terrible business," says Carol as she fills a cream kettle with a woodland scene depicted on the side. "They were a young couple, Frank and Julia were their names, and they lived next door but one."

"With a baby?" asks Jess.

Carol nods. "I didn't know them to speak to—I tend to keep myself to myself, even more so since I lost my Roy a few years back."

Lauren smiles sympathetically, but wishes she'd get to the point.

"So, anyways, they'd have these almighty rows—that we could hear from here—and every few weeks the police would show up, have a word with him, and things would quieten down for a bit. We'd not heard a peep out of them for a good few months before it happened."

Jess looks to Lauren. "Before what happened?" she asks impatiently.

Carol folds a cloth around the handle of the kettle and carefully pours the hot water into a floral teapot. Lauren can't help but smile as she puts what looks like a hand-knitted cozy over the top. The last time she'd seen anything like that was at her grandmother's house when she was a little girl. Carol goes into the cupboard and brings out an unopened biscuit selection box, tearing at the cellophane around it.

"Who would like a chocolate biccy?" she says to the children, who are just beginning to reach their boredom threshold. Noah's arm shoots up, while Emmy just waddles toward Carol with outstretched hands.

"Oh, please don't open those on our account," says Lauren, her relief at their attention being captured at odds with knowing the mess chocolate fingers can create.

"Don't be silly," says Carol. "This is exactly what they're for. They'll only sit in the cupboard for another year."

Lauren smiles, wondering when Carol last had a

visitor. The very least she can do is accept her courtesy with grace.

"So, about what happened," says Jess, pulling Carol back to the matter in hand.

"Ah yes," says Carol. "So one Thursday night, I think it was, there was this almighty commotion. We could hear shouting and screaming, and I said to Roy that we should call the police, but he told me not to get involved. Anyways, the very next morning, the place gets sealed off and poor Julia . . ."

Lauren looks at her wide-eyed, silently pleading with her not to say what she thinks she's about to say.

"She was . . . she was dead?" croaks Jess.

Carol nods. "And *he* did a runner, never to be seen again."

Lauren's heart sinks.

"So, he got away with it?" asks Jess. "But what about their baby? What happened to it? Did he take it with him?"

Carol shrugs her shoulders. "I don't know about the baby. There were all sorts of stories at the time, but I don't know that any of them were true."

Lauren can see all the connotations flickering behind Jess's eyes as her brain tries to process how *she* might fit into all of this.

They drink their teas quickly, making distracted small talk with the lonely old lady, before stepping back out into the heat of the afternoon.

"Well, that was a shock," whispers Lauren, as they put the children back in the buggy on the garden path. "I think we might have bitten off more than we can chew there."

"But what if there's something in it?" says Jess, making Lauren's head bang more than it is already. "What if that baby was me?"

"But you weren't *their* child," says Lauren, holding the gate open for Jess and the buggy. "We know that already, because you're genetically my half sister."

Jess nods, deep in thought. "But what if I'm *Julia's* child? What if I'm the result of an affair she had with your dad? What if *she's* who you saw your dad with?"

Lauren blanches, because despite *thinking* she knows what she saw, the reality of hearing it out loud still hurts.

"What if her husband found out?" Jess goes on. "What if he found out I wasn't his and killed her?"

"That's a lot of what ifs," says Lauren. "And besides, the only reason we're drawn to here is the vague memory that I *might* have seen him with a woman over twenty years ago."

"But it *might* have been Julia and me that you saw him with," insists Jess.

"It wouldn't make sense for you to be this woman's child," says Lauren, trying to stay patient. "If you were, you'd have disappeared with her husband when he went on the run."

"He wouldn't have taken me, if he knew I wasn't his," says Jess, playing devil's advocate.

"If that was the case, then the baby would probably have been placed with a family member. Maybe she had a sister that would have taken the baby in."

"Or, maybe the baby was put into foster care."

Lauren sighs. "Don't you think I would have known if my family were involved in this in any way? Don't you think my father would have moved heaven and earth to keep you with him once he found out what had happened to your mother?'"

"Maybe *he* killed her," says Jess, as casually as if she'd said, *Do you want a sugar in that?*

Lauren can't help but laugh, yet inside a bolt shoots across her chest, sending shockwaves up her neck and into her head. "You can't be serious."

Jess fixes her with an intense gaze. "Why not?"

"My father was a lot of things, but he wasn't a murderer."

"How would you *know*? How would *any* of us know what someone is capable of, until they find themselves in that unenviable position? People can make snap judgments. Maybe your dad just snapped."

"It was a mistake coming here," says Lauren. "I thought it would help you find closure, but it seems it's only served to open up new wounds." She takes Jess's hands in hers. "This is *not* your story. You were adopted by a loving couple who loved you as if you were their own. Why don't you focus on them, remember what they were to you, because you're never going to find what you're looking for here."

Jess nods her head solemnly and looks to the floor.

"They were everything I could have wished for and more."

"Exactly," says Lauren. "Don't ever lose sight of that."

"Until they told me I was adopted."

The hairs on Lauren's arms prickle as she imagines how hard that must have been, for both Jess *and* her parents.

"How old were you when you found out?" asks Lauren softly, wondering if there's ever a "good" age to be given that kind of information.

"I'd just turned eighteen."

It hits Lauren for the first time how it must feel to live a whole life before being told that everything you thought was true wasn't. It occurs to her then that the same could be said for Kate, who has had over thirty years of her life shattered, her love and respect for her father smashed into a million pieces. No wonder she doesn't want to believe it.

"How did they break it to you?" asks Lauren, hoping that it was gently.

Jess looks off into the distance. "They sat me down, just before I went off to university," she says. "They said that I'd always been their special girl and that no matter what they were about to tell me, nothing would ever change." A tear rolls down her cheek.

Lauren's heart feels as if it might break.

"They told me how proud they were of the woman I'd become and that seeing me go off to university was a dream come true. But that there was something that I needed to know."

"Why did they decide to tell you then?"

Jess shrugs her shoulders. "I guess they were worried that I'd somehow find out another way. I was going out into the big wide world for the first time."

"And how did you feel?" asks Lauren.

"Broken," says Jess. "I can't explain how it feels to discover that your parents aren't who you thought they were. You're probably feeling that in some small way now, having spent all these years thinking Harry was perfect, immortal even, only to find he was anything but—quite literally."

Lauren smiles wryly. "I never thought my father was perfect."

"What happened between you?" says Jess, tilting her head to one side. "I don't mean to talk out of turn, but I can sense an animosity there."

"We had our issues and our differences," says Lauren. "They were deeply rooted and were difficult to see past, but we tried to, especially in the last few years."

"And Kate?" asks Jess. "Did she have the same relationship?"

"Oh God, no!" exclaims Lauren. "They were as thick as thieves—always were."

"That must have been difficult," says Jess.

"For me, yes. I felt I was his testing ground, the one he got to practice his parenting on, and she was the one who benefitted from the mistakes he made."

Lauren wipes the tears that unexpectedly spring from her eyes.

"Hence why Kate's not as open to the idea of him having had an illegitimate child," says Jess.

"Exactly," says Lauren, sniffing. "But she's going to have to get used to it, because you're unequivocal proof that he did."

Jess's phone rings and she pulls it out of her bag. "Excuse me," she says, taking a couple of steps away before answering it.

"Hi," she says. There's a pause as she listens to the caller at the other end. "Do you even need to ask?" she says. "You know I'd love to."

As she turns around, Lauren can see her eyes sparkling and wonders who she's talking to.

"Okay," she goes on. "I'll meet you there."

"You look happy," says Lauren when she ends the call. "Good news?"

Jess nods enthusiastically.

Lauren smiles. "It's none of my business, but is there a guy on the scene?"

"There's someone at work," says Jess, coyly. "I don't know what's going to come of it but . . ."

"You really like him," says Lauren, finishing the sentence for her.

Jess nods. "Yes, but it's complicated. He's my boss so there's a lot that can go wrong."

"As long as he looks after you and treats you right, then he gets my vote."

"He's just asked me to meet him in Birmingham."

"What, now?" exclaims Lauren.

Jess nods. "It's a work thing, but it looks like it's going to be an over-nighter."

Lauren raises her eyebrows. "Will this be the first time you've done an over-nighter together?" She puts the pertinent phrase in speech marks with her fingers.

Jess smiles. "Yes!"

Butterflies flutter in Lauren's stomach on Jess's behalf as she remembers the intensity of emotions that she once felt for Justin. *Still* feels for Justin, so it seems.

"I'm so excited for you," she can't help herself from saying.

"Oh my God, I feel sick. This isn't how it was meant to be. I'm not prepared. I haven't got my make-up bag, a change of clothes, or even a toothbrush."

"Come on, quick," says Lauren, slipping her arm through Jess's and steering her back down the hill. "There's a couple of shops right opposite the station; if we hurry we can get you a few essentials."

"I'm really sorry to leave you here like this," says Jess. "Will you be all right?"

"Of course. I'm more worried about getting you what you need."

They run around the Sainsbury's Local as if they're taking part in *Supermarket Sweep*. Lauren tosses soap, deodorant and toothpaste into Jess's basket while *she* deliberates over what hair product will give her naturally straight hair a "voluminous lift."

"Yes or no," asks Lauren, holding up a packet of condoms.

"Oh my God," says Jess, her cheeks coloring. "I can't believe you're asking."

"I'll take that as a yes," says Lauren, throwing them in before Jess has a chance to change her mind. "Better to be safe than sorry."

Lauren feels like she's stuck in some weird cosmos where two worlds collide. She wants to keep Jess out of harm's way, like any mother would, but like a best friend, she also wants her to have a good time. *Isn't that in-between state called being a sister?* she wonders, the irony not lost on her.

"You're as prepared as you're ever going to be," says Lauren, smiling as she hands over the carrier bag laden with toiletries for every eventuality.

"Thanks a million," says Jess, pulling Lauren in for a hug. "I owe you one."

"Enjoy yourself," says Lauren.

"I will," says Jess excitedly and Lauren can't help but feel envious of the unencumbered life that allows Jess the freedom to do as she pleases.

I want to be you, she says after her.

But sometimes you need to be careful what you wish for.

26

KATE

Elm House is an imposing red-brick Victorian building, standing alone in the midst of a sprawling council estate. The cab driver joked to Kate on the two-mile journey inland that she should get out of there before it got dark, because no cabbie would be brave enough to come in and get her. As children circle her on bikes as she makes her way up the path to the house, she wonders that it might not have been a joke after all.

The stench of the overflowing bins makes her retch and she holds her breath until she's in the porch, where an ugly board of mismatched bells offers her nothing but the numbers of the flats. It's difficult to even know where to start. After all, what is she looking for? Who is she hoping to find if it isn't Jess? Or rather, Harriet.

In what feels like her previous life as a door-stepper, when she'd knocked on as many doors as it took to get the information she needed, she rings the top three bells, hoping that at least one of the residents will be willing to let her in and talk to her. The door buzzes and she pushes it open, stepping into the hallway.

"Who is it?" calls out a male voice from above her.

Kate positions herself at the base of the grand staircase that turns its way up three or four floors.

"Hello?"

"Who is it?" asks the same voice.

Kate can't see anyone, but presses on, refusing to be unnerved. "My name's Kate and I wondered if I could have a quick word?"

"What about? You the authorities?"

"Er no, I've just got a few questions about someone who used to live here."

"Fuck off," says the voice, before a door is slammed.

Undeterred, Kate steps back outside and presses the next three bells on the board. She'd noticed that there were a few windows open on the lower floors of the house, so *someone* must be in. She can't help but think their judgment is highly questionable if they're not.

The door buzzes again and Kate moves to the bottom of the stairs, waiting for someone to reveal themselves. A girl, barely out of her teens, peers over the banisters.

"Can I help you?" she asks hesitantly.

"Ah yes, hello," says Kate in her friendliest voice. "I'm looking for someone who used to live here and I just wondered if I might be able to ask you a couple of questions."

The girl pulls on the cuffs of her cardigan, making Kate feel even hotter than she already does. It must be thirty degrees in here.

"I don't know that many people," she says.

"Might you know a Harriet?" asks Kate hopefully.

Kate notices that the girl's expression changes fleetingly before she pulls it back.

"Who are you?" she asks.

"A friend," says Kate.

The girl nods. "Come up then."

It takes all of Kate's resolve not to balk as the fetid smell of overcooked vegetables mixed with the pungent odor of weed permeates her nostrils.

"My name's Kate," she says, holding out her hand when she reaches the top of the stairs.

"Finn," says the girl. "Come in—you'll have to excuse the mess."

There are wet clothes hanging off every surface in the room. It isn't until Finn hastily pulls a curtain partition across that Kate fleetingly notices the corner of a cot disappearing behind the makeshift screen. She can't imagine how you'd bring a baby up in these conditions.

"So is Harry okay?" asks the girl, as she moves a drying bedsheet from the only chair, nodding to Kate to sit down.

"Harry?" repeats Kate, momentarily stumped as to how this girl knows her father.

"Yeah, Harriet," says the girl.

Kate's stomach lurches as she acknowledges the similarities between her dad's name and that of the girl who's claiming to be his daughter. Had he given his illegitimate child his first name, knowing he could never give her his last?

What if he *did* have an affair which resulted in his mistress having a child? What if Jess really *is* his daughter?

No, Harriet or Jess, or whoever the hell she is, is not my father's daughter, Kate says to herself. *So why, then, is she trying so hard to pretend to be?*

"I hope Harriet's okay," she says to Finn. "I'm just trying to find her."

The girl seems to be sizing Kate up, as if working out whether to believe what she's saying.

"We met when we were both working at the university," Kate goes on. "She told me that she lived here, but I haven't heard from her since she left for London. I just wanted to make sure she was all right."

"I haven't heard from her in a while either," says Finn.

"But you've heard from her since she left here?"

"I've only heard through mutual friends—I don't have a phone," Finn says, shrugging her shoulders. "I can't afford one."

"But she's well, and chasing that dream of hers?"

"I guess so," says Finn, looking around the desolate place. "Though I imagine after living here, anything's a dream."

"And the baby?" asks Kate, nodding in the direction of the curtain partition. "Is that yours?"

Finn looks at her wide-eyed and nods. "You won't tell the authorities though, will you? They don't know that I'm living here."

Kate tilts her head, the journalist in her ever ready to pounce. "How do you mean?" she asks.

"Once I had the baby and turned eighteen, I had to leave foster care. Harry let me move in here with her, so that she could keep an eye on me."

"In *this* room?" exclaims Kate. "The three of you were living in this one room?" She looks around; the double bed, oven, fridge, sink and chair she's sitting on take up all the available floor space.

"The curtain helps," says Finn, as if it's a luxury item. "This place is a palace compared to our last foster home."

"So you'd been in foster care a while?" asks Kate.

Finn nods sadly. "Most of my life. I was adopted when I was two—that's when I met Harriet—when I went to live with the Oakleys. They adopted her at the same time. She's four years older than me, so became the big sister I never had."

"So neither of you knew your birth parents?" asks Kate, hoping that by making it sound more generic, Finn won't find it an odd question.

"No, we were both given up at birth," says Finn, and Kate gasps inwardly, relieved to know that if her dad *is* Jess's father, he hadn't been leading a double life. She hates herself for doubting him.

"We went into the foster system pretty quickly and thought all our prayers had been answered when the Oakleys took us in, but it wasn't to be."

"Why?" asks Kate. "What happened?"

"Our dad, Bill, got really sick about a year later. He had terminal lung cancer and when he died, his wife Patricia had a mental breakdown."

"I'm really sorry to hear that," says Kate. "That must have been terrible."

Finn nods. "It would have been if I didn't have Harry, but from that moment on she wouldn't let me out of her sight. We stayed in foster care together until she was eighteen and came here."

"What is this place?" asks Kate. "Some kind of halfway house?"

"Yeah, it's supposed to ease us into independent living, but once you come here, you very rarely leave."

"Unless you're Harriet," says Kate.

Finn smiles. "Unless you're Harriet," she says, before her face suddenly clouds over with worry. "But they don't know that she's gone. You won't tell them, will you? They'll throw me out if they know she's not living here, and she'll get into trouble."

Kate feels genuinely sorry for her, but her sympathy doesn't run to Jess. Why should it? When she's turned up out of the blue, wreaking havoc on her life. Everything she's said has been a lie and everything she's doing seems specifically targeted to inflict as much grief and pain as she possibly can.

"So, what dream is she chasing in London?" Kate asks casually.

"Oh, she's got big plans," says Finn, with a smile that creases her eyes. "She's got a great job, a new boyfriend . . . As you probably know, Harriet goes for what she wants . . ."

Kate smiles tightly.

"And usually gets it," says Finn, laughing.

Kate shivers involuntarily at the realization that it's *her* family that she's looking to get it from. Whatever "it" is.

27

LAUREN

Lauren's in the shower, with shampoo in her eyes, when she hears the ping of a text on her phone. She grabs at the towel hanging over the glass screen in an attempt to clear her vision, but the soap is still smarting as she blindly reaches out of the cubicle to where she'd left her phone balancing on the basin. She can't find it and risks a peek to give her some perspective. It's not there.

"Who's Sheila?" asks Simon.

She ducks her head back under the water, buying time. *Shit!*

"What's that?" she calls out, as nonchalantly as she can manage, even though her insides feel like they've been set alight.

"Sheila's asking about tomorrow night," says Simon, the tone of his voice loaded with cynicism.

Lauren turns the thermostat to cold in the hope that it's going to shock her brain into working. "One sec," she says, as she rinses the final traces of shampoo out.

The extra time that she thought she had is cut short

when Simon turns the shower off and hands her a towel.

"Let's have a look," she says, holding out her hand, the water still dripping from her hair.

Simon places her phone purposefully into her palm, its content weighing more than the device itself. He stands there, unmoving, watching her.

"Oh," she says, seeing the two-word message of *Tomorrow night?* "That's Sheila from work."

"From the hospital?" asks Simon.

She needs to think fast, but she feels wrong-footed, and vulnerable with no clothes on.

"Yeah, one of the girls was asking if any of us were about to cover her shift."

"But you're on maternity leave," says Simon gruffly.

"I know, it was just a round robin, and I guess I must still be on the list. Sheila's obviously checking that it's tomorrow they were talking about."

"I've not heard you mention a Sheila before," says Simon, eyes narrowed.

"She came just as I was going on maternity leave," says Lauren, covering her face with a towel as she dries her hair. It's easier to lie when he can't see her eyes.

"Did she come to your leaving drinks?"

Lauren does a quick mental scan of all the midwives sat around the table at the pub. They're all women Simon would know, and the two he didn't, he made a point of talking to when he came to pick her up, an hour early.

"I don't think so," she says warily.

"Well maybe you need to let whoever needs to know that you're not looking for any extra shifts. I'll do it." He starts to thumb instructions on the screen and Lauren makes a grab for it.

"Woah," says Simon, pulling it away and holding it up in the air, out of her reach. "What are *you* so tetchy about?"

She's not, because she *knows* she's deleted every single message that "Sheila" has ever sent, and all of her replies. But there's still that niggle, no matter how tiny, that she hasn't, and the thought of Simon seeing it sends her off-kilter. She gets hotter and hotter as she runs through their most recent communication in her head:

> *Sheila: I need to see you*
> *Lauren: I may be able to do Thursday night*
> *Sheila: Seriously?*
> *Lauren: Maybe. I'm not sure yet*
> *Sheila: I can't stop thinking about you*
> *Lauren: I'll let you know*
> *Sheila: Don't make me wait too long*

No matter how she comes at it, whichever way she plays it out in her head, there's no way that she could ever make it sound like an innocent conversation between two colleagues. She knows that it's not on there, but the thought of it keeps her reaching up for her phone.

"Give it to me," she says, making a grab for it.

"Me thinks she doth protest too much," says Simon, lowering it to read while holding Lauren firmly at arm's length. "What's on here that you're so worried about?"

"Nothing," she says, as she stops fighting for it, knowing that it's only piquing his interest. "It's my phone, my property."

"Well, actually I'm currently paying for it, so that's not strictly true."

God, how she hates having to be indebted to him. The sooner she gets back to work, the better.

"So is there anything on here that shouldn't be?" He waggles the phone within her reach but she forces herself not to react.

"No," she says, wrapping a towel around her and walking out onto the landing. She snags her toe on an exposed floorboard, and yelps, knowing it'll be another splinter. All Simon needs to do is lay the carpet that's been rolled up and standing in the corner for the past six months. But now is not the time to ask again. Maybe she'll go and buy a remnant tomorrow, just to tide them over.

"So you won't mind me looking then?" he says.

Her ears are burning. "Not at all."

He follows her, humming as he thumbs through her contacts and messages, her hatred for him growing with every second. The phone pings, a sign of a text coming in, and her bladder feels like it might give way. He raises his eyebrows as he reads it. "Interesting," he says.

Every fiber in her body is on high alert, as she imagines what it might say. Has Justin chosen this time to declare his undying love for her? Or has he been unusually intimate, writing in fine detail what he'd like to do to her? Lauren shudders at the thought, more out of fear than desire.

Simon's eyes are boring into her, but she will not give him the satisfaction of knowing how intimidated she feels. She will *not* ask who the text is from or what it says.

"Arrived safely in Birmingham," relays Simon. *"Thanks for today. Hope you got home okay."*

Lauren feels like she might cry with relief, but any respite is short-lived as her mind jumps to the very next problem of having to explain where she's been all day.

"Got home okay?" questions Simon. "Where have you been?"

Lauren had hoped to avoid this conversation, not least because she didn't want to have to explain herself or justify her actions. Though she'd allowed for the possibility that Noah would tell his dad about the trains he'd been on, as he'd spent most of the journey pretending to be the Fat Controller from *Thomas the Tank Engine.*

"Jess and I took the kids out for the day," she says.

"Where to?" asks Simon.

"Harrogate—to show her where I grew up." She bends the truth because it's easier. Because it means fewer questions, and that makes her life less stressful. "You know how Noah is with trains," she goes on with a forced smile. "He loved it."

Simon shrugs his shoulders and begrudgingly hands her phone back. "You do realize that if you're doing anything you shouldn't, I'll find out about it."

The threat weighs heavy on Lauren's shoulders. If whatever this is between her and Justin carries on, she's going to need a different plan going forward.

There is no going forward, she argues with herself. *This needs to stop. Now!*

But within seconds she's conspiring with herself—if Simon's out working tomorrow night, she *could* see Justin, even if it's just to say goodbye. It's not until her fantasy world collides with reality a few minutes later that she realizes that without a babysitter she's not going anywhere.

"I'll see you later," calls out Simon as he goes down the stairs. She hadn't even realized he was going out.

"Bye then," she whispers as the front door slams so hard it makes the whole house shudder.

She quickly scoops her hair up into a topknot and pulls on a T-shirt and leggings, desperate to get back to her phone.

Maybe, she texts "Sheila."

Where? comes back the speedy response.

She doesn't want to do what they did last time: hiding in dark corners, worrying about somebody seeing them.

Your place? she offers, before deleting it and tapping on the screen, deep in thought. What is she thinking? How can she even contemplate meeting Justin again? And at his place? That's asking for trouble. And anyway, she has no one to call on to have the children.

Yet, despite *all* of this, there's still a bubbling in her tummy that's telling her she will move heaven and earth to see him just one last time. She scrolls absently through her contacts, knowing that there are few people, if any, who she'd entrust with her children. It seems a pointless exercise, but then she sees it, and the answer suddenly dawns on her.

She types a message out, her thumb hovering perilously close to the "Send" button. No one is more surprised to hear that whoosh sound of it being sent than her.

"Come on, come on," she says, like a woman possessed, to the inanimate object in her hand. "Say something."

I'd love that! comes Jess's reply. *What time?*

Oh God. Does 8 p.m. suit? types Lauren before she has a chance to change her mind.

Perfect! See you then x

She lets out the breath she was holding in as she stares, transfixed by the text that is slowly appearing, as if by magic, across her phone screen. *Y-O-U-R* is being spelled out, but it doesn't feel like she's typing it. It's as if she's outside of herself, looking in.

P-L- Every letter she types makes her feel as if she's falling deeper into a hole, pulling her into a vortex she doesn't want to be pulled out of. She's still got time to change her mind, if she really wants to, but she knows she's not going to. *A-C-E* she adds, before sending it and covering her eyes with her hands.

She watches the three dots running across the page, knowing that Justin's typing his reply, desperate to know what he's going to say. The three dots disappear and she chastises herself. She's been too forward. He's going to think she does this kind of thing all the time. He won't want to know her now.

Looking forward to it flashes up his reply, and her stomach somersaults.

28

KATE

On the train back to London, Kate is buzzing. She feels more in control now that she has the proof that Jess isn't who she says she is. She has to remind herself to keep referring to her as Jess, because calling her Harriet will only serve to prove that she knows more than she should. Though it's how she's going to use that information that needs the most thought. Kate looks out the window as the open plains of the New Forest are left behind, replaced by the juxtaposition of an industrial park as the train moves across the River Test toward Southampton.

Her phone vibrates in her lap and, seeing that it's Matt, she picks up, momentarily forgetting where she is. As soon as she hears him say, "Hey, where are you?" her heart sinks.

"I've been trying to get hold of you," he continues, as she quickly looks at her watch, as if it will offer a justifiable excuse for where she's been. "I called the office, but they said you hadn't made it in. Are you okay? How are you feeling?"

The sound of the train speeding along the tracks is

unmistakable, yet still she wonders if she can get away without telling him where she is.

"Better," she says, answering one question that he's asked. "I did a bit of work this morning and went out for a walk at lunchtime. I actually feel better this afternoon than I have in a while." It's not an out-and-out lie. All of that has happened at *some* point today.

"Great," he says, sounding enthused. "So where are you now? At home?"

"I'm just on my way back now," she says, skirting the issue. "How's your day been?"

"Mad busy," he says. "And far from finished unfortunately. The PM's press conference isn't until this evening, and he's agreed to give me a one-to-one straight afterward."

"On the phone?" asks Kate.

"In person," says Matt.

Kate groans.

"Yeah, tell me about it," sighs Matt. "So I'm on a train to Birmingham after work."

"Okay," says Kate, nonplussed. She's used to dropping everything herself at a moment's notice—it comes with the territory.

"I'll keep you posted," says Matt. "Oh, and by the way, keep your eyes peeled for our center spread the day after tomorrow."

"Oh yeah," says Kate. "Why's that?"

"Didn't I tell you that the new girl had a good nose for a story?"

Kate's lungs feel like they're being squeezed. "Oh yeah?"

"She's sniffed out something that might be of interest to you."

"Meaning?" Kate presses.

"She's tracked down someone who's used those ge-nealogy websites to find their long-lost relatives."

Kate shudders involuntarily, her blood feeling like it's freezing over. "Wh-who's she found?"

"A woman who's been reunited with her sister by uploading her DNA—just like Lauren and that girl."

Kate's jaw spasms and there's a banging in her head as she imagines Jess's and Lauren's faces peering out at the five million people that read the *Echo*. Would they really be that stupid? Kate can't take the chance.

"My girl promises it's a corker," Matt goes on.

My girl? If Kate were in a forgiving mood, she'd acknowledge that it was a phrase he's used before, but right now it just leaves a sour taste in her mouth.

The noise in her head is getting louder, like a beat-ing drum that's getting closer and closer. She can see this spiraling out of control.

"You can't run it," she says.

"What? Why not?"

"Because . . . because we're running a similar story tomorrow."

"Oh shit!" groans Matt. "Are you kidding me?"

She hates lying to Matt, as they've always managed to give and take where work's concerned, both of them careful not to tread on the other's toes. But this is dif-ferent. This is personal.

"Yeah, sorry," she says. "I offered it up in confer-ence and the news team went with it. Their story's much stronger than *your girl's*, I'm afraid."

"What have you got?" he sighs, not picking up on Kate's sarcasm.

"Erm, I really can't say."

"Seriously?"

She needs to think quickly. "We've got a relative of someone who's been charged with an offense in the US," she says, biting down on her lip, hating herself. "A mother who the police were able to trace the criminal's DNA back to."

Matt lets out a long breath. "Is she even allowed to talk?"

"Seemingly so," says Kate, praying that he'll take the bait.

"And you're definitely running it tomorrow?"

"Yep, 'fraid so."

"Okay, I'll give you until then, but if it doesn't go to press, I'm printing mine the day after."

"Cool," she says, grateful for the extra twenty-four hours she's got to stop that from happening.

"You're a royal pain in my arse, d'you know that?"

Kate forces a laugh. "You wouldn't want me any other way."

By the time Kate gets off at Waterloo, she's caught up in the after-work throng that's spilling into the station. If she didn't have to get somewhere else urgently, she'd go for a walk along the South Bank, the need to not waste such a lovely evening at the forefront of her mind. She'd no doubt stop off to listen to one of the many buskers, each hoping to be the next Ed Sheeran. Kate always bought the home-burned CDs that were sold out of the musicians' empty instrument cases, mostly because she wants to support hard-working talent, but there's a little part of her that likes to think that maybe, one day, she'll own a rare recording of a global superstar.

She smiles at the thought, but then reality steps

in, and drags her kicking and screaming to the here and now.

She needs to stop that story from running, knowing that if it does, it will destroy her family once and for all.

29

LAUREN

Lauren's just put Jude to bed when the doorbell goes, and she knows that at gone 10 p.m., the only person she's going to answer the door to is Simon, who she assumes has forgotten his key. She does a cursory look out of the front bedroom window and is dismayed to see Kate standing on the pavement below. After the day she's had, she doesn't need this right now.

"Hello," she says wearily, as she opens the door.

"I need to talk to you," says Kate, stepping straight into the hallway.

Lauren probably has things she should tell *her*, but she's tired.

"Can we do this tomorrow?" she says, looking at the time on her phone to emphasize the point.

"There's something you need to know about Jess," blurts out Kate, seemingly unable to hold it in.

Lauren can't help but roll her eyes. "Seriously, Kate, can't you give it a rest?"

"I've been checking her out," says Kate, almost triumphantly. "And she's not who she says she is."

"I don't think even *she* knows who she is," says Lauren.

"No, you don't understand," Kate goes on. "She's lying to you, me, everyone. Jess Linley isn't even her real name. She's nothing but a fraud."

The words slice through Lauren as if cutting the very strings that are holding her up. She doesn't want to believe it. She *refuses* to believe it.

"I assume you've used your usual unethical methods to find this out?" asks Lauren, hoping to expose a weak link in the information that Kate thinks she's garnered.

"Does it matter?" asks Kate. "All you need to know is that Jess is up to something and you shouldn't trust her as far as you can throw her. She's playing us."

"What is *wrong* with you?"

"Me?" exclaims Kate. "You're the one who wants to believe everything she's telling you."

"Is this the person you've become?" says Lauren. "Forever the cynic, not wanting to believe anything anyone tells you." She laughs falsely. "D'you know what? I used to think your job made you better than me. That working among people deemed to be important made *you* more important by default. But I'm glad I'm me, because all your job has done is make you a mistrusting egotist who doesn't want to see the good in anyone."

"I'm a journalist," says Kate scathingly. "I seek out the truth, and if you're threatened by that, then that's your problem."

"Well whatever you *think* you've uncovered, I'm sure there's a very good reason for it."

"Oh yeah." Kate laughs bitterly. "She's got plenty good enough reasons. The first being that she's obtained a job under false pretenses."

Lauren feels a pang in her chest, not only at the revelation, but also because she'd not got around to finding out what exactly Jess did for work. All she knows is that she's doing a job she loves in Canary Wharf. It shames her that Kate appears to know more than she does. "Why would she need to do that?"

"You tell me," says Kate. "But she claims she's graduated from university."

"That's right," nods Lauren.

"Except she didn't *study* there; she *worked* there." Kate offers a cynical laugh. "In the cafeteria."

Relief floods out of Lauren. Kate has clearly got her facts wrong. "That's not Jess," she says, happy to set her straight. "She got a first-class honors degree."

"Is that what she *told* you?" asks Kate, with a wry smile.

Caught like a rabbit in headlights, Lauren doesn't know which way to turn. Her need to believe that Jess has told her the truth is far stronger than having to admit to Kate that she's been taken for a fool.

"Why is it so hard for you to take people at face value?" asks Lauren. "To accept that she's Dad's daughter?"

"Because I don't think she is," says Kate.

Lauren rolls her eyes and walks over to her laptop, perched on the end of the sofa. She hits a few buttons and turns the screen toward Kate. There's no denying that the first match under Lauren's profile page on the genealogy website is *Jessica Linley—Half sister.*

"Happy now?" asks Lauren. "What more proof do you need that Dad wasn't the man you thought he was?"

"That doesn't prove she's his daughter."

"For God's sake, Kate!" exclaims Lauren. "How many other options are there?"

"One," says Kate, locking eyes with her.

Lauren looks at her, open-mouthed. Is Kate honestly suggesting what Lauren thinks she is?

"While you're so quick to judge Dad, assuming he's the one who's been unfaithful, has it not occurred to you that Jess might be *Mum's* child?"

Lauren shakes her head disbelievingly. "You can't be serious," she says, barely audible. "Is that how desperate you've become to keep Dad's precious memory preserved? So much so that you're going to pretend it's Mum who was at fault?"

"It's a fifty-fifty chance, is all I'm saying," says Kate petulantly. "Why are you so quick to rule it out?"

"Be-because, that's preposterous!" exclaims Lauren, finding her voice. "How could she possibly have concealed a pregnancy, a birth, a child . . . ?"

"She may not have shown," says Kate, quick to answer, as if she's thought it all through. "She may have had the baby prematurely . . ."

"But even if she'd managed to keep it from us," says Lauren. "There's no way on earth Dad wouldn't have known about it."

Kate has clearly thought of that too. "Maybe, but if he knew it wasn't his . . . who knows what arrangement they may have come to?"

Lauren's eyes widen with bewilderment. "To have the baby *adopted*?" she asks incredulously. "You honestly think they would have gone to those lengths to keep an affair secret?"

"I think you'd be surprised how far Mum would go to keep this family together," says Kate.

"This is insane," says Lauren, scratching her head. "*You're* insane."

A key turns in the front door. "What are you two up to?" says Simon, coming into the room with an air of disdain about him.

"Nothing," says Lauren, far too quickly to be innocent.

"I suppose she's telling you all about her day out," he says.

Kate looks to Lauren expectantly.

"No," says Lauren, hoping that the retort will stop him from saying anything more. She doesn't need to give Kate any more reason to get on her back right now.

"Why didn't *you* go?" Simon says to Kate, despite Lauren looking at him with widened eyes. "Sounds like it would have been the perfect family day trip."

"Where did you go?" asks Kate.

"I, erm, I saw Jess today," mumbles Lauren. She tries to pretend that she doesn't see Kate's hackles rise.

"Oh," says Kate, tightly. "What for?"

God, she wished Simon hadn't got her into this. "We just went out," she says. "That's all."

"All the way to Harrogate," says Simon.

Lauren can feel Kate's eyes immediately snap onto her and that panicky feeling returns, sucking the breath out of her.

"Harrogate?"

"Mmm," is all Lauren can say.

An ominous silence hangs heavily in the air before

Simon sniggers and says, "Well, this is awkward," before falling down heavily on the sofa.

"So, do you want to tell me what you and Jess were doing in Harrogate?" asks Kate, her face flushed.

"We were, erm, just checking a few things out," says Lauren, ushering Kate into the kitchen. "She had a day off, so we thought it was a good opportunity. She's had to go into work now, by all accounts something came up, so we weren't really up there very long at all." She's well aware that she's waffling, trying to downplay what really went on.

Kate's gaze is unfaltering. "So what did the pair of you discover up there?" she asks tightly.

Lauren shrugs her shoulders, aware that now is not the time to divulge what Carol had told them. It's not as if it's relevant anyway. "Nothing much," she says.

"Perhaps if you'd invited me, I could have saved you the trouble," says Kate, scathingly. "I could have told you that Jess is not who you think she is."

Lauren grits her teeth, refusing to rise to the bait again.

"Where is she anyway?" asks Kate, turning to leave. "I'm surprised that you didn't want to bring her back to have tea with the kids, get them acquainted with their new aunty." Her tone is dripping with sarcasm.

"As I say, she was called away on business," says Lauren.

"What business is that, then?" asks Kate.

Lauren wonders what difference it makes to Kate.

"Her boss asked her to go to Birmingham with him," says Lauren.

30

KATE

Kate puts a hand out to steady herself on the wall as Lauren's words reverberate around her head.

There was a part of her that had felt relieved to see the connection between Lauren and Jess in black and white on Lauren's computer screen. She'd been comforted to know that whatever Jess was up to, Lauren wasn't a part of it; that they weren't colluding to bring Kate down. Because in her darker moments, that's what she feared was happening.

But now, at the mention of Birmingham, Lauren's sent her straight back there. If she's aware of the fuse she's just lit, she doesn't show it.

"What's she gone to Birmingham for?" croaks Kate.

"She said she needed to go for work," says Lauren, with the merest hint of a smile playing on her lips. "But I have a feeling that it was a bit of a ruse on her boss's part."

Kate feels dizzy, and an overwhelming heat begins to envelop her. "Oh yeah," she manages, hoping that it sounds nonchalant, but if Lauren knows her as well as she should, the waver is immediately obvious.

"Yeah, it sounds to me as if something's going on," she says. "She seems pretty excited . . ."

Lauren is still talking, but although Kate can see her lips moving, she can't hear anything she's saying— her ears momentarily not working, as if to protect her from the truth.

"I need to go," she says, interrupting Lauren mid-flow. "I'll speak to you later."

As soon as she's in her car, hot tears spring to her eyes and her throat constricts as she battles to hold back the deluge she knows is imminent as soon as she acknowledges the facts. The screen on her phone looks blurry as she types "Where is the PM's press conference today?" into Google, hoping that she'd somehow misheard where Matt had said he was going earlier. Might he be heading to *Brighton*, *Bolton* or *Burnley* perhaps? She knows she's grasping at straws, but she so doesn't want him to be in the same place as Jess. A tear escapes as *Birmingham* fills the search engine results page.

She doesn't even remember thinking it, so is surprised to find herself driving through the Blackwall Tunnel, the gateway between southeast London and its northeastern counterpart. It's also the most direct route to Jess's place, the address on her CV committed to Kate's memory.

When she pulls up outside the shoddy-looking parade of shops, she doesn't even notice the state of disrepair, or the hooded figures hanging around outside the Chinese takeaway. All she can see is number 193, and all she can think about is how she's going to get inside it. She rings all four bells and waits for what

feels like an inordinate amount of time before someone comes down the stairs.

"Hey," says a man with dreadlocked hair and a roll-
up between his lips. He holds out a twenty-pound note
before quickly pulling it back. "No pizza?"

Kate holds up her arms and gives him a regretful
look. "'Fraid not," she says. "Visiting Jess in Flat C."

"Oh man," he groans, before turning around and
walking back up the stairs.

"Jess, it's me," she says, for effect, as she knocks on
her flat door. She waits until she hears the one above
her closing before lifting the wheel brace from her car
boot out of her bag. Wedging the straight end between
the door frame and the flimsy lock, she applies pressure until she feels it give, then uses her shoulder to
push her way in.

Kate quickly evaluates the apartment, noticing that
all four doors leading from the hallway are closed. She
doesn't know what she's looking for, but she knows
she won't find it behind the first door, which leads her
into a windowless bathroom. The second is the living
room, and if *she* had anything to hide, she wouldn't
put it in here. Her stomach is tied up in knots, a tangle
of nerves that she usually only experiences when she's
sitting in Dr. Williams' office.

The next room, with clothes in the wardrobe and
personal effects on top of a mismatched chest of drawers, is clearly Jess's bedroom. Kate's eyes are automati-
cally drawn to the hairbrush and she takes a tissue from
her bag to fold around the loose strands, which together
with the DNA she's taken from her parents' house will
determine, once and for all, whose daughter Jess is.

She pulls the drawers open, one by one, and furtively rifles through their contents. Jumpers, tops and underwear are displaced in her efforts to find . . . what? What is it she's looking for that will give her answers to the questions resounding in her head, such as *why* Jess has targeted Matt and is clearly out to entrap him in her web of deceit? *Why* has Lauren been indoctrinated to believe that Jess is their father's child? *Why* is she, Kate, the common denominator between the two people that Jess has chosen to prey on?

The last thought takes Kate by surprise, as if she's only just made the connection. She falls down heavily onto the bed and screams, "What the hell is going on?" banging her fists onto the mattress in frustration.

She takes deep breaths, forcing herself to stay calm and think logically. What if the DNA match *has* been falsified? Kate already knows it's possible, even if Lauren is blissfully unaware of Jess's duplicitous plan. She could easily have obtained Kate's DNA if she'd wanted to, from a discarded water bottle or half-eaten sandwich. Christ, she might even have broken in and taken something from the flat. Kate shudders at the thought of Jess going through her and Matt's belongings—the irony somehow lost on her.

But even if Jess *had* used Kate's DNA as her own, it would have shown that she and Lauren were sisters, not half sisters. *Unless* . . . says Kate to herself, unable to bat away the abhorrent possibility that maybe *she's* not her father's daughter either.

"No!" she says aloud, refusing to give the thought room to breathe.

Jess *must* be their half sister, otherwise what's the

box of baby mementos all about? And why was Rose's reaction to it so extreme if she had nothing to hide? Kate's head falls into her hands as she acknowledges the only other possibility: that if Jess *isn't* her half sister, then not only are her mother and father exonerated, but the campaign that Jess has been inflicting on Kate's loved ones is aimed solely at one person. Her.

Kate feels like she might be sick as she wonders why anyone would have such an axe to grind. Were there people in her past who hated her enough to go to such lengths?

She thinks about the stories she's written and the enemies she may have made along the way, but apart from a few erstwhile PRs who'd lost their jobs for not managing to contain a juicy scoop on their client, there were few people in the entertainment world who would take umbrage to this degree. Even those she'd inadvertently got fired had eventually been lauded; the global superstar that had been pictured snorting cocaine off a naked woman's breast had enjoyed his biggest album success the following year. *All* publicity was good publicity, it seemed.

She remembers the undercover sting she did on a group of far-right activists some years back, before she decided that showbusiness was a safer option. But aside from the initial death threat and a talking to by the police, she'd never heard anything more. She feels strangely comforted that the queue to witness her downfall is surprisingly short.

As she gets up from the bed, conspiracy theories abound, bogging Kate down with the what ifs, making her brain feel as if it's banging against the inside of her skull in her efforts to work it all out. Hot tears of hurt and frustration run down her cheeks as she realizes how futile this all is.

She picks her handbag up from the hall floor, having resigned herself to at least telling Matt who his junior reporter really is. Once he knows that she's lied about her past, he won't hesitate to fire her, and that will leave Kate with one less problem to worry about.

As she walks down the hall, she absently turns the door handle to the only room she hasn't yet been in. When she finds it locked tight, her interest is piqued. Adrenaline courses through her veins as she imagines what might lie beyond it. A grotesque image of her dad, gagged and bound to a chair, immediately flashes into her head—a recollection of another dream she's recently had. Getting the wheel brace back out of her bag, she jimmies open the door with a renewed sense of purpose, desperate to see what Jess is so keen to keep hidden.

She feels for the light switch and peers around, through half-closed eyes, as if waiting for something to jump out at her. But instead of the dark dungeon-like room she'd expected, it's oddly serene. A bed adorned with a pretty floral duvet cover; a scented candle stands unused on the bedside. It isn't until Kate walks into the room that she sees a cot behind the door.

With her heart hammering through her chest, she reaches in to pick up a toy bunny rabbit that's sitting in the corner. Its floppy ears fall forward and Kate absently runs its soft fur against the skin of her cheeks, her tears making its glass eyes glisten.

She still has the rabbit in her hand as she slowly opens the wardrobe doors, now more scared than ever of what she's going to find. There, stacked in neat piles, are a dozen or so sleepsuits, perfectly folded muslin squares, an unopened pack of nappies, a breast pump—in fact, everything that a woman with a baby could possibly need. There's just one problem; Jess isn't a woman with a baby.

Kate tenderly runs a hand over her stomach, desperately trying to stay calm while she works out what all this means. Why would Jess have a locked bedroom, dedicated to a baby she doesn't have?

She frantically pulls at the drawers at the bottom of the wardrobe, tipping the soft embroidered blankets out onto the floor. She yanks a bedside cabinet drawer from its runners, and a jewelry box falls to the floor, its contents upending onto the spotless carpet.

Tiny human teeth lose themselves between the weave of the wool, and Kate finds herself wondering whether there's anything to gain from taking one with her to check its DNA. *That's* the way her mind now thinks—*that*'s what Jess has done to her.

It's then she notices the little hospital tag, lying face down among the spilled contents of the box. Her hands are trembling as she picks it up. Feeling as if she's handling a newborn baby, she slowly turns it over and takes a deep breath. And there, written in faded blue ink, are the numbers that are already indelibly etched on her mind.

15/09/96

The date goes around and around in Kate's head. She can hear it so clearly, as if each number is blaring out in stereo, shutting out the sound of the passing traffic and the heavy footsteps from the flat above.

The sudden heat is oppressive, holding her down, making her feel as if she can't breathe. *I need to get out of here*, she says to herself as she gets up and stumbles toward the front door. She's sure that she can feel a pain shoot across her stomach and she cradles it as she makes her way down the stairs.

Disoriented, she steps out onto the pavement, unable to remember how she got here, let alone where she parked the car. The young men, with their hoods up, eye her up and down as she falters, unsure of which way to go. She feels faint and needs to stop and take a breath, but her surroundings are unforgiving and bear no resemblance to how they looked on her way in. She walks a few meters before diving into an alleyway, the coolness of the shadows wrapping themselves around her, making her shiver.

She crouches down on bent knees, getting down low in case she passes out. It feels like she may go any second and she lets her head fall back onto the bare brick wall.

Breathe, just breathe, she says to herself, inhaling and exhaling as deeply as she can.

"Hey lady," says a hooded figure standing over her.

Fear seeps into her veins as she looks up at the face, concealed by a bandana.

The figure bears down on her and she flinches, waiting for whatever's going to happen. A strong hand reaches under her arm, lifting her up onto her feet.

"Bro," calls out the young man.

"Please," says Kate. "I just . . ."

"Where you going, lady?"

"I . . . I just need to get to my car."

"Bro, hurry up," he calls up the alley again. "This lady needs some water."

The boy supports her as she gingerly puts one foot in front of the other, telling her to take her time. Just before she reaches her car, another similarly dressed boy appears with a small bottle of water.

"You sure you're going to be all right?" he says as Kate gets in.

She nods and smiles gratefully, feeling both relieved and guilty that she'd jumped to the wrong conclusion.

Though what she *hadn't* been wrong about was that the hospital tag in the box she salvaged all those years ago *was* Jess's. Usually, she'd feel a sense of satisfaction when proved right—after all, this is the proof she's been waiting for, *wanting* even. Because this means that the box she'd held on to *was* worthy of the credence she'd given it, and not the disrespect Rose had showed it. As soon as she catches her breath, she thumbs through the contacts on her phone and connects the call to the loud-speaker in her car.

"DS Labs," answers the woman at the other end of the line.

"Hi, Nancy?"

"Yes."

"It's Kate from the *Gazette*. How's things?"

"Oh hi, Kate. Good. You?"

"Not bad. Listen, I've got a personal favor to ask." She explains what she needs. "I need this super fast," says Kate.

"It'll be a couple of days at least," says Nancy.

"If you can do it any quicker than that, I'd really

appreciate it. I'll make sure to put a good word in with the editor."

"No worries, I'll see what I can do."

Getting the DNA results back won't explain what the hell Jess is playing at, but it *will* provide unequivocal proof that Harry *isn't* her dad.

31

LAUREN

A text lights up the bedroom.

Bleary-eyed, Lauren instinctively turns to see if Simon is asleep, before unplugging her phone and taking it into the bathroom.

It's just gone midnight, but she's not yet been able to sleep—her mind too busy working over the events of the day, her body too alert to what tomorrow may bring.

Are you still up? reads the text. She doesn't know whether to respond or how—not yet having processed what's happened and whether or not it changes anything between them. She doesn't suppose it should, but still there's a sense of uneasiness.

Yes, she eventually types, as she closes the lid of the toilet and sits down.

I desperately need to talk to you.

Lauren rubs at her temple. *Where are you?*

In a bar and far drunker than I should be. Can you talk?

Lauren gets up and peers around the door to where Simon is snoring. *Yes—what's going on?*

Well, I've finished work and am now doing tequila shots!

Alone?

Lauren knows there are more pertinent questions she should be asking, but now doesn't seem the right time, and there's not much point, seeing as Jess is probably three sheets to the wind.

No—with him! And he's even more gorgeous than when he's sober!

Lauren can't help but smile. *That's because you're not looking at him through sober eyes!* she types.

We're going back to the hotel now, texts Jess.

Lauren imagines herself in Jess's position: the excitement of a burgeoning relationship—the anticipation of what's to come. Simon had taken her to a romantic hotel for the night when they'd wordlessly decided to consummate their relationship. Unlike the numerous casual liaisons she'd had after Justin, when she would unhappily admit that she'd mistaken sex for love in her quest to replace him, she'd gone on four dates with Simon before they spent the night together. She wonders what had made him stand out from the rest. Was it the fact that when he looked at her, he had made her feel like she was the only woman in the world? Was it that she had felt safe, knowing he would protect her? It had been good once, so how come he can now barely bring himself to look at her at all, and he's the only person she's scared of?

Are you sure you want to do this? asks Lauren, her innate mothering instinct kicking in. Or maybe it's just her attempt at making sure Jess doesn't get sucked in the same way she had—knowing that that would be the first mistake if she did.

Do *you* think I should do this? asks Jess.

What an impossible question to answer.

You have to be sure it's what you want.

More than anything I've wanted for a long time, says Jess.

Well, then do it, but please be careful.

You won't think any less of me?

Lauren can't believe she'd even ask. *Of course not!*

OK, types Jess with a sideways laughing emoji.

Night, types Lauren, before adding *Have fun!* But something doesn't sit quite right. It feels as if she's encouraging her own daughter to go and get laid. She deletes the last two words and says *Speak to you tomorrow* instead. Because they *do* need to speak, one way or another, about what Kate had told her.

It doesn't surprise her that Jess might have changed her name—she could have done so for myriad reasons, but she has never lied about it because it had never occurred to Lauren to ask. Why would she? Jess was well within her rights to do whatever she wanted. Lauren can't pretend to understand how it must feel to live eighteen years as one person, only to find out you're someone completely different. The ancestry, history and bloodline that Jess thought had bound her to those around her had been severed in the most brutal fashion.

Lauren wonders, not for the first time, why Jess's adoptive parents chose to tell her when they did. Perhaps one of them *knew* they were ill and thought it best, and fairer, to tell Jess the truth while they were both still able—together. Or maybe they felt they *had* to tell her, before somebody else did. Either way, it must have been the most impossible decision to make, knowing that such a secret hung over your family's head, waiting for it to be exposed, either accidentally or on purpose. Or as Kate's cynical mind would probably deduce, accidentally-on-purpose.

She wishes Kate could just be her sister for once, instead of forever being in reporter mode—constantly chasing the story that she thinks everyone is hiding. Maybe she should have put her investigative skills to the test when their father was alive, because quite clearly there's a truth there that she missed.

But no matter what Kate *thinks* she's found out, Lauren is sure of one thing; Jess *did* go to university. That's what she'd told her and she had no reason to lie.

"What are you doing?" asks Simon, walking into the bathroom. The illuminated screen on Lauren's phone casts a white light that is impossible to disguise.

"I was just . . . just . . ." she stutters, hunched over on the lid of the toilet seat in darkness.

"Are you texting?" he asks.

Even in Lauren's head, everything about the scene makes it look clandestine, as if she's doing something she shouldn't be.

"It's nothing," she says, in a clumsy attempt to over-emphasize her innocence. She immediately chastises herself—it's the worst thing she could say. *Nothing* about what she's doing makes it look like she's doing nothing.

"Who are you talking to?"

"It's . . . it's just Jess," she says.

"What does *she* want at this time in the morning?" he barks.

"She just wanted some advice," offers Lauren, hating him for making her justify herself when she's not doing anything wrong. *But you are*, her inner voice

says, referring to Justin. She can't help but acknowledge how much worse this would be if it had been *him*
she was talking to.

Simon snatches the phone out of her hand and she
instinctively wants to snatch it back, but she forces
herself to play the tactical game. Is that what their
marriage has become? A tactical game?

She watches powerlessly as Simon thumbs over the
screen to read the messages that have gone back and
forth between her and Jess.

"You're encouraging her to *sleep* with somebody?"
he asks incredulously.

"No . . . no of course not."

"Well, that's exactly what it sounds like you're doing."

Lauren can't believe that he's going to make an argument out of this.

"Is that what *you'd* do? If *you* were in her position?"

Lauren looks at him, dumbfounded. Less than a
minute ago he was asleep and now he's looking for
a row. It's almost as if it's become his default setting,
whenever he's conscious. What is it, Lauren wonders,
that's dented his male pride to such a degree that he
so often feels he has to exert his masculinity in other
ways? Maybe it's his inability to hold down a perma-
nent job. *Maybe it's a whole host of things*, she muses.

"Please don't start."

"Don't start?" he hisses, his face close to hers. "I
wake up in the middle of the night to find my wife hiding in the bathroom, secretly texting, and you're telling me not to start."

I wasn't hiding and I'm not secretly texting.

She pulls herself up from the toilet in an effort
to feel more in control, but Simon's looming bulk,

silhouetted against the window blind, doesn't feel any less intimidating.

"Go back to bed," she says wearily.

He laughs falsely and goes to walk away, but then, as if he thinks better of it, he turns back around and grabs her arms, digging his nails into her bare skin. "Who do you think you're talking to?" he bellows.

Lauren freezes, momentarily lost for words, but the pressure of his fingers, tightly holding her, gradually seeps into her consciousness and something inside her snaps.

"Get your hands off of me," she says calmly, surprising herself with the control in her voice.

Simon laughs that manic laugh again. "Or what?"

"Does this make you feel like more of a man?" she asks.

"You need to shut up," says Simon, tightening his grip.

"Is this what you have to do now? To feel like a real man." She sounds braver than she feels.

Even in the darkness, she can see the glassiness of his eyes as he glares at her—the sliver of moonlight emphasizing his disbelief as his wife, fueled by months of animosity and isolation, dares to fight back.

"I'm warning you," says Simon. "Shut up."

He pushes her and she stumbles backward, catching her foot on the base of the toilet. She tries to right herself but it's too late—she's in freefall and it takes a second or two for her to react, throwing her hands out. She lands awkwardly, half in, half out of the bathtub, and in her effort to break her fall, she's jarred her wrist. It throbs like something out of a *Tom and Jerry* cartoon.

Lauren looks up at the shadow looming over her,

sure that, even if the lights were on, she'd still not recognize the man she's been married to for six years.

"If you *ever* touch me again," she says breathlessly, "I swear to God I'll take the kids and leave."

It feels strangely euphoric to have finally found her voice after months of fearing she'd lost it.

"You wouldn't dare," he sneers.

She lifts herself up, grimacing as she puts weight on her pulsing wrist, and reaches for the light pull.

"Try me," she says, locking eyes with him as the tiny room is illuminated. "Just try me."

32

KATE

Kate wakes up, feeling as if she's just fallen asleep. For a split second, she thinks that everything that played out last night was a dream—a horrific one, but a dream nonetheless. The creeping realization that all the thinking, shouting and crying happened in real life chokes her mind and body with a grip so tight that she can barely breathe.

As soon as she got home from Jess's flat she'd called Matt, desperate to hear his voice, desperate to tell him what was going on and desperate for him to tell her that she'd got it all wrong. But instead, he'd said he couldn't talk and that he'd probably need to stay in Birmingham overnight.

"I want you to come home," she'd said.

"Has something happened?" he asked, his voice thick with concern. "Are you okay?"

For a moment she considered saying no, but she knew what he was referring to and she could never demand his presence under *that* pre-requisite.

"The baby's fine," she'd said. "But I'd like you to come home once you've done what you need to do."

Matt had laughed awkwardly. "Darling, you know how these things work. I could be here all night, but I'll make sure I'm back in time for our hospital appointment in the morning."

"It's got nothing to do with that," snapped Kate.

"So what's up?"

She'd thought about telling him over the phone, but knew that whatever was going on, needed to be spoken about face-to-face. And besides, what was she supposed to say? *I think the woman who is there with you, hundreds of miles away from me, is actively looking to destroy my world?* At best it sounded melodramatic and at worst needy, neither of which she was prone to being.

"Why don't you go to your mum's?" he'd offered. "If you don't want to be on your own."

"I don't want to go to my fucking mother's," she'd said, battling to keep the lid on the pressure cooker she felt she was submerged in. "I want you to come home."

"But darling, I—"

"D'you know what?" she yelled. "Don't fucking bother. Stay there. Do what you want—I don't care."

She'd thrown herself onto the bed, unaccustomed to feeling so vulnerable and out of control. She wanted to blame Jess; after all, if she hadn't have turned up, Matt wouldn't be with her. But then it occurred to her that it was Lauren's fault for bringing her into the fold. If she hadn't had gone looking, then they would still be blissfully ignorant, pretending that their family held no more secrets than any other. Though if it wasn't for Rose, Jess wouldn't exist for Lauren to have found.

All of a sudden, Kate's whole world had felt as if

it was tumbling down. It seemed that everyone she loved, and had thought she could rely on, was actually working against her. And the one person who would always have her back, no matter what, was dead.

As the night had worn on and her toxic thoughts had poisoned her brain, she'd called Matt again and again, looking to trade her paranoia for his reassurance, but every time, his phone had gone straight to voicemail.

She'd spent the next two hours scanning Jess's Instagram feed, which was being constantly uploaded with stories of her drinking and dancing. Kate didn't know what she was looking for—perhaps a flash of Matt's face or a flit of his hand in the corner of a shot. Either of which, in her saner moments, would mean nothing—yet right there and then it would have confirmed her worst fear: that the husband she trusted and adored was having an affair with her half sister.

She imagined the pair of them stumbling back to their hotel and kissing in the lift, unable to control themselves for a moment longer. They'd have gone to Matt's room and Kate wondered what he would have thought about as he lowered himself on top of her. She doubts it would have been his baby's scan the next morning.

"Stop!" she'd screamed out loud, in the hope that it would knock some sense into her. And for a second it did, but just as soon as she'd managed to banish *that* thought from her mind, she was hit with a barrage of others.

There was seemingly no doubt now that Jess was her half sister—two hospital tags with the same date, had to be more than coincidental. But she still refused to believe she could be her father's child. It'd be the more obvious choice of course, but as far as Kate's concerned, he would never have betrayed his family. Betrayed *her*. No, if anyone was capable of doing that, it was her mother. But how had she managed to keep her pregnancy secret? Or had her husband known? Had he known that she'd been unfaithful, and been complicit in hiding the pregnancy, birth *and* adoption in order to keep their family unit together? That sounded more like him. But Rose had look so terrified when Kate had shown her the box from the loft, as if she'd seen a ghost, and the only reason for that would have been that she thought her world was about to implode. By inadvertently discovering the only memory her mother had of her third child, Kate had so nearly torn their family apart. Rose would have known that— that's why she had snatched it from Kate's grasp.

She'd almost felt sorry for her mother, responsible for forcing her to discard the cherished memento. But then she was reminded of how quickly Rose had pointed the finger at their father when Jess turned up—so eager to cast aspersions that she knew weren't true—yet if it kept her secret safe, it seemed she had no moral responsibility to the man she'd been married to for forty years.

None of this explained what Jess actually wanted from them of course, though to cause as much distress and conflict as possible certainly seemed to be at the top of her agenda. Otherwise, why was she working with Matt? Why was she infiltrating Lauren's life? Why was her flat set up for a baby?

"And what the hell is she doing shacked up with my husband a hundred and fifty miles away?" Kate had asked herself out loud.

The never-ending questions had circled in Kate's head for most of the night, until she'd finally fallen asleep at dawn, wondering whether it was the past she should be worried about at all—because it seemed to be the future that was under threat.

She turns to Matt's side of the bed now and hopes against hope that he's there. When he's not, she's consumed not with a sense of foreboding, as she'd expected, but a sudden determination to find out exactly what Jess is up to. Because whatever it is, Kate will not let it beat her. "I'm a journalist, for God's sake," she says under her breath.

She pulls her laptop toward her with a renewed sense of purpose and looks up the government website for births, deaths and marriages. It turns out it's relatively easy to get a copy of an adoptee's birth certificate, but not without their original surname and adopted parents' names.

So she calls Jared, an old colleague of hers and a fearsome investigative reporter who leaves no stone unturned in his quest for the truth.

"Hey stranger," he says as he picks up, making her feel as if she only ever calls him when she wants something. She resolves to call him more often when she doesn't. "It's a bit early for you, isn't it?"

"Hey, how you doing?" says Kate. "Are you okay to talk?"

"Always," he says, making Kate feel even worse.

"I need to trace someone's back story, but I don't have their birth name."

"That shouldn't be a problem," he says confidently. "Are they adopted or have they changed their name?"

"Yes," says Kate, before thinking about it. "No, I don't know."

Jared laughs. "Well, which is it?"

She thinks back to what Finn told her. "Her adopted name is Harriet Oakley, but she's been living as Jessica Linley more recently. I'm not sure if she's changed it by deed poll or not."

"Sounds interesting."

You have no *idea.*

"Do you have a date of birth?"

"Yes, fifteenth of September, 1996."

"Okay, but no birth name?"

Kate sighs. "I can have a guess, but it would be a real stab in the dark."

"Anything might help," says Jared.

"Okay, can you try Harriet Alexander?" asks Kate, though even as she says it, she knows it's highly unlikely. Firstly, she's not her father's child and why would her mother give Harry's name to a child she was giving up for adoption? Even if her husband *did* know about it?

"Anything else you can tell me?" asks Jared.

"Actually, can you also look at Harriet Grainger?" adds Kate, wondering if her mother would have given the child *her* maiden name rather than that of her lover. It occurs to her for the first time to wonder whether Rose even told Jess's father that she was pregnant with his child.

How is she going to deal with that *when the time comes?*

"Okay," says Jared. "Let me talk to my contact at the adoption bureau and if she needs any further information, can I give her your number to call?"

"Of course," says Kate.

"Great, leave it with me for a day or two."

"Thanks Jared, I owe you one."

"Yeah, yeah," he says, as if she already has an out-standing debt.

She'd hate for him to think she won't pay it—that's the way it works in journalism. *You scratch my back and I'll scratch yours.* "We should get a date in the diary," she says before he hangs up. "Maybe grab a meal."

"That would be great," says Jared warmly. "If I trace your girl, it'll be on you."

"Deal!" says Kate, laughing, momentarily forgetting that this isn't someone else's story she's chasing. This is *her* life. It's funny how different it feels when it's happening to you.

She gets in the shower and imagines the water, hot-ter than feels comfortable, washing away her troubles. She groans as it stings her eyes, reminding her how much she'd cried last night.

There's a tap on the glass screen and she jumps, her heart skipping a beat.

"Jesus!" she says, as Matt's smiling face peers through the condensation.

She wipes a circle with her hand, but even through the fogginess, he still looks like he's been up all night. His eyes are heavy-lidded and his hair unkempt, mak-ing her suspect him of things she doesn't want to suspect him of.

"Surprise!" he says, handing her a towel as she steps out of the shower. He tries to kiss her, but she turns her head.

"You made good time," she says, coldly.

"Good to see you too," he says, sarcastically. "I cadged a lift with Oddie—thought it might get me home quicker than waiting for the trains to start up this morning."

Oddie? The Political Editor on the Gazette? The thought of Matt being with a colleague from her own newspaper makes her feel better, though she doesn't know why. She tries to convince herself that it means he'd never be foolish enough to do anything untoward in front of someone who knows his wife so well. But the very next minute, she's consumed with shame, knowing that if he has, everyone in the office will know about it except for her.

"Just the two of you?" she asks.

"And a couple of the others."

There's her nemesis—clumsily thrown in as a casual aside.

"That must have been a fun ride," she says, reaching for her hairbrush and dragging it forcefully through her hair.

Matt laughs as he takes off his shirt, rolling it up and throwing it into the laundry basket. "It was a *quiet* ride," he says. "It was a long night and some of the newbies aren't quite as robust as us."

"Why, what happened?" she asks.

"It was just the normal government press office debacle," he says.

Kate stares into the mirror as she vigorously rubs cream into her face. She can't look at him, because if he's lying, she's going to know by the look in his eyes.

"Did Jess go?" she asks, as he puts his head under the shower and groans in pleasure.

"What's that?" he says.

"I said, did Jess go?" Her tone is acerbic. "Was she one of the newbies?"

"Er, yeah . . . yeah, she was there."

"How did she get on?"

"Yeah, all right," says Matt, shampooing his hair.

Kate can't help but notice how short and clipped his answers are.

"So, was she a help?" she pushes on. "Was she able to take up some of the slack? Take the pressure off you."

Kate tries not to picture the ways she might achieve that.

"She was okay," he says. "Though I'm not sure politics is going to be her forte."

"Oh really?" says Kate. "What do you suppose *is* her forte?"

"Pass me that towel," he says, a classic diversion tactic if ever Kate heard one.

She stands there with crossed arms, knowing he's on the ropes. "What *is* her forte?" she repeats.

Matt looks at her with a vexed brow. "Since when have *you* been so interested?"

"Since you decided to hire the girl who's claiming to be my half sister." She'd not meant to say it like that. In fact, she's not sure she'd meant to say it at all. If she'd had her way, she would have carefully revealed who Jess really was and what she wanted in her own time, but she'd felt suddenly compelled.

"Wait!" he says, laughing nervously. "*What* did you just say?"

Kate looks away, chewing on the inside of her cheek. "You heard."

"Jess?!" he exclaims. "*She's* the girl who turned up at your mum's? She's the one who's claiming to be your father's daughter?"

"She is *not* my father's daughter," snaps Kate, seeing red. "Why is everyone so happy to assume that?"

"Hold on," says Matt, shaking his head and putting his hand in the air. "You're saying that Jess is that woman?"

"There *is* another option you know," barks Kate, ignoring the question. "You of all people should know that my father would never have deceived his family."

Matt looks like his head is about to explode as he tries to put all the pieces together. "Are you honestly expecting me to believe that Jess is the same girl?" he asks, clearly struggling with the admission. "Why would you think that? I mean, how have you come to that conclusion?" He's beginning to pace the floor, which means he's unable to comprehend what Kate's suggesting.

"Because I've seen her," she says. "And because that's her name."

Matt laughs in a way that Kate can't help but find patronizing. "Do you find this funny?" she asks incredulously. She'd thought, hoped, that when she eventually told him who Jess was, he'd immediately try to help her solve the problem. But he seems to find it more amusing than worrying, and Kate feels bitterly disappointed.

"So, you're putting two and two together and coming up with five."

"Do you really think I'm that stupid?" she yells, unable to hold her frustration in. "Do you honestly think I haven't checked her out?"

"And what did you find?" he asks, with what Kate's sure is the tiniest of smiles playing on his lips.

"That the woman you hired—the woman who says she went to Bournemouth University—did no such thing. She doesn't have a degree in journalism—in fact, she has never even studied journalism."

"What are you even talking about?" says Matt, an air of impatience to him now. "Of course she did. I've got her CV—I've seen her qualifications, I've got her references."

Kate allows herself a wry smile. "But did you think to actually check them out? Did it occur to you to call the uni up and make sure she was a bona fide student?"

"Not yet," he says, clearly affronted by her accusing tone.

"Well, maybe if you had, it would have saved us all a lot of trouble . . ."

"Are you insinuating that this is somehow *my* fault?"

Is it? If he's sleeping with her, then yes, he damn well needs to take responsibility for his actions. Whether Jess is her half sister or not.

Kate looks him in the eye. "Are you . . . are you having a relationship with her?"

"*What?*" he squeals, throwing his hands in the air.

"I want to know . . . are you sleeping with her?"

His pace quickens and he runs a hand through his hair. "This is fucking insane."

"I needed you last night," she says, refusing to let the tears that are prickling her eyes fall. "I was trying to get hold of you all night, but it seems you were otherwise engaged."

"Hold on a second," he says, as if sensing the seriousness of the situation for the first time. "You were mightily pissed off when I *did* speak to you, and after that I couldn't take your calls."

"And *why* couldn't you take my calls?" she shouts.

"Because I was tied up with other things," he says.

"Oh, I *bet* you were."

"Let me tell you about last night," he says, his jaw clenching involuntarily. "I was promised an interview with the PM at ten, which got pushed back to midnight, which then got moved to one a.m. And at the same time, I'm trying to schedule talks with the Home Secretary and Education Minister. I've had no sleep and I feel like shit, but *you* think it's because I've been . . . I've been . . ." He laughs sarcastically, unable to finish the sentence. "And to top it all off, you're now telling me that she's your *sister.*"

"It's not a coincidence," she says, letting the first tear fall onto her cheek.

"What isn't?" says Matt irritably.

"All this!" she exclaims, throwing her arms up. "Jess turning up at Mum and Dad's after supposedly being reeled in by Lauren, and then ending up working with you."

"Does she know who I am?" asks Matt. "Does she know who you are to me?"

"I honestly don't know," says Kate. "I've had all these mad conspiracy theories going around in my head, thinking this is all part of a bigger picture. That she's somehow out to get me. I can't help but feel that she's after something from us."

Matt stops pacing and sits down beside Kate on the edge of the bath. "But why would she be doing that? Surely this is just a huge coincidence."

"I want it to be, but I can't help thinking it's something more."

"Like what?" asks Matt.

She wants to tell him about the bizarre set-up she'd found at Jess's flat, as if she's waiting for a baby to arrive. But what it might mean, and how it might involve her and Matt, makes it difficult to put into words. It also means she'll have to admit to breaking in, and that's a new low, even for a journalist.

She shivers, as if someone's walked over her grave. "What she's doing is premeditated and intended to cause me maximum hurt and distress."

Matt looks at her as if she's completely mad. "Are you serious?" he says. "You think this is all about *you*?"

"Who else is it about?" says Kate, her hackles rising.

"Might it be that she's just a confused young woman who's trying to make the best of the unfortunate situation she finds herself in?"

Kate looks at him, open-mouthed. "Are you *honestly* going to stand there and defend her?" she asks incredulously.

As if sensing the minefield he's about to stand on, Matt takes a physical step back and runs a hand through his hair. "I just think we need to take stock," he says. "She's a nice girl and I can't see any reason why she would have any ulterior motive here. I agree that it seems hugely coincidental that she's wound up working with me, but it's a bit of a leap to suggest that it's got anything to do with you."

"She shows up at *my* parents'. She appears at *my* office. She's going out on day trips with *my* sister. She's working with *my* husband. What fucking part of this sounds like it's got nothing to do with me?" A vivid image of the wardrobe in Jess's flat, adorned with nappies and romper suits, flashes into Kate's head. "What will she want next, Matt?" she yells. "*My* baby?"

Matt looks at her dumbfounded. "Can you even hear yourself?" he says, when he eventually finds his voice.

Of all the things Kate thought he might do, doubting *her* wasn't one of them.

"I don't want you there," says Kate, without looking at him.

"*What?*"

"I don't want you at the scan." Even as she's saying it, she knows she's biting her nose off to spite her face, but she just can't stop herself.

"You can't possibly be serious."

"I'm going on my own," she says, stepping into a maxi dress.

"This is crazy," he says, with both hands on his head. "What are you doing?"

Honestly? She doesn't know. All she *does* know is that she needs to be as far away from Matt as possible right now.

"You can't do this," he barks. "You have no right."

"I have *every* right," cries Kate, knowing she's gone too far down the rabbit hole to back out now. "I don't even know if I want you in this flat. I most certainly don't want you anywhere near that hospital."

"But we've waited so long for this," he says, as tears spring to his eyes. "It's what we've been dreaming of, planning for . . . you can't just shut me out."

"I can do what the hell I like," barks Kate as she storms around the bedroom, throwing things she doesn't need into her oversized handbag.

"I won't let you do this," says Matt. "I won't let you

ruin this moment, because we will never get this time back again and we'll regret it for the rest of our lives."

"Well you should have thought about that . . ."

"Please, Kate," Matt begs, taking hold of her arm. "I've driven through the night to make sure I could get to the hospital in time."

She shakes him off as she heads for the door.

"Please, don't do this. Let me come with you."

"No," she chokes.

It feels as if she might break in two as she slams the door shut.

3 3

KATE

As soon as Dr. Williams sees her, his smile dissipates and he looks around, confused.

"No Matt?" he asks, clearly surprised. Him and her both. If someone had told her a month ago she'd be attending this scan on her own, she would have laughed in their face. It wouldn't have seemed remotely possible— not after everything she and Matt had gone through to get here. But that was before Jess turned up.

For some reason, Kate feels obliged to pretend to Dr. Williams that everything is fine and dandy in her world. As if, in *not* doing so, she would be letting him and his team down. They'd all worked so hard to get her pregnant, having been convinced that she and Matt as a couple were worthy of their time and expertise, that she couldn't bear to tell him that they weren't.

"Something came up at work," she says, furiously batting away the tears that are so close to falling.

He looks shocked and Kate feels immediately guilty, though she can't determine whether it's on behalf of the doctor or Matt.

"Knowing Matt, I presume it must be extremely

important, as I can't imagine he'd miss this for all the tea in China."

Kate smiles tightly.

"Anyway, it can't be helped," he says.

A sense of unease swirls in the pit of her stomach, as she remembers Matt's words. *We will never get this time back again and we'll regret it for the rest of our lives.*

"Are you excited?" he asks, as he leads her down the corridor toward the by-now-familiar ultrasound suite.

I was, she thinks. *More than you could ever know, but without Matt, it suddenly seems futile, as if none of it is really very important anymore.*

"Of course," she says instead. "I can't wait."

He smiles broadly. "Okay, so you know the form."

Kate slips off her ballet pumps as he rolls a sheet of what looks like oversized kitchen towel down the length of the narrow bed.

"Make yourself comfortable and we'll see what's going on in there."

He dims the lights as Kate lies down and her hand veers to her side, where it's normally clutched tightly by Matt. But today it just falls listlessly into the abyss before she places it down on the bed. A single tear runs into her ear.

"So how have you been feeling?" asks Dr. Williams.

"Emotional," says Kate, honestly.

"Ah, that is a universal symptom, I'm afraid," the doctor laughs. "And how's your diet? Are you eating any better?"

"Not as well as I'd like," comes a breathless voice.

"Ah, you made it!" says Dr. Williams, through a wide grin. "Just in time."

Matt immediately takes Kate's hand in his. It feels warm and reassuring—her safe place in a storm—the very thing she needs most right now. He looks down and smiles at her. "I wouldn't have missed it for the world," he says.

"Thank you," mouths Kate, and Matt catches another tear that escapes toward her hairline before kissing her forehead.

"Okay, so there's baby," says Dr. Williams, as a beating heartbeat reverberates around the room.

Matt's face crumples as Kate looks up at him and in that moment, she knows that no matter what, they'll find a way to get through this together. Because now there is so much more at stake than just him and her.

"Have you got time for a coffee?" Matt asks tentatively, as they step out into the sunshine afterward.

Kate looks at her watch. She doesn't know whether she wishes she did or not.

"I promised I'd pop to Mum's," she says. "Lauren's meeting me there."

"Is it about . . . ?"

She nods, neither of them needing him to finish the sentence.

"Okay, but we obviously need to talk," says Matt. "Shall we catch up later? If it stays like this, maybe you can get off work early and we can go up to Greenwich Park."

Kate smiles at the thought. They've always enjoyed lazy Sundays there, lying on a blanket, looking down on the ever-changing city they love. Kate can picture her head resting in Matt's lap as he runs his hand over her swollen belly—the two of them excitedly talking through their birth plan.

They'd not really had conversations like that, not since the very beginning, when they'd naively thought that they'd get pregnant immediately. Though they probably wouldn't be having conversations like that tonight either, as there were more pressing issues that needed to be discussed.

"I'm sorry," says Matt. "I shouldn't have . . ."

"No, *I'm* sorry," says Kate, cutting him off. "I'm expecting you to be telepathic. It's not your fault."

He nods and for a moment they stand there in the middle of the hospital concourse, as if weighing up the right thing to do next. Normally, in this situation, they wouldn't think twice. They'd casually lean in toward one another and share a chaste kiss—a "see you soon" peck that would send them both on their way, satisfied. But, right now, it feels as if there's a six-foot brick wall between them.

"Right then," says Matt awkwardly. "I'll see you later then."

"Let's aim for seven-ish," she says, keen to head off. She wants to be the first to get to her parents' house to give her mother one last chance to be honest before Lauren shows up.

"Oh, my darling, that's wonderful news," shrills Rose as she hugs Kate to her. "Truly wonderful."

The moment isn't how Kate imagined it would be. After all that they'd been through to get pregnant, she dreamed of her and Matt announcing their news together at a celebratory family gathering. Not on her own, on her mother's doorstep, earlier than she'd wanted to. But if Jess hadn't forced her hand, she wouldn't be in this position.

Rose holds Kate at arm's length, looking at her as if through new eyes. "You are going to make the most amazing mum," she says.

"It's funny," says Kate, as tears immediately spring to her eyes. "I've waited all this time, but now it's here, I feel nervous and a little bit scared."

"That's only natural," says Rose, as she leads her inside and into the living room. "But I promise you, as soon as this little one comes along, it will all fall into place."

"How will I know what to do?" asks Kate.

"It's instinct," says Rose. "It will kick in as soon as you give birth. Of course, there will be practical things you need help with, but you've got me and your sister to show you the ropes. Lord knows you've been around Lauren's children for long enough, so that'll give you a head start."

"But what if I don't bond with the baby? What if I don't feel what I'm supposed to feel?"

"You may not," says Rose. "You'll get plenty of people telling you how you *should* feel after having a baby, but for some new mothers, it's not always that straightforward."

"What do you mean?" Kate asks, wondering whether her mother is about to impart the reason she gave Jess up.

"Well, sometimes that feeling—that immediate bond

of unconditional love—doesn't come until later," says Rose. "So much happens to our bodies and our emotions that it's tough sometimes. There's all the hormones of the pregnancy, then the trauma of the birth, and while you're recovering from all that, you suddenly find yourself alone with this little human being who is solely dependent on you to survive."

"Did you struggle with me and Lauren?" asks Kate, lowering herself onto the sofa.

Rose looks away as she sits in the armchair beside her.

"Mum?"

"Look, this is happy news," says Rose after a long pause. "You don't have to worry—you'll be a natural, I know you will."

"So, you found it hard?" presses Kate. "Was it more so with Lauren, being your first?"

"I found it difficult in the beginning," admits Rose. "But they were different times then. Women were having babies in the morning and expected to be back at their desks in the afternoon."

Kate offers a weak smile.

"You've got to remember, this was the eighties, when magazines like *Cosmopolitan* were telling us we could have it *all*. If you weren't in a high-powered job, with a baby hanging off your hip, and still having great sex, then there was deemed to be something very wrong with you."

"So, what happened?" asks Kate, keen to take advantage of her mum's affable mood.

Rose looks off, out of the window, as if lost in thought. "You're made to feel as if it should be the happiest time of your life," she says eventually. "And for a few days it was blissful. Your dad took some time off work, the house was full of visitors and flowers and Lauren was such a good baby."

"But?"

"But I felt detached, as if it was all happening to someone else. When your dad went back to work, I begged him not to go. I remember crying and holding on to him at the front door, asking him what I was supposed to do on my own."

Despite herself, the admission brings tears to Kate's eyes. "Didn't you think you'd be able to cope?"

"I just didn't feel I was qualified to be left alone with a baby," says Rose. "I was scared of what I might do, or *not* do, whichever is the greatest evil."

"But you're a strong, capable woman," says Kate.

"Well, that's the thing with post-natal depression. It's pretty indiscriminate in who it chooses to affect. From the outside looking in, I had a husband who adored me, a lovely house, a supportive family—but inside I was a wreck who was having trouble functioning on any level. I didn't trust myself or anybody else and I was so paranoid that I was doing something wrong or not doing something right, that I thought Lauren would be taken away from me. There were times when I thought I'd save everyone the trouble and just end it, but the shocking thing was, hand on heart, I didn't know whether that meant hurting me or hurting her."

"So, what did you do?" asks Kate.

Rose gives a little laugh. "I muddled on for a year or so, living two lives: the one, on the face of it, that everyone saw, and the other, that gave me palpitations and disturbed thoughts. I knew it was happening, I just couldn't do anything about it."

"Did you go to your doctor?"

Rose shakes her head vehemently. "No, there was still a stigma attached to it back then. It wasn't like today—when we're all encouraged to talk about our emotions."

"Weren't you scared?" asks Kate. "When you found out you were pregnant with me?"

"Terrified!" says Rose, half smiling. "But I couldn't deny Lauren a sibling just because I had difficulty coping. I had to give myself some tough love and accept that everyone else was clearly managing, so I just had to pull myself together and get on with it."

"And was it as bad the second time around?"

Rose grimaces. "Worse, unfortunately."

Kate can't help but feel hurt that she was difficult to love. Maybe that explained why she'd always felt closer to her father. If Rose realizes what she's implied, she doesn't show it.

"And . . . the third time?" asks Kate, hesitantly.

Rose looks at her quizzically, tilting her head to the side. "The third time . . . ? I only have you and Lauren," she says, laughing. "In case you hadn't noticed."

Kate gets up and walks to the fireplace, picking up the Order of Service for her dad's funeral. She wonders if her mother can't bear to put it away for the same reason she can't. As if doing so would mean that she doesn't think about him, and if he's looking down, she doesn't *ever* want him to think she's forgotten him.

Kate smiles back at his grinning face, knowing that the reason he looks so happy is because his grandchildren, who were cut out of the shot, are playing at his feet. A crushing feeling descends on her as she acknowledges that it will never be *her* children who make him laugh like that.

"Did you love him?" asks Kate.

"You know I did," says Rose. "More than life itself."

"Were you faithful?" Kate asks, without turning around. It feels easier not to see her mother's face, especially if she's going to lie.

There's a stunned silence.

"Why on earth would you ask me something like that?" says Rose. "Why would you even *think* it?"

Kate's mouth feels as if it's full of cotton wool. This is her opportunity to backtrack. But that's not what she's come here for. She won't leave without the truth. She can't.

"Hey," calls out Lauren as she lets herself in.

"We're in here," says Rose, her voice resounding with relief.

"Sorry I'm late," offers Lauren nonchalantly, as if they're here to discuss the weather.

Kate suddenly wishes they were.

"So I've asked you both here because there's something I need to tell you," says Rose, wasting no time in getting to the point.

Lauren and Kate exchange a look. It feels as if they're about to find out the competition winner; will Lauren win the prize for rightly guessing that Jess is their father's daughter? Or will Kate, the outside favorite, romp home after trusting her hunch that Jess is their mother's child? Either way, it's a sick game.

"This is really hard for me, and I never imagined I'd ever have to do this, but you've given me no choice."

Kate bristles at the suggestion that it's somehow their fault that she abandoned her child.

"Jess turning up has brought back a lot of bad memories for me, of a time that I'd much rather forget."

Lauren falls heavily onto the sofa, as if signaling she's here for the long haul. Kate would prefer to get this over and done with as quickly as possible and stands straight-backed in front of the fireplace.

"There *was* a woman," starts Rose, slowly and deliberately. "Her name was Helen Wilmington and she was your father's secretary."

Kate's sure she's stopped breathing.

"Just before we moved down here from Yorkshire, your father wasn't his normal self," says Rose, sniffing. "He'd always worked hard, but suddenly he was working all hours God sent. One night, after telling me he was staying at the office, I decided to surprise him by taking his dinner in to him."

Kate grimaces, knowing the lie her mother is about to tell.

Rose bites down on her lip as she looks at the girls in turn, checking that she has their undivided attention.

"Was he not there?" asks Lauren naively.

"Oh, he was there all right," says Rose, attempting to laugh, though it sounds hollow. "She was there too, though, and there was no doubt in my mind what she was there for."

Lauren covers her mouth with her hand. "You *saw* them?"

Rose nods solemnly.

"Did they see *you*?" asks Lauren.

"No, no, I got out of there without them noticing me."

"Did you ever confront him? Did you ever tell him what you'd seen?"

Rose reaches across to Lauren and puts a hand over hers. When she looks up, her eyes are glistening with tears. "No, because I didn't want anything to change. You have to understand; I loved your father with all my heart, and I knew that if I told him what I'd seen, things would never be the same again. I didn't want that for our family—it was too important to me. It's *still* important to me."

Rose looks sadly around the place they'd called home for almost a quarter of a century. The peach-colored front room, with its mahogany units displaying porcelain figurines, is a little dated, but it has been beautifully kept.

Kate remembers the Saturday mornings when her mother would be hoovering along to Radio 2 as she and her father ran in from the garden, both of them wearing muddied boots and even dirtier grins.

"Don't you be coming through here with all that mud on you," Rose had cried, as Kate and her father looked at each other conspiratorially and giggled.

Had he been seeing another woman, then? Making a child with her? Kate refuses to believe it, yet tears still spring to her eyes.

"I'm sorry," says Rose. "I would never want you to think badly of your dad, but you've given me no choice. You wouldn't let it drop—you've forced my hand."

"So, you think Jess is Helen Wilmington's daughter?" asks Lauren.

"I hope so," says Rose, "Because if she's anybody else's then I've been far more naive than I would care to admit."

Lauren is wide-eyed as a thought occurs to her. "Do

you know where she is now? Perhaps Jess can track her down and be reunited with her mum."

Rose looks down, picking at the tissue she's holding in her lap. "I heard she died," she says quietly. "About four years ago."

"Why didn't you tell us all this when Jess first turned up?" asks Kate.

"Because . . . because I didn't want you to hate your father," cries Rose.

Kate feels winded. She could never hate her father, no matter what lies her mother told. It takes all her willpower not to applaud her stellar performance.

"How long did it take you to come up with this story?" she asks.

Lauren gasps at her sister's audacity. "Kate!"

Kate turns to face Lauren, her features hardened. "Before you jump on the bandwagon, why don't you ask Mum about the baby mementos that I found in the loft?"

Rose's eyes widen, but she quickly pulls herself back together, presenting the pitiful face of the grieving widow again.

"What baby mementos?" asks Lauren, looking from Kate, to their mother, and back again.

"Do you remember, Mum?" asks Kate. "Do you remember the little pink sleepsuit and teddy bear?"

A look of utter panic descends on Rose's face as she gets up from her chair, brusquely shaking her head from side to side. "No, no," she says, one too many times—each denial countered by Kate's resolute belief that she's lying. "I don't know what you're talking about."

"Sure you do," says Kate confidently, though inside

her stomach is in knots. "I showed them to you, and you promptly threw them in the bin."

Rose lets out a strangled guffaw. "I really don't remember that. Are you sure you didn't dream it?"

"I'm sure," mutters Kate, cocking her head.

"Well, perhaps you imagined it. You always had such an overactive imagination when you were little."

"You haven't even asked me how old I was at the time."

"Kate, that's enough," says Lauren.

"So you're denying any knowledge of it," Kate presses on, ignoring her sister. "You don't remember the box, any of its contents, throwing it in the bin . . . nothing at all."

"No, darling, I don't," says Rose, reaching for Kate's hand. She pulls it away and sits down on the sofa next to Lauren.

Kate considers telling her about the hospital tags bearing the same date—the strongest proof yet that, one way or another, Rose knows *exactly* who Jess is. But she decides to hold back, fearing that she won't be able to offer a justifiable explanation as to how she came about the information. It's going to be pretty irrelevant anyway, once the DNA results come in. Rose won't be able to wriggle her way out of that one.

"So you're going to carry on with this charade?" says Kate. "How could you do this to Dad? I thought you loved him."

"Oh darling, I did," says Rose. "Sometimes I think I loved him too much. I would have done anything for him."

"Having a sordid liaison in the office was not the man he was," says Kate, resolutely.

"That's not the man you *wanted* him to be," says Rose. "There's a difference."

Lauren puts a hand on Kate's back. "You had a very special relationship—we could all see that, but ultimately you weren't *in* a relationship with him, Kate. Mum was his wife, the person who saw what was going on."

"That's not the man he was," Kate repeats. "And I'm going to prove it."

34

LAUREN

As the day wears on, Lauren has discovered that being a faithful wife and mummy to three children doesn't sit comfortably alongside knowing you may be about to do something that could throw a grenade into your life.

She tries to convince herself, as she burns the kids' fish fingers—even the most perfunctory tasks are proving impossible—that it's all this business with Kate that's messing with her head. She tries to pretend that it's not the thought of seeing Justin tonight that's made her put Noah's red T-shirt in with Jude's white sleepsuits. Why would it? The only reason she's going to see him is for closure—to wrap up the unfinished business that stands between them, so they can both move on with their lives. She'll not go into his flat—there's no need to—they can say their goodbyes on the threshold. That's all they need to do. So why, then, does she put on matching underwear?

As she stands in front of the full-length mirror in her bedroom, adjusting her pose in an effort to turn herself into something she's not, she wonders when time had caught up with her. When she was last with Justin, all she'd wanted was to look like a *real* woman, instead of the teenager that she was. But now, as she lifts her bra strap up so her breast sits where it used to, and runs her fingers over the creped skin on her stomach, she yearns for the taut skin of her youth. *It seems we're never happy.*

"Are you going out, Mummy?" asks Noah from the doorway.

"Hey," she says, rushing to him and picking him up. "You're supposed to be asleep by now." She carries him to his bed and gently lays him down.

"But if you're going out, who's going to look after me?" he asks, rubbing the blanket he's had since he was born against his cheek.

She weighs up the pros and cons of telling him the truth, but coupled with not having told Simon she's going out, she opts for the path of least resistance.

"I'm not going anywhere," she says, hating herself. "Now snuggle back down."

He offers an angelic smile as Lauren kisses him and it feels as if her heart is about to break. She can't do whatever this is; it's madness. Even leaving Jess in charge of the kids—regardless of who she is—goes against the grain. Lauren has never left the children with anyone other than her parents since Noah was born. She'd balked at babysitters—no matter how highly recommended they were—because she could never truly trust a stranger. *But isn't that ultimately who Jess is?* she asks herself. She doesn't know what life she's led, the people she's in with, the bad habits she's picked up along the way.

She might take drugs. She might have been in trouble with the police. What if this guy she's seeing at work is a thief or a con artist on the side? Jess had mentioned he might pop in later—she'd sounded so excited that Lauren hadn't wanted to burst her bubble and say no, despite how uncomfortable she felt. But what if he was a criminal who just happened to hold down a day job as well? What if he and Jess were both professional scammers who attach themselves to a mark by pretending to be related to them? Suppose they wheedle their way into people's lives by preying on their vulnerability and strip them of everything they've got. The admission that she's questioning Jess's motives for the first time shames her. How can she leave her children with her now?

Going back into her bedroom, she calls Jess as she ruefully picks up the black jumpsuit that she'd laid on the bed. She's just about to put it back in the wardrobe when the doorbell rings. Jess's phone goes to voicemail and being the nearest thing to hand, Lauren hastily pulls the outfit from the hanger and steps into it. She's still doing up the buttons as she opens the door.

"Jess!"

"Sorry I'm a bit early, the trains were running on time for once."

"Oh, I was just about to . . ." says Lauren, staring at the phone in her hand, knowing that it's too late to call her off now.

"You look gorgeous," says Jess, looking Lauren up and down.

I look awful, Lauren says to herself, before remembering what Kate told her. "Thank you," she says out loud.

"So, what do I need to know?" asks Jess, as she steps into the hall.

"Mmm, do you know what?" says Lauren. "I'm not in the mood to go out so I think I'm just going to cancel. You should stay though—we can open a bottle of wine."

"You can't stay in when you look like *that*!" exclaims Jess with a smile. "People need to see you."

Lauren laughs awkwardly.

"I hope Simon knows how lucky he is," says Jess. "He should be very proud to have you on his arm tonight. Now go and get your shoes!"

Guilt engulfs Lauren as she goes back up the stairs, her fingers trailing the chipped paint as she goes. While Simon's out there, working through the night, she's getting ready to go and meet another man. Yes, he's chauvinistic, moody and sometimes loses his temper, but is it any surprise? She's on his case 24/7; asking him to fix the shower, put the kitchen door on, paint the staircase. Why isn't *she* painting the staircase instead of nagging her husband, who's busy trying to earn enough money to look after his family?

She's doing her utmost to convince herself that Simon deserves better, but for every reason that goes in his favor, she can think of two that don't. While they struggle to pay the bills, he could make it a lot easier if he didn't go down the pub most nights and visit the bookies every Saturday. And on the rare occasion he takes her out, it would be nice if he talked to her, instead of looking at his phone or accusing her of flirting with the waiter.

Her only heeled shoes sit next to her slippers at the bottom of her wardrobe, seemingly offering Lauren a symbolic choice between doing what's right or what's wrong. It doesn't take her long to pick the pair she wants to wear.

"Okay, so Noah and Emmy are in bed and should be asleep," she says, as she carefully makes her way back down the narrow stairs in feet adorned with black patent. "It's unlikely they'll wake up, but if they do it will only be for the toilet or a drink."

Jess nods confidently. "And Jude?"

Lauren looks at him, gurgling away contentedly in front of a colorful mobile on the living room floor. "There's a bottle in the fridge, which he's due to have at ten, but I'm sure I'll be home by then."

Jess looks at her watch. "It's almost eight now," she says. "At this rate you'll be coming home before you've even gone out."

Lauren smiles as she walks away from Jess and into the kitchen, surreptitiously sweeping up the mug that holds the paltry housekeeping money that Simon deems to give her every week. She puts the forty pounds into her pocket and tucks the laptop she shares with Simon under her arm. She'd rather take it with her than run the risk of Jess and her boyfriend using it to their advantage.

"Are you sure you're okay to do this?" asks Lauren as she walks back into the living room.

"I'm actually incredibly flattered that you've asked," says Jess. "And anyways"—she scuffs the floor with her feet while Lauren looks at her expectantly—"this is what sisters are for."

The words slice through Lauren's psyche, an image of Kate infiltrating her brain. Jess is right, this *is* what sisters are for, so why isn't hers here for her now? Lauren should be able to call on Kate to help with the children, but ever since little Noah came along, she feels that her relationship with Kate has paid the price. With every child that Lauren has been blessed with, she's felt that Kate has removed herself step by step, and now with Jess turning up, Lauren wonders if they'll ever be how they used to be again.

Lauren pulls Jess into her, hugging her tight. "I'm so pleased I've got *you*," she says, her eyes shining.

"And I'm pleased I've got you," says Jess.

"Ring me if you need me," calls out Lauren as she gets in the car.

"Will do," smiles Jess. "Have a good time."

Lauren watches the front door close with conflicted emotions. How had she deemed it necessary to safeguard her laptop by bringing it with her, while leaving the children—her most treasured possessions—there?

She shudders involuntarily as she pulls away, still thinking about Kate and how they might possibly begin to repair their fractured relationship. If she ever finds out about what she's doing now, she'll *never* be forgiven. There's no love lost between her husband and her sister, but Kate believes in the sanctity of marriage, and is happy to call out anyone who dares to cross the holy line. You only have to look at the headlines attached to her byline every day to know that she doesn't suffer cheaters gladly.

"But I'm not going to cheat," says Lauren to herself, as she pulls up in a road parallel to where Justin lives.

You'll not be able to park in Butler's Wharf itself, so just get as close to it as you can and walk the rest, Justin's last text had read. Lauren chooses not to recall his sign-off: *I can't wait to see you x*

Her heels don't lend themselves to the cobbled passageways of Shad Thames and she almost loses her footing as she passes under the arches of the old spice mills. She stops momentarily to lean on a wall, though she's not sure if it's a bid to slow down her feet or her heart. By the time she reaches Justin's door, with its twenty or so shiny intercom buttons, her mouth is dry and she's wishing she hadn't come. No part of this seems like a good idea right now. Her finger shakes as she trails the numbers, looking for number twelve.

"Hi, it's me," she says.

"Come on up," says Justin. "It's the top floor."

Okay, so you just knock on his door, she says to herself as the lift travels up. *And you say, "It was lovely to bump into you again, but I don't think it's a good idea to see each other anymore."*

She smooths down the front of her jumpsuit and swallows the lump in her throat. *Got it?* she asks herself, just to double-check. *Got it*, comes the convincing reply.

"Hi," says Justin as the lift doors open, and her legs immediately turn to jelly. His dancing eyes meet hers and the jolt sends a quiver through her. He brushes her cheek lightly with a kiss and her knees threaten to give way, reminding her how it's supposed to feel when you're with someone you want to be with. The last time she'd felt like this was with . . . well, Justin. God, this is going to be harder than she thought.

"Hi, listen," she says, aware of his hands lingering on her waist. "I should have called, but I thought I owed you the respect of coming here and . . ."

His lips are on hers and his hands are entwined in her hair before she can even finish the sentence. He kisses her softly, as if testing the waters. She desperately wants him to continue, but her brain is screaming at her to stop this while she can. But how can she when she doesn't want to? She bites down on his lip, playing for time. "I need to tell you something," she whispers.

He pulls back to look at her, concern etched on his face. "Okay," he says, taking her by the hand and walking her toward the open door of his apartment. Her legs don't feel like her own, and her chest is heavy, but strangely light at the same time, as if there are a hundred butterflies preparing to take flight.

"Oh my goodness," she exclaims as she walks into the vast open-plan living area, with floor-to-ceiling windows perfectly framing Tower Bridge. It's so close that she can see the expression on pedestrians' faces as they cross it. "It's beautiful."

"Wait until the lights come on," says Justin.

"Look . . ." she starts, knowing that every second she drags this out will just make it harder. She turns around, to where he's holding out a chair at a perfectly laid table for two. This isn't what she wanted. *It's exactly what you wanted*, says another voice in her head.

"I'm sorry, I shouldn't have kissed you," says Justin. "But why don't we sit down and talk? You've clearly got something on your mind and I'm all ears. Just as soon as I get the dinner out of the oven."

Lauren smiles, grateful to him for injecting some much-needed humor into the situation, but hating him for it at the same time because it makes her love him all the more.

She watches as he pours her a glass of red. "Or would

you prefer white?" he asks halfway through. "I assume you're driving?"

She nods. "Red's fine—just the one though."

He fills the glass and, with a flourish of a tea towel, retreats into the adjoining kitchen. Lauren smiles after him. "So do you own this place?" she calls out as she takes a sip. It would be polite to wait, but she needs all the Dutch courage she can get.

"No, I'm just renting at the moment," he says, before adding, "Shit!"

"You okay?" Lauren asks. "Do you need any help?"

"Just dropped a potato on the floor, but it's yours so it's okay."

Lauren laughs.

"So, yeah, I'm just renting it until I sort out what I'm doing. I've only been back a few months and this suits me for now, but going forward, what with the kids and all . . ."

Lauren breathes in sharply, waiting for him to carry on, not sure that she wants to hear what he's going to say.

"I'm hoping that they'll want to spend some time over here, so . . ."

"You'll probably want a garden then," says Lauren, finishing the sentence for him.

"Garden?" he says laughing. "That's not my sixteen-year-old's main priority anymore. I'm more concerned with him having too much of what London's got to offer by living so close."

"Sixteen?" says Lauren, feeling a little winded, but she doesn't know why. "And how old's your other child?"

"He's just turned eighteen," says Justin, as he comes in carrying two plates laden with a traditional roast dinner.

"Oh," stutters Lauren.

"What, you don't like it? Don't tell me you've gone vegetarian."

"Erm, no . . . no it's lovely," says Lauren. "So you had your children quite quickly after . . ."

"Yes," he says.

Lauren doesn't know if that surprises her in a good way or bad.

"Of course, I don't regret having them, but I wished I'd waited a while."

"Why?" she asks.

He sits down heavily opposite her. "I think I should have taken more time to . . . to get over you and us . . ."

Lauren looks down at the plate of food on the table.

"And, selfishly, I suppose if I'd had them later, they'd be younger now and I'd still have little nippers running around instead of ninety-kilo man mountains. I miss those times."

Lauren smiles uncomfortably as a slow grip snakes its way around her chest. "So, two boys then?"

Justin nods. "And you? Why didn't you have children? Or is that too personal a question?"

A potato lodges in Lauren's throat as she formulates an answer. This is it. This is her chance to be honest. If she tells the truth now, he might *just* forgive her. If she lets this opportunity slide, there'll be no coming back from it.

She clears her throat and puts her knife and fork down. "There's something I need to tell you."

He sits up and mirrors her actions, dabbing his mouth with a napkin.

"I *do* have children," she says, looking past him and out the window onto Tower Bridge.

"But I thought—"

"I don't know why I said I didn't," she goes on, still unable to look at him for fear of seeing what's behind his eyes. "When I saw you . . . I just . . . I just panicked, and everything came out wrong . . ."

"But why didn't you just tell me?" he says, sounding as confused by her actions as she is.

"I just . . ." she murmurs. "I'm sorry, I don't know why I didn't tell you the truth." She forces herself to look at him, expecting to see loathing, but is surprised to see a softness there. Buoyed by the glimmer of hope, she presses on. "I have three children: Noah, Emmy and Jude."

Justin sits back in his chair. If he feels anything like Lauren, he'll have lost his appetite.

"And may I . . ." he chokes. "May I ask how old they are?"

She reaches across the table to take hold of his hand, knowing what he must be thinking.

"Noah's five, Emmy is eighteen months and Jude is five months."

Justin lets out a long breath and pinches the bridge of his nose.

"So you have a partner?"

Lauren nods.

Justin gets up from the table and walks over to the window, looking out onto the River Thames.

"I didn't think I'd ever be able to forgive you for

what you did," he says, with his hands on his hips. "I hated you so much."

Lauren silently pushes her chair away from the table and goes to join him, putting a hand on his back.

"Yet here I am, seemingly still in love with you," he goes on.

"Why did you hate me so much?"

"You know why." His voice is strained, as if he's struggling to sound normal.

She moves around to face him, putting herself in the firing line, inviting him to take a shot.

"What did you expect me to do?" she says, taking hold of his hands.

"It was supposed to be a joint decision," he chokes.

Her hands fall away from his and she's unable to keep her brow from scowling. "It would have been if you'd have stayed around for long enough."

He laughs unkindly. "Are you kidding me?"

"You abandoned me when I needed you," she says, conscious of the change in atmosphere. "I pleaded with you to talk to me, but you cut me off, as if I was dead to you."

"You were," he says, his face close to hers.

A tear unexpectedly falls onto her cheek and she quickly wipes it away.

"I'm going to go now," she says, shaking herself down. "But know one thing: I *never* stopped loving you, and I honestly believe that if you'd stayed with me, our baby would be here today."

He grabs hold of her arm as she moves past him, spinning her around. "You'd already got rid of it before I even had a chance to talk to you. What difference would *I* have made?"

"What?" exclaims Lauren, pulling back, away from his grasp. "What are you talking about? I begged you to come over, to talk to my parents. I swore to them that you'd stand by me, that we'd work it out, together, but you left me there to face it alone." The tears fall with no apologies and she pummels his chest with her closed fists. "I needed you, but you weren't there. Why weren't you there?"

Justin grabs hold of her flailing arms and stares intently into her eyes. "I was told you'd already had an abortion," he says loudly. "*That's* why I left you. You took away our right to choose together."

"No, no, no," Lauren cries, shaking her head manically. "That's not what happened. You left me *before* I had made a decision. And without you there I just couldn't . . ."

The pair of them lock eyes, their pupils dilated with shock as they both suddenly realize that they were played off against one another in a wicked game of he said, she said.

Justin takes her head in his hands and kisses her hard, as if trying to quell the years of hurt and frustration that had built up between them.

"I swear to you—" starts Lauren, breaking away from him.

He kisses her again and she responds, his tongue, his touch, his smell, taking her back to the happiest and saddest time in her life.

"I have never stopped loving you," he breathes, as his lips and fingers trail her neck, his feather-like touch setting her skin alight.

"Make love to me," she whispers tearfully.

He picks her up and she wraps her legs around him,

their kissing not stopping until he lays her gently on his bed. She can feel his weight on top of her, his desire evident.

"Are you sure?" he says.

She nods, just like she did the last time he asked that question twenty-two years ago.

3 5

KATE

"I need the copy for the glamour show business model piece," shouts Lee across the news floor.

Kate looks at the clock on the wall—it's after seven and she's not yet had time to focus on what matters most. Instead she's having to file a depressingly predictable interview about a forty-year-old's fifth boob job. She's either getting too cynical or too long in the tooth to want to be writing such an inane piece.

"It's coming across now," she calls back.

As soon as she hits send, she picks up her phone and takes it with her to the stairwell, where she'll be afforded marginally more privacy.

"Hi, Nancy, it's Kate—I just wondered if you had any results on those DNA samples I sent over last night."

"Oh hi, Kate—not just yet, but we're getting there. I hope to have them in the next few hours."

"Great, let me know as soon as they're in, will you?"

"Will do," says Nancy, before hanging up.

Kate taps her phone on her chin as she wonders what she's going to do with the results if they go the way she's expecting them to. Her mother certainly won't be surprised—she'll just be shocked that Kate's gone to such lengths to get to the truth, though if she'd been honest in the first place, Kate wouldn't have felt the need to have done it. But Lauren is going to be stunned by the turn of events—Jess too, no doubt.

Once again, Kate is ashamed to admit that she's relieved that her father isn't here to witness Jess's arrival. If he was truly in the dark about what Rose had done, how would he feel to know that the wife he's loved and adored for forty years has been unfaithful and disloyal in the cruellest of ways.

What had happened to make her mother cheat on the best husband she could have ever wished for? What could he possibly have done to justify her actions?

If he was still here, Kate would ask him. She stares down at her bag on the floor and wonders if she still can.

She hurriedly swings the oversized bucket bag onto the desk and rummages through it, unable to believe that she'd forgotten the letter that she'd taken from her parents' wardrobe. Caught up with an electricity bill and a used tissue, the envelope, that might hold the answers or at least go some way to explaining the situation they now all found themselves in, is stained from the lipstick in her purse that has no lid. The symbolic weight of the blood-red blotted paper sits heavily on Kate's shoulders as her eyes scan the page.

Dear Harry,

I know what I've done is wrong, but you left me with no choice. What else was I supposed to do? We can get through this—I know we can—it's you and me together, with the girls. We're a fam-

*ily and one day, in the not too distant future, I
ask that you find it in your heart to forgive me,
as I will forgive you.*

All my love, as always,
Rose x

It creates more questions than answers, leaving Kate
desperate to know what they needed to forgive each
other for.

It didn't look like it was going to be quite the evening she and Matt had hoped for, but as guilty as she
feels, there are even more important issues she needs
to deal with right now.

I'm going to have to take a rain check on tonight, she
texts, as she heads to the station. *Something's come up.*

She jumps on the tube just as the doors are closing
and finds herself squashed between two rotund men.
Her only air channel is via their armpits, precisely at
her nose height. She balks at the odor emanating from
them and is attempting to turn herself around when
she feels a pull on her skirt. She can make out an
anonymous hand appearing through the bodies, as if
looking to be slapped down. But tracing it to its owner
is like unravelling an eight-player game of Twister.

"'Ere love, d'you wanna seat?" comes a gruff voice
through the limbs. The hand is still tugging on her
skirt, desperately trying to attract her attention. "Move
outta the way and let the lady sit down."

She doesn't know if she's eternally thankful or
mildly perturbed that it's being directed at her. Still,
she smiles gratefully at the man in a baseball cap, who
gets up from his coveted seat and brings the roll-up

from behind his ear into his mouth. Kate can feel the ripple of surprise as the juxtaposition of his manner and his deed seeps into people's consciousness.

You should never judge a book by its cover, her father used to say, and it was a rule she tried to live by, revelling in the pleasant surprises that it often bestowed. But what happens when it's the other way around? What happens when you're taken in by a wolf in sheep's clothing?

Kate rings the doorbell of her parents' home, not knowing if she wants her mother to be there or not. There's no answer, so she lets herself in and calls out, just in case. There's a stillness to the house that is only achieved when it's empty.

She takes the stairs two at a time, taking care to step over the creaky floorboard on the landing—it's a force of habit. She goes into her parents' bedroom and heads straight for the wardrobe door, sliding it silently across. She moves the bag that's standing in front of where she'd found the hat box. She knows, before she can even see, that the box is no longer there.

She frantically searches for it at the back of her mother's shoe racks and delves behind her stacked jumpers. It's got to be here somewhere.

Having exhausted the cupboards, Kate pulls on the handles of the dressing table, knowing that it's nigh on impossible for the box to fit into its shallow drawers. She searches under the bed, before heading to the airing cupboard on the landing, wondering why her mother would find it necessary to move it. She reaches behind the neat piles of towels and runs her hands all around the pipework of the dark cupboard, burning her fingers on the hot water inlet.

"Shit," she says aloud, though she's not sure whether it's because it hurt or because she's frustrated.

The pole hook for the loft hatch stands in the corner and she snatches a glance at the square door in the ceiling of the landing. *Could it be?* Would her mother have gone to the trouble of putting the box up there? And if so, why?

As she slides the ladder down, she remembers how her father had told her many a bedtime story about the loft monster, who everyone feared, yet when they were asleep, he'd come down in the dead of night to make their family's life easier. Kate would give her dad a skeptical sideways glance until the night she'd gone to bed without doing her history project.

"It's too late to do it now," her father had said as he'd tucked his distraught daughter in.

"But I'm going to get a respect task," Kate had cried, unable to understand how she could have forgotten it. "My name will go in the report book."

"Well, maybe it'll teach you to be more organized in future," he'd said.

The next morning, she'd gone down to breakfast to find the most intricate castle, made entirely out of recycled cardboard, sitting on the kitchen table. Foil-covered toilet roll holders had crenels cut into them for turrets and a string-operated drawbridge had been created out of a cereal box.

"Where did this come from?" Kate had asked, with tears of happiness rolling down her cheeks.

Her father had shrugged his shoulders nonchalantly.

"I have no idea," he'd said, flicking his broadsheet newspaper out in front of him. "Must have been the loft monster."

Kate smiles as she climbs the ladder, amazed that she'd fallen for it for so long, but it seems that if it came from her father's mouth, she believed it. The irony weighs heavy on her shoulders.

The rudimentary light casts an ominous glow over the eaves, as Kate carefully makes her way across the beams, bending down low to get into the far corner, where everything seems to be stored. Her back aches as she flashes her phone light into the dark, the need to stand up to full height overwhelming. She can see the hatbox sitting on top of a larger box and she edges her way toward it.

"Hello?" comes her mother's voice from somewhere beyond the hatch.

Kate's head bangs on a beam in panic.

"Hello, who's there?"

Kate considers not answering, but contemplating her position, she doubts a stand-off would work in her favor.

"Mum, it's me," she calls out.

"*Kate?* What on earth are you doing up there?"

She needs to think quickly. She looks at the box under her arm and a carrier bag of tinsel on the floor, wondering whether emptying the letters into a bag would be less conspicuous.

"I'm . . . erm, I'm just looking for the baby clothes you kept of ours," she says. "I won't be long, go back downstairs and put the kettle on."

"I'll do no such thing," says Rose. "What are you thinking, going up there in your condition?"

Damn. "I'm pregnant, not disabled," says Kate.

"Well you shouldn't be doing it, especially if you're alone in the house. Anything could happen. Come on down now. I'll hold the ladder for you."

Kate wonders what would be worse. Taking the letters and incurring the wrath of her mother if she discovers what she's up to, or not taking them and never really knowing the truths they may hold. She feels she's in too far not to at least take the chance.

"I've got you," says Rose, as Kate backs herself down the ladder. "Pass me the bag."

Kate holds on to it unwaveringly.

"Give me the bag," repeats Rose. "You'll be able to hold on better."

There's a tussle as they fight for the innocuous-looking carrier, and it knocks Kate off balance. There're only a few more steps until ground level, but it could still cause some serious damage if she falls. She resignedly gives the bag up, but as Rose pulls it toward her, the letters spill out and fall onto the carpet. The two women look at each other, both seemingly too shocked to speak.

"Wh-what's going on?" says Rose, bending down to pick them up. "What are you doing with these?"

Kate looks at the floor, her cheeks red with shame. "I just . . . I just . . ."

"You just what?" says Rose acerbically.

"I just wanted to . . ."

Rose puts a hand to her head. "What are you looking for, Kate? What are you hoping to find?"

"I just want to know the truth."

"And what are you going to do with it once you have it? When it's not what you want to hear?"

"Why did Dad need to forgive you?" asks Kate, taking the carefully folded letter out of her pocket.

"You had no right," says Rose, reaching out to grab it.

Kate holds it out of her reach.

"Give it to me," says Rose. "It's private."

"What did Dad need to forgive you for?" Kate asks again.

"You need to stop this now, for all our sakes," says Rose.

"Jess is *your* child, Mum. I know that much. But what I don't know is why you gave her up."

Rose takes a sharp breath and holds a hand to her chest. "You need to leave this alone now, Kate."

"I won't stop until I know the truth," says Kate.

"Not even if it destroys this family?" says Rose, staring intently at her daughter. "Not even if it destroys Lauren's family?"

Kate looks at her, taken aback. Of all the people in this sorry state of affairs, her sister is the one least affected.

"Lauren?" asks Kate wearily. "What's *she* got to do with any of this?"

Rose looks away, as if doing so will make it easier not to say anything.

"*What* has Lauren got to do with it?" Kate asks again, her voice rising.

Rose fixes her with a stare. "*I* wasn't the one who was pregnant. *She* was."

36

LAUREN

"Do you feel guilty?" Justin asks, caressing Lauren's hair as she lies on his chest.

It had felt as if the twenty-two years that stood between them last being together and now had evaporated into thin air. It was as if she was sixteen again, with the same hopes and aspirations of an unknown life before her. She'd lost herself in the idea that they could run away together, live somewhere on a remote island, where no one could find them. His question brings her back to earth with a bump.

"Guilty? No. Scared? Yes," she says truthfully.

"Scared?" asks Justin, tipping her chin up to face him. "Of what?"

"Of what I've done and what it means."

"What *does* it mean?" he asks.

She props herself up on her elbow, exposing her breast, and hurriedly pulls at the sheet to cover herself up. Justin gently takes it away again.

"It means that I'm an unfaithful wife and a selfish mother. It means that I'm no better than the husband I've grown to hate."

She bats away the threat of tears. She will not play the victim. This was her decision, and she needs to take ownership of it.

"Has he cheated on you?" asks Justin, tracing his finger down the side of her face.

"I don't know," she says honestly. "But if he has, that's not why I hate him."

"Does he treat you badly?"

She nods. "He's not happy and he takes it out on me."

"Physically?"

"Sometimes, but the emotional abuse is just as hard to take. But I won't let him break me because I have the children to think about—they're my world."

"Would you leave him?" asks Justin earnestly.

She falls back onto the pillow and sighs. "If I was brave enough, but it would break the kids' hearts and I don't think I could ever do that to them."

"I thought that staying with my wife until my youngest left high school was the best thing to do," says Justin. "But in reality, it just prolonged the agony for all of us. The boys have both since told me that they wished we'd called it a day well before we did, to spare them all the arguments and uncomfortable silences."

"They sound like sensible kids," says Lauren.

"They are," smiles Justin. "I'm very lucky."

Lauren sits up and swings her legs onto the floor. "I should go. I need to get home before Simon does."

Justin trails a finger down her spine, making her whole body tingle. "Where does he think you are?"

"He doesn't know I've gone anywhere. He's working in town tonight on a shop fit and I'm hoping that he'll be none the wiser when he comes in."

"Maybe he's not where he says *he* is either," says Justin with raised eyebrows.

Lauren quickly steps into her jumpsuit, not wanting Justin to see any more of her than he has already.

"Do you not think I've seen it all?" he asks, as if reading her mind.

Lauren laughs nervously. "Of me or women in general?"

"Of you," he says, smiling. "Do you think I don't know every inch of your body?"

"That was a long time ago," she says.

"And yet it's still exactly the same."

She's about to give a self-deprecating retort but stops and smiles instead. Maybe Kate's finally getting through to her. The thought of her sister brings with it a fresh surge of hurt and regret, that seems to settle in her chest. She pads barefoot into the living room to find her handbag, aware of Justin watching her every move.

"When can I see you again?" he calls out after her.

She looks at her phone and sees six missed calls from Kate and two from Simon. "Oh my God!" she exclaims, feeling as if the air's being sucked out of her. "Something's happened."

"What's wrong?" asks Justin.

"I need to go," she says, in a blind panic to get her shoes on. "I shouldn't be here."

Justin jumps up out of bed and takes hold of her, pleading with her to look at him. She shakes her head. "I shouldn't have come. What the hell was I thinking?"

"Hey, it'll be okay," he says.

An impending sense of doom bears down on her,

and she can't see straight. "That's easy for you to say," she says, turning away from him.

Justin looks hurt—the bubble they were so happily cocooned in well and truly burst. "Don't leave like this," he says, as she pulls away.

She needs to get away from him. She needs to get away from here, back to her babies—where she belongs.

"This was a mistake," she says brusquely. "A terrible mistake."

"That's not how it felt to me," says Justin, pulling on a pair of sweatpants.

"That's because you're not married, with children who depend on you," she snaps, close to tears. "Who right now need their mum."

"Calm down," he says. "You're jumping to conclusions."

"Look!" she shrieks, showing her phone to him. "Something's happened and I'm not there, because I'm here fucking you."

He looks as if he's been slapped.

"What kind of mother does that make me?"

"This isn't about you and me," he says. "You've got to try and keep the two things separate."

"It's one and the same thing," she says, moving toward the front door. "If Simon finds out about this, he'll kill me, just before he kills you."

"Don't let other people tear us apart again," he pleads. "We've let them do it once and look at what we've missed out on."

She stops at the door and slowly turns around with tears in her eyes. "I'm sorry for what my father did," she cries. "I will never forgive him for lying to you and telling you that I'd had an abortion, but we're deluding ourselves if we believe that we'd still be together today if he hadn't."

Justin looks at her with a vexed brow.

"We were young," she goes on, oblivious to his be-musement. "You were my first love and I will always love you, but it was a mistake to think we could recapture what we had."

"Take whatever time you need to get this all straight in your head," he says. "But know that I'll be here, waiting for you."

She looks at him, knowing that he means it, and if it were possible for a heart to literally break, she's sure she's just felt the first crack. She kisses him long and deep, as if it is the last time she'll ever see him, before opening the door and running down the corridor.

"Lauren," he calls out after her. "It wasn't your father who told me. It was your mother."

37

"Lauren!" Kate shouts through the letterbox, while simultaneously banging on the door with her hand. "Open the door!"

The rage that she had largely managed to contain from her mother's house to here is threatening to boil over. How could they have kept this vital piece of information secret for all this time? While Kate is running all over the country, desperate to uncover the truth and vindicate her father, Lauren and their mother have known from the outset *exactly* who Jess is.

Suddenly everything seems to make perfect sense; their closeness back then and as they were growing up; the colossal rows that Kate would cover her ears to; the seemingly natural pairings of Lauren and Rose versus Kate and Harry. It's all so crystal clear. Except now, instead of believing that the special relationship she'd shared with her father was what he wanted, it now feels as if it was forced, exiled by his wife and firstborn. How could they have done this? How could they have left Jess to a life of foster care and misery? No wonder she had come looking for answers, prepared to take anyone down who came between her and the truth.

Tears of fury run down Kate's face as she continues to slam her palm against the door. "Lauren!" she shouts.

The door opens and Kate almost falls into the woman on the other side. But it's not Lauren.

"Kate! What on earth's wrong?"

"You!" cries Kate. "What the hell are you doing here?"

Jess puts a finger to her lips. "Please, I've just managed to get Jude asleep."

"What?" says Kate. "Are you here alone? Where's Lauren?"

"She's gone out," says Jess. "With Simon."

"You're looking after the children?" says Kate in utter disbelief.

Jess looks at the floor. "Well, yes, I . . ."

Kate gives a hollow laugh. "Oh my God, this is insane. So you know? You're in on it as well? Everybody knows but me, it seems." She swallows the acrid taste in her mouth that makes her feel like she's drowning. "Where is she?" asks Kate, lowering her voice, if not for Jess, then for the children. "Where's Lauren?"

"I . . . I don't know," stutters Jess. "She went out a couple of hours ago. She didn't say where—I assume she was meeting Simon in town."

Kate shakes her head numbly as she calls Lauren for the seventh time.

"What's wrong?" asks Jess. "What's happened?"

"Who *are* you?" hisses Kate, leaning in close.

"I . . . I'm sorry, I don't . . ."

"You're not Jess Linley at all, are you?"

Jess recoils, physically backstepping into the living room as Kate follows her.

"I've been to visit some of your old friends in Bournemouth."

Jess's eyes widen. "You have? W-why?"

"Because I knew something wasn't right. Your story just didn't add up and now I know why."

Jess raises her eyebrows in question, but it doesn't look as though she wants to hear the answer.

"There was no way my dad would have done what everyone's been accusing him of."

"But Harry *was* my dad," says Jess, laughing nervously. "It's been proven by DNA testing."

Kate looks at Jess as if seeing her for the vulnerable young woman she is for the first time.

"They haven't told you, have they?" she asks incredulously, almost to herself.

"What the hell's going on?" cries Lauren as she comes through the door that Kate hadn't yet had a chance to shut.

The anger that Kate feels toward her sister knows no bounds. "How *could* you?" she spits.

"How could I *what*?" says Lauren in a high-pitched voice. "Jess, why haven't you answered my calls? I've been ringing and ringing."

Jess looks from one sister to the other in confusion. "I'm sorry, my phone must be in my bag."

"Where are the children? Are they all right?"

Jess nods. "Yes, of course, everything's fine."

Lauren slumps forward, as all the adrenaline that has put her on high alert drains out of her body.

"Oh my God, I thought something had happened,"

she breathes. "So, what's going on? Why are you here, Kate? Why have you been calling me incessantly?"

"If you'd answered, you'd have found out."

"Please," says Lauren, rubbing at her head. "Just tell me what's going on? Is it Simon? Where is he?"

"Oh," says Jess. "I thought he was with you."

Lauren shakes her head. "Er, no, he's working. I went out with a friend."

"I've just come from Mum's . . ." starts Kate.

Lauren raises her eyebrows expectantly.

Kate throws a sideways glance at Jess. It's taking all of her resolve not to launch into a blistering attack on Lauren, because, despite herself, she doesn't think it's fair on Jess. Then she remembers that Jess hasn't exactly played by the rules either, so the game still feels as if it needs to be won.

"She told me what happened when you were sixteen," Kate says, leaving it hanging there.

"Wh-at?" says Lauren, choking on the word.

"Does Jess know?" shouts Kate, unable to contain herself.

Lauren looks to her pleadingly, as if begging her to stop. "Does Jess know what?"

"That you've uploaded Emmy's DNA instead of your own?"

"What?" shrieks Lauren. She's a good liar, Kate has to give her that, but there is no denying the truth now—it all makes perfect sense. "Why would I do that?"

"Because it would be the only way to show Jess as your half sister when she's not."

Jess looks to Lauren and back to Kate with a manic expression. "What are you saying?" she says, her voice verging on the hysterical. "What's going on?"

"Lauren has used her own child's DNA to prove a match with yours."

Lauren shakes her head as she looks at Jess imploringly, reaching toward her with her hands. "Don't listen to her. She doesn't know what she's talking about."

"So you were prepared to drag Dad's good name and reputation through the mud, inventing a past he never had, all to protect your own."

"What is going on?" asks Jess, her face etched with confusion.

"Are you going to tell her, or am I?"

"Tell me what?" cries Jess.

Kate looks to Lauren, who merely shrugs her shoulders, leaving Kate with no choice. "You're not Harry's daughter," she says to Jess, before laughing sarcastically and shaking her head. "My God, you're not even Rose's."

"Will someone please tell me what the hell is going on?" says Jess.

Kate raises her eyebrows at Lauren, giving her one last chance. Her sister remains silent.

"You're *her* daughter," Kate says, as Lauren's eyes widen.

Jess's head swivels toward Lauren, her mouth opening and closing, but no words come out.

"You . . . you can't possibly think that's true," stutters Lauren, looking between them.

"You were pregnant at sixteen," barks Kate, her anger at the injustice her father's suffered so close to the surface. "Jess is twenty-two, you're thirty-eight. You do the maths."

"You honestly think I'd get Jess here under false

pretenses? That I'd palm her off as Dad's, when all along I've known she was mine?"

"If you wanted to be reunited with Jess and have her in your life, but didn't want to admit to the part you played in bringing her into the world, then yes. I think you'd be capable of anything."

Jess falls down onto the sofa, agog, as she watches Kate and Lauren battle it out. "Is that . . . is that true?"

"Of course it's not!" exclaims Lauren. "Why would you even think I would do something like that?"

"To get back at Dad," says Kate, brusquely. "To get back at me. All the while keeping your secret safe."

Lauren breaks down, clamping a hand to her mouth. "I can't believe you'd think I was capable of that."

Kate's breath catches in her throat as she contemplates for the first time the consequences of what she's done. A tear springs to her eye at the thought of her relationship with Lauren never recovering.

"I don't know what *anyone's* capable of anymore," says Kate.

38

LAUREN

"I don't even know what to say," whispers Lauren, unable to understand how she's found herself in this situation. How her own mother could have betrayed her so badly.

"You could start by telling us both why you lied," says Kate. "How you could deny Jess knowing who her birth mother is."

"I'm not her mother," Lauren says, wiping her eyes with a tissue. She turns to Jess. "I'm not *your* mother."

"How do we know that?" shouts Kate. "How do we know that this hasn't all been worked to your advantage?"

Lauren looks her in the eye, her bottom lip wobbling. "Because I had an abortion."

Just saying it out loud threatens to break Lauren. They're words she's never uttered and now that she has, she stands there as if waiting for the Devil to commit her to hell.

"I had an abortion," she says again, tearfully.

"But Mum implied—" starts Kate.

The mention of her mother makes Lauren's insides

feel as if they're twisting against each other, making it difficult to breathe. "Mum has implied a lot of things," she says, not wishing to embellish, because if she does, she's going to have to admit to where she's been.

The shock of Justin's parting words had stopped her in her tracks, midway down the corridor of his apartment block.

"What did you say?" she had said, turning slowly around to face him.

"I said: it wasn't your father who told me that you'd had an abortion, it was your mother."

Lauren had shaken her head. "That can't be right. Mum told me that she would support me with whatever decision I made. And that *wasn't* what I'd chosen to do." Tears came to her eyes. "I wanted our baby, Justin, really wanted it."

"So what happened?" he'd asked, pulling her back toward him, the pair of them standing on the threshold of his flat.

She had forced herself to go back in time, to a place she's never dared revisit.

"When I told them I was pregnant, I knew the reaction I was going to get," she'd said. "No parent wants to be told that their sixteen-year-old daughter is pregnant. But out of the two of them, Dad was the one who seemed to take it better, at least at first. It wasn't until a couple of days later that he sat me down and told me that he thought an abortion would be the best option."

"And what was Rose's stance during this time?" Justin had asked.

"Dad was supposedly the spokesperson for both of them, but she told me that she just wanted me to be happy, and would gladly support whatever decision I made, but feared it had been taken out of my hands."

"By your dad?" asked Justin.

"Yes." Lauren nodded.

"Well, it was definitely your mother who called me," said Justin. "I will never forget it—just the day before, we'd sat in your room and decided that we were going to keep it. You even called me the next night to tell me how much you loved me."

Lauren had nodded again, remembering.

"But in that short window of time, you'd already got rid of it—well, that's what Rose said anyway."

"But that just doesn't make any sense," Lauren had replied. "That only happened *after* you told me that you didn't love me anymore and wouldn't take my calls."

"I wouldn't return your calls *because* you'd had the abortion. I was told you'd done it without me, that you'd made the decision by yourself."

"But you know I would never have done that," cried Lauren.

"Well then your mother has a lot to answer for," Justin had said.

"I don't care what Mum implied," Lauren says now. "I'll talk to her in my own time about what she's done, but all you need to know now is that Jess is Dad's daughter."

"Lauren saw him with me," pipes up Jess, and Lauren wishes she hadn't.

"Sorry, what?" asks Kate.

"When I was a baby, Lauren saw him walking me in my pram, with my mum."

Kate turns to Lauren as a searing heat rises up her neck. "Did you?"

The question is asked with such intensity that Lauren feels claustrophobic. She looks to Jess, who is urging her on with unbridled enthusiasm, and she is suddenly aware of the very different answers the two women in front of her want to hear. It pains her that she can't please them both.

She nods, hoping that no one will ask for clarification.

"And you've waited until now to tell me?" asks Kate.

"I didn't want to hurt you," says Lauren.

Kate lets out a sardonic laugh. "So, you decide to go out and dig up the past by inviting Jess to turn up at our parents' house not even a year after we lost Dad. Who were you thinking of *then,* Lauren? Because it certainly wasn't me. And it certainly wasn't Mum."

"Mum already knew," says Lauren quietly.

"What?" snaps Kate.

"I told Mum at the time," says Lauren, not supposing it matters much anymore who knew what, and when. "When I saw them together."

"So, Rose knew your dad was having an affair?" says Jess, her voice high.

Lauren nods. "I told her what I'd seen."

"So, she *knew* about me?" ask Jess.

"I didn't know what it meant—I don't think either of us did, until now. But yes, I told her I'd seen him with a woman and a baby."

"And it didn't occur to you to talk to me about *any* of this?" chokes Kate. "Before a girl turns up on the doorstep claiming to be my half sister."

"I'm sorry," says Lauren. "I should have told you, but none of this was done to hurt you. I was, selfishly, only thinking about myself, wondering whether I *did* have a brother or sister out there."

"Am I not enough?" asks Kate.

Lauren looks at her, exasperated. "Let's face it, we've not been close for a long time. If we're honest, our problems go back to before I had Noah. I thought having children would bring us together, but it's only served to push us further apart."

"Did you ever think why that may have been?" asks Kate.

Lauren *knows* what it is, but needs to word it carefully. She doesn't want it to come out wrong and make matters worse. "Metaphorically, we just live poles apart," she says. "I don't think you can relate to what it's like having a kid because your life is so carefree and glamorous. You're able to flit off to LA at the drop of a hat to hang out with really cool people, and visiting your sister in her terraced house on the outskirts of London doesn't feature very highly on your list. And I get that, I really do, but how do you think that makes *me* feel?" *There.* She's said what's been eating her up for years and it feels surprisingly good to get it out.

Kate rubs at her head. "You honestly think that I look forward to another long-haul flight to go and interview a reality star whose only talent is displayed on a 'leaked' sex video? And while I sit there, having my intelligence insulted and battling mind-numbing jetlag, my husband is stuck thousands of miles away, meaning any minute chance that we have of conceiving that month is ruined. All I've ever wanted to be is you, but do you have any idea how hard that is?" She's crying by the end of the sentence.

Lauren breathes in sharply at Kate's admission. "I'm sorry," she says, somehow unable to think of anything more adequate. "I had no idea."

"Well, it doesn't matter anymore, because after three years of IVF, we're finally pregnant."

Lauren feels winded. She had always assumed that Kate was concentrating on her career, happy to overlook any maternal urges that she may have had in favor of the next celebrity scoop. Her heart aches at how wrong she'd got it.

"Oh my goodness, that's wonderful!" says Lauren, going to Kate, who despite her frosty expression, hugs her back tightly. "I'm sorry that it's been so tough for you both."

"Congratulations," says Jess, awkwardly.

Lauren turns to Jess. "This is all my fault. If it weren't for me, then we wouldn't be in this mess."

"If it weren't for you, I'd have no idea who I was," says Jess quietly.

"You're not exactly winning at that though, are you?" says Kate. "You seem to be getting further away from the truth with every passing day."

"Meaning?" asks Lauren,

"Her real name is Harriet Oakley," says Kate, soberly. "She's been in foster care most of her life and didn't go to university, despite claiming she did."

Jess's eyes fill with tears as Lauren stares at her, open-mouthed.

"That's not possible," says Lauren eventually. "Jess's *flatmate* is called Harriet Oakley. Jess was adopted by a loving family. Weren't you?"

Jess looks down at the floor.

"Weren't you?" cries Lauren.

"I . . . I'm sorry," sniffs Jess.

"What?" chokes Lauren. "But I thought—"

"I wanted you to think I had the perfect life," cries Jess. "I didn't want you to feel sorry for me or think that I came here for any other reason than to get to know my family."

"But you said your parents—" starts Lauren.

"I know, and I'm sorry for lying to you."

"Everything she's told you is a lie," says Kate, not getting as much satisfaction from revealing the truth as she thought she would.

"Is that true?" asks Lauren, dumbfounded, more hurt than angry.

Jess nods.

"So Harriet Oakley is your real name?"

"It's my adopted name," says Jess. "The Oakleys adopted me when I was six and I lived with them for a year or two before going back into foster care."

"Why did you change your name to come up here?"

"Because I wanted a new start," says Jess. "I wanted to wipe the slate clean of my old life and start afresh."

"But you can't just make qualifications up and cite universities that you never went to," says Kate. "That's fraud."

"How did you know to go to Bournemouth University?" asks Jess.

"Because I'm a journalist," says Kate. "When I smell a rat, I tend to follow its trail."

"And what did you find?" asks Jess.

"Let's just say you're leaving plenty of victims in

your wake. Us, your employers . . . we're all being fed a pack of lies."

"I just wanted the chance of a new life."

"I don't know why you would have lied," says Lauren. "What difference do you think it would have made to us . . . to me?"

"I wanted you to like me. I thought that if I told you the truth, you wouldn't think I was good enough. You've both got such amazing lives—your jobs, husbands, children—your worlds are perfect. It was going to be hard enough to endear myself to you as it was, without the added stigma of a foster-care background and the most basic of schooling. I wanted you to think I was as personable and educated as you—not from the wrong side of the tracks."

There's a tension in Lauren's neck that's working its way up into her head, setting every muscle alight. She can't believe that just an hour ago she was lying in Justin's arms, thinking the only problem she had was wondering how she was going to keep away from the only man she'd ever loved. Back then, even that had seemed insurmountable, but how she wished now that it was her only problem.

"Look, it's late," says Lauren, holding her hands up in defeat. "I think we should take some time out."

"But what happens now?" asks Jess forlornly. "Now you know the truth."

"Nothing's changed," says Lauren softly, taking a stray piece of hair and tucking it behind Jess's ear, like only a mother would.

"But will you still help me find my mother? She might still be out there."

Lauren can feel Kate bristling beside her. "I'll do everything I can to help you, but right now I need to speak to Kate."

Jess looks at her, wide-eyed. "Will you call me in the morning?" she asks, almost inaudibly.

"Yes," says Lauren.

"Promise," asks Jess, sounding like a little girl.

Lauren's heart feels like it might break. "I promise."

39

KATE

"So, where were you tonight?" asks Kate. They may not be as close as they used to be, but Kate knows her sister well enough to know when she's lying.

Lauren goes into the kitchen and comes back with a glass of water for Kate and a half-drunk bottle of red wine. She pours herself a generous glass and slumps down on the sofa.

Kate looks at her. "Lauren, I know you. There's no way you would have left the children with a virtual stranger unless it was an emergency. So what were you doing?" She raises her eyebrows, waiting for an answer.

Lauren takes a large glug of wine. "I need you to tell me exactly what Mum said," she says. "About me, about the pregnancy . . . because I just don't understand why that would come up now."

Kate looks at her, unable to believe that Lauren could have carried such a heavy secret around with her for so long. "And I don't understand how you could have kept that to yourself for all this time."

"It's been hard," says Lauren, "my biggest regret.

But having my three has helped me come to terms with it."

"So Mum and Dad were against you keeping it?"

"Dad certainly was, and Mum too, apparently."

"How do you mean?"

Lauren drains her glass before answering. "It doesn't matter—that's a conversation for another time."

"Did you talk to Dad about how you felt?" asks Kate. "Did you tell him you wanted to keep it?"

"I tried, and he tried to listen." Lauren laughs scornfully. "And for a while, I really thought he was getting it. He was shocked, of course—we all were, but he told me that although it wasn't what he had wanted or planned for me, once I'd thought about the consequences, he'd support my decision."

"So what changed?" asks Kate.

Lauren shrugs. "I honestly don't know—I'll never know. But all of a sudden, it went from being what felt like my decision, to me doing what he wanted with no questions asked."

"That doesn't sound like Dad," offers Kate gently, noticing the tears that are forming in Lauren's eyes. "He was reasonable, compassionate . . ."

Lauren snorts derisorily. "You and I had very different relationships with him."

"But you must know that that was who he truly was," says Kate.

"Maybe the man *I* saw was the real him," says Lauren bluntly, looking straight at Kate. "And the version *you* saw was the fake, because for a good few years after that, I only remember a controlling man who always got his own way."

Kate can't believe what she's hearing; it's so far removed from the man she knew.

"He'd stop me from going out," Lauren goes on. "Dictate who I was allowed to be friends with, forced me to go to sixth form when I really didn't want to . . ."

"But . . ." starts Kate, thinking it all sounds like a dad who cared, rather than one who didn't.

Lauren's lips thin as she empties the bottle into her glass. "He even put me in an institution for two weeks."

Kate's addled brain stops dead in its tracks. "He did *what*?"

"Yep, he took it upon himself to admit me to residential care."

"What for?"

Lauren shifts in her chair. "He thought I had an eating disorder."

Kate recalls a period when she was fourteen or fifteen and Lauren going away for a while. She thought she'd gone on holiday with friends—in fact, she's sure that's what their mother had told her. "And did you?" she asks.

"I had an unhealthy relationship with food for a bit, but I didn't need to go into hospital—it could have been dealt with at home."

Kate is beginning to see a pattern emerging of a scared, confused and unwell young woman, and a father who was doing his best to protect her. Though she can understand how their father's duty of care could have been portrayed by Lauren as Machiavellian.

"Did you ever wonder . . ." she starts, knowing she has to tread lightly if she's to get her point across before Lauren shuts her down, ". . . if Mum might have been the driving force?"

Lauren pulls herself up, Kate notices, and looks at her, suddenly alert.

"How do you mean?"

"Well, for as many reasons as you didn't always get along with Dad, I've never felt as close to Mum."

"Perhaps it was just naturally geared up that way," offers Lauren.

"Perhaps," admits Kate. "But I'm wondering if she had more control than we thought—now I know what I know."

Lauren leans in. "Go on," she presses.

Kate remembers back to the argument she witnessed when she was younger, the context of which is only becoming clear to her now. "We were in the New Forest . . ."

Lauren furrows her brow.

"It must have been when it was all kicking off about the baby."

Lauren nods and looks at the tattered tissue in her hands.

Kate leans her elbows on the table and holds her fingers at her temples, desperately trying to delve into the deepest corners of her mind to recall what happened next. The outline is there, she just needs to fill in the detail. "We were in the house and you stormed out."

"That's when Justin and I had decided to keep it," says Lauren.

Hearing the boy's name takes Kate back. "Mum and Dad rowed after you'd left," she says. "She accused him of not doing enough."

"Enough what?" asks Lauren.

"I don't know," says Kate. "I thought she'd meant he'd not done enough to stop you from leaving. She said something like, 'if you don't put a stop to this, I will not be held accountable for my actions.'"

Lauren screws her face up. "She must have been telling him to stop treating me like a child, to stop trying to control me."

She *could* have been, but now it doesn't ring quite true to Kate. "I wonder if she was talking about you and Justin—that Dad hadn't done enough to discourage you from seeing him, or . . ." She trails off, not wanting to state what appears to be blatantly obvious.

Lauren fixes her with a hard stare. "Or . . . ?"

"Or maybe she thought he hadn't done enough to stop you going ahead with the pregnancy."

"But that doesn't make any sense," says Lauren. "She told me that she was sorry but there was nothing she could do. She said that Dad had made his mind up and that was the end of it."

Kate's brain feels like it's banging against the inside of her skull. "But after she'd gone to find you, I found Dad crying. He was in the study; you remember that room at the end of the corridor with the big open fire."

Lauren nods. "What was he crying about?"

"He just said that he was sad that we weren't his little girls anymore. That all he'd ever wanted was for us to be happy."

"It was probably his guilty conscience," says Lauren, but Kate shakes her head.

"Come on, had you ever seen him cry before?"

"No."

"They were proper tears, Lauren. He was a broken man."

"Well, it wasn't my fault that he couldn't live with his decision."

"I don't think it was his decision," says Kate, looking at Lauren. "I think Mum was telling him that he had to put a stop to it."

Lauren shakes her head. "I think it's more likely she had found out about his affair. It was all happening around that time."

Kate takes a sip from her glass of water, wishing that it was a magic potion that would return her family to how it used to be. Somehow, it was easier to get along when all of their secrets were still hidden.

"Had you told her you'd seen him with another woman by then?" she asks.

Lauren thinks before answering. "No, that was after the summer holidays when I was in sixth form."

"Why would you do that?" asks Kate, unable to keep the accusatory tone from her voice. "When you had no idea what was really going on?"

"Because he'd just played the hand of God," cries Lauren. "How was it fair that he'd taken my baby away from me, then had a baby of his own behind our backs? How come he got to play happy families, when he'd left a trail of destruction behind him?"

"What did Mum say when you told her?"

"She fobbed me off and told me that it wasn't what it seemed," says Lauren. "That she knew the woman."

"Well there you go then," says Kate, breathing out her relief. "How much more proof do you need, to know that Dad wouldn't cheat? On Mum or us."

"Jess is proven to be our half sister by her DNA," says Lauren sympathetically.

"I'm running my own DNA test," says Kate.

Lauren looks at her quizzically. "What for?"

"Just to be sure," says Kate. "I'm waiting for the results as we speak."

"Well, if you've sent off Dad's DNA, hoping that it's not going to be a match to Jess, then I'm afraid you're going to be bitterly disappointed."

Kate looks Lauren in the eyes. "It's not Dad's I'm testing, it's Mum's."

"Have you gone completely mad?" gasps Lauren. "You can't honestly think that's a possibility?"

"I've thought it was a possibility from the minute Jess turned up," says Kate, unapologetically. "That's why I got so mad when you were insisting she was Dad's, aside from the simple fact that I didn't want her to be. You may have seen stuff, but I saw stuff too."

Lauren swallows hard. "You really think Mum's hiding something?"

"Yes," says Kate forthrightly. "I just don't know what."

40

"Kate, what's going on?" asks Matt, when she eventually gets home. "Even a Hollywood drugs bust wouldn't have kept you at the office for *this* long." He turns down the volume on the TV and sits forward on the couch, holding a bottle of beer.

"I've been with Lauren and Jess," she says.

Matt puts the beer down on the table and looks at her earnestly.

"And how did that go?"

"She wants to find her mother."

"I know," says Matt. "She wrote the feature I told you about."

"I knew it," says Kate. "As soon as you told me she had a lead on a DNA piece, I knew it was going to be her own story."

"Well, you had more information at your disposal than I did. I've only just been made aware this afternoon that it's her own story she pitched."

Kate's sure her heart's stopped beating. "You can't run it!"

Matt gets up and goes toward her. "I realize that. It

was scheduled for tomorrow, but I've pulled it. I noticed *your* scoop didn't run today, either." He raises his
eyebrows knowingly, but then smiles gently and takes
Kate's hands in his.

She gives an apologetic shrug. "I'm sorry . . ."

"It's okay," he says, pulling her into him and kissing
the top of her head. "I understand why you did it, but
I wish you'd told me the truth." He attempts to laugh.
"We could have sent the entire nation out looking for
Jess's mother."

Kate coughs as a strangled snigger catches in her
throat. "We already know who Jess's mother is."

Matt cocks his head back in astonishment. "We do?"

"Yep," she says, as her phone rings in her pocket.

She sees that it's Nancy from DS Labs and holds
her hand up. "I've got to take this," she says to Matt.

"Hi, Kate, it's Nancy. I've just got the preliminary
results back in."

Kate holds her breath, knowing from experience
that preliminary will be good enough. She'd commis-
sioned several DNA tests on behalf of women who al-
leged they'd had a child with a celebrity. An allegation
was a good enough story, but having the proof was
sensational; well, it would have been if it weren't for
the fact that, every time, the results proved otherwise.

"O-kay," says Kate, hesitantly. Her heart's pounding as the ramifications of what Nancy's about to say
reverberate around her brain.

"So, the initial findings are . . ."

Kate wishes she'd hurry up, but at the same time
doesn't want her to say what she's about to say.

". . . that there's *no* match."

The words swim as Kate tries to put them in the

order she wants them. If she could lose the "no" and put an "a" in its place, it would make all the difference.

"Are you . . . are you absolutely sure?" she stutters, shocked by the strength of feeling that is pooling in her intestines and flowing through her veins—unable to comprehend how it could make such a difference to know that it's her dad who has fathered a child, rather than her mother who has given birth to one. How had it felt easier to accept the latter?

"99.9 percent sure," says Nancy. "But as soon as the comprehensive results are in, I'll send them over."

"Th-thanks," says Kate, ending the call and looking at Matt numbly.

"What is it?" he asks.

"Maybe you *should* run Jess's article after all."

41

LAUREN

Lauren can't sleep. She looks at the time on her phone again, its digits goading her as they move ever closer to dawn. Her eyes are heavy, but every time they close, she pictures herself lying in Justin's arms, wondering how on earth she could have done it. As wonderful as it was, she's a married mother of three small children who depend on her. They deserve a mother they can rely on, not a woman who is prepared to leave them with someone she clearly knows nothing about so she can make a pathetic attempt to recapture her youth.

She feels sick as she thinks of the chaos she's wreaked by bringing Jess into the family. She'd naively thought it would be a good thing, that finding her would bring them closer together, yet it seems it's only torn them even further apart.

She catches her breath as she hears Simon come home from his night shift. His heavy work boots scuff the flimsy linoleum as he no doubt makes himself a hot drink in the kitchen. She only saw him a few hours ago, but so much has changed in that time. *She's* changed in that time.

"What's going on?" he says gruffly as he walks into their dark bedroom.

Lauren's under the duvet, pretending to be asleep, but she's sure he must be able to hear her heart hammering.

"Lauren!" he barks.

"What?" she says croakily, her throat dry. "What's the matter?"

"What the hell went on last night?"

Every muscle in her body tenses as she wonders what part he's talking about.

"What do you mean?" she says. "Nothing, why?"

Her mind races. He can't possibly know.

"Where were you?"

It's as if she's been hit by a stun gun, paralyzing everything but her raging thoughts. "I was here," she says, with a nervous laugh. "Where else?" She stays put under the duvet, not brave enough, or incapable perhaps, of coming out.

Simon snaps the light on and sits down heavily on her side of the bed.

"What's going on?" she says, shielding her eyes.

He taps on his phone and holds it to her ear. The message plays out in stereo around the room.

"Simon, it's Kate. Is Lauren with you? I need to talk to her urgently and she's not picking up her mobile or the landline. I'm on my way round to your place now, but if she's with you, can you get her to call me back?"

Lauren wants to snatch the phone from him and make it stop.

"So, I'll ask again; where were you?"

"I . . . I popped round to Mum's," she stutters.

"So why didn't you answer your phone?" he asks, staring at her intently.

She forces herself to come up with something feasible, but she can't think quickly enough. "I didn't even hear it ring. It must have been on silent."

Simon reaches for Lauren's phone on the bedside table and attempts to bring it to life with her passcode. She flinches as *Try Again* lights up the screen, knowing that he's going to be more suspicious of her changing it than anything he might find. She'd taken great care to delete any messages between her and Justin.

Try Again.

Try Again.

She feels sick as he turns to look at her. "What the fuck's going on?"

She sits up and holds her hand out, hoping he doesn't notice it shaking. "I changed it," she says.

"Why would you need to do that?"

"Because Noah knew my PIN," she says, as light-heartedly as she can. "He was playing games on it whenever I turned my back." She wants to say, *It's none of your damn business. It's my phone and you've got no right to look at it*, but she knows there's nothing to gain by riling him when he's in this mood.

"So what's the new code?" he asks, still holding on to it.

"Give it here and I'll do it."

His eyes narrow. "How about you tell me what it is, and *I'll* do it."

"Fine," she says. "1921."

His face flashes with satisfaction as the phone lights up, before clouding over again. "You've got eight missed calls from Kate and five from me."

Shit, that's something she hadn't cleaned up. "Really? I had no idea."

"What time did you get back from your mum's?"

"Erm, I don't know," she says. "Around eight, but then Kate caught up with me here, so it's all good."

He's still looking intently at the phone, making Lauren's nerves jangle. "What was so urgent?" he asks without looking up.

"Eh?"

He turns to face her. "What did Kate need to talk to you about so urgently?"

She slides back down the bed. "Oh, it was just something about Jess," she says, faking a yawn. "She's got a bee in her bonnet—you know Kate."

"So what time did Kate come here then?"

His questioning makes her feel as if she's on the stand, in front of a judge and jury. She needs to tread carefully because like the best of lawyers, Simon's good at catching her out.

"I can't remember," she says. "Probably about nine-ish."

Simon's brow furrows. "That's odd, because she left that message on my phone at nine thirty."

An overwhelming heat engulfs Lauren's body, instantaneously making every pore prickle with sweat.

"And she last tried you at ten," Simon goes on. "So that doesn't add up, does it?"

"I'm tired," says Lauren, bringing the duvet up over her head. "Can we talk about the semantics in the morning?"

"It *is* morning," says Simon, pulling the cover off her. "And I want to know where you were."

"I already told you, I was at Mum's."

"Until ten o'clock?" asks Simon.

"I can't remember the exact timings, but if that's when Kate last called, then yes."

"So you took the kids with you?" asks Simon.

He knows she would never keep the children up that late. "No," she says hesitantly. "I left them here . . . with Jess."

Simon leaps up from the bed. "You left my kids with a fucking stranger?"

"She's not a stranger, she's my sister."

"All to go to your mother's?" Simon's jaw tightens as he shakes his head. "Nah, I'm not buying it."

Lauren swallows hard as she backs up onto the headboard.

"Do you know where I think you really went?" he says. "I think you went and covered that shift."

"What?" exclaims Lauren, wondering what on earth he's talking about.

"The shift that woman was going on about yesterday," he goes on. "Sheila, or whatever her name was."

Lauren didn't know it was possible to feel relief and an impending sense of dread at the same time. She weighs up which answer will get him off her back faster.

"I . . . I didn't want you to get mad," she says, seeing a way out. "It was only for a few hours and I thought we could do with the money."

"Why do you think I'm out all night? Providing for my family."

"Yes, I know," says Lauren, reaching out and holding on to his arm. "And I'm very grateful, but it doesn't hurt to have a little bit extra, does it?"

He falls heavily back onto the bed. "I don't want you having to work. Your place is here at home with the kids."

She nods enthusiastically in agreement. "You're right, and I'm sorry." She hadn't realized she could be so manipulative.

"I'm sorry I woke you," he says, suddenly conciliatory. "I was just worried."

"That's okay," she says. "I may as well jump in the shower before Jude wakes up."

She sees her phone on the bed, but there's no good excuse to take it into the bathroom with her, so she leaves it where it is.

She showers as quickly as she can, sticking her head out the door to listen for any sounds from the children as soon as she's finished. Even with Simon in the house, she's always felt the children are her responsibility. She doesn't know if that's the innate instinct of a mother or if it's the way Simon *makes* her feel.

There's total silence, though, and she revels in the last few minutes of peace before her day becomes overrun with the physical demands of three children. However, she fears it may be the incessant noise of her thoughts that will be her greatest distraction today. If she could just stop thinking about the way Justin's touch had set her skin alight, how his lips on hers had felt like the most natural thing in the world. *Stop!* It is done, but it must *never* be repeated. It was a mistake, and she now needs to focus on her family and husband, who is trying *so* hard to keep their boat afloat.

As soon as she banishes Justin from her mind, the next thought gets in line, desperate for her attention. She roughly blow-dries her hair, her hands working ever more feverishly as she thinks about the pact she made with her mother and father all those years ago. The three of them vowed never to talk of it again, not with each other, and least of all with anyone else. As far as she knows, her dad had kept his promise, but her mum had broken hers in the cruellest way. How *could* she? Lauren won't let this slide. She can't. She'll go round there, as soon as she's dropped Noah at school.

She'd thought Simon would go to sleep for a couple of hours, but their bedroom's empty when she walks back in; so Jude *did* wake up after all. The black jumpsuit that she'd worn last night hangs prominently in her open wardrobe, prickling her conscience. She tucks it out of sight, knowing she'll never be able to wear it again.

Stepping into her more usual attire of leggings and baggy T-shirt, she hastily makes the bed, lifting the duvet into the air. A dull thud hits the floor and she instinctively knows it's her phone and groans. It's landed face down and Lauren turns it over slowly, grimacing at the potential cost of a replacement. But when she sees what's written on the screen, no amount of money could possibly repair the damage caused.

42

KATE

The headline on the double-page spread in the *Echo* reads:

I Found My Sister, But Who's My Mother?

"It looks good," says Matt as he stands against the kitchen counter, spooning cornflakes into his mouth.

Seeing Jess's picture staring out at her from Matt's laptop unnerves Kate, and she swallows the doubt that she's done the right thing by letting him run it.

"Are you absolutely sure you want to do this?" he'd asked late last night.

Kate had thought about it for a few seconds longer, knowing that once she gave him the go-ahead, he'd push the button to go to press. But they'd both decided that if they couldn't prevent the fire, they could at least try to control the flames.

"For better or worse, we now know Jess is my father's daughter," she'd said resignedly. "She deserves to know who her mother is and hopefully this will find her."

Kate's phone rings now and she watches as it vibrates away from her on the worktop.

"It's your sister," says Matt.

"Uh-oh," says Kate, taking a deep breath. "Here we go."

She'd thought about ringing Lauren last night to warn her that Jess's story was running, but it was late, and besides, she didn't think she'd have a problem with it. In fact, Kate imagined that Lauren would be thrilled that steps were being made to help find Jess's mother. After all, hadn't that been her intention all along?

"Kate! Kate!" Lauren is screaming down the phone. "He's taken the kids. I don't know what to do!"

Kate looks at Matt, wide-eyed.

"What do you mean?" she says, feeling as if the breath is being sucked out of her.

"Simon! He's taken the kids and I don't know where he is."

"Are you at home?" asks Kate, running into the bedroom and reaching for the first pair of sweatpants she can find.

"Yes," sobs Lauren. "I don't know what to do."

Kate slings a T-shirt on. "Okay, stay where you are. I'm on my way."

Matt wordlessly falls into line with her as she grabs her car keys and makes her way out of the flat.

Not surprisingly, Lauren's a wreck when they reach her ten minutes later, collapsing into Kate's arms as soon as she walks through the door.

"What's happened?" she asks. "What's going on?"

"He's gone, and taken the children with him," cries Lauren.

Kate steers Lauren onto the very sofa they were sitting on last night. How can so much change in such a short space of time?

"But why?" asks Kate. "When did he leave?"

Lauren passes her sister her phone and sobs even harder.

"Do you want me to call the police?" asks Matt.

Kate shakes her head as she reads the texts on Lauren's phone.

Lauren: Happy I could help out last night
Sheila: Help out? I'm not sure that's what I'd call it! I can't stop thinking about you. Hope everything was okay at home?
Lauren: I need to see you again
Sheila: You have no idea how happy that makes me. When?

"I'm sorry, I don't understand," says Kate, reading the messages over again. "Who's Sheila? And what's she got to do with Simon and the kids?"

Lauren's head falls into her hands. "Sheila's Justin," she says.

Kate's mind feels frazzled. "*Your* Justin?"

Lauren nods.

"You've been *seeing* him?" Kate asks incredulously, as the pieces begin to fall into place.

"Just twice," says Lauren quietly.

"So that's where you were last night? And now Simon's seen your messages?"

"They're not my messages. He was on to me this morning, when he got back from work, and while I was in the shower, he must have started this chat, checking that my story stacked up. I told him that Sheila was a midwife and I'd helped out on the ward last night."

"Shit!"

"And by the time I'd come out of the bathroom, he'd gone, and taken the children with him."

"I assume you've tried ringing him," says Matt.

Lauren nods and wipes her nose with a tissue. "I don't know what he'll do. I don't know what he's capable of."

"What do you mean?" asks Kate, taken aback.

"You don't know him." Lauren sounds broken. "He has a temper—that he struggles to control."

"Are you saying you're *frightened* of him?"

Lauren nods.

Kate is lost for words. How did she not know that her sister had been enduring this?

"If he's so much as laid a hand on you . . ." says Matt, his nostrils flaring.

Lauren looks at the floor, almost as if she's ashamed. It makes Kate hate Simon all the more.

"Lauren, why haven't you spoken to me about this before?" asks Kate. "I thought you were happy. I thought you had the perfect family."

"It's funny what we both thought the other one had," says Lauren.

It's a flippant remark, but as the two women look at one another, as if seeing each other properly for the first time, the truth of Lauren's words burrows deep into Kate's psyche.

"So what are we going to do?" asks Matt, breaking the spell. "I can't see that the police are going to do much at the moment. For all they know he's a dad who's just taken his kids out for an hour."

There's a screech of brakes from outside and they all freeze, looking at each other. Matt is the first to move toward the front door, throwing it open and leaving it swinging on its hinges.

"Be careful," says Kate, going after him.

"Where's my wife?" Simon shouts, as he gets out of the car and strides up to Matt, their noses just inches apart.

Kate puts a hand on Matt's arm for reassurance, but her insides have turned to jelly.

"How about we all calm down and sort this out?" says Matt.

"Calm down?" shouts Simon. "My wife's been sleeping around and you want me to calm down?"

Kate can see the children in the car and inches her way toward them, closely followed by Lauren, whose breath she can feel on her neck. She admires her sister's restraint. If it were *her* kids, she'd be like a screaming banshee, but Lauren obviously knows the best way to handle her husband. It pains Kate that she's clearly had years of practice.

"Come inside," says Matt, taking hold of Simon's arm. "Let's talk about this."

Simon shakes him off and moves toward Lauren, his eyes blazing. Kate pulls herself up and stands tall between them, blocking his way.

"How long's it been going on?" he shouts. "Did you honestly think you were going to get away with it? That I wouldn't find out?"

He takes a step closer and Kate instinctively puts a hand across her stomach.

"Who *is* he?" Simon yells. "Tell me who he is, because I'll fucking kill him."

He raises his right arm and Kate can feel, in slow motion, the rush of air as he swings it down. She ducks, pushing Lauren away, and flinches as she waits for contact to be made. With her eyes squeezed shut, the split second feels like an eternity, not knowing who he's going to strike or where. Another whoosh and a slap of skin, but it's not hers, it's Matt's, as he takes hold of Simon's forearm just before it crashes down on top of her.

"I'm gonna kill him, then you," shouts Simon, as Matt pulls his arm behind his back and frogmarches him into the house.

"Mummy," cries Noah from inside the car.

Lauren pulls open the door and holds the little boy to her. "It's okay," she says with tears rolling down her face. "Everything's going to be okay."

Kate looks across the backseat to see Jude and Emmy sleeping, blissfully unaware that their parents' marriage has just ended. Though if the truth be told, it sounds like it was over long ago.

"You can't stay here," says Kate, rubbing her hand up and down Lauren's back.

"I know . . . I'll go to Mum's for a bit—wait for the dust to settle."

"I'll come with you," says Kate.

"No, I'll be fine, you need to get to work."

"I'm sure the front line of show business can wait." Kate smiles.

"Here," says Matt, throwing a bunch of keys at her.

"I'm going to take everyone to Mum's," says Kate, catching them. "Will you be all right?"

He nods. "Just make sure Lauren and the kids are okay."

A warmth runs through Kate as Matt's selflessness

hits home. That's the kind of man he is. That's why she fell in love with him. She silently apologizes for suspecting he was anything else.

"Be careful," she says to him.

"Call me once you're at your mum's," he says.

And she would have done if Rose hadn't answered the door to them and said, "What the hell have you done?"

43

KATE

The *Echo* is laid out on Rose's kitchen table, with Jess's photo peering up at them.

The similarities between her and Lauren, who sits down beside it, are striking. The blonde hair that rests on their shoulders, their perfect noses, their wide-set eyes, making them look vulnerable and aggressive all at the same time.

"I can't believe you'd do this," says Rose. "I mean, what were you thinking?"

Lauren swivels the paper around to face her. "Wow," she says, her voice hoarse from crying. "When did Jess agree to do this?"

"A couple of days ago," says Kate.

Lauren looks at her with a perplexed expression.

"It turns out she works at the *Echo*," says Kate, by way of explanation. "With Matt."

Kate watches as Lauren's eyes move frantically back and forth, trying to make sense of what she's hearing. "But . . ." she starts, before her mouth drops open.

"She was with him in Birmingham," says Kate.

Lauren's hand flies to her mouth and her eyes search Kate's.

"I know," says Kate, reading her mind. "But it's not what you think."

"B-but she was there with her boss," says Lauren. "There's something going on between them."

"She's seeing Matt's deputy," says Kate, thankful that they'd had that conversation as they'd lain in bed last night. "His name's Ryan and apparently she was all over him like a cheap suit." She offers a weak smile, keen for the comment to come across as light-hearted.

Lauren exhales. "Oh my God, why didn't you say something? When I said . . . you must have thought . . ."

"I did," admits Kate. "But it's okay. I jumped to conclusions and it wasn't what I thought. Thankfully."

"I'm so sorry, I had no idea. If I'd have known they worked together, I would never have . . ."

"I know," says Kate, instinctively touching her sister's shoulder. She'd forgotten how good it felt to be close to her, both physically and emotionally.

"Does she know?" asks Lauren. "That Matt is your husband."

"We don't think so. She's certainly never broached the subject with him and although I've suspected her motives behind her being there, they're yet to be proven. I'd like to think it's all just a happy coincidence."

"What else would it be?" asks Lauren flippantly, as if there's no other option. Kate wishes she shared her sister's naivety.

"Why would you let her do something like this?" cries Rose, coming between them. "What purpose can it possibly serve?"

"We now know she's Dad's child," says Kate, each word slicing through her very being. "But he's not here. So let her find her mum."

"I *told* you," Rose says bitterly. "Her mother's dead."

Kate's jaw clenches involuntarily, not wanting to say what needs to be said.

"Might there . . ." she starts. "Might there have been anyone else?"

Rose looks at her open-mouthed. "Why would you even think to ask that?"

"Because I ran a check on Helen Wilmington before letting Matt run the story."

"And?" asks Lauren, hopefully.

"I've drawn a blank. There was only one Helen Wilmington in the Harrogate area and Mum's right; she died four years ago. I've checked the birth records for both Wilmington and Alexander and no babies were registered with either name around that time. That's why I thought the article was a good idea, to see if anyone else came crawling out of the woodwork."

"But like *this*?" says Rose scathingly, as she picks up the offending newspaper and throws it back down on the table. "You think that having our family's dirty laundry aired in public is the right way to go about things?"

"There's nothing in there to connect her to us," says Kate. "All of our names have been changed."

"She says she was born in Harrogate," says Rose, her voice high-pitched. "It won't take folk long to put two and two together."

"Mum . . . ?" starts Lauren, hesitantly. "Do you think the woman I saw him with was Helen Wilmington?"

Rose glares at her. "*What? What* woman?"

"The woman I told you about," says Lauren. "The woman and the baby."

Rose's lips pull back, exposing the top line of her gums. "I have no idea what you're talking about."

Lauren looks at her, pole-axed. "But Mum, you must remember. I can't imagine it's something you'd forget. I was seventeen . . ."

"You must be mistaken," says Rose emphatically. "As you say, I'd remember something like that, but I don't, so . . ."

Lauren takes her mother's hand in hers. "I know how hard this must be for you and I'm really sorry, but we owe it to Jess to help her. Do you remember anything else from that time? Anything at all?"

Rose shakes her head. "It was only ever Helen," she says. "Your father wasn't some kind of philanderer who was sleeping with anyone who took his fancy whenever my back was turned." A sob escapes from deep within her chest. "Perhaps she registered the baby under her maiden name or maybe she passed the child off as her boyfriend's—I'm sure she had one at the time."

Kate can't bear to impart the news that Matt had already spoken to a couple of Helen's old neighbors last night, and they didn't recall her ever having had any children either.

"He made a mistake," sniffs Rose, picking at the tissue in her lap with trembling hands. "A moment of madness with *one* woman who took advantage of him. He learned from it and vowed never to do it again, and he never did. So before you start thinking that he didn't love us and was sowing his seed with whoever turned his head, he wasn't." A tear falls onto Rose's cheek and she quickly wipes it away. "That's not the man he was."

Ironically, it's in that moment that Kate realizes that that's *exactly* the man he was, and as she watches him topple from the pedestal she's put him on for the past thirty-four years, her heart feels as if it's being torn in two.

44

LAUREN

"What an almighty mess this all is," says Lauren with a heavy sigh, once Kate has gone. "I'm truly sorry."

Rose looks at her, with tears still in her eyes. "Well, I hate to say it, but if it weren't for you dredging all this up, we wouldn't be in this situation. Everyone is entitled to have secrets, Lauren, and it's not *your* place to reveal those that don't belong to you."

"I couldn't have said it better myself. So why did you feel the need to tell Kate about . . ." Lauren coughs. As much as she tries, she still finds it so bloody hard to say the words. "About what happened when I was sixteen."

Rose's head falls into her hands. "I honestly don't know," she says. "She was pushing me about your dad, and I didn't want to hurt her any more than she was already. It just came out, I'm so sorry."

"I thought we'd agreed to keep it just between us three," says Lauren, treading carefully. "And Justin, of course."

"If he'd bothered to stick around," says Rose, with

a pinched expression. "I wonder what became of him. Not much, I wouldn't have thought, if he's still the type to run at the first sign of trouble."

Is her mum *really* going to persist with that lie? "Do you regret making me have an abortion?" she asks, indignation beginning to creep into her veins.

"Oh darling, let's not do this now. It was a long time ago."

"But it was a big part of my life," says Lauren. "It's made me who I am today."

"You know how your father could be. I tried to make him see sense, but he could be so obstinate sometimes."

"You say that, but I've been thinking about it a lot lately, and do you know what?"

Rose raises her eyebrows.

"I've spent all these years believing that Dad forced me to do it, blaming him. But when I really think about it, I don't once remember him telling me I *had* to do it."

"He tried to make you believe it was for the best," says Rose. "That your life would be very different if you had the baby."

"But he didn't *once* say I *had* to have an abortion." Lauren fixes Rose with an unflinching glare. "I did it because Justin didn't want to be with me anymore, and I couldn't see a way forward. I've blamed Dad for all these years, thinking all our rows were about him forcing me to do something I didn't want to do, but he was only ever trying to explain the consequences of my actions."

"He was an expert at coercive control," says Rose.

"That's why he was so good at his job. You wouldn't have even known it was happening."

"So, you're saying he didn't want me to have the baby?" asks Lauren.

"Good grief no," exclaims Rose. "You were too young. You had your whole life ahead of you. Why would you want to tie yourself to a commitment like that at *that* age?"

"Is this Dad talking, or you?"

"Darling, you know I've only ever wanted you to be happy, and if having a baby at sixteen was your happiness, then I would have supported you. I did everything I could to make your father see, but with hindsight, he was probably right."

"Meaning?" says Lauren coldly.

"Well, look how quickly Justin ducked out of his responsibilities. As soon as the going got tough, he was gone. Would you really have wanted a life with someone like that?"

"But I loved him."

"You *thought* you loved him," says Rose, patronizingly. "But you were young—you both were. You didn't know what love was."

Lauren remembers how she felt last night, with Justin's arms wrapped around her as she lay on his chest. How she knew she shouldn't be there but couldn't bear to tear herself away. How the intensity in his eyes as he'd made love to her had made her cry. How her heart races at the mere thought of him. It may be twenty-two years later, but nothing has changed. That's what love feels like, whether you're sixteen or thirty-eight.

"I saw him," says Lauren quietly, almost to herself.

"What's that, darling?"

Lauren takes a deep breath in an effort to stop the words that are threatening to tumble out. "I saw Justin," she says.

Rose's eyes blink too many times. "Oh," she says through a fixed grin. "Didn't he go abroad?"

Lauren nods.

"So, what did he make of his life?" asks Rose. "I assume not very much."

"He got married, had two children and is an executive at an American company." She refuses to give her mother the satisfaction of knowing that he's now divorced, and his sons live halfway across the world.

"Well imagine that," Rose says almost triumphantly. "If you'd stayed with him, you could have ended up all the way over in America. You wouldn't have met your wonderful husband; you wouldn't have your three beautiful children—"

"I'm leaving Simon," says Lauren, matter-of-factly. She didn't even know she'd made the decision until she said it.

Rose's face freezes, as if unable to compute what she's just heard. "Wh-what?"

"I'm leaving Simon," she says again.

"But . . . but why?" gasps Rose. "I thought . . . I mean, you're so good together."

Were they? Perhaps they were from an outsider's viewpoint. It's funny what people choose to see and the assumptions they make when they have no idea what goes on behind closed doors. They may mistake the look in her eye as pride in her husband, instead of the desperate need to please him. They may hear her agreeable voice as one half of an equal partnership, instead of the conciliatory tone of someone who's learned to be submissive.

"It's . . . not working," says Lauren.

"It didn't occur to me that anything was wrong," cries Rose. "I honestly thought you were happy."

Well, clearly you don't know me as well as you thought you did, Lauren wants to scream. *Because Justin made me happy. Justin still makes me happy.*

Rose clasps her hands over Lauren's. "I'm so sorry," she says. "What can I do to help?"

Lauren remembers a night long ago when her mother had held her, asking her the same question. "Just tell me what I can do to help you," she'd said, as Lauren cried into her arms.

"Make Justin come back to me."

"I'm sorry, darling, but I can't make him do something he doesn't want to do."

"But he said he loved me," Lauren had wept. "He said that he'd stand by me and we'd do this together."

"I'm afraid you'll learn that boys say a lot of things they don't mean."

Lauren's chest had convulsed, her shoulders caving in. "I can't do it without him," she'd sobbed.

"Well I think you have your answer," said Rose. "But don't worry, because I'll be there every step of the way."

And she had been, Lauren couldn't fault her for that. Her mother had been the glue that had kept them all together, though the bond between her and her father was never very tight after that. The thought that, for all these years, she'd blamed him for something he didn't do, makes Lauren feel physically sick.

"There *is* something you can do to help me," says Lauren now.

Rose tilts her head, raising her eyebrows expectantly.

"Can you watch the children?"

Rose's shoulders visibly relax. "Of course, darling. Are you going to see Simon? You mustn't let all these years go to waste. He's a good man."

Lauren smiles and shakes her head. "You're not a very good judge of character, are you?"

"What do you mean?" asks Rose, clearly affronted.

"You backed the wrong horse," says Lauren, getting up and walking out.

"Wait! Where are you going?"

"I'm going to see Justin," says Lauren. "The man I *should* have been with for all these years. The man *you* took away from me."

45

KATE

"Kate, it's me," says Matt. His voice is heavy down the phone.

"Hey," she says, wearily.

It has been an exhausting few days and she feels like she could sleep standing up, yet oddly when sleep *has* been available, she's not been able to take it, her mind keeping her awake as it frantically searched for an excuse for her father. But now, it seems that he doesn't need one. He'd been the man Lauren had accused him of being all along. She coughs to clear the overwhelming hurt that is stuck in her throat.

"Have you got a minute?" asks Matt.

"Yeah, sure, fire away."

"No, I mean, can you come down here? To my office."

Kate pulls herself up, immediately on the defense. "Why?" she asks.

"It's about Jess's story," says Matt. "There's somebody here I think you need to talk to. I'll explain when you get here."

"Okay, I'm on my way," she says, grabbing her handbag and heading for the door.

In the two minutes it takes for her to walk to Matt's offices, she runs through who it might be. She groans at the thought of it being a ne'er-do-well, who fancies having a go at passing herself off as Jess's mum. She'd probably spent half the morning concocting an elaborate backstory in the hope that it would make her sound plausible. But Matt had seen enough fame-hungry story chasers to know one when he saw one. She can't imagine he'd drag her down here for that.

She sees him, with his back to her in the lobby, talking to a man and a woman. She stops dead in her tracks for a moment as she quickly deduces that they look like police officers. The man, slightly smaller than Matt, and dressed in navy chinos and a white shirt, looks up, prompting her to carry on walking. She's just a few feet away when his female companion sees her, and looks her up and down.

"Er, Kate, this is Detective Sergeant Connolly," says Matt awkwardly. Kate leans across to shake the woman's hand.

"Detective Constable Stephens," says the man, extending his.

"Pleased to meet you," she says, shaking it.

Her mouth has instantaneously dried up, her lips sticking to her gums. She throws Matt a cautious look, silently asking what they're doing here and what it's got to do with Jess. DS Connolly is the one to answer.

"We read the piece by Jessica Linley in today's *Echo*," she says.

Kate nods, not trusting herself to speak.

"It's a very moving story."

"Mmm," manages Kate.

"I told them that Jess, *Jessica*, works here, but isn't in today," offers Matt.

Kate's eyes widen as she tries to read whether he's telling the truth or not. It's impossible to tell.

"Mr. Walker tells us you have a personal connection to Miss Linley," DS Connolly goes on.

"Er, possibly," says Kate. "It's a little contentious."

As soon as she says it, she wants to claw it back in. You should never use the word "contentious" when talking to the police—it opens up a whole host of questions.

DS Connolly raises her eyebrows in interest, as if proving the point. "Really?" she asks. "In what way?"

Kate looks helplessly from one detective to another. "Can I just ask what this is about?"

"We're investigating cold cases," pipes up DC Stephens. "And this article has piqued our interest. We just wondered if we could ask you a couple of questions."

Kate nods. "What's the case?" she asks, her voice wavering.

Stephens looks to his superior for permission to tell her. She gives a little nod.

"We're trying to trace a baby found abandoned in Harrogate in 1996," he says. "And Miss Linley says she was born there, around that time, to unknown parents. Is that true?" asks DC Stephens.

"It's *her* truth," says Kate, as a heat creeps slowly up from her toes, burning her skin from the inside out as it travels.

"What do you mean by that?" steps in DS Connolly.

"I mean, it's what she believes to be true," says Kate. "It may not prove to be the case, but it's what she believes, at this moment in time, given the information available to her."

She wonders if she's talking too much. Saying too many words when a few would be enough.

"Are you familiar with the town at all?"

Kate nods, as pinpricks of sweat spring to every pore. "I spent my early childhood there," she says, trying to ignore the split-second glance between the two detectives.

"Can I ask what time period that was?" asks Stephens.

Kate looks up at the treble-height ceiling and the marble-wrapped pillars that hold it up. "Erm, I was born there in 1984 and left to come to London in 1996."

"So around the same time that Ms. Linley was born?" Stephens asks rhetorically. "Did you move down with your family?"

Kate's fast losing the ability to talk, her throat feeling as if it's closing in on itself.

"Mmm."

"And your family are?"

"Erm, there's me, my sister, my mother and my late father."

"Can I just take down their names?" asks Stephens, reaching into his back trouser pocket and pulling out a notebook.

She glances at Matt, whose unchanged features send a surge of calmness through her addled brain.

"My sister is Lauren Carter, my mother is Rose, and my late father was Harry."

"And your parents' surname?" asks Stephens, with pen poised.

"Do you mind if we sit down?" asks Kate, feeling herself swaying.

"She's pregnant," says Matt, taking hold of her elbow and guiding her over to the modern leather couches that look far too small for the vast space. Kate watches as he goes to fetch her a glass of water, willing him to hurry up.

"And as I understand it," Stephens goes on, "Miss Linley has uploaded her DNA onto a genealogy website and has discovered that she has a half sister. Would that be Mrs. Carter?"

Kate nods.

"And yourself, of course, though I notice you're not referred to in the article."

Kate stays silent.

"Were you perhaps not quite as accepting of the situation as Mrs. Carter?"

"Well, it's not exactly ideal," admits Kate, coughing to clear her throat.

"That *your* father was *her* father?"

"Yes," says Kate quietly. "It's not easy to accept that your father could have had an affair."

"Especially difficult to discover this after his passing, I must imagine," says Stephens, almost to himself.

Kate bristles at his clumsy attempt at sincerity.

"But you accept it to be the case?" asks Stephens.

"I can't argue with science," she says, smiling tightly.

Stephens returns her smile, though it doesn't quite reach his eyes.

"Do you have any reason to believe that your father *knew* of his third daughter's existence?"

Yes. No. I don't know. They all reverberate around her head on a loop, as her, Lauren's, and their mother's different theories abound.

"No," she says, because it feels the safest answer to give until she knows exactly what's going on here. Relief floods through her as Matt returns and sits down next to her.

"And you don't remember the case of an abandoned baby when you were living in Harrogate at the time?"

"No," she says honestly.

"You would have been eleven or twelve?" says Stephens, needlessly reminding her of her age.

"That's correct," she says.

"And your sister, Lauren?" says Stephens, referring to his notebook. "She's a few years older than you."

"Yes, four." Kate is now worried that her answers are too short and clipped.

"So, she might have some memory of it. Or indeed your mother, Mrs. . . ." He looks at his notebook. "I'm sorry, I didn't quite catch your parents' surname."

"Alexander."

"And Mrs. Alexander is still in London?" DS Connolly asks.

Kate nods.

"Can I get an address for her please? We might need to ask her a few questions too."

"About what?" says Kate, her hackles rising as well as her heart rate.

"We just need to eliminate everyone from our

inquiries," says Stephens, sounding as if he's reading from a script for a TV show.

"Inquiries for what?" chokes Kate. "What is it that you're investigating exactly?"

DS Connolly looks at her. "A murder, Mrs. Walker. We're investigating a murder."

46

LAUREN

"I'm truly sorry," says Justin, taking Lauren's hand in his as they sit in a cafe at the foot of the Shard. "I had no idea I was talking to him."

"Why would you?" she says, as she swipes her tears away, not knowing whether she's crying for her marriage or the new life she's about to embark on. "It's my own stupid fault. I should never have let him anywhere near my phone." Though even as she's saying it, she knows she had no choice.

Justin looks at her intently. "You never *know*, it might be a good thing."

Lauren laughs cynically. "How can two parents breaking up *ever* be a good thing?"

"Because he's a violent bully, Lauren! You and the children are so much better off away from him."

Lauren nods. In her head she knows he's right but, despite herself, in her heart she's still not sure she completely agrees with him.

"I want to look after you, Lauren. If you want that too."

"I've got a lot to sort out, both practically and emotionally," says Lauren. "But in time, yes."

"We can figure that out. But first things first," says Justin. "Where are you and the children going to live?"

Lauren looks at him wide-eyed, suddenly overwhelmed by the enormity of the situation she's in. There were practical reasons she'd stayed in a marriage so toxic; having a roof over her children's heads was one of them.

"I'm going to have to take some advice," she says, feeling fresh tears spring to her eyes when she realizes that her one true advocate is no longer here. How she wishes she could roll back a year, to when her dad was still alive. Or even better, roll back twenty-two years, to a time when she was daddy's girl just as much as Kate was. Before she fell pregnant, before Justin left her, before she gave up their baby and blamed her dad for it all. Now she's discovered that the resentment she's been carrying around for all that time was misplaced. Yes, he may have had an affair and yes, it seems he had a baby with another woman, but that didn't detract from the father he was to *her*—the father he tried so very hard to be, if only she'd let him. And now it's too late.

He will never know how much she wished she'd gone into the office with him whenever he asked, instead of crying at home and regretting saying no. He will never know how much she'd have loved him to pop round to *her* place on his way home from a football match, instead of always going to Kate's. He will never know her regret at not telling him she loved him when she naively believed she had all the time in the world.

"Legal advice, you mean?" asks Justin, bringing her back.

Lauren nods. "I can stay with Mum for a bit, but it's not ideal, especially in the current circumstances, and Kate's not got enough room for us all."

"Well, if you need somewhere to stay, there's plenty of room at mine."

Lauren looks at him as if he's mad. "I can't move myself and three children into yours. This isn't your problem."

"Your problems are my problems. I want to help you in any way I can, and if the apartment isn't right, and I understand why it might not be, let me find you somewhere to rent while you're sorting yourself out."

"I'm not working at the moment," says Lauren. "I can't afford to rent anywhere."

"So let me help you then, at least until you're back on your feet."

"Justin, that's very kind of you, but honestly I don't need you to—"

"I want to," he says, taking her hand in his. "This could be a new beginning for both of us—"

Lauren's phone interrupts him and she looks at him apologetically. "I'm sorry, I need to get this," she says. She walks out of the cafe, sidestepping the bodies that are dispersing from London Bridge station.

"Hi," she says, as she teeters on the curb.

"Are you okay?" asks Kate.

"Getting there. You?"

"Yeah, listen, something's come up and I wondered if you could get across to Canary Wharf?"

Lauren instinctively looks at her watch, though she doesn't know why. "What now?" she says.

"Yes, if you can. It's important."

It doesn't occur to Lauren to ask any more questions. Mostly out of fear of what the answers will be. She's not quite sure how much more she can take at the moment.

"I need to go," she says to Justin when she walks back into the cafe.

"Is everything all right?" he asks. "Do you want me to come with you? I don't want you having to face him on your own."

"It's not Simon," she says. "It's Kate. I'll call you later."

Lauren wonders, as she goes the three stops on the Jubilee line, what Kate has to say that's so important. She hopes she's not going to slate their father, because for the first time, Lauren doesn't want to hear it. She's spent all these years waiting for everyone else to feel the way she did, but now that they do, she wishes they didn't. Kate, on the other hand, has had all the good things she thought about her father turned upside down. The irony of how they've changed sides isn't lost on her.

Lauren walks into the intimidating lobby at the *Echo* offices fifteen minutes later, feeling instantly out of place. This isn't where she wants to be, no matter how much she'd tried to convince herself that it was. It had felt so glamorous whenever Kate talked about it, but in reality, it feels threatening and highly pressured. Seeing Kate waving from the corner eases her anxiety.

"What's going on?" she says as confidently as she can as she approaches the group of four.

"Lauren, this is DS Connolly and DC Stephens," says Kate. "They're . . ."

"Thank you . . ." says Connolly, cutting Kate off. "They're just preliminary inquiries at the moment, Mrs. Carter, but we'd like to ask you some questions all the same."

"Of course," says Lauren, looking at Kate wide-eyed, trying to read her mind.

"They're investigating the murder of a woman in Harrogate in 1996," says Kate quickly, in answer to her silent questioning.

Lauren's palms instantly go clammy.

"The article implies that you uploaded your DNA onto a genealogy site," says Stephens. "Did you know that you might have another sibling?"

"N-no," stutters Lauren. "I was just doing it for a bit of fun, really. I didn't have any expectations other than perhaps building our family tree."

"So you were surprised when Miss Linley showed as a match?"

Not remotely, she wants to say, but instead says, "Absolutely."

"So it didn't occur to you that your dad, Mr. Harry Alexander, might have fathered another child?"

"No," she says, feeling sick. "Not at all."

The two detectives look at each other, making Lauren feel as if they know everything already and are just seeing how long it takes her to admit it.

"Did your father have any violent tendencies?" asks DS Connolly, bringing her back.

"Now, hang on a minute," says Kate, answering on Lauren's behalf. "Whatever's going on here has got absolutely nothing to do with my father."

Lauren looks, panic-stricken, between her sister and the officer.

"I'm sure it hasn't," says DS Connolly. "But, as we said, we need to eliminate everyone from our inquiries."

"No," says Lauren, truthfully. "Never."

Stephens jots down Lauren's answer in his notebook.

"I'm sorry, can you tell me more about what this is all about?" says Lauren, finally finding her voice. She will not allow assumptions to be made about her father. She's made enough of those for everyone.

"Back in 1996, a woman was attacked in her own home, sustained serious head injuries and died shortly after," says DS Connolly.

"And you think Jess is her baby?" Lauren asks, instinctively.

She knows, even before the two detectives look at each other with raised eyebrows, what she's done.

"Her baby?" asks Stephens through narrowed eyes,

"The woman's baby," she says, feeling an oppressive heat bearing down on her. "Didn't you say she had a baby?" Kate's eyes are burning into her.

"Her baby was found abandoned shortly after the murder," says Stephens. "May I ask how you knew that the victim had a baby?"

Lauren's eyes flicker from the detective to Kate and back again. "I . . . we . . . Jess and I went up there . . . earlier this week."

"What for?" asks DS Connolly.

"We just thought it might be a good idea to go back and knock on a few doors to see if anyone remembered my dad or Jess. We just wanted to see if we could find something that might lead us to Jess's mum."

"And did you?"

"We spoke with someone who told us about the Woods family," offers Lauren. "They said he'd killed his wife and disappeared."

DS Connolly raises her eyebrows. "That was one theory, but there are other lines of inquiry we need to pursue."

"Why?" says Lauren. "It seems everyone knew that he was violent—he had previous instances, and then he disappeared immediately after his wife's murder. It couldn't be any more clear-cut, *could* it?"

"Mr. Woods has since been cleared of any involvement," says Connolly, and Lauren feels like she's suddenly teetering on a precipice. She tries to stop the internal swaying that's threatening to knock her off balance.

"Since when?" she manages, her tongue feeling as if it's too big for her mouth.

"Since he returned to the UK two years after the murder and provided DNA and an alibi," says Connolly.

"So why wait until now to trawl it all up again?" asks Lauren.

"Well, we'd always believed the abandoned baby to be that of Mr. Woods, but if it comes to pass that it isn't, then we've got a whole new motive on our hands."

Lauren catches Kate closing her eyes.

"So, what are you going to do now?" asks Lauren.

"We need to talk to Miss Linley to see if she would be willing to have her DNA analyzed against that of Julia Woods," says Stephens. "And then we'll confirm the match between Miss Linley and your father, just to be sure."

"And if it's proven that Jess *is* their daughter?" asks Matt.

"Then it looks like we might not only have a new *motive*, but a new *suspect*," says Connolly.

47

KATE

"Kate! Kate! Can you hear me?" says Matt.

It sounds like he's calling her from miles away, yet she can see the outline of his face, the color of his eyes as he draws in close to her.

"Do you need to go to the hospital?" asks a woman's voice. It doesn't sound like Lauren's, but Kate so desperately wants it to be. Otherwise it will mean that she didn't dream what just happened.

"Do you want me to call an ambulance?" asks the same voice, and her heart falls into her stomach. It's not Lauren. It's DS Connolly, and any notion of her having imagined their conversation is thwarted.

"N-no, I'm fine," Kate manages. "I'm honestly fine."

"Okay, maybe we can wrap this up now," says Matt, but Kate doesn't know who he's saying it to. She just looks around aimlessly at all the faces peering into the bubble that she's created around herself.

"Of course," says DS Connolly. "We'll be on our way, just as long as Mrs. Walker is okay."

"She'll be fine," says Matt.

Kate's head is thumping as she's helped up from the floor and sits back in the chair she can't even remember falling out of. Lauren takes hold of her hand as they sit huddled on the sofa, watching the officers retreat.

"What the hell's going on?" asks Lauren breathlessly. "What are they trying to imply? That Dad's got something to do with it?" She laughs nervously. "As if. Surely all fingers have got to point to the woman's husband. He'd been violent before—their neighbor told me that the police were called several times."

The more Lauren's talking, the more claustrophobic Kate feels.

"We need to find Jess," croaks Kate, almost to herself. "We need to get to her before the police do." She turns to Matt. "Where is she?"

"I don't know," he says. "She called in sick this morning."

"Call her, Lauren," says Kate authoritatively, standing up and striding unsteadily toward the revolving doors. "Find out where she is."

Lauren rings her number as they rush across Cabot Square. Engaged. She tries again. Engaged.

"Shit!" says Kate, as they reach the station. "What's the quickest route to Hackney?"

"Light rail to Stratford," says Matt.

"She doesn't deserve this," says Lauren as they scramble down the escalator of Canary Wharf station. "She feels alone and lost enough as it is, but if the police tell her what they've just told us . . ."

"That's why we need to get to her first," says Kate, as Matt takes hold of her hand, making her feel more secure, both literally and figuratively.

"And what are we going to say to her?" asks Lauren.

"She doesn't know what *we* know," says Kate, breathlessly. "So, we have that advantage."

Kate's phone rings just as they reach the platform and, seeing that it's Jared, she slides to answer it. "I need to take this," she says, as they all stop for breath.

"Hey Kate, it's only me," he says. "I just wanted to get back to you with what I've found out about your girl so far."

Kate can't help but wonder if it's even relevant anymore.

"So?" she snaps, without meaning to.

"So, she was adopted when she was six by Mr. and Mrs. Oakley down in Bournemouth and it appears she kept their name even though she went back into the foster system a short while after. It seems that the ill health of her adoptive parents brought that on."

"Okay," says Kate, not hearing anything she doesn't already know. She can't decide if that's a good thing or not.

"But her papers show that up until she was adopted, she was living with various foster parents across the north of England."

"Yep, that seems to add up," says Kate. "And do you have the name she was living under?"

"Yeah, it seems she kept her birth name until she was adopted," says Jared.

"Which was?" asks Kate, feeling as if there's something lodged in her throat.

"Which was . . ." says Jared, without any sense of urgency. "Ah, here it is . . ." Kate can hear the rustle of paper at his end and doesn't know whether she wants him to hurry up or slow down. "Woods," he declares, oblivious to its significance. "Her birth name was Harriet Woods."

She ends the call and looks to Matt, who, judging by the fact that he has his hands on his head, is one step ahead.

"It's her, isn't it?" he says.

Kate types *Woods Murder Harrogate* into her phone's search engine. A flurry of archived articles flood her screen.

Woman murdered—husband and baby missing.
Husband prime suspect in woman's murder.
Baby found abandoned.
Woods murder—husband cleared.

The salacious headlines are mainly from Yorkshire's local newspapers, but "*Killer on the loose*" ran in her own paper. "Shit!" she says before reading the body of the article to Lauren and Matt.

"Frank Woods, the husband of Julia Woods, who was found murdered in her home in Harrogate, Yorkshire, two years ago, has been released without charge. Mr. Woods was the prime suspect for his wife's murder since absconding and being traced to Spain. But following his extradition and subsequent questioning, Yorkshire police have said that he is no longer part of their inquiries. The hunt for Mrs. Woods's killer goes on."

None of them say a word. Their expressions say more than enough.

48

LAUREN

Now that Lauren's stopped moving, sweat is springing to her pores, making a track down the length of her spine. She fans out her shirt with one hand, while the other trembles as she dials Jess's number again, not sure whether she wants her to pick up or not.

She answers on the third ring, but now that she has her, Lauren doesn't know what to say and looks to Kate wide-eyed.

"Find out where she is," hisses Kate under her breath.

"Listen, where are you?" starts Lauren. "I need to see you."

"Did you see the article?" asks Jess, ignoring the question.

"Yes, I did," says Lauren.

"It's caused quite a stir," says Jess tightly.

Lauren wants to ask how, but she doesn't want to alert her to anything she doesn't already know.

"I'm sure," she says.

Kate nods at her and rolls her hand over to encourage her to get to the point.

"Look, I really do need to see you," she says. "*We* need to see you."

"*We?*" asks Jess, and Lauren grimaces. She should have kept it simple, not made it out to be the big deal that it is. Kate looks as if she's holding her breath. "Me and Kate," Lauren goes on. "Are you at home?"

"Aren't I the popular one?" Jess says. "First the police and now you and Kate."

Lauren's sure her heart's stopped beating. "The police?" she says numbly, and Kate closes her eyes, letting her head fall backward. "What did *they* want?"

"They think they might have some news on my mother," says Jess.

Lauren goes into fight or flight mode, her head battling against itself to do the right thing. Does she offer this young girl solace in a world that has been so cruel to her? Or does she protect her family, at all costs, no matter what they may have done?

"Wow . . . that's amazing news!" she says, trying her best to sound upbeat, but the pretense lies thick on her tongue.

"Yeah," agrees Jess somberly. "I'm going down to the police station now as they want to take a DNA sample and tell me what's going on."

"Why don't I come with you?" says Lauren, at a loss for anything else. She can't let Jess, a young girl she's come to care a great deal about, face the news of her mother's murder alone. "Where are you? I'll come and meet you. You don't want to do this on your own."

Jess sniggers. "You make it sound like I'm a lamb going to slaughter. Do you know something I don't?"

An oppressive heat bears down on Lauren and she's

grateful for the rush of air the oncoming train brings with it. Kate and Matt look at her with raised eyebrows, both of them questioning whether they're getting on or not.

"Of course not," laughs Lauren awkwardly, shrugging her shoulders. "I just think you should have somebody with you. Tell me which police station you're heading to and I'll meet you there."

"Oh that's really sweet of you," gushes Jess. "I'm going to—"

"Jess?" calls out Lauren as a silence fills the line. "Jess?"

"What's going on?" asks Kate. "Where is she?"

The doors of the train begin to slide shut. "Lauren, where is she?" Kate shouts, jamming her foot in between them to stop them from closing.

"Hey!" says Matt, pulling Kate free. "Nothing's worth killing yourself for. We'll get the next one."

"Shit! Shit! Shit!" says Lauren as she jabs at her phone again and again, only to hear the busy tone. "She's on her way to talk to the police now, but I've no idea what station she's heading to."

"Okay," says Kate. "She's going to have to find out in her own way now, so we need to think about damage limitation from our point of view."

"How do you mean?" asks Lauren, wondering how they can protect themselves from the fallout that looks to be heading their way. Even if Jess takes the news she's about to get well, the police are still going to be knocking on their door again, wanting to know more. What started out as someone else's adventure now feels like Lauren's very own nightmare.

"I think we need to go and see Mum," says Kate. "We need to prepare her for what might be coming her way."

"Agreed," says Lauren, as they rush across the footbridge and onto the opposite platform where a southbound train is waiting. "But how the hell are we going to tell her that the woman her husband's had a child with was murdered?"

"Do you think Dad knew?" asks Kate, stepping on just as the door alarm sounds.

"That he had a child or that her mother was killed?" asks Lauren.

"Either," says Kate.

"I'm still sure I saw him with a woman and a baby, and I know I told Mum, despite her not remembering."

"So if he knew he had a baby, then he'd know that child's mother was dead. Even if they weren't in a relationship—weren't even on speaking terms—he'd know because it was all over the local paper."

Lauren's head falls back against the glass partition. "It doesn't look very good, does it?" she says, not wanting to state the obvious, but unable to ignore it. "Especially given we moved to London that same year."

It hits her then that this is all her fault. If she hadn't uploaded her DNA, hadn't persisted in bringing Jess into the family, hadn't upset Kate and her mother with her insistence that Jess's story was worth listening to . . . and now it's out there and look what's happened. Lauren feels as if the air is being squeezed out of her as she acknowledges that she may have served her father's head on a silver platter.

"Let's not jump to conclusions," says Matt, without any real conviction. "I'm sure there's a perfectly good explanation for all of this. We just need to let the police join up the dots. At the moment they've got to follow every line of inquiry, so all we need to do is tell them what we know . . . and support your mum, until they realize that they're barking up the wrong tree." He offers a smile of reassurance, but Lauren gleans none.

"Do you think they know who killed her already?" asks Kate.

Matt looks at her. "I think they have someone's DNA, other than the husband's."

"What, so now all they need to do is match it up?" asks Lauren, somewhat naively.

"All they need is a name," says Kate dourly.

Lauren can't bear to imagine it's one they all know.

They walk from Greenwich station to their parents' house in silence, playing out the next few minutes in their heads.

Lauren presumes it will largely fall to *her* to tell their mother about the secrets from the past, to destroy the love she's held for her husband all these years. Because whichever way you look at this, the absolute best-case scenario is that their father was a serial philanderer—firstly with Helen Wilmington, then Julia Woods, and God knows how many other women. They're the cold, hard facts that are about to crush their mother's world. The worst case doesn't even bear thinking about.

Lauren's mouth instantaneously dries up as she turns into her parents' quiet cul-de-sac, and by the time she reaches their house, it's nigh on impossible to swallow.

In the summer sunshine, with its manicured garden and flowering hanging baskets, the house looks the epitome of the suburban dream. She shudders as she imagines what's about to go on behind its perfect facade.

49

KATE

"Mum!" shouts Kate as she lets herself in with her key. She can hear Noah crying, calling out for his mummy.

"Ssh," says Rose. "Just be quiet, it'll be all right."

"But I want my mummy," the little boy cries.

Kate looks at Lauren and in that split second, they share a look of utter confusion.

"Noah!" yells Lauren, as she flies into the living room.

Kate's right behind, but it doesn't shield her from what greets them. Her knees lock and her heart jumps into her mouth as Jess stands in front of them, holding Jude.

"Jess!" cries out Kate, unable to comprehend the scene that is playing out in front of her. Rose is sitting on the floor, backed up in the corner of the room, with Noah on her lap. Emmy is sitting with them, looking up at Jess with fascination.

"Mummy!" squeaks Noah through his tears.

"Stay here!" says Rose abruptly, gripping his arm tightly.

"But I want Mummy," he cries, trying to pull away from her.

"Don't come any closer," says Jess, as Lauren instinctively moves toward her son's open arms.

"What?" manages Lauren, sounding as if someone has their hands around her throat. "Wh-what are you doing? Give me my baby."

"Stay where you are," says Jess, holding Jude tighter to her.

"Jess, please!" shrieks Lauren.

"I mean it," says Jess.

Kate edges forward, out of Matt's cautionary grasp, with her arms aloft.

"Jess, what's going on?" she says. "What are you doing here?"

"I thought I'd pay your mother a visit," says Jess acerbically.

"But I thought you were going to the police station?" says Kate, choosing her words carefully. "I thought you were going to give a DNA sample."

"What, to find out if I'm my mother's daughter?" Jess lets out a hollow laugh that ricochets around Kate's whole being. "I don't need a DNA test to prove who I am."

"I-I don't understand," stutters Lauren.

Kate has no idea what's going on, but she needs to get control before this all becomes so much worse than it already is. "Jess, just give Jude to me," she says, forcing herself to sound conciliatory when all she wants to do is scream. She inches ever closer toward her precious nephew, who's gurgling away contentedly, thankfully oblivious to the hostility surrounding him.

"I'm warning you," says Jess. "Stay where you are."

Kate weighs up what's the worst Jess can do if she just makes a lunge for Jude and snatches him out of her grasp. They might grapple for a few seconds and he *could* get pushed and pulled, but it wouldn't take much to overwhelm Jess's slight frame.

She leaps forward, flinching in anticipation of the resistance she's going to come up against. Jess raises her right hand and Kate stops dead in her tracks, so close to Jess that she can feel her breath on her face. It feels like it's all happening in slow motion as the metal blade catches the sunlight filtering through the net curtains. In that moment, Kate finds herself wondering how on earth this can be going on behind the doors of such an ordinary house.

"Kate!" barks Matt, bringing her out of her momentary trance.

"Ah, Matt!" exclaims Jess.

Kate can't compute what's going on.

"So, you know exactly who I am?" he asks.

Jess laughs cynically. "What? You thought *you* were the one holding all the cards?"

Kate feels as if her lungs might burst as she holds her breath.

"I . . ." he starts. "I don't understand."

"Well, then maybe you're not quite the intrepid journalist you *think* you are," says Jess.

"Whatever this is, you need to stop," he warns.

Jess laughs and grips hold of Jude even tighter. "It hurts, doesn't it? Not knowing what someone would do to a defenseless baby."

Kate remembers the room in Jess's flat, perfectly

prepared for the arrival of a little one, with its baby clothes and nappies. Had this been what it was all about from the beginning? Was Jess looking to get an eye for an eye? One baby's sacrifice for another's?

"Okay, listen to me," says Kate, forcing herself to stay calm amid Lauren's desperate cries. "No good can ever come of this. Whatever it is you want, we need to sit down and talk it through."

"I want the truth!" Jess screams, her ice-cold facade momentarily giving way to a show of raw emotion.

"And we can find it," offers Kate. "But not like this."

Jess's shoulders slump and Kate gets ready to snatch Jude from the arms of defeat, but then Jess shakes her head and any chance of a truce crumbles.

"*This*," she says, pointing the knife at Jude, "is the only way I'm going to find out what really happened, because that's the way you seem to do things around here. You think babies are collateral damage. That they can be sacrificed if it means you get what you want."

Lauren lets out a heart-wrenching sob from somewhere behind Kate. "We can find the truth together," says Kate, her voice trembling. "Whatever it is you need to know, we'll help you find it."

Jess scoffs. "Funny how you're all so interested now, isn't it? Now *you've* got something to lose."

"Let us help you," says Kate.

"*Help* me?" Jess snorts. "You've done nothing but hinder me since the day I arrived."

Kate knows she can't argue with that. She's going to have to try a different tack. "I understand that," she says, edging slowly forward again, hoping Jess won't notice. "But we now have unequivocal proof that you're our father's child and I will do everything I can to help you find whatever it is you're looking for."

"I gave you that opportunity three months ago," sneers Jess.

Kate shakes her head, unable to make sense of what she means. It had only been a month since Jess had turned up at her parents' front door.

"I came to your offices and spoke to you about a story I had," says Jess, smiling wryly.

Kate's head feels as if it's about to explode.

"Don't you remember?" Jess goes on. "I told you that my mother had been murdered and I'd been abandoned."

Kate delves into the depths of her mind, desperately searching for something of any relevance.

"So, you've known all along who your mother is?" asks Lauren incredulously.

"*Was*," sneers Jess correcting her. "I know who my mother *was*, because she's dead now, isn't she?" A flash of pain crosses Jess's features, but she quickly pulls herself together.

"Wh-when did you find out?" Kate stutters, unable to think straight.

"When I was eighteen and able to get a copy of my birth certificate," says Jess. "I only needed to do some basic research to find out what had happened to her."

Lauren looks at her, open-mouthed.

Jess turns to Kate. "I asked you to help me find my mother's murderer—that there was a good news angle to it—but you dismissed me out of hand. You said you had people turning up every day of the week, claiming to have the next front page up their sleeve."

Kate can hear herself saying it.

"I gave you the chance to narrate your *own* story, but you weren't interested, so I had to find a way of doing it myself."

"So you *lied* your way onto Matt's paper?" says Kate, unable to keep the contempt from her voice. "To get back at me?"

"Partly," says Jess. "But it wasn't only about you. I needed to find a way to get my story out there."

"Why didn't you just go to the police?" asks Matt.

"I did," says Jess. "As soon as I found out who my mother was, but they weren't interested. It was a cold case, they said. They had reduced resources . . . they didn't have the manpower . . . it wasn't in the public's interest . . ." She laughs. "Well it looks like it *is* now."

Kate feels Matt shift beside her as they both realize that they've fallen head first into Jess's trap.

"So have you even spoken to the police today?" asks Kate. "Since the article came out?"

"They've called me and asked me to go in." She looks at Matt. "I assume you've spoken to them too?"

"They've brought us up to speed," he says, and Kate prays that he leaves it there. This is Jess's stage—let *her* do the performing.

"If only you'd listened," says Jess threateningly. "None of this would have happened."

"I'm sorry," says Kate. "*We're* sorry. But we're listening now."

"But it's not *my* turn to talk," says Jess, "is it, Rose?"

Rose holds Noah and Emmy closer to her. "I don't know what you want me to say," she says shakily.

"Well, you must have *something* to offer," says Jess.

"You knew your husband was having an affair, knew he'd had a baby . . ."

"No," says Rose, shaking her head manically. "No, I didn't."

"Sure you did," says Jess, gripping Jude tighter and making him cry. His distress makes Kate's chest feel as if it's being ripped open.

"Lauren told you she'd seen Harry with me and my mum, didn't you, Lauren?"

Kate looks at her sister wide-eyed, not knowing what answer she wants her to give.

"Y-yes," stutters Lauren, her voice sounding as if she's gargling blood.

"Okay, I had my suspicions that he was having an affair," Rose blurts out, "but I swear I didn't know about you."

"You sure about that?" questions Jess, making Jude cry even louder.

"Tell her!" barks Kate, unable to listen to her nephew's pitiful sobs any longer. "Tell her about the hospital tag."

Rose looks at her, dumbstruck. "I don't know what . . ." she starts.

"I *saw* it!" exclaims Kate, wanting to scream, but mindful of not frightening the children any more than they already are. "It has Jess's date of birth on it. Just tell her what you know."

Rose's head drops and her chest heaves. "I'm sorry," she cries.

"You *knew* Jess's mum wasn't Helen Wilmington, didn't you?" says Kate tightly, as the truth begins to dawn on her.

Rose makes a strange noise in the back of her throat.

"You gave us that name, hoping that it would be enough to throw us off the scent. Thinking that we'd run with it, find out she'd died and that would be the end of it."

Rose looks at her imploringly, silently begging her to understand why.

"So you knew all along that Jess's mum was Julia Woods? That Dad's lover had been murdered?"

A sob catches in Rose's chest. "Yes. I just didn't want you to find out, and start asking questions that I couldn't answer."

"So what do you know about my mum?" asks Jess.

"Not much," Rose whimpers. "Nothing at all in fact, apart from what happened to her."

"And how did you find out about *that*?" presses Jess.

"From the paper, like everyone else," offers Rose.

"So you and Harry never discussed what happened?"

Rose shakes her head emphatically. "No, never. I knew that her husband had gone on the run and I assumed he'd taken the baby with him."

"So even though you knew your husband was having an affair with a woman who'd been murdered, and thought his child had disappeared with someone other than its father, you never gave it another thought?"

"Well . . . I . . . I . . . thought it was over," stutters Rose.

"So you didn't know that my mother's husband was cleared of any involvement?"

Rose's eyes widen. "N-no, I didn't."

"It didn't occur to you to read the newspaper to keep up to date over the years?" asks Jess sardonically. "It's all there on the internet, Rose."

Rose remains tight-lipped.

"And now the police have a new lead, *me*, and they're going to be sniffing around you and your family until they find out what really went on."

Rose looks between Jess, Lauren and Kate, her eyes flitting wildly. "I only did it to protect you."

"We don't need *protecting*," cries Lauren. "We need the *truth*. Because the sooner you tell it, the sooner I'll get my babies back." It sounds as if Lauren's insides are being ripped out. "Please, Mum."

Rose closes her eyes and takes a deep breath. "Your dad wasn't always the person you thought he was."

Kate looks at her mother contemptuously.

"He wasn't always the man that you saw on the outside," Rose goes on. "He could be manipulative and controlling—that's what made him so good at his job, but sometimes he'd bring it home with him."

Kate shakes her head. She can't remember a single time, not one, when her father wasn't the most loving, caring person she could possibly imagine.

"He was never that person," she says. "He loved us unconditionally."

"*If* everything was going his way," says Rose. "You only have to ask Lauren what he was capable of when it wasn't. *She* knows how he could be."

Kate looks to Lauren with raised eyebrows. She wonders if her sister is going to be brave enough to tell *her* truth.

"Tell her," urges Rose, looking at Lauren. "Tell her what he made you do."

"About the abortion?" asks Lauren.

Rose nods encouragingly.

"You want me to say that he gave me no choice, that he manipulated the whole situation, that he called the father of my baby to tell him I'd already had the operation, when I hadn't?"

"Exactly," says Rose, looking at Kate imploringly. "I'm sorry, darling—I can only imagine how hard this must be for you to hear, but *that's* the kind of man he could be sometimes."

"Except he wasn't," says Lauren, choking back tears. "He was never that man. He was your puppet, and when you told him to jump, the only question he ever asked was, *how high?*"

Rose turns to look at Lauren with a confused expression.

"I *know*, Mum," says Lauren. "I know you were the one behind him, pulling his strings, all the while telling me that I should do whatever *I* wanted to do."

Rose shakes her head. "No darling, that's not how it was. See how coercive he was? That's what he wanted you to think. I only ever wanted you to be happy."

"Did you think making Justin walk away from me would make me happy?" Lauren cries.

"Of course not, but as much as I tried to reason with your father, sometimes I just couldn't make him see sense. I didn't even know that he'd called Justin, not until afterward, when it was too late."

Lauren rushes forward toward her mother and Kate's hand instinctively reaches out and grabs hold of her wrist.

"*You* were the instigator!" Lauren shouts. "You didn't want *my* mistake to upset the equilibrium of the perfect family you thought you had!"

"It wasn't about *me*," says Rose, aghast. "You were too young to be tied down with a baby, and with a boy who couldn't support you. It was the right thing to do for *all* of us."

"Except it sent *me* off the rails, and your *husband* into the arms of another woman."

Rose's lip quivers and she pulls Noah and Emmy closer to her, as if goading Lauren. "Women were your father's weakness."

"Don't you dare!" hisses Kate. "Don't you dare try and justify your actions by blaming him. All he ever wanted to do was help people."

Rose laughs bitterly. "Oh yes, he was very good at helping people, especially women whose husbands were beating them up. Your father liked to play the martyr and be on hand for his clients when they came out of hospital."

"Are you referring to my mother?" asks Jess.

Kate had almost forgotten she was there.

Rose looks at Jess—her eyes silently saying *yes*.

"So, you *did* know my mother?" says Jess.

"I knew *of* your mother," says Rose, correcting her.

"Who are you lying for?" asks Jess. "Your husband or yourself?"

"Your father was going to leave us to be with Julia," says Rose, looking directly at Kate. "He wanted to be with her and the baby and there was nothing I could do to make him see sense."

If it were possible for blood to freeze, Kate imagines this is what it would feel like. "He would never have left us!" she shouts. "You know he wouldn't!"

"*This* is why I didn't want to tell you anything,"

cries Rose. "I didn't want to hurt you. I was only ever trying to protect you from knowing what your father was really like. But the reality was that he and Julia were going to make a new life together in London, with the baby." She throws Jess a disdainful look.

"So what happened?" presses Jess, when it looks like Rose has offered all that she's going to.

"Th-that was it," stutters Rose. "Your mother was killed and I presumed it was by her husband, who found out what she was planning to do."

Kate looks at her mother paralyzed with fear on the floor. She can't tell whether it's because Jess is holding her grandson hostage, or she knows she's sitting on a ticking timebomb.

"The police are going to be crawling all over this now," says Jess. "And I'll make sure that they don't rest until they find out who killed my mother. So if there's anything you're not telling me . . ." Jess raises the knife, her eyes never leaving Rose.

"Okay, okay!" calls out Rose, closing her eyes and shaking her head, as if trying to dislodge a deeply buried memory. "Harry packed his bags and said he was leaving—I pleaded with him not to go, but his mind was made up. When he got to Julia's, she said she couldn't do it—that her husband had found out and threatened to kill her and the baby if she went."

Tears fall onto Rose's cheek and Noah turns to look at his nana, momentarily forgetting the hostile situation he finds himself in. "What's wrong, Nana?" he asks innocently, dabbing at her cheek with the sleeve of his top.

"Please, Jess, let me take him," says Lauren, falling onto her knees. "None of this is the children's fault."

"Go on!" barks Jess, ignoring her.

"They rowed," says Rose, "and there was a scuffle. Harry said that she lost her footing and fell, hitting her head as she went down."

A stunned silence descends on the room.

"How *could* you!" cries Kate. "How could you make up such wicked lies?" It feels as if there's an obstruction in her airways. She closes her eyes and forces herself to breathe in for three, and out for three.

Rose's chest heaves as she sobs. "I'm sorry. I'm so sorry, but it was an accident—he never meant for it to happen."

"So why didn't he just call the police?" asks Jess, almost robotically. "If it was an accident."

"How *could* he?" cries Rose. "He was a highly regarded lawyer. Imagine the investigation that would have had to be done. He could have lost everything: his job, his family and, if they didn't believe him, his liberty."

"They'd know if it was an accident," says Jess. "An accident is an accident, but murder is murder."

"It *was* an accident," says Rose. "A terrible accident."

"And you're prepared to take your husband at his word, are you?" asks Jess. "The man who cheated on you, fathered a child, was going to live with someone else . . . you're willing to believe his version of events?"

Rose nods. "Yes."

"Well I guess it'll be down to the forensics now," says Jess, visibly relaxing, but not quite enough for Kate to feel confident to make a grab for Jude. "They'll prove what really happened."

"I *know* what really happened," says Rose.

"They won't go on the hearsay of a scorned wife," says Jess, acerbically. "No matter how much she wants to believe it."

"I *know* what really happened . . ." Rose says again, ". . . because I was there."

50

ONE YEAR LATER

"How's it going?" Kate asks, as she sits down next to Lauren on the bench in Court One.

"I didn't think you'd come," says Lauren, leaning in for a kiss.

"I had to force myself. I don't know how I'm going to look her in the eye."

"It's been a long time," says Lauren, rubbing her younger sister's arm. "But she'll be pleased to see you're here."

"I'm not here for *her*," says Kate tightly, before offering a weak smile. "I'm here for *you*."

"Well, I appreciate it," says Lauren, taking hold of Kate's hand and giving it a squeeze.

"Are you still okay for Sunday?" asks Kate, absently swiping a photo of a beaming Matt holding their baby, Charlie, from her phone's home screen. She checks for any last-minute texts and emails before turning it off.

"Yes, the kids are looking forward to it. It's supposed to be Simon's weekend to have them, but he's been unusually civil and agreed to swap it."

"Wonders will never cease."

"Don't hold your breath," says Lauren. "He's still a bastard most of the time."

"I was going to suggest a barbecue if the weather stays like this," says Kate. "It'll be our first chance to use the garden since we moved in. It also means we can put Matt and Justin in charge of the grill, while we put our feet up with a bottle of wine."

"Sounds like my kind of afternoon," says Lauren.

The banality of the conversation jars against the seriousness of their surroundings.

"What do you think's going to happen?" asks Kate, suddenly conscious.

"Well, she's still maintaining that Dad called her in a panic and asked her to meet him at Julia's house. And that when she got there, he told her there'd been an accident and gave her the baby."

Kate shakes her head. "Does that sound like Dad?"

"No doubt we'll find out. But I can see that he would have wanted to get the baby away from the scene."

"And she's still claiming she left Jess at a church?"

Lauren nods. "She said that Dad told her to put the baby somewhere safe and the church was the first place she could think of."

The gallery door opens and in walk Jess and Finn. Jess gives a polite nod and sits down on the back row.

"Have you spoken to her yet?" asks Kate.

"Only briefly, this morning, after the jury were sworn in and the opening speeches had been made." Lauren sighs. "It's funny, but despite everything that's gone on, it's good to see her. With each day that passes, the more I understand why she felt the need to do what she did, and if I'm really honest with myself, there's a part of me that still misses her."

"Did she say what she's doing with herself?" asks Kate.

"Finn's moved in with her now, but I think that was always the plan, and she's got a new job in a restaurant in town."

"Do you want to invite them over on Sunday?" asks Kate. Lauren turns to look at her with a smile.

The court hushes as Rose shuffles into the dock, looking like a shadow of the woman she was: her shoulder-length auburn hair is cut short and graying at the sides; her once vibrant skin is sallow and pale; even her height seems to have diminished. Though when she looks up to the gallery and sees Kate, she instantly stands taller, buoyed by her daughter's presence.

As soon as the judge is seated, the prosecution calls the forensic investigator to the witness box and after the formal introductions, the wigged barrister approaches the stand.

"Can you confirm that the defendant Rose Alexander's DNA was found at the scene of Julia Woods's murder?" he says.

"Yes," says the bespectacled man, before leaning in closer to the small microphone perched in front of him and repeating himself.

"And can you confirm that the same DNA was found close to the body of the deceased, even though the defendant claims in her written statement that she didn't enter the house?"

"Yes, that's correct."

"While we could allow the benefit of the doubt to some extent, it's unlikely in this event, is it not?"

"Highly unlikely," says the witness.

"And can you explain why that's the case on this particular occasion?"

The man clears his throat and Lauren squeezes Kate's hand tighter. "Because the defendant's DNA was found under the victim's fingernails."

There are audible gasps from the gallery and Kate and Lauren lock eyes.

"And just for the record," the Crown Prosecutor goes on, twisting the knife until it has nowhere else to go. "Is it conceivable that anyone else was present at the time of the murder, apart from the defendant, Mrs. Alexander?"

"Absolutely not."

"Thank you." The barrister grins. "I have no further questions."

ACKNOWLEDGMENTS

Writing *one* book was a dream come true, and writing a second and third—with a fourth in the offing—is beyond anything I could have possibly imagined. And it's all thanks to my agent, Tanera Simons at Darley Anderson, who spends her days mixing magic potions into life-changing concoctions. Her colleagues, Mary Darby, Georgia Fuller, and Kristina Egan, have ensured that my novels have reached far and wide, having been translated into fourteen languages and counting. And Sheila David is the visionary who floats the idea of an altogether different format—thank you all.

Like most novels, this book is far removed from the first draft that I sent to my editors, Catherine Richards at Minotaur Books and Vicki Mellor at Pan Macmillan. Together they've helped me hone this final draft—for, in my eyes, it will always be a draft, as writing is so infinite—into the best shape it can possibly be. I am sure it could always be better, but there comes a point when you have to hand your baby over, as otherwise you will coo, fuss, and fret over it for far longer than you should. Thank you both for guiding it through that difficult teething stage!

So much goes on behind the scenes to turn words into a book, and to get that book into retailers and to encourage you, the readers, to choose yours from all the thousands available. Many thanks to Nettie Finn, Natalie Young, Joseph Brosnan, Sarah Melnyk, Matthew Cole, Becky Lloyd, and Fraser Crichton for all that you do.

Thank you to my wonderful friends and family for their patience and understanding, and for having the forethought to know that when I'm killing someone, I mustn't be interrupted!

But the biggest thank-you of all, as always, is to *you*, for taking the time to read my ramblings and enjoy them enough to write reviews, blog, and recommend to others. I am eternally grateful.

Read on for an excerpt from

THE BLAME GAME

the next novel from Sandie Jones,
available soon from Minotaur Books!

PROLOGUE

She wants to be everything to everyone, but making yourself indispensable is dangerous.

It means you're party to secrets that others don't want you to know. It means you'll go to any length to keep your own close to your chest. It means that everyone around you becomes collateral damage.

But she'll not bring me down. I'll get to her, before she gets to me.

Her need to be essential is about to make her an accessory.

1

I'm sure, as soon as I see the door ajar, that something has happened. I never leave my garden office unlocked overnight, not because there's anything in there worth stealing, but there's been a spate of petty shed burglaries around here recently and I don't need my clients' files strewn across the manicured lawns of Tattenhall in the hapless pursuit of a mower or power tool.

Though you'd have to be pretty stupid if you honestly thought that the sprawling estate was tended to by a hand-held strimmer kept in my pimped-up shed. The fifty acres of rolling land that surround our cottage are maintained and nurtured by a team of three full-time greenkeepers, who you're more likely to see astride a sit-on John Deere than hovering a Flymo.

I remember Leon showing me the barn where all the machinery is kept, when we first moved here after he'd become the estate's manager. My eyes had stood out on stalks, as I'd always been a tomboy growing up and one of the best days I remember having as a child was being taken to Diggerland, where I was allowed to operate a JCB. I'd patiently waited in line for over an hour, just so I could pick up dirt from one pile with the giant bucket and move it onto another. My dad was infuriated that a theme park would charge for such an inane activity, but I'd been delighted.

Pushing the memory to the back of my mind, before it turns sour, I tentatively pull the door open and peer inside the converted outbuilding I've grown to love. I expect to see my desk upturned and its drawers thrown across the room in frustration, as the low-life realized that there wasn't as much as a skateboard on which he could make his getaway. But my workstation is still upright; the framed certificates proving my right to practice as a psychologist still hang, dead straight, on the wall, and the vase of flowers that I'd been sent by a grateful client still blossom, their optimism jarring against the unnerving sensation that is coiling around my stomach.

My eyes travel to the salmon-colored couch, where many a life story has been shared, but its cushions remain perfectly plumped and the magazines on the coffee table are fanned out just as I had left them after my last appointment on Friday.

Nothing looks to have been disturbed and I allow a little frisson of relief to ease its way across my shoulders, loosening the knot that has so quickly tightened there. Maybe I had carelessly left the door unlocked and the breeze had just taken it off the latch, leaving it swaying in the brisk morning air.

I admonish myself, promising that I will pay more attention in future. There might not be anything in here to entice an opportunist looking for an easy grab and sell, but there is still incredibly sensitive information held within the drawers of the cabinets that, in the

wrong hands, could have far more damaging consequences.

I take a sip of my coffee and turn the electric heater
on, just to take the edge off. It's forecast to be a warm
day, but the overnight coolness has made its presence
felt. *Not helped by leaving the door open*, I say scathingly to myself.

I shiver involuntarily as I open my diary, though I
can't tell whether it's because of the very real chill in
the air or seeing who my first appointment is.

Jacob.

My chest tightens and I ask myself for the hun-
dredth time whether I've done the right thing by him.
I know I certainly haven't done right by Leon, but then
I wonder if that's not his own fault.

If he hadn't been so distracted lately, I would have
found it easier to tell him. But the job that we thought
would give us more time together has actually resulted
in exactly the opposite. Because even when he's home,
he's on constant call, and the summer concert that he's
spent the last four months organizing is fast approach-
ing, leaving him with even less time, and certainly less
patience.

I've wanted to tell him about Jacob, tried to several
times, but he's never listened long enough for me to get
to the important part. But maybe that's just me choosing to see it that way, because I know how he's going
to react when I do. He'll no doubt take me to task for
caring too much and going beyond the call of duty. But
there's a reason for that.

I knew as soon as Jacob started coming to see me three
months ago that his story was different. Although he,

like all of my clients, had reached the point where he felt able to put his pride aside and bravely ask for help, the irony of his situation was that he wasn't looking to save himself; he wanted to save the woman who had been abusing him for ten years.

"If I don't get out now, I'm terrified of what I might do," he'd said when I asked why he'd come to see me, during our first session. "For the first time ever, I was going to retaliate and it scared me because I didn't know what I might be capable of."

I'd looked at him, curiously, unable to recall another client who thought they were the one who needed help, instead of the person who'd been making their life hell.

"Can you tell me what happened to make you feel this way?" I'd asked softly.

He'd looked down at his intertwined fingers in his lap. "She stayed out last Saturday," he started. "All night."

"OK," I said. "And do you know where she'd been?"

He'd laughed cynically. "Oh, she made sure to tell me all the details." He shifted on the sofa, pulling a scatter cushion onto his lap, as if it were a metaphorical barrier.

I'd sat back in my chair opposite him, giving him the time and space to decide whether he wanted to elaborate.

"She'd been with another man," he'd said eventually. "Having the best sex she's ever had."

I'd recoiled inwardly, unable to imagine how it must feel to be told something like that by the person you thought you were going to spend the rest of your life with.

"She told you that?" I'd asked incredulously, seemingly still capable of being shocked by the sadistic behavior of some people, despite being in the job for over ten years.

He'd nodded. "Yes, just before she straddled me and attempted to force herself on me."

"And what happened?"

"Absolutely nothing," he said. "I could still smell him on her, for God's sake. But regardless, I could no longer convince my body that making love to her was what I wanted to do. It had listened to the call to action for so long, ever ready to perform when she wanted it to, but eventually, my brain just said, 'Enough, I can't do this any more.'"

His lips had closed and he'd grimaced. "She told me I was an embarrassment to mankind, unable to perform the most primitive of functions."

"How did that make you feel?" I'd asked.

"Less of a man," he said. "Though I guess she's ingrained it in me to such an extent that it's impossible to feel any other way."

"So your relationship has affected your masculinity?" I'd asked.

"Of course," he'd said, sighing. "How can it not? The stereotype is that a real man should be in charge, be the breadwinner."

I couldn't help but cringe at his misguided definition. "Don't you think that's a rather outdated stereotype these days?"

"Is it?" he'd asked, seeming genuinely out of touch. "That gives me some hope then, as I'm not like that."

"I think masculinity's more about how you feel."

"Well, that morning, I couldn't have felt any less of

a man if I'd tried. Maybe that's why I almost did what I did."

He'd wiped a tear away and I pushed the box of tissues on the table closer to him.

"What did you *almost* do?" I asked.

His jaw tensed, the bristles of his beard pulsing.

"When she got off me and walked toward the bathroom, I reached for the baseball bat that we keep beside the bed. I've let her rain down blow after blow, insult after insult, without so much as a retort, but that morning, everything that I've held in over the years just rose to the surface."

"What were you thinking you would do?" I'd asked.

He took a deep breath. "I wanted to kill her," he said, before looking at me as if to gauge my reaction. When I didn't give him one, he'd forged on. "It felt like the only way out and I remember thinking that all I had to do was swing it once and it would all be over. I was walking up behind her, having this internal dialogue with myself, wondering how bad it would be if I just did it."

"So what stopped you?" I asked.

"As much as I so desperately wanted to do it, all the time I was rationalizing it in my head, it wasn't going to be an instinctive act, was it?"

"I'm going to ask the question that I'm sure you've asked yourself a thousand times," I'd said.

"Why haven't I left her?" he sighed, beating me to it.

I'd nodded.

"I will, but it's going to take some organization. I've been applying for new jobs in Canterbury as I can't risk her finding me once I've gone."

"What is it you do?" I asked.

"I'm a school teacher," he said. "For my sins."

I'd offered a small smile.

"And what about accommodation?" I'd asked.

"I haven't got anything lined up, but if I get offered any of the positions I've applied for, I'll have to get something sorted out pretty quickly, even if it's just something temporary, until I'm able to get myself properly settled."

I'd been tempted to offer him our flat, which was standing empty just a few miles down the coast, there and then. We were planning on decorating it, ready for the onslaught of tourists that descend on Whitstable for the holiday season, but somehow summer is already upon us and we haven't got around to it yet. It's in a great little spot, just two roads back from the beach, and has served us well these past six years while Leon and I have been commuting into nearby Canterbury: him to his job as events manager at the cathedral and me to my gray little windowless box in the council offices.

But when the opportunity to live in a grace and favor cottage at Tattenhall had presented itself, it had been a no-brainer. Not least because it gave me the chance to set up my own practice in the outbuilding, which, seeing as I was embroiled in a stand-off with my line manager, couldn't have come at a better time.

"You've crossed the line," he'd said, when he discovered I'd helped a woman seek sanctuary from her violent husband in the middle of the night.

"She was in imminent danger," I'd retorted. "Are we really such slaves to bureaucracy that we're prepared to risk a woman being killed?"

"Red tape's there for a reason," he'd barked as I walked away.

Well, if it was there, I chose not to see it when I slipped out of the house and drove the four miles to where Sarah lived. That's not to say fear wasn't coursing through my veins as I sat there with my lights and engine off, surrounded by what felt like an invisible trip wire that would set off a deafening alarm as soon as she crossed it. But my stomach was in knots for her, not myself.

I watched with my heart in my mouth as she came out and carefully closed the door behind her. Just one forced error, and her husband would be down those stairs and dragging her back up to give her the beating of her life.

"You can do this," I'd said out loud, as she momentarily hesitated in the porch. "Come on, Sarah, just a few more steps."

She silently ran toward the car without looking back, but just as she reached the passenger door, an upstairs light went on.

"Get in, get in," I whispered, my voice hoarse with terror.

I'd managed to get her to the safehouse, but two days later her husband had paid me a visit in the underground car park at work, demanding to know where she was.

I wasn't going to tell Leon, but I was still trembling when I got home, unable to shake the memory of a double-barrelled shotgun being pressed against my temple.

"Promise me you'll never do anything like that again, Naomi," he'd said, as he pulled me close and wrapped himself around me. Right there, nestled in my safe place, I never imagined I would.

Yet here I am, once again, with the weapon's indentation not yet forgotten, finding myself unable to deny someone in need.

"Are we still going to rent the flat out?" I'd mooted to Leon a few weeks ago, when Jacob told me he'd been offered a new job.

"Yeah, as soon as the concert's out of the way," Leon had said. "I'll look at getting it ready for the summer season. I think it will do well as a holiday rental."

"Yes, but that could be unpredictable," I'd said. "Not to mention hard work for me and you. Wouldn't it make more sense to rent it out on a six-month contract, or even three? At least we'd know we had that guaranteed income."

"I'm not sure there's anyone around here who would take it on that basis," he said, his tone already distracted by something he was looking at on his laptop.

"Well, one of my clients might be interested," I said, turning my back, conscious of what I was plotting being written all over my face.

"I don't think that's a good idea," he'd said. "Do you not think it would be better to keep your work and the flat separate?"

"Not when it's someone as desperate as he is."

"*He?*" Leon repeated, suddenly giving me his undivided attention. Was that what it took these days?

"Yes," I said, wishing I'd kept Jacob gender neutral.

"So what's his story?" he'd asked, his interest piqued.

"He's been abused by his wife for the past ten years and he's finally had enough," I said. "Whenever he dares to fall asleep before her, she'll pour freezing cold water over him or run razors across the soles of his feet. They leave just the tiniest of nicks that can barely be seen by the naked eye, but you try walking on a hundred paper cuts."

Leon had looked at me with confusion etched across his brow. "And you want him to live in our flat?"

I'd nodded.

He'd shaken his head. "She sounds like a complete nutter."

"She is," I'd said, thinking he was finally beginning to understand the need to get Jacob somewhere safe.

"I don't think that's something you should involve yourself in," he said. "God knows what she's capable of."

My heart had sunk. "But she won't know where he is."

"Yeah, but still—it's probably best we stay out of it."

"He doesn't have anywhere else to go," I said.

"Why is that suddenly your problem?"

"I just want to be able to help, that's all, and the flat's sitting there empty . . ."

"I think you do enough for your clients," he'd said. "You're paid an hour for just that, an hour."

He'd made it sound so easy, but I defy anyone with half a heart to listen to what my clients say, and not think about it for long after they've left. It's a bit like reading a book. You know that feeling you get when you're so fully invested in the characters that you have to read one more page? And then another and another, until you find out what happens to them, even when you know you can't do anything to change their fate and what the author has already written on the pages.

But what if you *could* change the end of the story? What if you had the chance to change somebody's life, at no cost to your own? You would, wouldn't you?